Robert E. Howard's Favorite Yarns and Rimes

Edited by

Willard M. Oliver

A Sepulcher Press Book

Copyright © 2021 by Willard M. Oliver

All rights reserved.

ISBN: 978-0-578-82710-0

Dedication

To Cross Plains Project Pride

For keeping Robert E. Howard's memory alive

Robert E. Howard's

Favorite Yarns and Rimes

Contents

	Introduction	1
1	The Rubáiyát (ca. 1100) by Omar Khayyám	5
2	Heimskringla (King Olaf's Saga) (ca. 1200) by Snorri Sturluson	7
3	Grettir the Outlaw (The Vampire Chapters) (ca. 1400) by Unknown	17
4	The Fall of the House of Usher (1839) by Edgar Allan Poe	31
5	The Novel of the Black Seal (1895) by Arthur Machen	53
6	The Star Rover (1915) by Jack London	101
7	The Parrot (1925) by Alfred Noyes	123
8	The Call of Cthulhu (1928) by H.P. Lovecraft	125
9	Cravetheen the Harper (1928) by A. Leslie	161
10	A Jest and a Vengeance (1929) by E. Hoffmann Price	163
11	The Silver Key (1929) by H.P. Lovecraft	181

12	Thirsty Blades (1930) by Otis Adelbert Kline and E. Hoffmann Price	197
13	The Rats in the Walls (1930) by H.P. Lovecraft	235
14	Teotíhuacán (1931) by Alice I'Anson	259
15	Doom around the Corner (1931) by Wilfred Blanch Talman	261
16	The Return of the Sorcerer (1931) by Clark Ashton Smith	269
17	The Little Gods Wait (1932) by Donald Wandrei	289
18	The Last of Placide's Wife (1932) by Kirk Mashburn	291
19	Death (1932) by Wilfred Blanch Talman	317
20	Isle of Torturers (1933) by Clark Ashton Smith	319
21	Ismeddin and the Holy Carpet (1933) by E. Hoffmann Price	339
22	The Seed from the Sepulcher (1933) by Clark Ashton Smith	377
23	The Festival (1933) by H.P. Lovecraft	393
24	Revenant (1934) by Clark Ashton Smith	405

25	The Dweller (1934) by William Lumley	409
26	Through the Gates of the Silver Key (1934) by H.P. Lovecraft & E. Hoffmann Price	411
27	Out of the Eons (1935) by Hazel Heald (& H.P. Lovecraft)	455
28	Dominion (1935) Clark Ashton Smith	487
29	The Haunter of the Dark (1936) by H.P. Lovecraft	489
30	Ennui (1936) by Clark Ashton Smith	519
31	Bride of Baal (1936) by Edgar Daniel Kramer	521
32	Night-Gaunts (1936) by H.P. Lovecraft	523
	About the Editor	525

Robert E. Howard's

Introduction

Robert E. Howard (1906-1936) is most widely known for his character "Conan of Cimmeria," or, in terms of popular culture, "Co-nan the Barbarian." Still, he created many other characters, such as Solomon Kane and King Kull, and wrote in many different genres, including westerns, detective stories, humorous tall tales, boxing stories and tales of horror. Howard was also a naturally gifted and talented poet, and the lyrical cadence and feel of much of his poetry is on display in his prose. Because of his many talents and stories across genres—and often the mixing of genres—not everyone comes to Robert E. Howard in the same manner. Indeed, many have discovered his writing only through the popular culture aspects of his character Conan, either through the comics or the movies. Regardless of how people began reading Howard, those who have, more often than not, become fans of Howard.

After someone discovers an author for the first time, they often set about reading additional stories that include their beloved character before venturing down the path of reading other stories by their favorite author. Many people discovering Howard for the first time cannot wait to read more of his fiction. If the joy continues, readers often consider reading the author's entire canon. When thinking about Robert E. Howard, the benefit today is the fact it is now possible to find and read everything he wrote thanks in large part to the efforts of the people behind the Robert E. Howard Foundation. Once the author's canon has been exhausted, many will turn to reading pastiche stories, those written by other authors typically using their more popular characters, such as Howard's Conan. These stories are never quite as good as the originals—for as it has often been said, "No one writes like Howard, but Howard"—but they help keep the joy of their favorite character alive.

At this point, fans often seek to learn more about the author himself by reading articles and biographies. Once someone learns more about their treasured author as a person, the next natural progression is to see where the person grew up and lived. Ruth Stein, as quoted in Rusty Burke's *Robert E. Howard in Cross Plains*, once said, "Standing in a house where one's favorite author lived, or seeing the desk at which he or she wrote, or visiting the haunts the writer once knew established a certain kinship with him." This is so very true and fortunately the good people of Cross Plain's Project Pride purchased the house where Howard wrote his stories and have opened it up as a museum so visitors can see the room from which he wrote.

Although the museum is available for tours all year round, there is a special weekend in which Project Pride, along with members of The Robert E. Howard Foundation and the Robert E. Howard Universal Press Association, hosts Howard Days. This weekend is the second weekend of June, near the date of his death, June 11. Fans of Howard gather for tours of the house, take bus tours of Cross Plains and the surrounding area, attend presentations on Howard's life and writing, and gather socially at the pavilion, conveniently located on the property, to talk about their favorite author.

For those continuing to want to know more about their favorite author, many dive even deeper by either reading the works of the authors who influenced them or by reading the same stories and poems their author enjoyed. For Robert E. Howard, the former included authors such as Edgar Rice Burroughs, Jack London, and Talbot Mundy, while the latter were many of his contemporaries including H.P. Lovecraft, Clark Ashton Smith, and E. Hoffmann Price. And this brings us to the purpose of this edited collection—to share some of the authors who influenced Robert E. Howard's writing and to present the stories and poems that Howard enjoyed the most.

Now, when Howard wrote his stories, he typically referred to them as his "yarns," and when he wrote his poems, he called them his "rimes," so this edited collection encompasses *Robert E. Howard's Favorite Yarns and Rimes*. To do so, the book draws upon Howard's own letters in which he mentions a yarn or rime he really enjoyed. Because many of the authors are his *Weird Tales* colleagues, such as Lovecraft and Smith, there is the possibility Howard could have been offering praise on their recent publications just to be kind. However, I do not believe this to be the case, for as E. Hoffmann Price once said of Howard, "He meant precisely what he said, and he said exactly what he meant, no more, no less." So, I am fairly confident these are the yarns and rimes that he truly enjoyed reading.

This is not a complete collection. First, the collection is only based on what he mentioned in his letters, and there is little doubt there were others he enjoyed that he did not mention. Second, it is not entirely complete due to both length and copyright constraints. There are some yarns Howard enjoyed that are book-length treatments and are far too long to be reprinted here, such as Ray Cummings' novella *Explorers into Infinity* (serialized in *Weird Tales* beginning April 1927). Others remain under copyright protection today. The copyright law at the time stated that an author received a copyright for 28 years and had to renew the copyright for an additional 28 years. Some authors, such as August Derleth, had the copyright on their stories renewed since they were around to do so.

Still, as a whole, most of the yarns and rimes Howard mentioned in his letters are included in this edited reader. The versions that are reprinted here are the ones Howard most likely would have read. For instance, "The Rats in the Walls" by H.P. Lovecraft first appeared in the March 1924 issue of *Weird Tales*, and was reprinted in the June 1930 issue. It is the latter that Howard read, so it is this version that was used for this reader. Moreover, the versions of such book publications as Omar Khayyám's *The Rubáiyát* and Jack London's *The Star Rover*, are based on the most widely popular versions available during Howard's lifetime.

Each of the yarns and rimes in this collection feature an introduction that presents Howard's praise as well as some

Robert E. Howard's

background on the story or poem itself, along with its publication information. Every effort was made by the editor to ensure that copyright was not violated in gathering this collection based on research into the publication history of the yarn or rime, as well as their copyright status according to the U.S. copyright office.

For the fan of Robert E. Howard, it is hoped that reading these together in one volume will present a unique perspective on the yarns and rimes Howard enjoyed.

It should also be noted that all sales of this edited collection will go to Cross Plains' Project Pride to help support their efforts in preserving both the home and memory of Robert E. Howard.

The editor would like to thank Rob Roehm and the Robert E. Howard Foundation for making this publication possible with their own publication of *The Collected Letters of Robert E. Howard*. I would also like to thank Ronda Harris for donating her time by providing copy-editing assistance.

-Willard M. Oliver

1
The Rubáiyát
Omar Khayyám
(ca. 1100)

"I have carefully gone over, in my mind, the most powerful men—that is, in my opinion—in all of the world's literature and here is my list," wrote Robert E. Howard to his best friend, Tevis Clyde Smith, in February of 1928. "Jack London, Leonid Androyev [Andreiev], Omar Khayam [Khayyám], Eugene O'Neill, William Shakespeare." Howard then added this qualification: "All these men, and especially London and Khayam, to my mind stand out so far above the rest of the world that comparison is futile, a waste of time. Reading these men and apprecíateing them makes a man feel life not altogether useless." The Rubáiyát, written circa 1100 A.D., did not become popularized in the West until the 19th century and was widely read in the early 20th century. Howard adopted a series of quatrains from the Rubáiyát to use as epigraphs for chapters one through four in his novella, *Skull-Face*. The story, first published in *Weird Tales* magazine in 1929, was serialized over the October, November, and December issues. The following selection, drawn from around the *Skull-Face* quatrains, are linked together by the lamp/lantern theme.

XXXI

Up from Earth's Centre through the Seventh Gate
rose, and on the Throne of Saturn sate;
And many a Knot unravel'd by the Road;
But not the Master-knot of Human Fate.

XXXII

There was the Door to which I found no Key;
There was the Veil through which I might not see:
Some little talk awhile of Me and Thee
There was—and then no more of Thee and Me.

XXXIII

Earth could not answer; nor the Seas that mourn
In flowing Purple, of their Lord forlorn;
Nor rolling Heaven, with all his Signs reveal'd
And hidden by the sleeve of Night and Morn.

XXXIV

Then of the Thee in Me works behind
The Veil, I lifted up my hands to find
A Lamp amid the Darkness; and I heard,
As from Without—"The Me Within Thee Blind!"

LXVIII

We are no other than a moving row
Of Magic Shadow-shapes that come and go
Round with the Sun-illumined Lantern held
In Midnight by the Master of the Show;

LXIX

But helpless Pieces of the Game He plays
Upon this Chequer-board of Nights and Days;
Hither and thither moves, and checks, and slays,
And one by one back in the Closet lays.

LXX

The Ball no question makes of Ayes and Noes,
But Here or There as strikes the Player goes;
And He that toss'd you down into the Field,
He knows about it all—He knows—HE knows!

2
Heimskringla: King Olaf's Story
Snorri Sturluson
(ca. 1200)

Snorri Sturluson wrote *Heimskringla*, the Icelandic sagas, around 1230 A.D. They are a collection of tales about Norwegian kings, beginning with the Ynglinga dynasty up to the death of Eystein Meyla in 1177. The tales, translated by Samuel Laing in the mid-19th century, became popular during the late 19th and early 20th centuries. Howard appears to have obtained a copy sometime in the spring/summer of 1935. In a July 1935 letter to H.P. Lovecraft, he wrote, "By the way, I recently got hold of a book that ought to be read by all writers who strive after realism, and by every man with a drop of Nordic blood in his veins—the 'Heimskirngla' by Snorre Sturlason. Reading his sagas of the Norse people, I felt more strongly than ever my instinctive kinship with them, and the kinship between them and frontier people of America. In many ways the Norsemen figuring in his history more resemble the American pioneers of the West more than any other European people I have ever read about. The main difference, as far as I could see, was that the Norsemen were more prone to break their pledged word than were the frontiersmen." The entire collection is book length, so the following excerpt comes from only one of the 16 sagas—"King Olaf Trygvason's Saga"—detailing his final days as king.

Of King Olaf
King Olaf stood on the *Serpent's* quarterdeck, high over the others. He had a gilt shield, and a helmet inlaid with gold; over his armour he had a short red coat, and was easy to be distinguished from other men. When King Olaf saw that the scatter-

ed forces of the enemy gathered themselves together under the banners of their ships, he asked, "Who is the chief of the force right opposite to us?"

He was answered, that it was King Svein with the Danish army.

The king replies, "We are not afraid of these soft Danes, for there is no bravery in them; but who are the troops on the right of the Danes?"

He was answered, that it was King Olaf with the Swedish forces.

"Better it were," says King Olaf, "for these Swedes to be sitting at home killing their sacrifices, than to be venturing under our weapons from the *Long Serpent*. But who owns the large ships on the larboard side of the Danes?"

"That is Earl Eirik Hakonson," say they.

The king replies, "He, methinks, has good reason for meeting us; and we may expect the sharpest conflict with these men, for they are Norsemen like ourselves."

The Battle Begins

The kings now laid out their oars, and prepared to attack (AD 1000). King Svein laid his ship against the *Long Serpent*. Outside of him Olaf the Swede laid himself, and set his ship's stern against the outermost ship of King Olaf's line; and on the other side lay Earl Eirik. Then a hard combat began. Earl Sigvalde held back with the oars on his ships, and did not join the fray. So says Skule Thorsteinson, who at that time was with Earl Eirik:

> "I followed Sigvalde in my youth,
> And gallant Eirik, and in truth
> The' now I am grown stiff and old,
> In the spear-song I once was bold.
> Where arrows whistled on the shore
> Of Svold fjord my shield I bore,

And stood amidst the loudest clash
When swords on shields made fearful crash."
And Halfred also sings thus:

"In truth I think the gallant king,
Midst such a foemen's gathering,
Would be the better of some score
Of his tight Throndhjem lads, or more;
For many a chief has run away,
And left our brave king in the fray,
Two great kings' power to withstand,
And one great earl's, with his small band,
The king who dares such mighty deed
A hero for his skald would need."

Flight of Svein and Olaf the Swede

This battle was one of the severest told of, and many were the people slain. The forecastle men of the *Long Serpent*, the *Little Serpent*, and the *Crane*, threw grapplings and stem chains into King Svein's ship, and used their weapons well against the people standing below them, for they cleared the decks of all the ships they could lay fast hold of; and King Svein, and all the men who escaped, fled to other vessels, and laid themselves out of bow-shot. It went with this force just as King Olaf Trygvason had foreseen. Then King Olaf the Swede laid himself in their place; but when he came near the great ships it went with him as with them, for he lost many men and some ships, and was obliged to get away. But Earl Eirik laid his ship side by side with the outermost of King Olaf's ships, thinned it of men, cut the cables, and let it drive. Then he laid alongside of the next, and fought till he had cleared it of men also. Now all the people who were in the smaller ships began to run into the larger, and the earl cut them loose as fast as he cleared them of men. The Danes and Swedes laid themselves now out of shooting distance all around Olaf's ship; but Earl Eirik lay always close alongside of the ships, and used hid swords and battle-axes, and as fast as people fell in his vessel others, Danes and Swedes, came in their place. So says Haldor, the Unchristian:

> "Sharp was the clang of shield and sword,
> And shrill the song of spears on board,
> And whistling arrows thickly flew
> Against the *Serpent's* gallant crew.
> And still fresh foemen, it is said,
> Earl Eirik to her long side led;
> Whole armies of his Danes and Swedes,
> Wielding on high their blue sword-blades."

Then the fight became most severe, and many people fell. But at last it came to this, that all King Olaf Trygvason's ships were cleared of men except the *Long Serpent*, on board of which all who could still carry their arms were gathered. Then Earl Eirik lay with his ship by the side of the *Serpent*, and the fight went on with battle-axe and sword. So says Haldor:

> "Hard pressed on every side by foes,
> The *Serpent* reels beneath the blows;
> Crash go the shields around the bow!
> Breast-plates and breasts pierced thro' and thro'!
> In the sword-storm the Holm beside,
> The earl's ship lay alongside
> The king's *Long Serpent* of the sea –
> Fate gave the earl the victory."

Of Earl Eirik

Earl Eirik was in the forehold of his ship, where a cover of shields had been set up. In the fight, both hewing weapons, sword, and axe, and the thrust of spears had been used; and all that could be used as weapon for casting was cast. Some used bows, some threw spears with the hand. So many weapons were cast into the *Serpent*, and so thick flew spears and arrows, that the shields could scarcely receive them, for on all sides the *Serpent* was surrounded by war-ships. Then King Olaf's men became so mad with rage, that they ran on board of the enemies ships, to get at the people with stroke of sword and kill them; but many did not lay themselves so near the *Serpent*, in order to escape the close encounter with battle-axe or sword; and thus the most of Olaf's men went overboard and sank under their weapons, thinking they were fighting on plain ground. So says Halfred:

> "The daring lads shrink not from death; –
> Overboard they leap, and sink beneath
> The *Serpent's* keel: all armed they leap,
> And down they sink five fathoms deep.
> The foe was daunted at the cheers;
> The king, who still the *Serpent* steers,
> In such a strait – beset with foes –
> Wanted but some more lads like those."

Of Einar Tambarskelver

Einar Tambarskelver, one of the sharpest of bowshooters, stood by the mast, and shot with his bow. Einar shot an arrow at Earl Eirik, which hit the tiller end just above the earl's head so hard that it entered the wood up to the arrow-shaft. The earl looked that way, and asked if they knew who had shot; and at the same moment another arrow flew between his hand and his side, and into the stuffing of the chief's stool, so that the barb stood far out on the other side. Then said the earl to a man called Fin, – but some say he was of Fin (Laplander) race, and was a superior archer, – "Shoot that tall man by the mast." Fin shot; and the arrow hit the middle of Einar's bow just at the moment that Einar was drawing it, and the bow was split in two parts.

"What is that."cried King Olaf, "that broke with such a noise?"

"Norway, king, from your hands," cried Einar.

"No! not quite so much as that," says the king; "take my bow, and shoot," flinging the bow to him.

Einar took the bow, and drew it over the head of the arrow. "Too weak, too weak," said he, "for the bow of a mighty king!" and, throwing the bow aside, he took sword and shield, and fought Valiantly.

Olaf Gives His Men Sharp Swords

The king stood on the gangways of the *Long Serpent*, and shot the greater part of the day; sometimes with the bow, sometimes with the spear, and always throwing two spears at once. He looked down over the ship's sides, and saw that his men struck briskly with their swords, and yet wounded but seldom. Then he called aloud, "Why do you strike so gently that you seldom cut?" One among the people answered, "The swords are blunt and full of notches." Then the king went down into the forehold, opened the chest under the throne, and took out many sharp swords, which he handed to his men; but as he stretched down his right hand with them, some observed that blood was running down under his steel glove, but no one knew where he was wounded.

The Serpent Boarded

Desperate was the defence in the *Serpent*, and there was the heaviest destruction of men done by the forecastle crew, and those of the forehold, for in both places the men were chosen men, and the ship was highest, but in the middle of the ship the people were thinned. Now when Earl Eirik saw there were but few people remaining beside the ship's mast, he determined to board; and he entered the *Serpent* with four others. Then came Hyrning, the king's brother-in-law, and some others against him, and there was the most severe combat; and at last the earl was forced to leap back on board his own ship again, and some who had accompanied him were killed, and others wounded. Thord Kolbeinson alludes to this:

"On Odin's deck, all wet with blood,
The helm-adorned hero stood;
And gallant Hyrning honour gained,
Clearing all round with sword deep stained.
The high mountain peaks shall fall,
Ere men forget this to recall."

Now the fight became hot indeed, and many men fell on board the *Serpent*; and the men on board of her began to be thinned off, and the defence to be weaker. The earl resolved to board the *Serpent* again, and again he met with a warm reception. When the forecastle men of the *Serpent* saw what he was doing, they went aft and made a desperate fight; but so many men of the *Serpent* had fallen, that the ship's sides were in many places quite bare of defenders; and the earl's men poured in all around into the vessel, and all the men who were still able to defend the ship crowded aft to the king, and arrayed themselves for his defence. So says Haldor the Unchristian:

> "Eirik cheers on his men, –
> 'On to the charge again!'
> The gallant few
> Of Olaf's crew
> Must refuge take
> On the quarter-deck.
> Around the king
> They stand in ring;
> Their shields enclose
> The king from foes,
> And the few who still remain

Fight madly, but in vain.
Eirik cheers on his men –
'On to the charge again!'"

The Serpent Decks Cleared

Kolbjorn the marshal, who had on clothes and arms like the kings, and was a remarkably stout and handsome man, went up to king on the quarter-deck. The battle was still going on fiercely even in the forehold. But as many of the earl's men had now got into the *Serpent* as could find room, and his ships lay all round her, and few were the people left in the *Serpent* for defence against so great a force; and in a short time most of the *Serpent's* men fell, brave and stout though they were. King Olaf and Kolbjorn the marshal both sprang overboard, each on his own side of the ship; but the earl's men had laid out boats around the *Serpent*, and killed those who leaped overboard. Now when the king had sprung overboard, they tried to seize him with their hands, and bring him to Earl Eirik; but King Olaf threw his shield over his head, and sank beneath the waters. Kolbjorn held his shield behind him to protect himself from the spears cast at him from the ships which lay round the *Serpent*, and he fell so on his shield that it came under him, so that he could not sink so quickly. He was thus taken and brought into a boat, and they supposed he was the king. He was brought before the earl; and when the earl saw it was Kolbjorn, and not the king, he gave him his life. At the same moment all of King Olaf's men who were in life sprang overboard from the *Serpent*; and Thorkel Nefia, the king's brother, was the last of all the men who sprang overboard. It is thus told concerning the king by Halfred:

"The *Serpent* and the *Crane*
Lay wrecks on the main.
On his sword he cast a glance, –
With it he saw no chance.

> To his marshal, who of yore
> Many a war-chance had come over,
> He spoke a word – then drew in breath,
> And sprang to his deep-sea death."

Report Among the People
Earl Sigvalde, as before related, came from Vindland, in company with King Olaf, with ten ships; but the eleventh ship was manned with the men of Astrid, the king's daughter, the wife of Earl Sigvalde. Now when King Olaf sprang overboard, the whole army raised a shout of victory; and then Earl Sigvalde and his men put their oars in the water and rowed towards the battle. Haldor the Unchristian tells of it thus:

> "Then first the Vindland vessels came
> Into the fight with little fame;
> The fight still lingered on the wave,
> Tho' hope was gone with Olaf brave.
> War, like a full-fed ravenous beast,
> Still oped her grim jaws for the feast.
> The few who stood now quickly fled,
> When the shout told – 'Olaf is dead!'"

But the Vindland cutter, in which Astrid's men were, rowed back to Vindland; and the report went immediately abroad and was told by many, that King Olaf had cast off his coat-of-mail under water, and had swum, diving under the longships, till he came to the Vindland cutter, and that Astrid's men had conveyed him to Vindland: and many tales have been made since about the adventures of Olaf the king. Halfred speaks thus about it:

> "Does Olaf live? or is he dead?
> Has he the hungry ravens fed?
> I scarcely know what I should say,

> For many tell the tale each way.
> This I can say, nor fear to lie,
> That he was wounded grievously –
> So wounded in this bloody strife,
> He scarce could come away with life."

But however this may have been, King Olaf Trygvason never came back again to his kingdom of Norway. Halfred Vandredaskald speaks also thus about it:

> "The witness who reports this thing
> Of Trygvason, our gallant king,
> Once served the king, and truth should tell,
> For Olaf hated lies like hell.
> If Olaf 'scaped from this sword-thing,
> Worse fate, I fear, befel our king
> Than people guess, or ever can know,
> For he was hemm'd in by the foe.
> From the far east some news is rife
> Of king sore wounded saving life;
> His death, too sure, leaves me no care
> For cobweb rumours in the air.
> It never was the will of fate
> That Olaf from such perilous strait
> Should 'scape with life! this truth may grieve –
> 'What people wish they soon believe.'"

3
Grettir the Outlaw: A Story of Iceland
(The Vampire Chapters)
S. Baring-Gould
(ca. 1400)

Robert. E. Howard, writing in *Weird Tales* magazine's letter-column, "The Eyrie," in May 1926, suggested the Old Norse sagas as an excellent possibility for inclusion in the magazine's reprint series. "The Saga of Grettir the Outlaw," he wrote, "while told in plain, almost homely language, reaches the peak of horror. You will recall the terrific, night-long battle between the outlaw and the vampire, who had himself been slain by the Powers of Darkness." Grettir's saga is part of the Sagas of Icelanders written in the 13th and 14th centuries. Baring-Gould translated the sagas then told them in his own style in what became a very popular edition published in 1889. While this may not be the version Howard read, it is the story he is referring to in his letter to "The Eyrie."

We have come now to an incident which formed a turning-point in Grettir's life. It is a very mysterious and inexplicable story, not one that can be put aside as we have that of his fight in the tomb with Karr the Old. This is a story even more gruesome. It relates to an event that so shook Grettir's nerves that he never after could endure to be alone in the dark, and would risk all kinds of dangers to escape solitude. How much of truth lies under this strange narrative we cannot now say, but that something really did take place is certain from the effect it had on Grettir ever after.

The richest valley for grass in all this quarter of Iceland, and the most peopled, is the Waterdale. On the east rises a mountain ridge of precipitous basaltic cliffs, down which leap waterfalls from the snows above. The river that flows through this valley is fed by two main streams that unite at the farm called Tongue. The stream on the east rises a long way inland in a mass of lava, and flows through a valley so narrow and so gloomy that it goes by the name of the Valley of Shadows. The high ranges of moor and waste to the south shut off the southern sun, and the lofty banks of mountain to east and west so close it in that it gets no sun morning or evening.

A little way up this valley—not far, and not where it is most gloomy—are now the scanty ruins of a farm called Thorhall's-stead. Above this the valley so contracts and the hills are so steep that it is only with great difficulty that a horse can be led along. This I know very well; for in crossing an avalanche slide my horse and I were almost precipitated into the torrent below. Further up the valley stands a tongue of high land with a waterfall on one side and the ravine on the other, and here at one time some robbers had their fortress who were the terror of the neighbourhood. No trace of their fortress remains at present, but it was to find this place that I explored the valley.

In the farm that is now but a heap of ruins lived a bonder named Thorhall and his wife. He was not a man of much consideration in the district, for he was planted on cold, poor land, and his wealth was but small. Moreover, he had no servants; and the reason was that his sheep-walks were haunted.

Not a herdsman would remain with him. He offered high wages, he threatened, he entreated, all in vain. One shepherd after another left his service, and things came to such a pass that he determined to have the advice of the law-man or chief judge at the next annual assize.

He saddled his horses and rode to Thingvalla. Skapti was the name of the judge then, a man with a long head, and deemed the best of men for giving counsel. Thorhall told him his trouble.

"I can help you," said Skapti. "There is a shepherd who has been with me, a rude, strange man, but afraid of neither man nor hobgoblin, and strong as a bull; but he is not very clear in his intellect."

"That does not matter," said Thorhall, "so long as he can mind sheep."

"You may trust him for that," said Skapti. "He is a Swede, and his name is Glam."

Towards the end of the assize two gray horses belonging to Thorhall slipped their hobbles and strayed; so, as he had no serving-man, he went after them himself, and on his way met a strange-looking fellow, driving before him an ass laden with faggots. The man was tall and stalwart; his face attracted Torhall's attention, for the eyes were ashen gray and staring. The powerful jaw was furnished with white protruding teeth, and about his low brow hung bunches of coarse wolf-gray hair.

"Pray, what are you called?" asked Thorhall, for he suspected that this was the man Skapti had spoken about.

"Glam, at your service."

"Do you like your present duties—wood-cutting?" asked the farmer.

"No, I do not. I am properly a shepherd."

"Then, will you come with me? Skapti has spoken of you and offered you to me."

"What are the drawbacks to your service?" asked Glam cautiously.

"None, save that my sheep-walks are haunted."

"Oh! is that all? Ghosts won't scare me. Here is my hand. I will come to you before winter."

They separated, and soon after the farmer found his horses; they had got into a little wood, and were nibbling the willow tops. He went home, having thanked Skapti.

Summer passed, then autumn, and nothing further was heard of Glam. The winter storms began to bluster up the valley from the cold Polar Sea, driving the flying snowflakes and heaping them in drifts at every turn of the vale. Ice formed in the shallows of the river, and the streams which in summer trickled down the sides were now turned to icicles. I was there the very end of June, and then the whole of the mountain flank to the west was covered with frozen streams spread like a net of icicle over the black and red striped bare rock.

One gusty night a violent blow at the door startled all in the farm. In another moment Glam, tall and wild, stood in the hall glowering out of his gray staring eyes, his hair matted with frost, his teeth rattling and snapping with cold, his face blood-red in the glare of the fire that glowed in the centre of the hall.

He was well received by Thorhall, but the housewife did not like the man's looks, and did not welcome him with much heartiness. Time passed, and the shepherd was on the moors every day with the flock; his loud and deep-toned voice was often borne down on the wind as he shouted to the sheep, driving them to fold. His presence always produced a chill in the house, and when he spoke it sent a thrill through the women, who did not like him.

Christmas-eve was raw and windy; masses of gray vapour rolled up from the Arctic Ocean, and hung in piles about the mountain tops. Now and then a scud of frozen fog, covering bar and beam with feathery hoar-frost, swept up the glen. As the day declined snow began to fall in large flakes.

When the wind lulled there could be heard the shout of Glam high up on the hillside. Darkness closed in, and with the darkness the snow fell thicker. There was a church then at Thorhall's farm; there is none there now, since the valley has been abandoned from its cold and ill name.

The lights were kindled in the church, and every snowflake as it sailed down past the open door burned like a golden feather in the light.

When the service was over, and the farmer and his party returned to the house, Glam had not come home. This was strange; as he could not live abroad in the cold, and the sheep would also require shelter. Thorhall was uneasy and proposed a search, but no one would go with him; and no wonder, it was not a night for a dog to be out in, and the tracks would all be buried in snow. So the family sat up all night listening, trembling and anxious.

Day broke at last faintly in the south over the great white masses of mountains. Now a party was formed to search for the missing man. A sharp climb brought them to the top of the moor above Tongue. Here and there a sheep was found shivering under a rock or half buried in a snowdrift, but of Glam—not a sign.

Presently the whole party was called together about a spot on the hilltop where the snow was trampled and kicked about, and it was clear that some desperate struggle had taken place there. There the snow was also dabbled with frozen blood. A red track led further up the mountain side, and the searchers were following it when a boy uttered a shriek of fear. In looking behind a rock he had come on the corpse of the shepherd lying on its back with the arms extended. The body was taken up and carried to the edge of the gorge, and was there buried under a pile of stones, heaped over it to the height of about six feet. *How* Glam had died, *by whom* killed, no one knew, nor could they make a guess.

Two nights after this one of the thralls who had gone for the cows burst into the hall with a face blank from terror; he staggered to a seat and fainted. On recovering his senses, in a broken voice he assured those who were round him that he had seen Glam walking past him, with huge strides, as he left the stable door. The shepherd had turned his head and looked at him fixedly from his great gray staring eyes. On the following day a stable lad was found in a fit under a wall, and he never after recovered his senses. It was thought he must have seen something that had scared him. Next, some of the women, declared that they had seen Glam looking in on them through a window of the dairy. In the dusk Thorhall himself met the dead man, who stood and glowered at him, but made no attempt to injure his master, and uttered not a word. The haunting did not end thus. Nightly a heavy tread was heard round the house, and a hand groping along the walls, and sometimes a hand came in at the windows, a great coarse hand, that in the red light from the fire seemed as though steeped in blood.

When the spring came round the disturbances lessened, and as the sun obtained full power, ceased altogether.

During the course of the summer a Norwegian vessel came into the fiord; Thorhall went on board and found there a man named Thorgaut, who had come out in search of work. Thorhall engaged him as a shepherd, but not without honestly telling him his trouble, and what there was uncanny about his sheep-walks, and how Glam had fared. The man did not regard this, he laughed, and promised to be with Thorhall at the appointed season.

Accordingly he arrived in autumn, and he soon established himself as a favourite in the house; he romped with the children, helped his fellow-servants, and was as much liked as his predecessor had been detested. He was such a merry careless fellow that he did not think anything of the risks that lay before him, and joked about them.

When winter set in strange sights and sounds began to alarm the folk at the farm, but Thorgaut was not troubled; he slept too soundly at night to be disturbed by the heavy tread round the house.

On the day before Yule, as was his wont, Thorgaut drove out the sheep to pasture. Thorhall was uneasy. He said to him: "I pray you be careful, and do not go near the barrow under which Glam was laid."

"Don't fear for me," laughed Thorgaut, "I shall be back in time for supper, and shall attend you to church."

Night settled in, but no Thorgaut arrived. There was little mirth at table when the supper was brought in. All were anxious and fearful.

The wind was cold and wetting. Blocks of ice were driving about in the bay, grinding against each other, and the sound could be heard far up the valley. Aloft, the aurora flames were lighting up the heavens with an arch of fire. Again this Christmas night the dwellers in the farm sat up and did not go to bed, waiting for the return of Thorgaut, but he did not arrive.

Next morning he was sought, and was found lying dead across the barrow of Glam, with his spine and one leg and one arm broken. He was brought home and laid in the churchyard.

Matters now rapidly became worse. Outbuildings were broken into of a night, and their woodwork was rent and shattered; the house door was violently shaken, and great pieces of it were torn away; the gables of the house were also pulled furiously to and fro.

Now it fell out that one morning the only man who remained in the service of the family went out early. Not another servant dared to remain in the place, and this man remained because he had been with Thorhall and with his father, and he could not make up his mind to desert his master in his need. About an hour after he had gone out Thorhall's wife took her milking cans and went to the cow-house that she might milk the cows, as she had now not a maid in the house, and had to do everything herself. On reaching the door of the cow-house she heard a terrible sound from within, the bellowing of the cattle, and the deep bell-notes of an unearthly voice. She was so frightened that she dropped her pails and ran back to the house and called her husband. Thorhall was in bed, but he rose instantly, caught up a weapon, and hastened to the cow-house.

On opening the door he found all the cattle loose and goring each other. Slung across the stone that separated their stalls was the old serving-man, perfectly dead, with his back broken. He had, apparently, been tossed by the cows, and had fallen on this stone backwards.

Neither Thorhall nor his wife explained his death in this way; they thought that Glam must have been there, have driven the cattle wild, and that just as he had broken the back of Thorgaut, so had he now broken that of the poor old serving-man.

It was impossible for the bonder to remain longer in that place; he and his wife therefore removed down to Tongue, which lies at the junction of the two rivers, and there things were quiet. There he was hospitably received by Jokull. Thorhall was able to persuade some of his runaway servants to come back to him, but no man all that winter would go near the moor where was the barrow of the shepherd Glam.

Not till the summer returned, and the sun had dispelled the darkness, did Thorhall venture back to the Vale of Shadows. In the meanwhile his daughter's health had given way under the repeated alarms of the winter; she became paler every day; with the autumn flowers she faded, and was laid in the churchyard before the first snowflakes fell. What was Thorhall to do through the winter? He knew that it was not possible for him to secure servants if he remained on his own farm; besides, he did not know what loss might come to his stock. Then, he could not spend the whole winter at Tongue, for that was another bonder's house, and though the farmer there had kindly received him and entertained him for three months the winter before, he could not ask him to give him houseroom to himself, his cattle, and servants for a whole long winter.

So he was in the greatest possible perplexity what to do. Help came to him from an unexpected quarter.

Grettir had heard the story of the hauntings, and he rode to Thorhall's farm and asked if he might be accommodated there for the night. He said that it was his great desire to encounter Glam.

Thorhall was surprised, but not exactly pleased, for he thought that the family at Biarg would attribute the wrong to him were anything to happen to Grettir.

Grettir put his horse into the stable, and retired for the night to one of the beds in the hall and slept soundly.

Next morning Grettir went with Thorhall to the stable for his horse. The strong wooden door was shivered and driven in. They stepped across it; Grettir called to his horse, but there was no responsive whinny. Grettir dashed into the stall and found his horse dead; its neck was broken.

"Now," said Thorhall, "I will give you a horse in exchange for that you have lost. You had better ride home to Biarg at once."

"Not at all. My horse has been killed, and I must avenge it." So Grettir remained.

Night set in. Grettir ate a hearty supper, and was right merry. But not so Thorhall, who had his misgivings. At bedtime the latter crept into a locked bedstead beside the hall; but Grettir said he would not go into a bed, he would lie by the fire in the hall. So he wrapped himself up in a long fur cloak and flung himself on a bench, with his feet against the posts of the high seat. The fur cloak was over his head, and he kept an opening through which he could look out.

There was a fire burning on the hearth, a smouldering heap of glowing embers, and by the red light Grettir looked up at the rafters of the blackened roof. The smoke escaped by a *louvre* in the middle. The wind whistled mournfully. The windows high up were covered with parchment, and admitted now and then a sickly yellow glare from the full moon, which, however, shone in through the smoke hole, silvering the rising smoke. A dog began to bark, then bay at the moon. Then the cat, which had been sitting demurely watching the fire, stood up with raised back and bristling tail, and darted behind some chests. The hall-door was in a sad plight. It had been so torn by

Glam that it had to be patched up with wattles. Soothingly the river prattled over its shingly bed as it swept round the knoll on which stood the farm. Grettir heard the breathing of the sleeping women in the adjoining chamber, and the sigh of the housewife as she turned in her bed.

Then suddenly he heard something that shook all the sleep out of him, had any been stealing over his eyes. He heard a heavy tread, beneath which the snow crackled. Every footfall went straight to Grettir's heart. A crash on the turf overhead. The strange visitant had scrambled on the roof, and was walking over that. The roofs of the houses in Iceland are of turf. For a moment the chimney gap was completely darkened—the monster was looking down it—the flash of the red fire illumined the horrible face with its lack-lustre eyes. Then the moon shone in again, and the heavy tramp of Glam was heard as he walked to the other end of the hall. A thud—he had leaped down.

Then Grettir heard his steps passing to the back of the house, then the snapping of wood showed that Glam was destroying some of the outhouse doors. Presently the tread was heard again approaching the house, and this time the main entrance. Grettir thought he could distinguish a pair of great hands thrust in over the broken door. In another moment he heard a loud snap—a long plank had been torn out of place, and the light of the moon shone in where the gap had been made. Then Glam began to unrip the wattles.

There was a cross-beam to the door, acting as bolt. Against the gray light Grettir saw a huge black arm thrust in trying to remove the bar. It was done, and then all the broken door was driven in and went down on the floor in shivers. Now Grettir could see a tall dark figure, almost naked, with wild locks of hair about the head standing in the doorway. That was but for a minute, and then Glam came in stealthily; he entered the hall and was illumined by the firelight. The figure Grettir now saw was unlike anything he had seen before. A few rags hung from the shoulders and waist, the long wolf-gray hair was matted. The eyes were staring and strange. Grettir could hear Thorhall within his locked bed trembling and breathing fast.

Presently Glam's eyes rested on the shaggy bundle by the high seat. He stepped towards it, and Grettir felt him groping about him. Then Glam laid hold of one end of the fur cloak and began to pull at it. The cloak did not come away. Another jerk. Grettir kept his feet firmly pressed against the posts, so that the fur was not pulled away. Glam seemed puzzled; he went to the other end of the bundle and began to pull at that. Grettir held to the bench, so that he was not moved himself, but the fur cloak was torn in half, and the strange visitant staggered back holding the portion in his hand wonderingly before his eyes. Before he could recover from his surprise, Grettir started to his feet, bent his body, flung his arms round Glam, and driving his head into the breast of the visitor, tried to bend him backward and so snap his spine. This was in vain, the cold hands grasped Grettir's arms and tore them from their hold. Grettir clasped them again about his body, and then Glam threw his also round Grettir, and they began to wrestle. Grettir saw that Glam was trying to drag him to the door, and he was sure that if he were got outside he would be at a disadvantage, and Glam would break his back. He therefore made a desperate effort not to be drawn forth. He clung to benches and posts, but the posts gave way, and the benches were torn from their places.

At each moment he was being dragged nearer to the door. Sharply twisting himself loose, Grettir flung his arms round a beam of the roof, for the hall was low. He was dragged off his feet at once. Glam clenched him about the waist, and tore at him to get him loose. Every tendon in Grettir's breast was strained; still he held on. The nails of Glam cut into his side like knives, then his hands gave way. He could endure the strain no longer, and Glam drew him towards the doorway, in so doing trampling over the broken fragments of the door, and the wattles that lay about. Grettir knew that the last chance was come for saving himself. Here, in the hall, he could hold to posts and beams, and so make some resistance; but outside he would have nothing to cling to, and strong though he was, his strength did not equal that of his opponent.

Now the door-posts were of stone, and the beam that had served as bolt went across the door, slid into a hollow on one side cut in the door-post, and was pulled across and fitted into another hollow in the other post. As the wrestlers neared the opening, Grettir planted both his feet against the stone posts, one against each, and put his arms round Glam. He had the enemy now at an advantage; but then, he merely held him, and could not hold him so for ever. He called to Thorhall, but Thorhall was too greatly frightened to leave his place of refuge.

"Now," thought Grettir, "if I can but break his back!" Then drawing Glam to him by the middle, he put his head beneath the chin of his opponent and forced back the head. If he could only drive the head far enough back he would break his neck.

At that moment one or both of the door-posts gave way; down crashed the gable-trees, ripping beams and rafters from their places, frozen clods of turf rattled from the roof and thumped into the snow.

Glam fell on his back outside the door, and Grettir on top of him. The moon was, as I said before, at her full; large white clouds chased each other across the sky. Grettir's strength was failing him, his hands quivered in the snow, and he knew that he could not support himself from dropping flat on the mysterious and dreadful visitant, eye to eye, lip to lip.

Then Glam said: "You have done ill matching yourself with me; now know that never shall you be stronger than you are to-day, and that, to your dying day, whenever you are in the dark you will see my eyes staring at you, so that for very horror you will not dare to be alone."

At this moment Grettir saw his short sword in the snow, it had slipped from his belt as he fell. He put out his hand at once, clutched the handle, and with a blow cut off Glam's head, and at once laid it beside his thigh.

Thorhall came out at this juncture, his face blanched; but when he saw how the fray had ended, he joyfully assisted Grettir to roll the dead man to the top of a pile of faggots that had been collected for winter fuel. Fire was applied, and soon far down the Waterdale the flames of the pyre startled folks, and made them wonder what new horror was being enacted in the Vale of Shadows.

Next day the charred bones were conveyed a long way—some hours' ride—into the great desert in the interior, and in one of the most lonely spots there a cairn or pile of stones was heaped over them. I have seen this mound, which is still pointed out as that under which the redoubted Glam lies.

And now we may well ask, what truth is there in the story? That there is a basis of truth can hardly be denied. The facts have been embellished, worked up, but not invented. The only probable explanation of the story is this.

As already said, further up the valley, in a spot difficult to be reached, stood the old fortress of some robbers, with many caves in the sandstone about it very convenient for shelter. Now, it is not improbable that some madman may have taken refuge in this safe retreat, and may have come out at night in search of food, and carried off the sheep of Thorhall. It may be that Glam caught him attempting to steal a sheep, and fought with him, and was killed, and that in like manner Thorgaut was killed. Then when people saw a great wild man wandering about they thought it was Glam, whereas it was the man who had haunted the region before Glam came there, and had killed Glam. This is the simplest and easiest explanation of this wild and fearful tale.

Robert E. Howard's

4
The Fall of the House of Usher
Edgar Allan Poe
1839

In the April-May 1931 issue of *Weird Tales* magazine, Robert E. Howard published one of his best Cthulhu Mythos yarns, "The Children of the Night." At one point in the story, the character Tavrel makes mention of three stories that he thinks are masterpieces: "I will admit that few writers of fiction touch the true heights of horror—most of their stuff is too concrete, given too much earthly shape and dimensions. But in such tales as Poe's *Fall of the House of Usher*, Machen's *Black Seal* and Lovecraft's *Call of Cthulhu*—the three master horror-tales, to my mind—the reader is borne into dark and *outer* realms of imagination." While this is a fictitious character, one would have to wonder if it was Howard's own personal sentiment. Well, it was, or at least that is what he told H.P. Lovecraft in a June 1931 letter: "As regards my mention of the three foremost weird masterpieces—Poe's, Machen's and your own—it's my honest opinion that these three are the outstanding tales."

Son coeur est un luth suspendu; (His heart is a poised lute;)
Sitôt qu'on le touche il résonne. (As soon as it is touched, it resounds.)
  -De Béranger.

During the whole of a dull, dark, and soundless day in the autumn of the year, when the clouds hung oppressively low in the heavens, I had been passing alone, on horseback, through a singularly dreary tract of country; and at length found myself, as the shades of the evening drew on, within view of the melancholy House of Usher. I know not how it was—but, with the first glimpse of the building, a sense of insufferable gloom pervaded my spirit. I say insufferable; for the feeling was unrelieved by any of that half-pleasurable, because poetic, sentiment, with which the mind usually receives even the sternest natural images of the desolate or terrible. I looked upon the scene before me—upon the mere house, and the simple landscape features of the domain—upon the bleak walls—upon the vacant eye-like windows—upon a few rank sedges—and upon a few white trunks of decayed trees—with an utter depression of soul which I can compare to no earthly sensation more properly than to the after-dream of the reveller upon opium—the bitter lapse into everyday life—the hideous dropping off of the veil. There was an iciness, a sinking, a sickening of the heart—an unredeemed dreariness of thought which no goading of the imagination could torture into aught of the sublime. What was it—I paused to think—what was it that so unnerved me in the contemplation of the House of Usher? It was a mystery all insoluble; nor could I grapple with the shadowy fancies that crowded upon me as I pondered. I was forced to fall back upon the unsatisfactory conclusion, that while, beyond doubt, there *are* combinations of very simple natural objects which have the power of thus affecting us, still the analysis of this power lies among considerations beyond our depth. It was possible, I reflected, that a mere different arrangement of the particulars of the scene, of the details of the picture, would be sufficient to modify, or perhaps to annihilate its capacity for sorrowful impression; and, acting upon this idea, I reined my horse to the precipitous brink of a black and lurid tarn that lay in unruffled lustre by the dwelling, and gazed down—but with a shudder even more thrilling than before—upon the remodelled and inverted images of the gray sedge, and the ghastly tree-stems, and the vacant and eye-like windows.

Nevertheless, in this mansion of gloom I now proposed to myself a sojourn of some weeks. Its proprietor, Roderick even with effort, connect its Arabesque expression with any idea of simple humanity.

In the manner of my friend I was at once struck with an incoherence—an inconsistency; and I soon found this to arise from a series of feeble and futile struggles to overcome an habitual trepidancy—an excessive nervous agitation. For something of this nature I had indeed been prepared, no less by his letter, than by reminiscences of certain boyish traits, and by conclusions deduced from his peculiar physical conformation and temperament. His action was alternately vivacious and sullen. His voice varied rapidly from a tremulous indecision (when the animal spirits seemed utterly in abeyance) to that species of energetic concision—that abrupt, weighty, un-hurried, and hollow-sounding enunciation—that leaden, self-balanced and perfectly modulated guttural utterance, which may be observed in the lost drunkard, or the irreclaimable eater of opium, during the periods of his most intense excite-ment.

It was thus that he spoke of the object of my visit, of his earnest desire to see me, and of the solace he expected me to afford him. He entered, at some length, into what he conceived to be the nature of his malady. It was, he said, a constitutional and a family evil, and one for which he despaired to find a remedy—a mere nervous affection, he immediately added, which would undoubtedly soon pass. It displayed itself in a host of unnatural sensations. Some of these, as he detailed them, interested and bewildered me; although, perhaps, the terms, and the general manner of the narration had their weight. He suffered much from a morbid acuteness of the senses; the most insipid food was alone endurable; he could wear only garments of certain texture; the odours of all flowers were oppressive; his eyes were tortured by even a faint light; and there were but peculiar sounds, and these from stringed instruments, which did not inspire him with horror.

To an anomalous species of terror I found him a boun-den slave. "I shall perish," said he, "I *must* perish in this deplorable folly. Thus, thus, and not otherwise, shall I be lost. I dread the events of the future, not in themselves, but in their results. I shudder at the thought of any, even the most trivial, incident, which may operate upon this intolerable agitation of soul. I have, indeed, no abhorrence of danger, except in its absolute effect—in terror. In this unnerved—in this pitiable condition—I feel that the period will sooner or later arrive when I must abandon life and reason together, in some struggle with the grim phantasm, FEAR."

I learned, moreover, at intervals, and through broken and equivocal hints, another singular feature of his mental condition. He was enchained by certain superstitious impressions in regard to the dwelling which he tenanted, and whence, for many years, he had never ventured forth—in regard to an influence whose supposititious force was conveyed in terms too shadowy here to be re-stated—an influence which some peculiarities in the mere form and substance of his family mansion, had, by dint of long sufferance, he said, obtained over his spirit—an effect which the *physique* of the gray walls and turrets, and of the dim tarn into which they all looked down, had, at length, brought about upon the *morale* of his existence.

He admitted, however, although with hesitation, that much of the peculiar gloom which thus afflicted him could be traced to a more natural and far more palpable origin—to the severe and long-continued illness—indeed to the evidently approaching dissolution—of a tenderly beloved sister—his sole companion for long years—his last and only relative on earth. "Her decease," he said, with a bitterness which I can never forget, "would leave him (him the hopeless and the frail) the last of the ancient race of the Ushers." While he spoke, the lady Madeline (for so was she called) passed slowly through a remote portion of the apartment, and, without having noticed my presence, disappeared. I regarded her with an utter astonishment not unmingled with dread—and yet I found it impossible to account for such feelings. A sensation of stupor oppressed me, as my eyes followed her retreating steps. When a door, at length, closed upon her, my glance sought instinctively and eagerly the countenance of the brother—but he had buried his face in his hands, and I could only perceive that a far more than ordinary wanness had overspread the emaciated fingers through which trickled many passionate tears.

The disease of the lady Madeline had long baffled the skill of her physicians. A settled apathy, a gradual wasting away of the person, and frequent although transient affections of a partially cataleptical character, were the unusual diagnosis. Hitherto she had steadily borne up against the pressure of her malady, and had not betaken herself finally to bed; but, on the closing in of the evening of my arrival at the house, she succumbed (as her brother told me at night with inexpressible agitation) to the prostrating power of the destroyer; and I learned that the glimpse I had obtained of her person would thus probably be the last I should obtain—that the lady, at least while living, would be seen by me no more.

For several days ensuing, her name was unmentioned by either Usher or myself: and during this period I was busied in earnest endeavours to alleviate the melancholy of my friend. We painted and read together; or I listened, as if in a dream, to the wild improvisations of his speaking guitar. And thus, as a closer and still closer intimacy admitted me more unreservedly into the recesses of his spirit, the more bitterly did I perceive the futility of all attempt at cheering a mind from which darkness, as if an inherent positive quality, poured forth upon all objects of the moral and physical universe, in one unceasing radiation of gloom.

I shall ever bear about me a memory of the many solemn hours I thus spent alone with the master of the House of Usher. Yet I should fail in any attempt to convey an idea of the exact character of the studies, or of the occupations, in which he involved me, or led me the way. An excited and highly distempered ideality threw a sulphureous lustre over all. His long improvised dirges will ring forever in my ears. Among other things, I hold painfully in mind a certain singular perversion and amplification of the wild air of the last waltz of Von Weber. From the paintings over which his elaborate fancy brooded, and which grew, touch by touch, into vaguenesses at which I shuddered the more thrillingly, because I shuddered knowing not why;—from these paintings (vivid as their images now are before me) I would in vain endeavour to educe more than a small portion which should lie within the compass of merely written words. By the utter simplicity, by the nakedness of his designs, he arrested and overawed attention. If ever mortal painted an idea, that mortal was Roderick Usher. For me at least—in the circumstances then surrounding me—there arose out of the pure abstractions which the hypochondriac contrived to throw upon his canvas, an intensity of intolerable awe, no shadow of which felt I ever yet in the contemplation of the certainly glowing yet too concrete reveries of Fuseli.

One of the phantasmagoric conceptions of my friend, partaking not so rigidly of the spirit of abstraction, may be shadowed forth, although feebly, in words. A small picture presented the interior of an immensely long and rectangular vault or tunnel, with low walls, smooth, white, and without interruption or device. Certain accessory points of the design served well to convey the idea that this excavation lay at an exceeding depth below the surface of the earth. No outlet was observed in any portion of its vast extent, and no torch, or other artificial source of light was discernible; yet a flood of intense rays rolled throughout, and bathed the whole in a ghastly and inappropriate splendour.

I have just spoken of that morbid condition of the auditory nerve which rendered all music intolerable to the sufferer, with the exception of certain effects of stringed instruments. It was, perhaps, the narrow limits to which he thus confined himself upon the guitar, which gave birth, in great measure, to the fantastic character of his performances. But the fervid *facility* of his *impromptus* could not be so accounted for. They must have been, and were, in the notes, as well as in the words of his wild fantasias (for he not unfrequently accompanied himself with rhymed verbal improvisations), the result of that intense mental collectedness and concentration to which I have previously alluded as observable only in particular moments of the highest artificial excitement. The words of one of these rhapsodies I have easily remembered. I was, perhaps, the more forcibly impressed with it, as he gave it, because, in the under or mystic current of its meaning, I fancied that I perceived, and for the first time, a full consciousness on the part of Usher, of the tottering of his lofty reason upon her throne. The verses, which were entitled "The Haunted Palace," ran very nearly, if not accurately, thus:

I.
In the greenest of our valleys,
  By good angels tenanted,
Once a fair and stately palace—
  Radiant palace—reared its head.
In the monarch Thought's dominion—
  It stood there!
Never seraph spread a pinion
  Over fabric half so fair.

II.
Banners yellow, glorious, golden,
  On its roof did float and flow;
(This—all this—was in the olden
  Time long ago)
And every gentle air that dallied,
  In that sweet day,
Along the ramparts plumed and pallid,
  A winged odour went away.

III.
Wanderers in that happy valley
   Through two luminous windows saw
Spirits moving musically
    To a lute's well-tunèd law,
Round about a throne, where sitting
   (Porphyrogene!)
In state his glory well befitting,
    The ruler of the realm was seen.

IV.
And all with pearl and ruby glowing
   Was the fair palace door,
Through which came flowing, flowing, flowing,
   And sparkling evermore,
A troop of Echoes whose sweet duty
   Was but to sing,
In voices of surpassing beauty,
    The wit and wisdom of their king.

V.
But evil things, in robes of sorrow,
   Assailed the monarch's high estate;
(Ah, let us mourn, for never morrow
   Shall dawn upon him, desolate!)
And, round about his home, the glory
    That blushed and bloomed
Is but a dim-remembered story
    Of the old time entombed.

VI.
And travellers now within that valley,
   Through the red-litten windows, see
Vast forms that move fantastically

> To a discordant melody;
> While, like a rapid ghastly river,
> Through the pale door,
> A hideous throng rush out forever,
> And laugh—but smile no more.

I well remember that suggestions arising from this ballad led us into a train of thought wherein there became manifest an opinion of Usher's which I mention not so much on account of its novelty, (for other men have thought thus,) as on account of the pertinacity with which he maintained it. This opinion, in its general form, was that of the sentience of all vegetable things. But, in his disordered fancy, the idea had assumed a more daring character, and trespassed, under certain conditions, upon the kingdom of inorganization. I lack words to express the full extent, or the earnest *abandon* of his persuasion. The belief, however, was connected (as I have previously hinted) with the gray stones of the home of his forefathers. The conditions of the sentience had been here, he imagined, fulfilled in the method of collocation of these stones—in the order of their arrangement, as well as in that of the many *fungi* which overspread them, and of the decayed trees which stood around—above all, in the long undisturbed endurance of this arrangement, and in its reduplication in the still waters of the tarn. Its evidence—the evidence of the sentience—was to be seen, he said, (and I here started as he spoke,) in the gradual yet certain condensation of an atmosphere of their own about the waters and the walls. The result was discoverable, he added, in that silent, yet importunate and terrible influence which for centuries had moulded the destinies of his family, and which made *him* what I now saw him—what he was. Such opinions need no comment, and I will make none.

Our books—the books which, for years, had formed no small portion of the mental existence of the invalid—were, as might be supposed, in strict keeping with this character of phantasm. We pored together over such works as the Ververt et Chartreuse of Gresset; the Belphegor of Machiavelli; the Heaven and Hell of Swedenborg; the Subterranean Voyage of Nicholas Klimm by Holberg; the Chiromancy of Robert Flud, of Jean D'Indaginé, and of De la Chambre; the Journey into the Blue Distance of Tieck; and the City of the Sun of Campanella. One favourite volume was a small octavo edition of the *Directorium Inquisitorum*, by the Dominican Eymeric de Gironne; and there were passages in Pomponius Mela, about the old African Satyrs and OEgipans, over which Usher would sit dreaming for hours. His chief delight, however, was found in the perusal of an exceedingly rare and curious book in quarto Gothic—the manual of a forgotten church—the *Vigilae Mortuorum secundum Chorum Ecclesiae Maguntinae.*

I could not help thinking of the wild ritual of this work, and of its probable influence upon the hypochondriac, when, one evening, having informed me abruptly that the lady Madeline was no more, he stated his intention of preserving her corpse for a fortnight, (previously to its final interment) in one of the numerous vaults within the main walls of the building. The worldly reason, however, assigned for this singular proceeding, was one which I did not feel at liberty to dispute. The brother had been led to his resolution (so he told me) by consideration of the unusual character of the malady of the deceased, of certain obtrusive and eager inquiries on the part of her medical men, and of the remote and exposed situation of the burial-ground of the family. I will not deny that when I called to mind the sinister countenance of the person whom I met upon the staircase, on the day of my arrival at the house, I had no desire to oppose what I regarded as at best but a harmless, and by no means an unnatural, precaution.

At the request of Usher, I personally aided him in the arrangements for the temporary entombment. The body having been encoffined, we two alone bore it to its rest. The vault in which we placed it (and which had been so long unopened that our torches, half smothered in its oppressive atmosphere, gave us little opportunity for investigation) was small, damp, and entirely without means of admission for light; lying, at great depth, immediately beneath that portion of the building in which was my own sleeping apartment. It had been used, apparently, in remote feudal times, for the worst purposes of a donjon-keep, and, in later days, as a place of deposit for powder, or some other highly combustible substance, as a portion of its floor, and the whole interior of a long archway through which we reached it, were carefully sheathed with copper. The door, of massive iron, had been, also, similarly protected. Its immense weight caused an unusually sharp grating sound, as it moved upon its hinges.

Having deposited our mournful burden upon tressels within this region of horror, we partially turned aside the yet unscrewed lid of the coffin, and looked upon the face of the tenant. A striking similitude between the brother and sister now first arrested my attention; and Usher, divining, perhaps, my thoughts, murmured out some few words from which I learned that the deceased and himself had been twins, and that sympathies of a scarcely intelligible nature had always existed between them. Our glances, however, rested not long upon the dead—for we could not regard her unawed. The disease which had thus entombed the lady in the maturity of youth, had left, as usual in all maladies of a strictly cataleptical character, the mockery of a faint blush upon the bosom and the face, and that suspiciously lingering smile upon the lip which is so terrible in death. We replaced and screwed down the lid, and, having secured the door of iron, made our way, with toil, into the scarcely less gloomy apartments of the upper portion of the house.

And now, some days of bitter grief having elapsed, an observable change came over the features of the mental disorder of my friend. His ordinary manner had vanished. His ordinary occupations were neglected or forgotten. He roamed from chamber to chamber with hurried, unequal, and objectless step.

The pallor of his countenance had assumed, if possible, a more ghastly hue—but the luminousness of his eye had utterly gone out. The once occasional huskiness of his tone was heard no more; and a tremulous quaver, as if of extreme terror, habitually characterized his utterance. There were times, indeed, when I thought his unceasingly agitated mind was labouring with some oppressive secret, to divulge which he struggled for the necessary courage. At times, again, I was obliged to resolve all into the mere inexplicable vagaries of madness, for I beheld him gazing upon vacancy for long hours, in an attitude of the profoundest attention, as if listening to some imaginary sound. It was no wonder that his condition terrified—that it infected me. I felt creeping upon me, by slow yet certain degrees, the wild influences of his own fantastic yet impressive superstitions.

It was, especially, upon retiring to bed late in the night of the seventh or eighth day after the placing of the lady Madeline within the donjon, that I experienced the full power of such feelings. Sleep came not near my couch—while the hours waned and waned away. I struggled to reason off the nervousness which had dominion over me. I endeavoured to believe that much, if not all of what I felt, was due to the bewildering influence of the gloomy furniture of the room—of the dark and tattered draperies, which, tortured into motion by the breath of a rising tempest, swayed fitfully to and fro upon the walls, and rustled uneasily about the decorations of the bed. But my efforts were fruitless. An irrepressible tremour gradually pervaded my frame; and, at length, there sat upon my very heart an incubus of utterly causeless alarm. Shaking this off with a gasp and a struggle, I uplifted myself upon the pillows, and, peering earnestly within the intense darkness of the chamber, hearkened—I know not why, except that an instinctive spirit prompted me—to certain low and indefinite sounds which came, through the pauses of the storm, at long intervals, I knew not whence. Overpowered by an intense sentiment of horror, unaccountable yet unendurable, I threw on my clothes with haste (for I felt that I should sleep no more during the night), and endeavoured to arouse myself from the pitiable condition into which I had fallen, by pacing rapidly to and fro through the apartment.

I had taken but few turns in this manner, when a light step on an adjoining staircase arrested my attention. I presently recognised it as that of Usher. In an instant afterward he rapped, with a gentle touch, at my door, and entered, bearing a lamp. His countenance was, as usual, cadaverously wan—but, moreover, there was a species of mad hilarity in his eyes—an evidently restrained *hysteria* in his whole demeanour. His air appalled me—but anything was preferable to the solitude which I had so long endured, and I even welcomed his presence as a relief.

"And you have not seen it?" he said abruptly, after having stared about him for some moments in silence—"you have not then seen it?—but, stay! you shall." Thus speaking, and having carefully shaded his lamp, he hurried to one of the casements, and threw it freely open to the storm.

The impetuous fury of the entering gust nearly lifted us from our feet. It was, indeed, a tempestuous yet sternly beautiful night, and one wildly singular in its terror and its beauty. A whirlwind had apparently collected its force in our vicinity; for there were frequent and violent alterations in the direction of the wind; and the exceeding density of the clouds (which hung so low as to press upon the turrets of the house) did not prevent our perceiving the life-like velocity with which they flew careering from all points against each other, without passing away into the distance. I say that even their exceeding density did not prevent our perceiving this—yet we had no glimpse of the moon or stars—nor was there any flashing forth of the lightning. But the under surfaces of the huge masses of agitated vapour, as well as all terrestrial objects immediately around us, were glowing in the unnatural light of a faintly luminous and distinctly visible gaseous exhalation which hung about and enshrouded the mansion.

"You must not—you shall not behold this!" said I, shudderingly, to Usher, as I led him, with a gentle violence, from the window to a seat. "These appearances, which bewilder you, are merely electrical phenomena not uncommon—or it may be that they have their ghastly origin in the rank miasma of the tarn. Let us close this casement;—the air is chilling and dangerous to your frame. Here is one of your favourite romances. I will read, and you shall listen;—and so we will pass away this terrible night together."

The antique volume which I had taken up was the "Mad Trist" of Sir Launcelot Canning; but I had called it a favourite of Usher's more in sad jest than in earnest; for, in truth, there is little in its uncouth and unimaginative prolixity which could have had interest for the lofty and spiritual ideality of my friend. It was, however, the only book immediately at hand; and I indulged a vague hope that the excitement which now agitated the hypochondriac, might find relief (for the history of mental disorder is full of similar anomalies) even in the extremeness of the folly which I should read. Could I have judged, indeed, by the wild over-strained air of vivacity with which he hearkened, or apparently hearkened, to the words of the tale, I might well have congratulated myself upon the success of my design.

I had arrived at that well-known portion of the story where Ethelred, the hero of the Trist, having sought in vain for peaceable admission into the dwelling of the hermit, proceeds to make good an entrance by force. Here, it will be remembered, the words of the narrative run thus:

"And Ethelred, who was by nature of a doughty heart, and who was now mighty withal, on account of the powerfulness of the wine which he had drunken, waited no longer to hold parley with the hermit, who, in sooth, was of an obstinate and maliceful turn, but, feeling the rain upon his shoulders, and fearing the rising of the tempest, uplifted his mace outright, and, with blows, made quickly room in the plankings of the door for his gauntleted hand; and now pulling therewith sturdily, he so cracked, and ripped, and tore all asunder, that the noise of the dry and hollow-sounding wood alarummed and reverberated throughout the forest."

At the termination of this sentence I started, and for a moment, paused; for it appeared to me (although I at once concluded that my excited fancy had deceived me)—it appeared to me that, from some very remote portion of the mansion, there came, indistinctly, to my ears, what might have been, in its exact similarity of character, the echo (but a stifled and dull one certainly) of the very cracking and ripping sound which Sir Launcelot had so particularly described. It was, beyond doubt, the coincidence alone which had arrested my attention; for, amid the rattling of the sashes of the casements, and the ordinary commingled noises of the still increasing storm, the sound, in itself, had nothing, surely, which should have interested or disturbed me. I continued the story:

"But the good champion Ethelred, now entering within the door, was sore enraged and amazed to perceive no signal of the maliceful hermit; but, in the stead thereof, a dragon of a scaly and prodigious demeanour, and of a fiery tongue, which sate in guard before a palace of gold, with a floor of silver; and upon the wall there hung a shield of shining brass with this legend enwritten –

Who entereth herein, a conqueror hath bin;
Who slayeth the dragon, the shield he shall win;

And Ethelred uplifted his mace, and struck upon the head of the dragon, which fell before him, and gave up his pesty breath, with a shriek so horrid and harsh, and withal so piercing, that Ethelred had fain to close his ears with his hands against the dreadful noise of it, the like whereof was never before heard."

Here again I paused abruptly, and now with a feeling of wild amazement—for there could be no doubt whatever that, in this instance, I did actually hear (although from what direction it proceeded I found it impossible to say) a low and apparently distant, but harsh, protracted, and most unusual screaming or grating sound—the exact counterpart of what my fancy had already conjured up for the dragon's unnatural shriek as described by the romancer.

Oppressed, as I certainly was, upon the occurrence of the second and most extraordinary coincidence, by a thousand conflicting sensations, in which wonder and extreme terror were predominant, I still retained sufficient presence of mind to avoid exciting, by any observation, the sensitive nervousness of my companion. I was by no means certain that he had noticed the sounds in question; although, assuredly, a strange alteration had, during the last few minutes, taken place in his demeanour. From a position fronting my own, he had gradually brought round his chair, so as to sit with his face to the door of the chamber; and thus I could but partially perceive his features, although I saw that his lips trembled as if he were murmuring inaudibly. His head had dropped upon his breast—yet I knew that he was not asleep, from the wide and rigid opening of the eye as I caught a glance of it in profile. The motion of his body, too, was at variance with this idea—for he rocked from side to side with a gentle yet constant and uniform sway. Having rapidly taken notice of all this, I resumed the narrative of Sir Launcelot, which thus proceeded:

> "And now, the champion, having escaped from the terrible fury of the dragon, bethinking himself of the brazen shield, and of the breaking up of the enchantment which was upon it, removed the carcass from out of the way before him, and approached valorously over the silver pavement of the castle to where the shield was upon the wall; which in sooth tarried not for his full coming, but fell down at his feet upon the silver floor, with a mighty great and terrible ringing sound."

No sooner had these syllables passed my lips, than—as if a shield of brass had indeed, at the moment, fallen heavily upon a floor of silver—I became aware of a distinct, hollow, metallic, and clangorous, yet apparently muffled reverberation. Completely unnerved, I leaped to my feet; but the measured rocking movement of Usher was undisturbed. I rushed to the chair in which he sat. His eyes were bent fixedly before him, and throughout his whole countenance there reigned a stony rigidity. But, as I placed my hand upon his shoulder, there came a strong shudder over his whole person; a sickly smile quivered about his lips; and I saw that he spoke in a low, hurried, and gibbering murmur, as if unconscious of my presence. Bending closely over him, I at length drank in the hideous import of his words.

> "Not hear it?—yes, I hear it, and have heard it. Long—long—long—many minutes, many hours, many days, have I heard it—yet I dared not—oh, pity me, miserable wretch that I am!—I dared not—I *dared* not speak! *We have put her living in the tomb!* Said I not that my senses were acute? I *now* tell you that I heard her first feeble movements in the hollow coffin. I heard them—many, many days ago—yet I dared not—*I dared not speak!* And now—to-night—Ethelred—ha! ha!—the breaking of the hermit's door, and the death-cry of the dr-

agon, and the clangour of the shield!—say, rather, the rending of her coffin, and the grating of the iron hinges of her prison, and her struggles within the coppered archway of the vault! Oh whither shall I fly? Will she not be here anon? Is she not hurrying to upbraid me for my haste? Have I not heard her footstep on the stair? Do I not distinguish that heavy and horrible beating of her heart? Madman!"—here he sprang furiously to his feet, and shrieked out his syllables, as if in the effort he were giving up his soul—"*Madman! I tell you that she now stands without the door!*"

As if in the superhuman energy of his utterance there had been found the potency of a spell—the huge antique pannels to which the speaker pointed, threw slowly back, upon the instant, their ponderous and ebony jaws. It was the work of the rushing gust—but then without those doors there *did* stand the lofty and enshrouded figure of the lady Madeline of Usher. There was blood upon her white robes, and the evidence of some bitter struggle upon every portion of her emaciated frame. For a moment she remained trembling and reeling to and fro upon the threshold—then, with a low moaning cry, fell heavily inward upon the person of her brother, and in her violent and now final death-agonies, bore him to the floor a corpse, and a victim to the terrors he had anticipated.

From that chamber, and from that mansion, I fled aghast. The storm was still abroad in all its wrath as I found myself crossing the old causeway. Suddenly there shot along the path a wild light, and I turned to see whence a gleam so unusual could have issued; for the vast house and its shadows were alone behind me. The radiance was that of the full, setting, and blood-red moon which now shone vividly through that once barely-discernible fissure, of which I have before spoken as extending from the roof of the building, in a zigzag direction, to the base. While I gazed, this fissure rapidly widened—there came a fierce breath of the whirlwind—the entire orb of the satellite burst at once upon my sight—my brain reeled as I saw the mighty walls rushing asunder—there was a long tumultuous shouting sound like the voice of a thousand waters—and the deep and dank tarn at my feet closed sullenly and silently over the fragments of the *"House of Usher."*

Robert E. Howard's

5
The Novel of the Black Seal
Related by the Young Lady in Leicester Square
Arthur Machen
1895

Arthur Machen's writing influenced the *Weird Tales* three: Clark Ashton Smith, H.P. Lovecraft, and, of course, Robert E. Howard. Many of Howard's yarns dealing with the "little people," show evidence of having been influenced by Machen, particularly by his "The Novel of the Black Seal." These yarns include: "The Children of the Night," "Worms of the Earth," and "The Little People." Arthur Machen and Robert E. Howard were, in many ways, kindred souls, for Howard had been fascinated by the "Picts" from a young age and Machen the "Little People," both describing a surviving strange, prehistoric, and subterranean race—both possibly one and the same. The following Machen story is one of the three tales Howard highlighted as being "master horror-tales," the others being Poe's "The Fall of the House of Usher" and Lovecraft's "The Call of Cthulhu."

Prologue

"I see you are a determined rationalist," said the lady. "Did you not hear me say that I have had experiences even more terrible? I too was once a sceptic, but after what I have known I can no longer affect to doubt."

"Madam," replied Mr. Phillipps, "no one shall make me deny my faith. I will never believe, nor will I pretend to believe, that two and two make five, nor will I on any pretenses admit the existence of two-sided triangles."

"You are a little hasty," rejoined the lady. "But may I ask you if you ever heard the name of Professor Gregg, the authority on ethnology and kindred subjects?"

"I have done much more than merely hear of Professor Gregg," said Phillipps. "I always regarded him as one of our most acute and clear-headed observers; and his last publication, the *Textbook of Ethnology*, struck me as being quite admirable in its kind. Indeed, the book had but come into my hands when I heard of the terrible accident which cut short Gregg's career. He had, I think, taken a country house in the west of England for the summer, and is supposed to have fallen into a river. So far as I remember, his body was never recovered."

"Sir, I am sure that you are discreet. Your conversation seems to declare as much, and the very title of that little work of yours which you mentioned assures me that you are no empty trifler. In a word, I feel that I may depend on you. You appear to be under the impression that Professor Gregg is dead; I have no reason to believe that that is the case."

"What?" cried Phillipps, astonished and perturbed. "You do not hint that there was anything disgraceful? I cannot believe it. Gregg was a man of clearest character; his private life was one of great benevolence; and though I myself am free from delusions, I believe him to have been a sincere and devout Christian. Surely you cannot mean to insinuate that some disreputable history forced him to flee the country?"

"Again you are in a hurry," replied the lady. "I said nothing of all this. Briefly, then, I must tell you that Professor Gregg left this house one morning in full health both in mind and body. He never returned, but his watch and chain, a purse containing three sovereigns in gold, and some loose silver, with a ring that he wore habitually, were found three days later on a wild and savage hillside, many miles from the river. These articles were placed beside a limestone rock of fantastic form; they had been wrapped into a parcel with a kind of rough parchment which was secured with gut. The parcel was opened, and the inner side of the parchment bore an inscription done with some red substance; the characters were undecipherable, but seemed to be a corrupt cuneiform."

"You interest me intensely," said Phillipps. "Would you mind continuing your story? The circumstance you have mentioned seems to me of the most inexplicable character, and I thirst for an elucidation."

The young lady seemed to meditate for a moment, and she then proceeded to relate the

Novel of the Black Seal

I must now give you some fuller particulars of my history. I am the daughter of a civil engineer, Steven Lally by name, who was so unfortunate as to die suddenly at the outset of his career, and before he had accumulated sufficient means to support his wife and her two children.

My mother contrived to keep the small household going on resources which must have been incredibly small; we lived in a remote country village, because most of the necessaries of life were cheaper than in a town, but even so we were brought up with the severest economy. My father was a clever and well-read man, and left behind him a small but select collection of books, containing the best Greek, Latin, and English classics, and these books were the only amusement we possessed. My brother, I remember, learnt Latin out of Descartes's *Meditationes*, and I, in place of the little tales which children are usually told to read, had nothing more charming than a translation of the *Gesta* Romanorum. We grew up thus, quiet and studious children, and in course of time my brother provided for himself in the manner I have mentioned. I continued to live at home: my poor mother had become an invalid, and demanded my continual care, and about two years ago she died after many months of painful illness. My situation was a terrible one; the shabby furniture barely sufficed to pay the debts I had been forced to contract, and the books I dispatched to my brother, knowing how he would value them. I was absolutely alone; I was aware how poorly my brother was paid; and though I came up to London in the hope of finding employment, with the understanding that he would defray my expenses, I swore it should only be for a month, and that if I could not in that time find some work I would starve rather than deprive him of the few miserable pounds he had laid by for his day of trouble. I took a little room in a distant suburb; the cheapest that I could find; I lived on bread and tea, and I spent my time in vain answering of advertisements, and vainer walks to addresses I had noted. Day followed on day, and week on week, and still I was unsuccessful, till at last the term I had appointed drew to a close, and I saw before me the grim prospect of slowly dying of starvation. My landlady was good-natured in her way; she knew the slenderness of my means, and I am sure that she would not have turned me out of doors; it remained for me then to go away, and to try to die in some quiet place. It was winter then, and a thick white fog gathered in the early part of the afternoon, becoming more dense as the day wore on; it was a Sunday, I remember, and the people of the house were at chapel. At about three o'clock I crept out and walked away as quickly as I could, for I was weak from abstinence. The white mist wrapped all the streets in silence, a hard frost had gathered thick upon the bare branches of the trees, and frost crystals glittered on the wooden fences, and on the cold, cruel ground beneath my feet. I walked on, turning to right and left in utter haphazard, without caring to look up at the names of the streets, and all that I remember of my walk on that Sunday afternoon seems but the broken fragments of an evil dream. In a confused vision I stumbled on, through roads half town and half country, grey fields melting into the cloudy world of mist on one side of me, and on the other comfortable villas with a glow of firelight flickering on the walls, but all unreal; red brick walls and lighted windows, vague trees, and glimmering country, gas-lamps beginning to star the white shadows, the vanishing perspectives of the railway line beneath high embankments, the green and red of the signal lamps—all these were but momentary pictures flashed on my tired brain and senses numbed by hunger. Now and then I would hear a quick step ringing on the iron road, and men would pass me well wrapped up, walking fast for the sake of warmth, and no doubt eagerly foretasting the pleasures of a glowing hearth, with curtains tightly drawn about the frosted panes, and the welcomes of their friends, but as the early evening darkened and night approached, foot-passengers got fewer and fewer, and I passed through street after street alone. In the white silence I stumbled on, as desolate as if I trod the streets of a buried city; and as I grew more weak and exhausted, something of the horror of death was folding thickly round my heart. Suddenly, as I turned a corner, some one accosted me courteously beneath the lamp-post, and I heard a voice asking if I could kindly point the way to Avon Road. At the sudden shock of human accents I was prostrated, and my strength gave way; I fell all huddled on the sidewalk, and wept and sobbed and laughed in violent hysteria. I had gone out prepared to die, and as I stepped across the threshold that had sheltered me, I consciously bade adieu to all hopes and all remembrances; the door clanged behind me with the noise of thunder, and I felt that an iron curtain had fallen on the brief passage of my life, that henceforth I was to walk a little way in a world of gloom and shadow; I entered on the stage of the first act of death. Then came my wandering in the mist, the whiteness wrapping all things, the void streets, and muffled silence, till when that voice spoke to me it was as if I had died and life returned to me. In a few minutes I was able to compose my feelings, and as I rose I saw that I was confronted by a middle-aged gentleman of pleasing appearance, neatly and correctly dressed. He looked at me with an expression of great pity, but before I could stammer out my ignorance of the neighbourhood, for indeed I had not the slightest notion of where I had wandered, he spoke.

"My dear madam," he said, "you seem in some terrible distress. You cannot think how you alarmed me. But may I inquire the nature of your trouble? I assure you that you can safely confide in me."

"You are very kind," I replied. "But I fear there is nothing to be done. My condition seems a hopeless one."

"Oh, nonsense, nonsense! You are too young to talk like that. Come, let us walk down here and you must tell me your difficulty. Perhaps I may be able to help you."

There was something very soothing and persuasive in his manner, and as we walked together I gave him an outline of my story, and told of the despair that had oppressed me almost to death.

"You were wrong to give in so completely," he said, when I was silent. "A month is too short a time in which to feel one's way in London. London, let me tell you, Miss Lally, does not lie open and undefended; it is a fortified place, fossed and double-moated with curious intricacies. As must always happen in large towns, the conditions of life have become hugely artificial, no mere simple palisade is run up to oppose the man or woman who would take the place by storm, but serried lines of subtle contrivances, mines, and pitfalls which it needs a strange skill to overcome. You, in your simplicity, fancied you had only to shout for these walls to sink into nothingness, but the time is gone for such startling victories as these. Take courage; you will learn the secret of success before very long."

"Alas! Sir," I replied, "I have no doubt your conclusions are correct, but at the present moment I seem to be in a fair way to die of starvation. You spoke of a secret; for Heaven's sake tell it me, if you have any pity for my distress."

He laughed genially. "There lies the strangeness of it all. Those who know the secret cannot tell it if they would; it is positively as ineffable as the central doctrine of freemasonry. But I may say this, that you yourself have penetrated at least the outer husk of the mystery," and he laughed again.

"Pray do not jest with me," I said. "What have I done, *que sçais-je?* I am so far ignorant that I have not the slightest idea of how my next meal is to be provided."

"Excuse me. You ask what you have done. You have met me. Come, we will fence no longer. I see you have self-education, the only education which is not infinitely pernicious, and I am in want of a governess for my two children. I have been a widower for some years; my name is Gregg. I offer you the post I have named, and shall we say a salary of a hundred a year?"

I could only stutter out my thanks, and slipping a card with his address, and a banknote by way of earnest, into my hand, Mr. Gregg bade me good-bye, asking me to call in a day or two.

Such was my introduction to Professor Gregg, and can you wonder that the remembrance of despair and the cold blast that had blown from the gates of death upon me made me regard him as a second father? Before the close of the week I was installed in my new duties. The Professor had leased an old brick manor-house in a western suburb of London, and here, surrounded by pleasant lawns and orchards, and soothed with the murmur of ancient elms that rocked their boughs above the roof, the new chapter of my life began. Knowing as you do the nature of the professor's occupation, you will not be surprised to hear that the house teemed with books, and cabinets full of strange, and even hideous, objects filled every available nook in the vast low rooms. Gregg was a man whose one thought was for knowledge, and I too before long caught something of his enthusiasm, and strove to enter into his passion of research. In a few months I was perhaps more his secretary than the governess of the two children, and many a night I have sat at the desk in the glow of the shaded lamp while he, pacing up and down in the rich gloom of the firelight, dictated to me the substance of his *Textbook of Ethnology*. But amidst these more sober and accurate studies I always detected a something hidden, a longing and desire for some object to which he did not allude; and now and then he would break short in what he was saying and lapse into reverie, entranced, as it seemed to me, by some distant prospect of adventurous discovery. The textbook was at last finished, and we began to receive proofs from the printers, which were entrusted to me for a first reading, and then underwent the final revision of the professor. All the while his weariness of the actual business he was engaged on increased, and it was with the joyous laugh of a schoolboy when term is over that he one day handed me a copy of the book. "There," he said, "I have kept my word; I promised to write it, and it is done with. Now I shall be free to live for stranger things; I confess it, Miss Lally, I covet the renown of Columbus; you will, I hope, see me play the part of an explorer."

"Surely," I said, "there is little left to explore. You have been born a few hundred years too late for that."

"I think you are wrong," he replied; "there are still, depend upon it, quaint, undiscovered countries and continents of strange extent. Ah, Miss Lally! believe me, we stand amidst sacraments and mysteries full of awe, and it doth not yet appear what we shall be. Life, believe me, is no simple thing, no mass of grey matter and congeries of veins and muscles to be laid naked by the surgeon's knife; man is the secret which I am about to explore, and before I can discover him I must cross over weltering seas indeed, and oceans and the mists of many thousand years. You know the myth of the lost Atlantis; what if it be true, and I am destined to be called the discoverer of that wonderful land?"

I could see excitement boiling beneath his words, and in his face was the heat of the hunter; before me stood a man who believed himself summoned to tourney with the unknown. A pang of joy possessed me when I reflected that I was to be in a way associated with him in the adventure, and I, too, burned with the lust of the chase, not pausing to consider that I knew not what we were to unshadow.

The next morning Professor Gregg took me into his inner study, where, ranged against the wall, stood a nest of pigeon-holes, every drawer neatly labelled, and the results of years of toil classified in a few feet of space.

"Here," he said, "is my life; here are all the facts which I have gathered together with so much pains, and yet it is all nothing. No, nothing to what I am about to attempt. Look at this"; and he took me to an old bureau, a piece fantastic and faded, which stood in a corner of the room. He unlocked the front and opened one of the drawers.

"A few scraps of paper," he went on, pointing to the drawer, "and a lump of black stone, rudely annotated with queer marks and scratches—that is all that the drawer holds. Here you see is an old envelope with the dark red stamp of twenty years ago, but I have pencilled a few lines at the back; here is a sheet of manuscript, and here some cuttings from obscure local journals. And if you ask me the subject-matter of the collection, it will not seem extraordinary—a servant-girl at a farmhouse, who disappeared from her place and has never been heard of, a child supposed to have slipped down some old working on the mountains, some queer scribbling on a limestone rock, a man murdered with a blow from a strange weapon; such is the scent I have to go upon. Yes, as you say, there is a ready explanation for all this; the girl may have run away to London, or Liverpool, or New York; the child may be at the bottom of the disused shaft; and the letters on the rock may be the idle whims of some vagrant. Yes, yes, I admit all that; but I know I hold the true key. Look!" and he held out a slip of yellow paper.

Characters found inscribed on a limestone rock on the Grey Hills, I read, and then there was a word erased, presumably the name of a county, and a date some fifteen years back. Beneath was traced a number of uncouth characters, shaped somewhat like wedges or daggers, as strange and outlandish as the Hebrew alphabet.

"Now the seal," said Professor Gregg, and he handed me the black stone, a thing about two inches long, and something like an old-fashioned tobacco-stopper, much enlarged.

I held it up to the light, and saw to my surprise the characters on the paper repeated on the seal.

"Yes," said the professor, "they are the same. And the marks on the limestone rock were made fifteen years ago, with some red substance. And the characters on the seal are four thousand years old at least. Perhaps much more."

"Is it a hoax?" I said.

"No, I anticipated that. I was not to be led to give my life to a practical joke. I have tested the matter very carefully. Only one person besides myself knows of the mere existence of that black seal. Besides, there are other reasons which I cannot enter into now."

"But what does it all mean?" I said. "I cannot understand to what conclusion all this leads."

"My dear Miss Lally, that is a question that I would rather leave unanswered for some little time. Perhaps I shall never be able to say what secrets are held here in solution; a few vague hints, the outlines of village tragedies, a few marks done with red earth upon a rock, and an ancient seal. A queer set of data to go upon? Half a dozen pieces of evidence, and twenty years before even so much could be got together; and who knows what mirage or *terra incognita* may be beyond all this? I look across deep waters, Miss Lally, and the land beyond may be but a haze after all. But still I believe it is not so, and a few months will show whether I am right or wrong."

He left me, and alone I endeavoured to fathom the mystery, wondering to what goal such eccentric odds and ends of evidence could lead. I myself am not wholly devoid of imagination, and I had reason to respect the professor's solidity of intellect; yet I saw in the contents of the drawers but the materials of fantasy, and vainly tried to conceive what theory could be founded on the fragments that had been placed before me. Indeed, I could discover in what I had heard and seen but the first chapter of an extravagant romance; and yet deep in my heart I burned with curiosity, and day after day I looked eagerly in Professor Gregg's face for some hint of what was to happen.

It was one evening after dinner that the word came.

"I hope you can make your preparations without much trouble," he said suddenly to me. "We shall be leaving here in a week's time."

"Really!" I said in astonishment. "Where are we going?"

"I have taken a country house in the west of England, not far from Caermaen, a quiet little town, once a city, and the headquarters of a Roman legion. It is very dull there, but the country is pretty, and the air is wholesome."

I detected a glint in his eyes, and guessed that this sudden move had some relation to our conversation of a few days before.

"I shall just take a few books with me," said Professor Gregg, "that is all. Everything else will remain here for our return. I have got a holiday," he went on, smiling at me, "and I shan't be sorry to be quit for a time of my old bones and stones and rubbish. Do you know," he went on, "I have been grinding away at facts for thirty years; it is time for fancies."

The days passed quickly; I could see that the professor was all quivering with suppressed excitement, and I could scarce credit the eager appetence of his glance as we left the old manor-house behind us and began our journey. We set out at midday, and it was in the dusk of the evening that we arrived at a little country station. I was tired and excited, and the drive through the lanes seems all a dream. First the deserted streets of a forgotten village, while I heard Professor Gregg's voice talking of the Augustan Legion and the clash of arms, and all the tremendous pomp that followed the eagles; then the broad river swimming to full tide with the last afterglow glimmering duskily in the yellow water, the wide meadows, the cornfields whitening, and the deep lane winding on the slope between the hills and the water. At last we began to ascend, and the air grew rarer. I looked down and saw the pure white mist tracking the outline of the river like a shroud, and a vague and shadowy country; imaginations and fantasy of swelling hills and hanging woods, and half-shaped outlines of hills beyond, and in the distance the glare of the furnace fire on the mountain, glowing by turns a pillar of shining flame and fading to a dull point of red. We were slowly mounting a carriage drive, and then there came to me the cool breath and the secret of the great wood that was above us; I seemed to wander in its deepest depths, and there was the sound of trickling water, the scent of the green leaves, and the breath of the summer night. The carriage stopped at last, and I could scarcely distinguish the form of the house, as I waited a moment at the pillared porch. The rest of the evening seemed a dream of strange things bounded by the great silence of the wood and the valley and the river.

The next morning, when I awoke and looked out of the bow window of the big, old-fashioned bedroom, I saw under a grey sky a country that was still all mystery. The long, lovely valley, with the river winding in and out below, crossed in mid-vision by a mediæval bridge of vaulted and buttressed stone, the clear presence of the rising ground beyond, and the woods that I had only seen in shadow the night before, seemed tinged with enchantment, and the soft breath of air that sighed in at the opened pane was like no other wind. I looked across the valley, and beyond, hill followed on hill as wave on wave, and here a faint blue pillar of smoke rose still in the morning air from the chimney of an ancient grey farmhouse, there was a rugged height crowned with dark firs, and in the distance I saw the white streak of a road that climbed and vanished into some unimagined country. But the boundary of all was a great wall of mountain, vast in the west, and ending like a fortress with a steep ascent and a domed tumulus clear against the sky.

I saw Professor Gregg walking up and down the terrace path below the windows, and it was evident that he was revelling in the sense of liberty, and the thought that he had for a while bidden good-bye to task-work. When I joined him there was exultation in his voice as he pointed out the sweep of valley and the river that wound beneath the lovely hills.

"Yes," he said, "it is a strangely beautiful country; and to me, at least, it seems full of mystery. You have not forgotten the drawer I showed you, Miss Lally? No; and you have guessed that I have come here not merely for the sake of the children and the fresh air?"

"I think I have guessed as much as that," I replied; "but you must remember I do not know the mere nature of your investigations; and as for the connection between the search and this wonderful valley, it is past my guessing."

He smiled queerly at me. "You must not think I am making a mystery for the sake of mystery," he said. "I do not speak out because, so far, there is nothing to be spoken, nothing definite, I mean, nothing that can be set down in hard black and white, as dull and sure and irreproachable as any blue-book. And then I have another reason: Many years ago a chance paragraph in a newspaper caught my attention, and focused in an instant the vagrant thoughts and half-formed fancies of many idle and speculative hours into a certain hypothesis. I saw at once that I was treading on a thin crust; my theory was wild and fantastic in the extreme, and I would not for any consideration have written a hint of it for publication. But I thought that in the company of scientific men like myself, men who knew the course of discovery, and were aware that the gas that blazes and flares in the gin-palace was once a wild hypothesis—I thought that with such men as these I might hazard my dream—let us say Atlantis, or the philosopher's stone, or what you like—without danger of ridicule. I found I was grossly mistaken; my friends looked blankly at me and at one another, and I could see something of pity, and something also of insolent contempt, in the glances they exchanged. One of them called on me next day, and hinted that I must be suffering from overwork and brain exhaustion. "In plain terms," I said, "you think I am going mad. I think not"; and I showed him out with some little appearance of heat. Since that day I vowed that I would never whisper the nature of my theory to any living soul; to no one but yourself have I ever shown the contents of that drawer. After all, I may be following a rainbow; I may have been misled by the play of coincidence; but as I stand here in this mystic hush and silence, amidst the woods and wild hills, I am more than ever sure that I am hot on the scent. Come, it is time we went in."

To me in all this there was something both of wonder and excitement; I knew how in his ordinary work Professor Gregg moved step by step, testing every inch of the way, and never venturing on assertion without proof that was impregnable. Yet I divined, more from his glance and the vehemence of his tone than from the spoken word, that he had in his every thought the vision of the almost incredible continually with him; and I, who was with some share of imagination no little of a sceptic, offended at a hint of the marvellous, could not help asking myself whether he were cherishing a monomania, and barring out from this one subject all the scientific method of his other life.

Yet, with this image of mystery haunting my thoughts, I surrendered wholly to the charm of the country. Above the faded house on the hillside began the great forest—a long, dark line seen from the opposing hills, stretching above the river for many a mile from north to south, and yielding in the north to even wilder country, barren and savage hills, and ragged commonland, a territory all strange and unvisited, and more unknown to Englishmen than the very heart of Africa. The space of a couple of steep fields alone separated the house from the woods, and the children were delighted to follow me up the long alleys of undergrowth, between smooth pleached walls of shining beech, to the highest point in the wood, whence one looked on one side across the river and the rise and fall of the country to the great western mountain wall, and on the other over the surge and dip of the myriad trees of the forest, over level meadows and the shining yellow sea to the faint coast beyond. I used to sit at this point on the warm sunlit turf which marked the track of the Roman Road, while the two children raced about hunting for the whinberries that grew here and there on the banks. Here, beneath the deep blue sky and the great clouds rolling, like olden galleons with sails full-bellied, from the sea to the hills, as I listened to the whispered charm of the great and ancient wood, I lived solely for delight, and only remembered strange things when we would return to the house and find Professor Gregg either shut up in the little room he had made his study, or else pacing the terrace with the look, patient and enthusiastic, of the determined seeker.

One morning, some eight or nine days after our arrival, I looked out of my window and saw the whole landscape transmuted before me. The clouds had dipped low and hidden the mountain in the west; a southern wind was driving the rain in shifting pillars up the valley, and the little brooklet that burst the hill below the house now raged, a red torrent, down to the river. We were perforce obliged to keep snug within-doors; and when I had attended to my pupils, I sat down in the morning-room, where the ruins of a library still encumbered an old-fashioned bookcase. I had inspected the shelves once or twice, but their contents had failed to attract me; volumes of eighteenth-century sermons, an old book on farriery, a collection of poems by "persons of quality," Prideaus's *Connection*, and an odd volume of Pope, were the boundaries of the library, and there seemed little doubt that everything of interest or value had been removed. Now, however, in desperation, I began to re-examine the musty sheepskin and calf bindings, and found, much to my delight, a fine old quarto printed by the Stephani, containing the three books of Pomponius

Mela, *De Situ Orbis*, and other of the ancient geographers. I knew enough of Latin to steer my way through an ordinary sentence, and I soon became absorbed in the odd mixture of fact and fancy—light shining on a little of the space of the world, and beyond, mist and shadow and awful forms. Glancing over the clear-printed pages, my attention was caught by the heading of a chapter in Solinus, and I read the words:

MIRA DE INTIMIS GENTIBUS LIBYAE. DE LAPIDE HEXECONTALITHO,
—"The wonders of the people that inhabit the inner parts of Libya, and of the stone called Sixtystone."

The odd title attracted me, and I read on:

> *Gens ista avia et secreta habitat, in montibus horrendis foeda mysteria celebrat. Dehominibus nihil aliud illi praeferunt quam figuram, ab humano ritu prorsus exulant, oderunt deum lucis.*

> *Stridunt potius quam loquuntur; vox absona nec sine horrore auditur. Lapide quodam gloriantur, quem Hexecontalithon vocant; dicunt enim hunc lapidem sexaginta notas ostendere.*

> *Cujus lapidis nomen secretum ineffabile colunt: quod Ixaxar.*

"This folk," I translated to myself, "dwells in remote and secret places, and celebrates foul mysteries on savage hills. Nothing have they in common with men save the face, and the customs of humanity are wholly strange to them; and they hate the sun. They hiss rather than speak; their voices are harsh, and not to be heard without fear. They boast of a certain stone, which they call Sixtystone; for they say that it displays sixty characters. And this stone has a secret unspeakable name; which is Ixaxar."

I laughed at the queer inconsequence of all this, and thought it fit for "Sinbad the Sailor," or other of the supplementary *Nights*. When I saw Professor Gregg in the course of the day, I told him of my find in the bookcase, and the fantastic rubbish I had been reading. To my surprise he looked up at me with an expression of great interest.

"That is really very curious," he said. "I have never thought it worth while to look into the old geographers, and I dare say I have missed a good deal. Ah, that is the passage, is it? It seems a shame to rob you of your entertainment, but I really think I must carry off the book."

The next day the professor called me to come to the study. I found him sitting at a table in the full light of the window, scrutinizing something very attentively with a magnifying glass.

"Ah, Miss Lally," he began, "I want to use your eyes. This glass is pretty good, but not like my old one that I left in town. Would you mind examining the thing yourself, and telling me how many characters are cut on it?"

He handed me the object in his hand. I saw that it was the black seal he had shown me in London, and my heart began to beat with the thought that I was presently to know something. I took the seal, and, holding it up to the light, checked off the grotesque dagger-shaped characters one by one.

"I make sixty-two," I said at last.

"Sixty-two? Nonsense; it's impossible. Ah, I see what you have done, you have counted that and that," and he pointed to two marks which I had certainly taken as letters with the rest.

"Yes, yes," Professor Gregg went on, "but those are obviously scratches, done accidentally; I saw that at once. Yes, then that's quite right. Thank you very much, Miss Lally."

I was going away, rather disappointed at my having been called in merely to count the number of marks on the black seal, when suddenly there flashed into my mind what I had read in the morning.

"But, Professor Gregg," I cried, breathless, "the seal, the seal. Why, it is the stone Hexecontalithos that Solinus writes of; it is Ixaxar."

"Yes," he said, "I suppose it is. Or it may be a mere coincidence. It never does to be too sure, you know, in these matters. Coincidence killed the professor."

I went away puzzled by what I had heard, and as much as ever at a loss to find the ruling clue in this maze of strange evidence. For three days the bad weather lasted, changing from driving rain to a dense mist, fine and dripping, and we seemed to be shut up in a white cloud that veiled all the world away from us. All the while Professor Gregg was darkling in his room, unwilling, it appeared, to dispense confidences or talk of any kind, and I heard him walking to and fro with a quick, impatient step, as if he were in some way wearied of inaction. The fourth morning was fine, and at breakfast the professor said briskly:

"We want some extra help about the house; a boy of fifteen or sixteen, you know. There are a lot of little odd jobs that take up the maids' time which a boy could do much better."

"The girls have not complained to me in any way," I replied. "Indeed, Anne said there was much less work than in London, owing to there being so little dust."

"Ah, yes, they are very good girls. But I think we shall do much better with a boy. In fact, that is what has been bothering me for the last two days."

"Bothering you?" I said in astonishment, for as a matter of fact the professor never took the slightest interest in the affairs of the house.

"Yes," he said, "the weather, you know. I really couldn't go out in that Scotch mist; I don't know the country very well, and I should have lost my way. But I am going to get the boy this morning."

"But how do you know there is such a boy as you want anywhere about?"

"Oh, I have no doubt as to that. I may have to walk a mile or two at the most, but I am sure to find just the boy I require."

I thought the professor was joking, but, though his tone was airy enough, there was something grim and set about his features that puzzled me. He got his stick, and stood at the door looking meditatively before him, and as I passed through the hall he called to me.

"By the way, Miss Lally, there was one thing I wanted to say to you. I dare say you may have heard that some of these country lads are not over-bright; 'idiotic' would be a harsh word to use, and they are usually called 'naturals,' or something of the kind. I hope you won't mind if the boy I am after should turn out not too keen-witted; he will be perfectly harmless, of course, and blacking boots doesn't need much mental effort."

With that he was gone, striding up the road that led to the wood, and I remained stupefied; and then for the first time my astonishment was mingled with a sudden note of terror, arising I knew not whence, and all unexplained even to myself, and yet I felt about my heart for an instant something of the chill of death, and that shapeless, formless dread of the unknown that is worse than death itself. I tried to find courage in the sweet air that blew up from the sea, and in the sunlight after rain, but the mystic woods seemed to darken around me; and the vision of the river coiling between the reeds, and the silver grey of the ancient bridge, fashioned in my mind symbols of vague dread, as the mind of a child fashions terror from things harmless and familiar.

Two hours later Professor Gregg returned. I met him as he came down the road, and asked quietly if he had been able to find a boy.

"Oh, yes." he answered; "I found one easily enough. His name is Jervase Cradock, and I expect he will make himself very useful. His father has been dead for many years, and the mother, whom I saw, seemed very glad at the prospect of a few shillings extra coming in on Saturday nights. As I expected, he is not too sharp, has fits at times, the mother said; but as he will not be trusted with the china, that doesn't much matter, does it? And he is not in any way dangerous, you know, merely a little weak."

"When is he coming?"

"To-morrow morning at eight o'clock. Anne will show him what he has to do, and how to do it. At first he will go home every night, but perhaps it may ultimately turn out more convenient for him to sleep here, and only go home for Sundays."

I found nothing to say to all this; Professor Gregg spoke in a quiet tone of matter-of-fact, as indeed was warranted by the circumstance; and yet I could not quell my sensation of astonishment at the whole affair. I knew that in reality no assistance was wanted in the housework, and the professor's prediction that the boy he was to engage might prove a little "simple," followed by so exact a fulfilment, struck me as bizarre in the extreme. The next morning I heard from the housemaid that the boy Cradock had come at eight, and that she had been trying to make him useful. "He doesn't seem quite all there, I don't think, miss," was her comment, and later in the day I saw him helping the old man who worked in the garden. He was a youth of about fourteen, with black hair and black eyes and an olive skin, and I saw at once from the curious vacancy of his expression that he was mentally weak. He touched his forehead awkwardly as I went by, and I heard him answering the gardener in a queer, harsh voice that caught my attention; it gave me the impression of some one speaking deep below under the earth, and there was a strange sibilance, like the hissing of the phonograph as the pointer travels over the cylinder. I heard that he seemed anxious to do what he could, and was quite docile and obedient, and Morgan the gardener, who knew his mother, assured me he was perfectly harmless. "He's always been a bit queer," he said, "and no wonder, after what his mother went through before he was born. I did know his father, Thomas Cradock, well, and a very fine workman he was too, indeed. He got something wrong with his lungs owing to working in the wet woods, and never got over it, and went off quite sudden like. And they do say as how Mrs. Cradock was quite off her head: anyhow, she was found by Mr. Hillyer, Ty Coch, all crouched up on the Grey Hills, over there, crying and weeping like a lost soul. And Jervase, he was born about eight months afterwards, and, as I was saying, he was a bit queer always; and they do say when he could scarcely walk he would frighten the other children into fits with the noises he would make."

A word in the story had stirred up some remembrance within me, and, vaguely curious, I asked the old man where the Grey Hills were.

"Up there," he said, with the same gesture he had used before; "you go past the 'Fox and Hounds,' and through the forest, by the old ruins. It's a good five mile from here, and a strange sort of a place. The poorest soil between this and Monmouth, they do say, though it's good feed for sheep. Yes, it was a sad thing for poor Mrs. Cradock."

The old man turned to his work, and I strolled on down the path between the espaliers, gnarled and gouty with age, thinking of the story I had heard, and groping for the point in it that had some key to my memory. In an instant it came before me; I had seen the phrase "Grey Hills" on the slip of yellowed paper that Professor Gregg had taken from the drawer in his cabinet. Again I was seized with pangs of mingled curiosity and fear; I remembered the strange characters copied from the limestone rock, and then again their identity with the inscription of the age-old seal, and the fantastic fables of the Latin geographer. I saw beyond doubt that, unless coincidence had set all the scene and disposed all these bizarre events with curious art, I was to be a spectator of things far removed from the usual and customary traffic and jostle of life. Professor

Gregg I noted day by day; he was hot on his trail, growing lean with eagerness; and in the evenings, when the sun was swimming on the verge of the mountain, he would pace the terrace to and fro with his eyes on the ground, while the mist grew white in the valley, and the stillness of the evening brought far voices near, and the blue smoke rose a straight column from the diamond-shaped chimney of the grey farmhouse, just as I had seen it on the first morning. I have told you I was of sceptical habit; but though I understood little or nothing, I began to dread, vainly proposing to myself the iterated dogmas of science that all life is material, and that in the system of things there is no undiscovered land, even beyond the remotest stars, where the supernatural can find a footing. Yet there struck in on this the thought that matter is as really awful and unknown as spirit, that science itself but dallies on the threshold, scarcely gaining more than a glimpse of the wonders of the inner place.

There is one day that stands up from amidst the others as a grim red beacon, betokening evil to come. I was sitting on a bench in the garden, watching the boy Cradock weeding, when I was suddenly alarmed by a harsh and choking sound, like the cry of a wild beast in anguish, and I was unspeakably shocked to see the unfortunate lad standing in full view before me, his whole body quivering and shaking at short intervals as though shocks of electricity were passing through him, his teeth grinding, foam gathering on his lips, and his face all swollen and blackened to a hideous mask of humanity. I shrieked with terror, and Professor Gregg came running; and as I pointed to Cradock, the boy with one convulsive shudder fell face forward, and lay on the wet earth, his body writhing like a wounded blind-worm, and an inconceivable babble of sounds bursting and rattling and hissing from his lips. He seemed to pour forth an infamous jargon, with words, or what seemed words, that might have belonged to a tongue dead since untold ages and buried deep beneath Nilotic mud, or in the inmost recesses of the Mexican forest. For a moment the thought passed through my mind, as my ears were still revolted with that infernal clamour, "Surely this is the very speech of hell," and then I cried out again and again, and ran away shuddering to my inmost soul. I had seen Professor Gregg's face as he stooped over the wretched boy and raised him, and I was appalled by the glow of exultation that shone on every lineament and feature. As I sat in my room with drawn blinds, and my eyes hidden in my hands, I heard heavy steps beneath, and I was told afterwards that Professor Gregg had carried Cradock to his study, and had locked the door. I heard voices murmur indistinctly, and I trembled to think of what might be passing within a few feet of where I sat; I longed to escape to the woods and sunshine, and yet I dreaded the sights that might confront me on the way; and at last, as I held the handle of the door nervously, I heard Professor Gregg's voice calling to me with a cheerful ring. "It's all right now, Miss Lally," he said. "The poor fellow has got over it, and I have been arranging for him to sleep here after tomorrow. Perhaps I may be able to do something for him."

"Yes," he said later, "it was a very painful sight, and I don't wonder you were alarmed. We may hope that good food will build him up a little, but I am afraid he will never be really cured," and he affected the dismal and conventional air with which one speaks of hopeless illness; and yet beneath it I detected the delight that leapt up rampant within him, and fought and struggled to find utterance. It was as if one glanced down on the even surface of the sea, clear and immobile, and saw beneath raging depths and a storm of contending billows. It was indeed to me a torturing and offensive problem that this man, who had so bounteously rescued me from the sharpness of death, and showed himself in all the relations of life full of benevolence, and pity, and kindly forethought, should so manifestly be for once on the side of the demons, and take a ghastly pleasure in the torments of an afflicted fellow creature. Apart, I struggled with the horned difficulty, and strove to find the solution; but without the hint of a clue, beset by mystery and contradiction. I saw nothing that might help me, and began to wonder whether, after all, I had not escaped from the white mist of the suburb at too dear a rate. I hinted something of my thought to the professor; I said enough to let him know that I was in the most acute perplexity, but the moment after regretted what I had done when I saw his face contort with a spasm of pain.

"My dear Miss Lally," he said, "you surely do not wish to leave us? No, no, you would not do it. You do not know how I rely on you; how confidently I go forward, assured that you are here to watch over my children. You, Miss Lally, are my rearguard; for let me tell you the business in which I am engaged is not wholly devoid of peril. You have not forgotten what I said the first morning here; my lips are shut by an old and firm resolve till they can open to utter no ingenious hypothesis or vague surmise, but irrefragable fact, as certain as a demonstration in mathematics. Think over it, Miss Lally; not for a moment would I endeavour to keep you here against your own instincts, and yet I tell you frankly that I am persuaded it is here, here amidst the woods, that your duty lies."

I was touched by the eloquence of his tone, and by the remembrance that the man, after all, had been my salvation, and I gave him my hand on a promise to serve him loyally and without question. A few days later the rector of our church—a little church, grey and severe and quaint, that hovered on the very banks of the river and watched the tides swim and return—came to see us, and Professor Gregg easily persuaded him to stay and share our dinner. Mr. Meyrick was a member of an antique family of squires, whose old manor-house stood amongst the hills some seven miles away, and thus rooted in the soil, the rector was a living store of all the old fading customs and lore of the country. His manner, genial, with a deal of retired oddity, won on Professor Gregg; and towards the cheese, when a curious Burgundy had begun its incantations, the two men glowed like the wine, and talked of philology with the enthusiasm of a burgess over the peerage. The parson was expounding the pronunciation of the Welsh *ll*, and producing sounds like the gurgle of his native brooks, when Professor Gregg struck in.

"By the way," he said, "that was a very odd word I met with the other day. You know my boy, poor Jervase Cradock? Well, he has got the bad habit of talking to himself, and the day before yesterday I was walking in the garden here and heard him; he was evidently quite unconscious of my presence. A lot of what he said I couldn't make out, but one word struck me distinctly. It was such an odd sound, half sibilant, half guttural, and as quaint as those double *l*s you have been demonstrating. I do not know whether I can give you an idea of the sound; 'Ishakshar' is perhaps as near as I can get. But the *k* ought to be a Greek *chi* or a Spanish *j*. Now what does it mean in Welsh?"

"In Welsh?" said the parson. "There is no such word in Welsh, nor any word remotely resembling it. I know the book-Welsh, as they call it, and the colloquial dialects as well as any man, but there's no word like that from Anglesea to Usk. Besides, none of the Cradocks speak a word of Welsh; it's dying out about here."

"Really. You interest me extremely, Mr. Meyrick. I confess the word didn't strike me as having the Welsh ring. But I thought it might be some local corruption."

"No, I never heard such a word, or anything like it. Indeed," he added, smiling whimsically, "if it belongs to any language, I should say it must be that of the fairies—the Tylwydd Têg, as we call them."

The talk went on to the discovery of a Roman villa in the neighbourhood; and soon after I left the room, and sat down apart to wonder at the drawing together of such strange clues of evidence. As the professor had spoken of the curious word, I had caught the glint in his eye upon me; and though the pronunciation he gave was grotesque in the extreme, I recognized the name of the stone of sixty characters mentioned by Solinus, the black seal shut up in some secret drawer of the study, stamped for ever by a vanished race with signs that no man could read, signs that might, for all I knew, be the veils of awful things done long ago, and forgotten before the hills were moulded into form.

When the next morning I came down, I found Professor Gregg pacing the terrace in his eternal walk.

"Look at that bridge," he said, when he saw me; "observe the quaint and Gothic design, the angles between the arches, and the silvery grey of the stone in the awe of the morning light. I confess it seems to me symbolic; it should illustrate a mystical allegory of the passage from one world to another."

"Professor Gregg," I said quietly, "it is time that I knew something of what has happened, and of what is to happen."

For the moment he put me off, but I returned again with the same question in the evening, and then Professor Gregg flamed with excitement. "Don't you understand yet?" he cried. "But I have told you a good deal; yes, and shown you a good deal; you have heard pretty nearly all that I have heard, and seen what I have seen; or at least," and his voice chilled as he spoke, 'enough to make a good deal clear as noonday. The servants told you, I have no doubt, that the wretched boy Cradock had another seizure the night before last; he awoke me with cries in that voice you heard in the garden, and I went to him, and God forbid you should see what I saw that night. But all this is useless; my time here is drawing to a close; I must be back in town in three weeks, as I have a course of lectures to prepare, and need all my books about me. In a very few days it will be all over, and I shall no longer hint, and no longer be liable to ridicule as a madman and a quack. No, I shall speak plainly, and I shall be heard with such emotions as perhaps no other man has ever drawn from the breasts of his fellows."

He paused, and seemed to grow radiant with the joy of great and wonderful discovery.

"But all that is for the future, the near future certainly, but still the future," he went on at length. "There is something to be done yet; you will remember my telling you that my researches were not altogether devoid of peril? Yes, there, is a certain amount of danger to be faced; I did not know how much when I spoke on the subject before, and to a certain extent I am still in the dark. But it will be a strange adventure, the last of all, the last demonstration in the chain."

He was walking up and down the room as he spoke, and I could hear in his voice the contending tones of exultation and despondence, or perhaps I should say awe, the awe of a man who goes forth on unknown waters, and I thought of his allusion to Columbus on the night he had laid his book before me. The evening was a little chilly, and a fire of logs had been lighted in the study where we were; the remittent flame and the glow on the walls reminded me of the old days. I was sitting silent in an armchair by the fire, wondering over all I had heard, and still vainly speculating as to the secret springs concealed from me under all the phantasmagoria I had witnessed, when I became suddenly aware of a sensation that change of some sort had been at work in the room, and that there was something unfamiliar in its aspect. For some time I looked about me, trying in vain to localize the alteration that I knew had been made; the table by the window, the chairs, the faded settee were all as I had known them. Suddenly, as a sought-for recollection flashes into the mind, I knew what was amiss. I was facing the professor's desk, which stood on the other side of the fire, and above the desk was a grimy-looking bust of Pitt, that I had never seen there before. And then I remembered the true position of this work of art; in the furthest corner by the door was an old cupboard, projecting into the room, and on the top of the cupboard, fifteen feet from the floor, the bust had been, and there, no doubt, it had delayed, accumulating dirt, since the early days of the century.

I was utterly amazed, and sat silent, still in a confusion of thought. There was, so far as I knew, no such thing as a step-ladder in the house, for I had asked for one to make some alteration in the curtains of my room, and a tall man standing on a chair would have found it impossible to take down the bust. It had been placed, not on the edge of the cupboard, but far back against the wall; and Professor Gregg was, if anything, under the average height.

"How on earth did you manage to get down Pitt?" I said at last.

The professor looked curiously at me, and seemed to hesitate a little.

"They must have found you a step-ladder, or perhaps the gardener brought in a short ladder from outside?"

"No, I have had no ladder of any kind. Now, Miss Lally," he went on with an awkward simulation of jest, "there is a little puzzle for you; a problem in the manner of the inimitable Holmes; there are the facts, plain and patent: summon your acuteness to the solution of the puzzle. For Heaven's sake," he cried with a breaking voice, "say no more about it! I tell you, I never touched the thing," and he went out of the room with horror manifest on his face, and his hand shook and jarred the door behind him.

I looked round the room in vague surprise, not at all realizing what had happened, making vain and idle surmises by way of explanation, and wondering at the stirring of black waters by an idle word and the trivial change of an ornament. "This is some petty business, some whim on which I have jarred," I reflected; "the professor is perhaps scrupulous and superstitious over trifles, and my question may have outraged unacknowledged fears, as though one killed a spider or spilled the salt before the very eyes of a practical Scotchwoman." I was immersed in these fond suspicions, and began to plume myself a little on my immunity from such empty fears, when the truth fell heavily as lead upon my heart, and I recognized with cold terror that some awful influence had been at work. The bust was simply inaccessible; without a ladder no one could have touched it.

I went out to the kitchen and spoke as quietly as I could to the housemaid.

"Who moved that bust from the top of the cupboard, Anne?" I said to her. "Professor Gregg says he has not touched it. Did you find an old step-ladder in one of the outhouses?"

The girl looked at me blankly.

"I never touched it," she said. "I found it where it is now the other morning when I dusted the room. I remember now, it was Wednesday morning, because it was the morning after Cradock was taken bad in the night. My room is next to his, you know, miss," the girl went on piteously, "and it was awful to hear how he cried and called out names that I couldn't understand. It made me feel all afraid; and then master came, and I heard him speak, and he took down Cradock to the study and gave him something."

"And you found that bust moved the next morning?"

"Yes, miss. There was a queer sort of smell in the study when I came down and opened the windows; a bad smell it was, and I wondered what it could be. Do you know, miss, I went a long time ago to the Zoo in London with my cousin Thomas Barker, one afternoon that I had off, when I was at Mrs. Prince's in Stanhope Gate, and we went into the snake-house to see the snakes, and it was just the same sort of smell; very sick it made me feel, I remember, and I got Barker to take me out. And it was just the same kind of smell in the study, as I was saying, and I was wondering what it could be from, when I see that bust with Pitt cut in it, standing on the master's desk, and I thought to myself, 'Now who has done that, and how have they done it?' And when I came to dust the things, I looked at the bust, and I saw a great mark on it where the dust was gone, for I don't think it can have been touched with a duster for years and years, and it wasn't like finger-marks, but a large patch like, broad and spread out. So I passed my hand over it, without thinking what I was doing, and where that patch was it was all sticky and slimy, as if a snail had crawled over it. Very strange, isn't it, miss? and I wonder who can have done it, and how that mess was made."

The well-meant gabble of the servant touched me to the quick; I lay down upon my bed, and bit my lip that I should not cry out loud in the sharp anguish of my terror and bewilderment. Indeed, I was almost mad with dread; I believe that if it had been daylight I should have fled hot foot, forgetting all courage and all the debt of gratitude that was due to Professor Gregg, not caring whether my fate were that I must starve slowly, so long as I might escape from the net of blind and panic fear that every day seemed to draw a little closer round me. If I knew, I thought, if I knew what there was to dread, I could guard against it; but here, in this lonely house, shut in on all sides by the olden woods and the vaulted hills, terror seems to spring inconsequent from every covert, and the flesh is aghast at the half-hearted murmurs of horrible things. All in vain I strove to summon scepticism to my aid, and endeavoured by cool common sense to buttress my belief in a world of natural order, for the air that blew in at the open window was a mystic breath, and in the darkness I felt the silence go heavy and sorrowful as a mass of requiem, and I conjured images of strange shapes gathering fast amidst the reeds, beside the wash of the river.

In the morning from the moment that I set foot in the breakfast-room, I felt that the unknown plot was drawing to a crisis; the professor's face was firm and set, and he seemed hardly to hear our voices when we spoke.

"I am going out for a rather long walk," he said, when the meal was over. "You mustn't be expecting me, now, or thinking anything has happened if I don't turn up to dinner. I have been getting stupid lately, and I dare say a miniature walking tour will do me good. Perhaps I may even spend the night in some little inn, if I find any place that looks clean and comfortable."

I heard this, and knew by my experience of Professor Gregg's manner that it was no ordinary business of pleasure that impelled him. I knew not, nor even remotely guessed, where he was bound, nor had I the vaguest notion of his errand, but all the fear of the night before returned; and as he stood, smiling, on the terrace, ready to set out, I implored him to stay, and to forget all his dreams of the undiscovered continent.

"No, no, Miss Lally," he replied, still smiling, "it's too late now. *Vestigia nulla retrorsum*, you know, is the device of all true explorers, though I hope it won't be literally true in my case. But, indeed, you are wrong to alarm yourself so; I look upon my little expedition as quite commonplace; no more exciting than a day with the geological hammers. There is a risk, of course, but so there is on the commonest excursion. I can afford to be jaunty; I am doing nothing so hazardous as 'Arry does a hundred times over in the course of every Bank Holiday. Well, then, you must look more cheerfully; and so good-bye till tomorrow at latest."

He walked briskly up the road, and I saw him open the gate that marks the entrance of the wood, and then he vanished in the gloom of the trees.

All the day passed heavily with a strange darkness in the air, and again I felt as if imprisoned amidst the ancient woods, shut in an olden land of mystery and dread, and as if all was long ago and forgotten by the living outside. I hoped and dreaded; and when the dinner-hour came I waited, expecting to hear the professor's step in the hall, and his voice exulting at I knew not what triumph. I composed my face to welcome him gladly, but the night descended dark, and he did not come.

In the morning, when the maid knocked at my door, I called out to her, and asked if her master had returned; and when she replied that his bedroom door stood open and empty,

I felt the cold clasp of despair. Still, I fancied he might have discovered genial company, and would return for luncheon, or perhaps in the afternoon, and I took the children for a walk in the forest, and tried my best to play and laugh with them, and to shut out the thoughts of mystery and veiled terror.

Hour after hour I waited, and my thoughts grew darker; again the night came and found me watching, and at last, as I was making much ado to finish my dinner, I heard steps outside and the sound of a man's voice.

The maid came in and looked oddly at me. "Please, miss," she began, "Mr. Morgan, the gardener, wants to speak to you for a minute, if you didn't mind."

"Show him in, please," I answered, and set my lips tight.

The old man came slowly into the room, and the servant shut the door behind him.

"Sit down, Mr. Morgan," I said; "what is it that you want to say to me?"

"Well, miss, Mr. Gregg he gave me something for you yesterday morning, just before he went off, and he told me particular not to hand it up before eight o'clock this evening exactly, if so be as he wasn't back again home before, and if he should come home before I was just to return it to him in his own hands. So, you see, as Mr. Gregg isn't here yet, I suppose I'd better give you the parcel directly."

He pulled out something from his pocket, and gave it to me, half rising. I took it silently, and seeing that Morgan seemed doubtful as to what he was to do next. I thanked him and bade him good night, and he went out. I was left alone in the room with the parcel in my hand—a paper parcel, neatly sealed and directed to me, with the instructions Morgan had quoted, all written in the professor's large, loose hand. I broke the seals with a choking at my heart, and found an envelope inside, addressed also, but open, and I took the letter out.

My dear Miss Lally it began—*To quote the old logic manual, the case of your reading this note is a case of my having made a blunder of some sort, and, I am afraid, a blunder that turns these lines into a farewell. It is practically certain that neither you nor any one else will ever see me again. I have made my will with provision for this eventuality, and I hope you will consent to accept the small remembrance addressed to you, and my sincere thanks for the way in which you joined your fortunes to mine. The fate which has come upon me is desperate and terrible beyond the remotest dreams of man; but this fate you have a right to know—if you please. If you look in the left-hand drawer of my dressing-table, you will find the key of the escritoire, properly labelled. In the well of the escritoire is a large envelope sealed and addressed to your name. I advise you to throw it forthwith into the fire; you will sleep better of nights if you do so. But if you must know the history of what has happened, it is all written down for you to read.*

The signature was firmly written below, and again I turned the page and read out the words one by one, aghast and white to the lips, my hands cold as ice, and sickness choking me. The dead silence of the room, and the thought of the dark woods and hills closing me in on every side, oppressed me, helpless and without capacity, and not knowing where to turn for counsel. At last I resolved that though knowledge should haunt my whole life and all the days to come, I must know the meaning of the strange terrors that had so long tormented me, rising grey, dim, and awful, like the shadows in the wood at dusk. I carefully carried out Professor Gregg's directions, and not without reluctance broke the seal of the envelope, and spread out his manuscript before me. That manuscript I always carry with me, and I see that I cannot deny your unspoken request to read it. This, then, was what I read that night, sitting at the desk, with a shaded lamp beside me.

The young lady who called herself Miss Lally then proceeded to recite

The Statement of William Gregg. F.R.S., etc.

It is many years since the first glimmer of the theory which is now almost, if not quite, reduced to fact dawned on my mind. A somewhat extensive course of miscellaneous and obsolete reading had done a great deal to prepare the way, and, later, when I became somewhat of a specialist, and immersed myself in the studies known as ethnological, I was now and then startled by facts that would not square with orthodox scientific opinion, and by discoveries that seemed to hint at something still hidden for all our research. More particularly I became convinced that much of the folk-lore of the world is but an exaggerated account of events that really happened, and I was especially drawn to consider the stories of the fairies, the good folk of the Celtic races. Here, I thought I could detect the fringe of embroidery and exaggeration, the fantastic guise, the little people dressed in green and gold sporting in the flowers, and I thought I saw a distinct analogy between the name given to this race (supposed to be imaginary) and the description of their appearance and manners. Just as our remote ancestors called the dreaded beings "fair" and "good" precisely because they dreaded them, so they had dressed them up in charming forms, knowing the truth to be the very reverse. Literature, too, had gone early to work, and had lent a powerful hand in the transformation, so that the playful elves of Shakespere are already far removed from the true original, and the real horror is disguised in a form of prankish mischief. But in the older tales, the stories that used to make men cross themselves as they sat around the burning logs, we tread a different stage; I saw a widely opposed spirit in certain histories of children and of men and women who vanished strangely from the earth.

They would be seen by a peasant in the fields walking towards some green and rounded hillock, and seen no more on earth; and there are stories of mothers who have left a child quietly sleeping, with the cottage door rudely barred with a piece of wood, and have returned, not to find the plump and rosy little Saxon, but a thin and wizened creature, with sallow skin and black, piercing eyes, the child of another race. Then, again, there were myths darker still; the dread of witch and wizard, the lurid evil of the Sabbath, and the hint of demons who mingled with the daughters of men. And just as we have turned the terrible "fair folk" into a company of benignant, if freakish elves, so we have hidden from us the black foulness of the witch and her companions under a popular *diablerie* of old women and broomsticks, and a comic cat with tail on end. So the Greeks called the hideous furies benevolent ladies, and thus the northern nations have followed their example. I pursued my investigations, stealing odd hours from other and more imperative labours, and I asked myself the question: Supposing these traditions to be true, who were the demons who are reported to have attended the Sabbaths? I need not say that I laid aside what I may call the supernatural hypothesis of the Middle Ages, and came to the conclusion that fairies and devils were of one and the same race and origin; invention, no doubt, and the Gothic fancy of old days, had done much in the way of exaggeration and distortion; yet I firmly believe that beneath all this imagery there was a black background of truth. As for some of the alleged wonders, I hesitated. While I should be very loath to receive any one specific instance of modern spiritualism as containing even a grain of the genuine, yet I was not wholly prepared to deny that human flesh may now and then, once perhaps in ten millions cases, be the veil of powers which seem magical to us—powers which, so far from proceeding from the heights and leading men thither, are in reality survivals from the depths of being. The amoeba and the snail have powers which we do not possess; and I thought it possible that the theory of reversion might explain many things which seem wholly inexplicable. Thus stood my position; I saw good reason to believe that much of the tradition, a vast deal of the earliest and uncorrupted tradition of the so-called fairies, represented solid fact, and I thought that the purely supernatural element in these traditions was to be accounted for on the hypothesis that a race which had fallen out of the grand march of evolution might have retained, as a survival, certain powers which would be to us wholly miraculous. Such was my theory as it stood conceived in my mind; and working with this in view, I seemed to gather confirmation from every side, from the spoils of a tumulus or a barrow, from a local paper reporting an antiquarian meeting in the country, and from general literature of all kinds. Amongst other instances, I remember being struck by the phrase "articulate-speaking men" in Homer, as if the writer knew or had heard of men whose speech was so rude that it could hardly be termed articulate; and on my hypothesis of a race who had lagged far behind the rest, I could easily conceive that such a folk would speak a jargon but little removed from the inarticulate noises of brute beasts.

Thus I stood, satisfied that my conjecture was at all events not far removed from fact, when a chance paragraph in a small country print one day arrested my attention. It was a short account of what was to all appearance the usual sordid tragedy of the village—a young girl unaccountably missing, and evil rumour blatant and busy with her reputation. Yet I could read between the lines that all this scandal was purely hypothetical, and in all probability invented to account for what was in any other manner unaccountable. A flight to London or Liverpool, or an undiscovered body lying with a weight about its neck in the foul depths of a woodland pool, or perhaps murder—such were the theories of the wretched girl's neighbours. But as I idly scanned the paragraph, a flash of thought passed through me with the violence of an electric shock: what if the obscure and horrible race of the hills still survived, still remained haunting wild places and barren hills, and now and then repeating the evil of Gothic legend, unchanged and unchangeable as the Turanian Shelta, or the Basques of Spain? I have said that the thought came with violence; and indeed I drew in my breath sharply, and clung with both hands to my elbow-chair, in a strange confusion of horror and elation. It was as if one of my *confrères* of physical science, roaming in a quiet English wood, had been suddenly stricken aghast by the presence of the slimy and loathsome terror of the ichthyosaurus, the original of the stories of the awful worms killed by valourous knights, or had seen the sun darkened by the pterodactyl, the dragon of tradition. Yet as a resolute explorer of knowledge, the thought of such a discovery threw me into a passion of joy, and I cut out the slip from the paper and put it in a drawer in my old bureau, resolved that it should be but the first piece in a collection of the strangest significance. I sat long that evening dreaming of the conclusions I should establish, nor did cooler reflection at first dash my confidence. Yet as I began to put the case fairly, I saw that I might be building on an unstable foundation; the facts might possibly be in accordance with local opinion, and I regarded the affair with a mood of some reserve. Yet I resolved to remain perched on the lookout, and I hugged to myself the thought that I alone was watching and wakeful, while the great crowd of thinkers and searchers stood heedless and indifferent, perhaps letting the most prerogative facts pass by unnoticed.

Several years elapsed before I was enabled to add to the contents of the drawer; and the second find was in reality not a valuable one, for it was a mere repetition of the first, with only the variation of another and distant locality. Yet I gained something; for in the second case, as in the first, the tragedy took place in a desolate and lonely country, and so far my theory seemed justified. But the third piece was to me far more decisive. Again, amongst outland hills, far even from a main road of traffic, an old man was found done to death, and the instrument of execution was left beside him. Here, indeed, there were rumour and conjecture, for the deadly tool was a primitive stone axe, bound by gut to the wooden handle, and surmises the most extravagant and improbable were indulged in. Yet, as I thought with a kind of glee, the wildest conjectures went far astray; and I took the pains to enter into corresponddence with the local doctor, who was called at the inquest. He, a man of some acuteness, was dumbfounded. "It will not do to speak of these things in country places," he wrote to me; "but frankly, there is some hideous mystery here. I have obtained possession of the stone axe, and have been so curious as to test its powers. I took it into the back garden of my house one Sunday afternoon when my family and the servants were all out, and there, sheltered by the poplar hedges, I made my experiments. I found the thing utterly unmanageable; whether there is some peculiar balance, some nice adjustment of weights, which require incessant practice, or whether an effectual blow can be struck only by a certain trick of the muscles, I do not know; but I can assure you that I went into the house with but a sorry opinion of my athletic capacities. I was like an inexperienced man trying "putting the hammer"; the force exerted seemed to return on oneself, and I found myself hurled backwards with violence, while the axe fell harmless to the ground. On another occasion I tried the experiment with a clever woodman of the place; but this man, who had handled his axe for forty years, could do nothing with the stone implement, and missed every stroke most ludicrously. In short, if it were not so supremely absurd, I should say that for four thousand years no one on earth could have struck an effective blow with the tool that undoubtedly was used to murder the old man." This, as may be imagined, was to me rare news; and afterwards, when I heard the whole story, and learned that the unfortunate old man had babbled tales of what might be seen at night on a certain wild hillside, hinting at unheard-of wonders, and that he had been found cold one morn ing on the very hill in question, my exultation was extreme, for I felt I was leaving conjecture far behind me. But the next step was of still greater importance. I had possessed for many years an extraordinary stone seal—a piece of dull black stone, two inches long from the handle to the stamp, and the stamping end a rough hexagon an inch and a quarter in diameter. Altogether, it presented the appearance of an enlarged tobacco stopper of an old-fashioned make. It had been sent to me by an agent in the East, who informed me that it had been found near the site of the ancient Babylon. But the characters engraved on the seal were to me an intolerable puzzle. Somewhat of the cuneiform pattern, there were yet striking differences, which I detected at the first glance, and all efforts to read the inscription on the hypothesis that the rules for deciphering the arrow-headed writing would apply proved futile. A riddle such as this stung my pride, and at odd moments I would take the Black Seal out of the cabinet, and scrutinize it with so much idle perseverance that every letter was familiar to my mind, and I could have drawn the inscription from memory without the slightest error. Judge, then, of my surprise when I one day received from a correspondent in the west of England a letter and an enclosure that positively left me thunderstruck. I saw carefully traced on a large piece of paper the very characters of the Black Seal, without alteration of any kind, and above the inscription my friend had written: *Inscription found on a limestone rock on the Grey Hills, Monmouthshire. Done in some red earth, and quite recent.* I turned to the letter. My friend wrote: "I send you the enclosed inscription with all due reserve. A shepherd who passed by the stone a week ago swears that there was then no mark of any kind. The characters, as I have noted, are formed by drawing some red earth over the stone, and are of an average height of one inch. They look to me like a kind of cuneiform character, a good deal altered, but this, of course, is impossible. It may be either a hoax, or more probably some scribble of the gipsies, who are plentiful enough in this wild country. They have, as you are aware, many heiroglyphics which they use in communicating with one another. I happened to visit the stone in question two days ago in connection with a rather painful incident which has occurred here."

As it may be supposed, I wrote immediately to my friends, thanking him for the copy of the inscription, and asking him in a casual manner the history of the incident he mentioned. To be brief, I heard that a woman named Cradock, who had lost her husband a day before, had set out to communicate the sad news to a cousin who lived some five miles away. She took a short cut which led by the Grey Hills. Mrs. Cradock, who was then quite a young woman, never arrived at her relative's house. Late that night a farmer, who had lost a couple of sheep, supposed to have wandered from the flock, was walking over the Grey Hills, with a lantern and his dog. His attention was attracted by a noise, which he described as a kind of wailing, mournful and pitiable to hear; and, guided by the sound, he found the unfortunate Mrs. Cradock crouched on the ground by the limestone rock, swaying her body to and fro, and lamenting and crying in so heart-rending a manner that the farmer was, as he says, at first obliged to stop his ears, or he would have run away. The woman allowed herself to be taken home, and a neighbour came to see to her necessities. All the night she never ceased her crying, mixing her lament with words of some unintelligible jargon, and when the doctor arrived he pronounced her insane. She lay on her bed for a week, now wailing, as people said, like one lost and damned for eternity, and now sunk in a heavy coma; it was thought that grief at the loss of her husband had unsettled her mind, and the medical man did not at one time expect her to live. I need not say that I was deeply interested in this story, and I made my friend write to me at intervals with all the particulars of the case. I heard then that in the course of six weeks the woman gradually recovered the use of her faculties, and some months later she gave birth to a son, christened Jervase, who unhappily proved to be of weak intellect. Such were the facts known to the village; but to me, while I whitened at the suggested thought of the hideous enormities that had doubtless been committed, all this was nothing short of conviction, and I incautiously hazarded a hint of something like the truth to some scientific friends. The moment the words had left my lips I bitterly regretted having spoken, and thus given away the great secret of my life, but with a good deal of relief mixed with indignation I found my fears altogether misplaced, for my friends ridiculed me to my face, and I was regarded as a madman; and beneath a natural anger I chuckled to myself, feeling as secure amidst these blockheads as if I had confided what I knew to the desert sands.

But now, knowing so much, I resolved I would know all, and I concentrated my efforts on the task of deciphering the inscription on the Black Seal. For many years I made this puzzle the sole object of my leisure moments, for the greater portion of my time was, of course, devoted to other duties, and it was only now and then that I could snatch a week of clear research. If I were to tell the full history of this curious investigation, this statement would be wearisome in the extreme, for it would contain simply the account of long and tedious failure. But with what I knew already of ancient scripts I was well equipped for the chase, as I always termed it to myself. I had correspondents amongst all the scientific men in Europe, and, indeed, in the world, and I could not believe that in these days any character, however ancient and however perplexed, could long resist the search-light I should bring to bear upon it. Yet in point of fact, it was fully fourteen years before I succeeded. With every year my professional duties increased and my leisure became smaller. This no doubt retarded me a good deal; and yet, when I look back on those years, I am astonished at the vast scope of my investigation of the Black Seal. I made my bureau a centre, and from all the world and from all the ages I gathered transcripts of ancient writing.

Nothing, I resolved, should pass me unawares, and the faintest hint should be welcomed and followed up. But as one covert after another was tried and proved empty of result, I began in the course of years to despair, and to wonder whether the Black Seal were the sole relic of some race that had vanished from the world, and left no other trace of its existence—had perished, in fine, as Atlantis is said to have done, in some great cataclysm, its secrets perhaps drowned beneath the ocean or moulded into the heart of the hills. The thought chilled my warmth a little, and though I still persevered, it was no longer with the same certainty of faith. A chance came to the rescue. I was staying in a considerable town in the north of England, and took the opportunity of going over the very creditable museum that had for some time been established in the place. The curator was one of my correspondents; and, as we were looking through one of the mineral cases, my attention was struck by a specimen, a piece of black stone some four inches square, the appearance of which reminded me in a measure of the Black Seal. I took it up carelessly, and was turning it over in my hand, when I saw, to my astonishment, that the under side was inscribed. I said, quietly enough, to my friend the curator that the specimen interested me, and that I should be much obliged if he would allow me to take it with me to my hotel for a couple of days. He, of course, made no objection, and I hurried to my rooms and found that my first glance had not deceived me. There were two inscriptions; one in the regular cuneiform character, another in the character of the Black Seal, and I realized that my task was accomplished. I made an exact copy of the two inscriptions; and when I got to my London study, and had the seal before me, I was able seriously to grapple with the great problem. The interpreting inscription on the museum specimen, though in itself curious enough, did not bear on my quest, but the transliteration made me master of the secret of the Black Seal. Conjecture, of course, had to enter into my calculations; there was here and there uncertainty about a particular ideograph, and one sign recurring again and again on the seal baffled me for many successive nights. But at last the secret stood open before me in plain English, and I read the key of the awful transmutation of the hills. The last word was hardly written, when with fingers all trembling and unsteady I tore the scrap of paper into the minutest fragments, and saw them flame and blacken in the red hollow of the fire, and then I crushed the grey films that remained into finest powder. Never since then have I written those words; never will I write the phrases which tell how man can be reduced to the slime from which he came, and be forced to put on the flesh of the reptile and the snake.

There was now but one thing remaining. I knew, but I desired to see, and I was after some time able to take a house in the neighbourhood of the Grey Hills, and not far from the cottage where Mrs. Cradock and her son Jervase resided. I need not go into a full and detailed account of the apparently inexplicable events which have occurred here, where I am writing this. I knew that I should find in Jervase Cradock something of the blood of the "Little People," and I found later that he had more than once encountered his kinsmen in lonely places in that lonely land. When I was summoned one day to the garden, and found him in a seizure speaking or hissing the ghastly jargon of the Black Seal, I am afraid that exultation prevailed over pity. I heard bursting from his lips the secrets of the underworld, and the word of dread, "Ishakshar," signification of which I must be excused from giving.

But there is one incident I cannot pass over unnoticed. In the waste hollow of the night I awoke at the sound of those hissing syllables I knew so well; and on going to the wretched boy's room, I found him convulsed and foaming at the mouth, struggling on the bed as if he strove to escape the grasp of writhing demons. I took him down to my room and lit the lamp, while he lay twisting on the floor, calling on the power within his flesh to leave him. I saw his body swell and become distended as a bladder, while the face blackened before my eyes; and then at the crisis I did what was necessary according to the directions on the Seal, and putting all scruple on one side, I became a man of science, observant of what was passing. Yet the sight I had to witness was horrible, almost beyond the power of human conception and the most fearful fantasy. Something pushed out from the body there on the floor, and stretched forth a slimy, wavering tentacle, across the room, grasped the bust upon the cupboard, and laid it down on my desk.

When it was over, and I was left to walk up and down all the rest of the night, white and shuddering, with sweat pouring from my flesh, I vainly tried to reason within myself: I said, truly enough, that I had seen nothing really supernatural, that a snail pushing out his horns and drawing them in was but an instance on a smaller scale of what I had witnessed; and yet horror broke through all such reasonings and left me shattered and loathing myself for the share I had taken in the night's work.

There is little more to be said. I am going now to the final trial and encounter; for I have determined that there shall be nothing wanting, and I shall meet the "Little People" face to face. I shall have the Black Seal and the knowledge of its secrets to help me, and if I unhappily do not return from my journey, there is no need to conjure up here a picture of the awfulness of my fate.

Pausing a little at the end of Professor Gregg's statement, Miss Lally continued her tale in the following words:

Such was the almost incredible story that the professor had left behind him. When I had finished reading it, it was late at night, but the next morning I took Morgan with me, and we proceeded to search the Grey Hills for some trace of the lost professor. I will not weary you with a description of the savage desolation of that tract of country, a tract of utterest loneliness, of bare green hills dotted over with grey limestone boulders, worn by the ravages of time into fantastic semblances of men and beast. Finally, after many hours of weary searching, we found what I told you—the watch and chain, and purse, and the ring—wrapped in a piece of coarse parchment. When Morgan cut the gut that bound the parcel together, and I saw the professor's property, I burst into tears, but the sight of the dreaded characters of the Black Seal repeated on the parchment froze me to silent horror, and I think I understood for the first time the awful fate that had come upon my late employer.

I have only to add that Professor Gregg's lawyer treated my account of what had happened as a fairy tale, and refused even to glance at the documents I laid before him. It was he who was responsible for the statement that appeared in the public press, to the effect that Professor Gregg had been drowned, and that his body must have been swept into the open sea.

Miss Lally stopped speaking, and looked at Mr. Phillipps, with a glance of some inquiry. He, for his part, was sunken in a deep reverie of thought; and when he looked up and saw the bustle of the evening gathering in the square, men and women hurrying to partake of dinner, and crowds already besetting the music-halls, all the hum and press of actual life seemed unreal and visionary, a dream in the morning after an awakening.

Robert E. Howard's

6
The Star Rover
Jack London
(1915)

Robert E. Howard considered Jack London to be one of the finest authors he had ever read and he had a particular affinity for two of London's books: *Martin Eden* (1909) and *The Star Rover* (1915). Both of these books clearly had a strong influence on both Howard's life and his writings. "London's *The Star Rover*," Howard wrote in a letter to friend Harold Preece, "is a book that I've read and re-read for years, and that generally goes to my head like wine." The chapter reprinted here from London's *The Star Rover* will no doubt be very familiar to fans of Robert E. Howard. Jack London's character, Darrell Standing, sits on death row awaiting execution and is able to project himself into the lives he had previously lived. Howard's character, James Allison, is similarly confined, though by his handicap rather than by imprisonment, and is also able to experience his past lives. Chapter XXI shows numerous parallels to Howard's works, particularly his stories "The Valley of the Worm" and "The Children of the Night."

Chapter XXI

Pascal somewhere says: "In viewing the march of human evolution, the philosophic mind should look upon humanity as one man, and not as a conglomeration of individuals."

I sit here in Murderers' Row in Folsom, the drowsy hum of flies in my ears as I ponder that thought of Pascal. It is true. Just as the human embryo, in its brief ten lunar months, with bewildering swiftness, in myriad forms and semblances a myriad times multiplied, rehearses the entire history of organic life from vegetable to man; just as the human boy, in his brief years of boyhood, rehearses the history of primitive man in acts of cruelty and savagery, from wantonness of inflicting pain on lesser creatures to tribal consciousness expressed by the desire to run in gangs; just so, I, Darrell Standing, have rehearsed and relived all that primitive man was, and did, and became until he became even you and me and the rest of our kind in a twentieth century civilisation.

Truly do we carry in us, each human of us alive on the planet to-day, the incorruptible history of life from life's beginning. This history is written in our tissues and our bones, in our functions and our organs, in our brain cells and in our spirits, and in all sorts of physical and psychic atavistic urgencies and compulsions. Once we were fish-like, you and I, my reader, and crawled up out of the sea to pioneer in the great, dry-land adventure in the thick of which we are now. The marks of the sea are still on us, as the marks of the serpent are still on us, ere the serpent became serpent and we became we, when pre-serpent and pre-we were one. Once we flew in the air, and once we dwelt arboreally and were afraid of the dark. The vestiges remain, graven on you and me, and graven on our seed to come after us to the end of our time on earth.

What Pascal glimpsed with the vision of a seer, I have lived. I have seen myself that one man contemplated by Pascal's philosophic eye. Oh, I have a tale, most true, most wonderful, most real to me, although I doubt that I have wit to tell it, and that you, my reader, have wit to perceive it when told. I say that I have seen myself that one man hinted at by Pascal. I have lain in the long trances of the jacket and glimpsed myself a thousand living men living the thousand lives that are themselves the history of the human man climbing upward through the ages.

Ah, what royal memories are mine, as I flutter through the æons of the long ago. In single jacket trances I have lived the many lives involved in the thousand-years-long Odysseys of the early drifts of men. Heavens, before I was of the flaxen-haired Aesir, who dwelt in Asgard, and before I was of the red-haired Vanir, who dwelt in Vanaheim, long before those times I have memories (living memories) of earlier drifts, when, like thistledown before the breeze, we drifted south before the face of the descending polar ice-cap.

I have died of frost and famine, fight and flood. I have picked berries on the bleak backbone of the world, and I have dug roots to eat from the fat-soiled fens and meadows. I have scratched the reindeer's semblance and the semblance of the hairy mammoth on ivory tusks gotten of the chase and on the rock walls of cave shelters when the winter storms moaned outside. I have cracked marrow-bones on the sites of kingly cities that had perished centuries before my time or that were destined to be builded centuries after my passing. And I have left the bones of my transient carcasses in pond bottoms, and glacial gravels, and asphaltum lakes.

I have lived through the ages known to-day among the scientists as the Paleolithic, the Neolithic, and the Bronze. I remember when with our domesticated wolves we herded our reindeer to pasture on the north shore of the Mediterranean where now are France and Italy and Spain. This was before the ice-sheet melted backward toward the pole. Many processions of the equinoxes have I lived through and died in, my reader . . . only that I remember and that you do not.

I have been a Son of the Plough, a Son of the Fish, a Son of the Tree. All religions from the beginnings of man's religious time abide in me. And when the Dominie, in the chapel, here in Folsom of a Sunday, worships God in his own good modern way, I know that in him, the Dominie, still abide the worships of the Plough, the Fish, the Tree—ay, and also all worships of Astarte and the Night.

I have been an Aryan master in old Egypt, when my soldiers scrawled obscenities on the carven tombs of kings dead and gone and forgotten aforetime. And I, the Aryan master in old Egypt, have myself builded my two burial places—the one a false and mighty pyramid to which a generation of slaves could attest; the other humble, meagre, secret, rock-hewn in a desert valley by slaves who died immediately their work was done. . . . And I wonder me here in Folsom, while democracy dreams its enchantments o'er the twentieth century world, whether there, in the rock-hewn crypt of that secret, desert valley, the bones still abide that once were mine and that stiffened my animated body when I was an Aryan master high-stomached to command.

And on the great drift, southward and eastward under the burning sun that perished all descendants of the houses of Asgard and Vanaheim, I have been a king in Ceylon, a builder of Aryan monuments under Aryan kings in old Java and old Sumatra. And I have died a hundred deaths on the great South Sea drift ere ever the rebirth of me came to plant monuments, that only Aryans plant, on volcanic tropic islands that I, Darrell Standing, cannot name, being too little versed to-day in that far sea geography.

If only I were articulate to paint in the frail medium of words what I see and know and possess incorporated in my consciousness of the mighty driftage of the races in the times before our present written history began! Yes, we had our history even then. Our old men, our priests, our wise ones, told our history into tales and wrote those tales in the stars so that our seed after us should not forget. From the sky came the life-giving rain and the sunlight. And we studied the sky, learned from the stars to calculate time and apportion the seasons; and we named the stars after our heroes and our foods and our devices for getting food; and after our wanderings, and drifts, and adventures; and after our functions and our furies of impulse and desire.

And, alas! we thought the heavens unchanging on which we wrote all our humble yearnings and all the humble things we did or dreamed of doing. When I was a Son of the Bull, I remember me a lifetime I spent at star-gazing. And, later and earlier, there were other lives in which I sang with the priests and bards the taboo-songs of the stars wherein we believed was written our imperishable record. And here, at the end of it all, I pore over books of astronomy from the prison library, such as they allow condemned men to read, and learn that even the heavens are passing fluxes, vexed with star-driftage as the earth is by the drifts of men.

Equipped with this modern knowledge, I have, returning through the little death from my earlier lives, been able to compare the heavens then and now. And the stars do change. I have seen pole stars and pole stars and dynasties of pole stars. The pole star to-day is in Ursa Minor. Yet, in those far days I have seen the pole star in Draco, in Hercules, in Vega, in Cygnus, and in Cepheus. No; not even the stars abide, and yet the memory and the knowledge of them abides in me, in the spirit of me that is memory and that is eternal. Only spirit abides. All else, being mere matter, passes, and must pass.

Oh, I do see myself to-day that one man who appeared in the elder world, blonde, ferocious, a killer and a lover, a meat-eater and a root-digger, a gypsy and a robber, who, club in hand, through millenniums of years wandered the world around seeking meat to devour and sheltered nests for his younglings and sucklings.

I am that man, the sum of him, the all of him, the hairless biped who struggled upward from the slime and created love and law out of the anarchy of fecund life that screamed and squalled in the jungle. I am all that that man was and did become. I see myself, through the painful generations, snaring and killing the game and the fish, clearing the first fields from the forest, making rude tools of stone and bone, building houses of wood, thatching the roofs with leaves and straw, domesticating the wild grasses and meadow-roots, fathering them to become the progenitors of rice and millet and wheat and barley and all manner of succulent edibles, learning to scratch the soil, to sow, to reap, to store, beating out the fibers of plants to spin into thread and to weave into cloth, devising systems of irrigation, working in metals, making markets and trade-routes, building boats, and founding navigation—ay, and organizing village life, welding villages to villages till they became tribes, welding tribes together till they became nations, ever seeking the laws of things, ever making the laws of humans so that humans might live together in amity and by united effort beat down and destroy all manner of creeping, crawling, squalling things that might else destroy them.

I was that man in all his births and endeavors. I am that man to-day, waiting my due death by the law that I helped to devise many a thousand years ago, and by which I have died many times before this, many times. And as I contemplate this vast past history of me, I find several great and splendid influences, and, chiefest of these, the love of woman, man's love for the woman of his kind. I see myself, the one man, the lover, always the lover. Yes, also was I the great fighter, but somehow it seems to me as I sit here and evenly balance it all, that I was, more than aught else, the great lover. It was because I loved greatly that I was the great fighter.

Sometimes I think that the story of man is the story of the love of woman. This memory of all my past that I write now is the memory of my love of woman. Ever, in the ten thousand lives and guises, I loved her. I love her now. My sleep is fraught with her; my waking fancies, no matter whence they start, lead me always to her. There is no escaping her, that eternal, spleendid, ever-resplendent figure of woman.

Oh, make no mistake. I am no callow, ardent youth. I am an elderly man, broken in health and body, and soon to die. I am a scientist and a philosopher. I, as all the generations of philosophers before me, know woman for what she is—her weaknesses, and meannesses, and immodesties, and ignobilities, her earth-bound feet, and her eyes that have never seen the stars. But—and the everlasting, irrefragable fact remains: *Her feet are beautiful, her eyes are beautiful, her arms and breasts are paradise, her charm is potent beyond all charm that has ever dazzled men; and, as the pole willy-nilly draws the needle, just so, willy-nilly, does she draw man.*

Woman has made me laugh at death and distance, scorn fatigue and sleep. I have slain men, many men, for love of woman, or in warm blood have baptized our nuptials or washed away the stain of her favor to another. I have gone down to death and dishonor, my betrayal of my comrades and of the stars black upon me, for woman's sake—for my sake, rather, I desired her so. And I have lain in the barley, sick with yearning for her, just to see her pass and glut my eyes with the swaying wonder of her and of her hair, black with the night, or brown or flaxen, or all golden-dusty with the sun.

For woman *is* beautiful . . . to man. She is sweet to his tongue, and fragrance in his nostrils. She is fire in his blood, and a thunder of trumpets; her voice is beyond all music in his ears; and she can shake his soul that else stands steadfast in the draughty presence of the Titans of the Light and of the Dark. And beyond his star-gazing, in his far-imagined heavens, Valkyrie or houri, man has fain made place for her, for he could see no heaven without her. And the sword, in battle, singing, sings not so sweet a song as the woman sings to man merely by her laugh in the moonlight, or her love-sob in the dark, or by her swaying on her way under the sun while he lies dizzy with longing in the grass.

I have died of love. I have died for love, as you shall see. In a little while they will take me out, me, Darrell Standing, and make me die. And that death shall be for love. Oh, not lightly was I stirred when I slew Professor Haskell in the laboratory at the University of California. He was a man. I was a man. And there was a woman beautiful. Do you understand? She was a woman and I was a man and a lover, and all the heredity of love was mine up from the black and squalling jungle ere love was love and man was man.

Oh, ay, it is nothing new. Often, often, in that long past have I given life and honor, place and power for love. Man is different from woman. She is close to the immediate and knows only the need of instant things. We know honor above her honor, and pride beyond her wildest guess of pride. Our eyes are far-visioned for star-gazing, while her eyes see no farther than the solid earth beneath her feet, the lover's breast upon her breast, the infant lusty in the hollow of her arm. And yet, such is our alchemy compounded of the ages, woman works magic in our dreams and in our veins, so that more than dreams and far visions and the blood of life itself is woman to us, who, as lovers truly say, is more than all the world. Yet is this just, else would man not be man, the fighter and the conqueror, treading his red way on the face of all other and lesser life—for, had man not been the lover, the royal lover, he could never have become the kingly fighter. We fight best, and die best, and live best, for what we love.

I am that one man. I see myself the many selves that have gone into the constituting of me. And ever I see the woman, the many women, who have made me and undone me, who have loved me and whom I have loved.

I remember, oh, long ago when human kind was very young, that I made me a snare and a pit with a pointed stake upthrust in the middle thereof, for the taking of Sabre-Tooth. Sabre-Tooth, long-fanged and long-haired, was the chiefest peril to us of the squatting place, who crouched through the nights over our fires and by day increased the growing shell-bank beneath us by the clams we dug and devoured from the salt mud-flats beside us.

And when the roar and the squall of Sabre-Tooth roused us where we squatted by our dying embers, and I was wild with far vision of the proof of the pit and the stake, it was the woman, arms about me, leg-twining, who fought with me and restrained me not to go out through the dark to my desire. She was part-clad, for warmth only, in skins of animals, mangy and fire-burnt, that I had slain; she was swart and dirty with camp smoke, unwashed since the spring rains, with nails gnarled and broken, and hands that were calloused like footpads and were more like claws than like hands; but her eyes were blue as the summer sky is, as the deep sea is, and there was that in her eyes, and in her clasped arms about me, and in her heart beating against mine, that withheld me . . . though through the dark until dawn, while Sabre-Tooth squalled his wrath and his agony, I could hear my comrades snickering and sniggling to their women in that I had not the faith in my emprise and invention to venture through the night to the pit and the stake I had devised for the undoing of Sabre-Tooth. But my woman, my savage mate held me, savage that I was, and her eyes drew me, and her arms chained me, and her twining legs and heart beating to mine seduced me from my far dream of things, my man's achievement, the goal beyond goals, the taking and the slaying of Sabre-Tooth on the stake in the pit.

Once I was Ushu, the archer. I remember it well. For I was lost from my own people, through the great forest, till I emerged on the flat lands and grass lands, and was taken in by a strange people, kin in that their skin was white, their hair yellow, their speech not too remote from mine. And she was Igar, and I drew her as I sang in the twilight, for she was destined a race-mother, and she was broad-built and full-dugged, and she could not but draw to the man heavy-muscled, deep-chested, who sang of his prowess in man-slaying and in meat-getting, and so, promised food and protection to her in her weakness whilst she mothered the seed that was to hunt the meat and live after her.

And these people knew not the wisdom of my people, in that they snared and pitted their meat and in battle used clubs and stone throwing-sticks and were unaware of the virtues of arrows swift-flying, notched on the end to fit the thong of deer-sinew, well-twisted, that sprang into straightness when released to the spring of the ask-stick bent in the middle.

And while I sang, the stranger men laughed in the twilight. And only she, Igar, believed and had faith in me. I took her alone to the hunting, where the deer sought the water-hole. And my bow twanged and sang in the covert, and the deer fell fast-stricken, and the warm meat was sweet to us, and she was mine there by the water-hole.

And because of Igar I remained with the strange men. And I taught them the making of bows from the red and sweet-smelling wood like unto cedar. And I taught them to keep both eyes open, and to aim with the left eye, and to make blunt shafts for small game, and pronged shafts of bone for the fish in the clear water, and to flake arrow-heads from obsidian for the deer and the wild horse, the elk and old Sabre-Tooth. But the flaking of stone they laughed at, till I shot an elk through and through, the flaked stone standing out and beyond, the feathered shaft sunk in its vitals, the whole tribe applauding.

I was Ushu, the archer, and Igar was my woman and mate. We laughed under the sun in the morning, when our man-child and woman-child, yellowed like honey-bees, sprawled and rolled in the mustard, and at night she lay close in my arms, and loved me, and urged me, because of my skill at the seasoning of woods and the flaking of arrow-heads, that I should stay close by the camp and let the other men bring to me the meat from the perils of hunting. And I listened, and grew fat and short-breathed, and in the long nights, unsleeping, worried that the men of the stranger tribe brought me meat for my wisdom and honor, but laughed at my fatness and undesire for the hunting and fighting.

And in my old age, when our sons were man-grown and our daughters were mothers, when up from the southland the dark men, flat-browed, kinky-headed, surged like waves of the sea upon us and we fled back before them to the hill-slopes, Igar, like my mates far before and long after, leg-twining, arm-clasping, unseeing far visions, strove to hold me aloof from the battle.

And I tore myself from her, fat and short-breathed, while she wept that no longer I loved her, and I went out to the night-fighting and dawn-fighting, where, to the singing of bowstrings and the shrilling of arrows, feathered, sharp-pointed, we showed them, the kinky-heads, the skill of the killing and taught them the wit and the willing of slaughter.

And as I died them at the end of the fighting, there were death songs and singing about me, and the songs seemed to sing as these the words I have written when I was Ushu, the archer, and Igar, my mate-woman, leg-twining, arm-clasping, would have held me back from the battle.

Once, and heaven alone knows when, save that it was in the long ago when man was young, we lived beside great swamps, where the hills drew down close to the wide, sluggish river, and where our women gathered berries and roots, and there were herds of deer, of wild horses, of antelope, and of elk, that we men slew with arrows or trapped in the pits or hill-pockets. From the river we caught fish in nets twisted by the women of the bark of young trees.

I was a man, eager and curious as the antelope when we lured it by waving grass clumps where we lay hidden in the thick of the grass. The wild rice grew in the swamp, rising sheer from the water on the edges of the channels. Each morning the blackbirds awoke us with their chatter as they left their roosts to fly to the swamp. And through the long twilight the air was filled with their noise as they went back to their roosts. It was the time that the rice ripened. And there were ducks also, and ducks and blackbirds feasted to fatness on the ripe rice half unhusked by the sun.

Being a man, ever restless, ever questing, wondering always what lay beyond the hills and beyond the swamps and in the mud at the river's bottom, I watched the wild ducks and blackbirds and pondered till my pondering gave me vision and I saw. And this is what I saw, the reasoning of it:

Meat was good to eat. In the end, tracing it back, or at the first, rather, all meat came from grass. The meat of the duck and of the blackbird came from the seed of the swamp rice. To kill a duck with an arrow scarce paid for the labor of stalking and the long hours in hiding. The blackbirds were too small for arrow-killing save by the boys who were learning and preparing for the taking of larger game. And yet, in rice season, blackbirds and ducks were succulently fat. Their fatness came from the rice. Why should I and mine not be fat from the rice in the same way?

And I thought it out in camp, silent, morose, while the children squabbled about me unnoticed, and while Arunga, my mate-woman, vainly scolded me and urged me to go hunting for more meat for the many of us.

Arunga was the woman I had stolen from the hill-tribes. She and I had been a dozen moons in learning common speech after I captured her. Ah, that day when I leaped upon her, down from the over-hanging tree-branch as she padded the runway! Fairly upon her shoulders with the weight of my body I smote her, my fingers wide-spreading to clutch her. She squalled like a cat there in the runway. She fought me and bit me. The nails of her hands were like the claws of a tree-cat as they tore at me. But I held her and mastered her, and for two days beat her and forced her to travel with me down out of the canyons of the Hill-Men to the grass lands where the river flowed through the rice-swamps and the ducks and the blackbirds fed fat.

I saw my vision when the rice was ripe. I put Arunga in the bow of the fire-hollowed log that was most rudely a canoe. I bade her paddle. In the stern I spread a deerskin she had tanned. With two stout sticks I bent the stalks over the deerskin and threshed out the grain that else the blackbirds would have eaten. And when I had worked out the way of it, I gave the two stout sticks to Arunga, and sat in the bow paddling and directing.

In the past we had eaten the raw rice in passing and not been pleased with it. But now we parched it over our fire so that the grains puffed and exploded in whiteness and all the tribe came running to taste.

After that we became known among men as the Rice-Eaters and as the Sons of the Rice. And long, long after, when we were driven by the Sons of the River from the swamps into the uplands, we took the seed of the rice with us and planted it. We learned to select the largest grains for the seed, so that all the rice we thereafter ate was larger-grained and puffier in the parching and the boiling.

But Arunga. I have said she squalled and scratched like a cat when I stole her. Yet I remember the time when her own kin of the Hill-Men caught me and carried me away into the hills. They were her father, his brother, and her two own blood-brothers. But she was mine, who had lived with me. And at night, where I lay bound like a wild pig for the slaying, and they slept weary by the fire, she crept upon them and brained them with the war-club that with my hands I had fashioned. And she wept over me, and loosed me, and fled with me, back to the wide sluggish river where the blackbirds and wild ducks fed in the rice swamps—for this was before the time of the coming of the Sons of the River.

For she was Arunga, the one woman, the eternal woman. She has lived in all times and places. She will always live. She is immortal. Once, in a far land, her name was Ruth. Also has her name been Iseult, and Helen, Pocahontas, and Unga. And no stranger man, from stranger tribes, but has found her and will find her in the tribes of all the earth.

I remember so many women who have gone into the becoming of the one woman. There was the time that Har, my brother, and I, sleeping and pursuing in turn, ever hounding the wild stallion through the daytime and night, and in a wide circle that met where the sleeping one lay, drove the stallion unresting through hunger and thirst to the meekness of weakness, so that in the end he could but stand and tremble while we bound him with ropes twisted of deer-hide. On our legs alone, without hardship, aided merely by wit—the plan was mine—my brother and I walked that fleet-footed creature into possession.

And when all was ready for me to get on his back—for that had been my vision from the first—Selpa, my woman, put her arms about me, and raised her voice and persisted that Har, and not I, should ride, for Har had neither wife nor young ones and could die without hurt. Also, in the end she wept, so that I was raped of my vision, and it was Har, naked and clinging, that bestrode the stallion when he vaulted away.

It was sunset, and a time of great wailing, when they carried Har in from the far rocks where they found him. His head was quite broken, and like honey from a fallen bee-tree his brains dripped on the ground. His mother strewed wood-ashes on her head and blackened her face. His father cut off half the fingers of one hand in token of sorrow. And all the women, especially the young and unwedded, screamed evil names at me; and the elders shook their wise heads and muttered and mumbled that not their fathers nor their fathers' fathers had betrayed such a madness. Horse meat was good to eat; young colts were tender to old teeth; and only a fool would come to close grapples with any wild horse save when an arrow had pierced it, or when it struggled on the stake in the midst of the pit.

And Selpa scolded me to sleep, and in the morning woke me with her chatter, ever declaiming against my madness, ever pronouncing her claim upon me and the claims of our children, till in the end I grew weary, and forsook my far vision, and said never again would I dream of bestriding the wild horse to fly swift as its feet and the wind across the sands and the grass lands.

And through the years the tale of my madness never ceased from being told over the camp-fire. Yet was the very telling the source of my vengeance; for the dream did not die, and the young ones, listening to the laugh and the sneer, redreamed it, so that in the end it was Othar, my eldest-born, himself a sheer stripling, that walked down a wild stallion, leapt on its back, and flew before all of us with the speed of the wind. Thereafter, that they might keep up with him, all men were trapping and breaking wild horses. Many horses were broken, and some men, but I lived at the last to the day when, at the changing of camp-sites in the pursuit of the meat in its seasons, our very babes, in baskets of willow-withes, were slung side and side on the backs of our horses that carried our camp-trappage and dunnage.

I, a young man, had seen my vision, dreamed my dream; Selpa, the woman, had held me from that far desire; but Othar, the seed of us to live after, glimpsed my vision and won to it, so that our tribe became wealthy in the gains of the chase.

There was a woman—on the great drift down out of Europe, a weary drift of many generations, when we brought into India the shorthorn cattle and the planting of barley. But this woman was long before we reached India. We were still in the mid-most of that centuries-long drift, and no shrewdness of geography can now place for me that ancient valley.

The woman was Nuhila. The valley was narrow, not long, and the swift slope of its floor and the steep walls of its rim were terraced for the growing of rice and of millet—the first rice and millet we Sons of the Mountain had known. They were a meek people in that valley. They had become soft with the farming of fat land made fatter by water. Theirs was the first irrigation we had seen, although we had little time to mark their ditches and channels by which all the hill waters flowed to the fields they had builded. We had little time to mark, for we Sons of the Mountain, who were few, were in flight before the Sons of the Snub-Nose, who were many. We called them the Noseless, and they called themselves the Sons of the Eagle. But they were many, and we fled before them with our shorthorn cattle, our goats, and our barleyseed, our women and children.

While the Snub-Noses slew our youths at the rear, we slew at our fore the folk of the valley who opposed us and were weak. The village was mud-built and grass-thatched; the encircling wall was of mud, but quite tall. And when we had slain the people who had built the wall, and sheltered within it our herds and our women and children, we stood on the wall and shouted insult to the Snub-Noses. For we had found the mud granaries filled with rice and millet. Our cattle could eat the thatches. And the time of the rains was at hand, so that we should not want for water.

It was a long siege. Near to the beginning, we gathered together the women, and elders, and children we had not slain, and forced them out through the wall they had builded. But the Snub-Noses slew them to the last one, so that there was more food in the village for us, more food in the valley for the Snub-Noses.

It was a weary long siege. Sickness smote us, and we died of the plague that arose from our buried ones. We emptied the mud-granaries of their rice and millet. Our goats and shorthorns ate the thatch of the houses, and we, ere the end, ate the goats and the shorthorns.

Where there had been five men of us on the wall, there came a time when there was one; where there had been half a thousand babes and younglings of ours, there were none. It was Nuhila, my woman, who cut off her hair and twisted it that I might have a strong string for my bow. The other women did likewise, and when the wall was attacked, stood shoulder to shoulder with us, in the midst of our spears and arrows raining down potsherds and cobblestones on the heads of the Snub-Noses.

Even the patient Snub-Noses we well-nigh out-patienced. Came a time when of ten men of us, but one was alive on the wall, and of our women remained very few, and the Snub-

Noses held parley. They told us we were a strong breed, and that our women were men-mothers, and that if we would let them have our women they would leave us alone in the valley to possess for ourselves and that we could get women from the valleys to the south.

And Nuhila said no. And the other women said no. And we sneered at the Snub-Noses and asked if they were weary of fighting. And we were as dead men then, as we sneered at our enemies, and there was little fight left in us we were so weak. One more attack on the wall would end us. We knew it. Our women knew it. And Nuhila said that we could end it first and outwit the Snub-Noses. And all our women agreed. And while the Snub-Noses prepared for the attack that would be final, there, on the wall, we slew our women. Nuhila loved me, and leaned to meet the thrust of my sword, there on the wall. And we men, in the love of tribehood and tribesmen, slew one another till remained only Horda and I alive in the red of the slaughter. And Horda was my elder, and I leaned to his thrust. But not at once did I die. I was the last of the Sons of the Mountain, for I saw Horda, himself fall on his blade and pass quickly. And dying with the shouts of the oncoming Snub-Noses growing dim in my ears, I was glad that the Snub-Noses would have no sons of us to bring up by our women.

I do not know when this time was when I was a Son of the Mountain and when we died in the narrow valley where we had slain the Sons of the Rice and the Millet. I do not know, save that it was centuries before the wide-spreading drift of all us Sons of the Mountain fetched into India, and that it was long before ever I was an Aryan master in Old Egypt building my two burial places and defacing the tombs of kings before me.

I should like to tell more of those far days, but time in the present is short. Soon I shall pass. Yet am I sorry that I cannot tell more of those early drifts, when there was crushage of peoples, or descending ice-sheets, or migrations of meat.

Also, I should like to tell of Mystery. For always were we curious to solve the secrets of life, death, and decay. Unlike the other animals, man was for ever gazing at the stars. Many gods he created in his own image and in the images of his fancy. In those old times I have worshipped the sun and the dark. I have worshipped the husked grain as the parent of life. I have worshipped Sar, the Corn Goddess. And I have worshipped sea gods, and river gods, and fish gods.

Yes, and I remember Ishtar ere she was stolen from us by the Babylonians, and Ea, too, was ours, supreme in the Under World, who enabled Ishtar to conquer death. Mitra, likewise, was a good old Aryan god, ere he was filched from us or we discarded him. And I remember, on a time, long after the drift when we brought the barley into India, that I came down into India, a horse-trader, with many servants and a long caravan at my back, and that at that time they were worshipping Bodhisatwa.

Truly, the worships of the Mystery wandered as did men, and between filchings and borrowings the gods had as vagabond a time of it as did we. As the Sumerians took the loan of Shamashnapishtin from us, so did the Sons of Shem take him from the Sumerians and call him Noah.

Why, I smile me to-day, Darrell Standing, in Murderers' Row, in that I was found guilty and awarded death by twelve jurymen staunch and true. Twelve has ever been a magic number of the Mystery. Nor did it originate with the twelve tribes of Israel. Star-gazers before them had placed the twelve signs of the Zodiac in the sky. And I remember me, when I was of the Assir, and of the Vanir, that Odin sat in judgment over men in the court of the twelve gods, and that their names were Thor, Baldur, Niord, Frey, Tyr, Bregi, Heimdal, Hoder, Vidar, Ull, Forseti, and Loki.

Even our Valkyries were stolen from us and made into angels, and the wings of the Valkyries' horses became attached to the shoulders of the angels. And our Helheim of that day of ice and frost has become the hell of to-day, which is so hot an abode that the blood boils in one's veins, while with us, in our Helheim, the place was so cold as to freeze the marrow inside the bones. And the very sky, that we dreamed enduring, eternal, has drifted and veered, so that we find to-day the scorpion in the place where of old we knew the goat, and the archer in the place of the crab.

Worships and worships! Ever the pursuit of the Mystery! I remember the lame god of the Greeks, the master-smith. But their vulcan was the Germanic Wieland, the master-smith captured and hamstrung lame of a leg by Nidung, the kind of the Nids. But before that he was our master-smith, our forger and hammerer, whom we named Il-marinen. And him we begat of our fancy, giving him the bearded sun-god for father, and nursing him by the stars of the bear. For, he, Vulcan, or Wieland, or Il-marinen, was born under the pine tree, from the hair of the wolf, and was called also the bear-father ere ever the Germans and Greeks purloined and worshipped him. In that day we called ourselves the Sons of the Bear and the Sons of the Wolf, and the bear and the wolf were our totems. That was before our drift south on which we joined with the Sons of the Tree-Grove and taught them our totems and tales.

Yes, and who was Kashyapa, who was Pururavas, but our lame master-smith, our iron-worker, carried by us in our drifts and re-named and worshipped by the south-dwellers and the east-dwellers, the Sons of the Pole and of the Fire Drill and Fire Socket.

But the tale is too long, though I should like to tell of the three-leaved Herb of Life by which Sigmund made Sinfioti alive again. For this is the very soma-plant of India, the holy grail of King Arthur, the—but enough! enough!

And yet, as I calmly consider it all, I conclude that the greatest thing in life, in all lives, to me and to all men, has been woman, is woman, and will be woman so long as the stars drift in the sky and the heavens flux eternal change. Greater than our toil and endeavor, the play of invention and fancy, battle and star-gazing and mystery—greatest of all has been woman.

Even though she has sung false music to me, and kept my feet solid on the ground, and drawn my star-roving eyes ever back to gaze upon her, she, the conserver of life, the earth-mother, has given me my great days and nights and fulness of years. Even mystery have I imaged in the form of her, and in my star-charting have I placed her figure in the sky.

All my toils and devices led to her; all my far visions saw her at the end. When I made the fire-drill and fire-socket, it was for her. It was for her, although I did not know it, that I put the stake in the pit for old Sabre-Tooth, tamed the horse, slew the mammoth, and herded my reindeer south in advance of the ice-sheet. For her I harvested the wild rice, tamed the barley, the wheat, and the corn.

For her, and the seed to come after whose image she bore, I have died in tree-tops and stood long sieges in cave-mouths and on mud-walls. For her I put the twelve signs in the sky. It was she I worshipped when I bowed before the ten stones of jade and adored them as the moons of gestation.

Always has woman crouched close to earth like a partridge hen mothering her young; always has my wantonness of roving led me out on the shining ways; and always have my star-paths returned me to her, the figure everlasting, the woman, the one woman, for whose arms I had such need that clasped in them I have forgotten the stars.

For her I accomplished Odysseys, scaled mountains, crossed deserts; for her I led the hunt and was forward in battle; and for her and to her I sang my songs of the things I had done. All ecstasies of life and rhapsodies of delight have been mine because of her. And here, at the end, I can say that I have known no sweeter, deeper madness of being than to drown in the fragrant glory and forgetfulness of her hair.

One word more. I remember me Dorothy, just the other day, when I still lectured on agronomy to farmer-boy students. She was eleven years old. Her father was dean of the college. She was a woman-child, and a woman, and she conceived that she loved me. And I smiled to myself, for my heart was untouched and lay elsewhere.

Yet was the smile tender, for in the child's eyes I saw the woman eternal, the woman of all times and appearances. In her eyes I saw the eyes of my mate of the jungle and tree-top, of the cave and the squatting-place. In her eyes I saw the eyes of Igar when I was Ushu the archer, the eyes of Arunga when I was the rice-harvester, the eyes of Selpa when I dreamed of bestriding the stallion, the eyes of Nuhila who leaned to the thrust of my sword. Yes, there was that in her eyes that made them the eyes of Lei-Lei whom I left with a laugh on my lips, the eyes of the Lady Om for forty years my beggar-mate on highway and byway, the eyes of Philippa for whom I was slain on the grass in old France, the eyes of my mother when I was the lad Jesse at the Mountain Meadows in the circle of our forty great wagons.

She was a woman-child, but she was daughter of all women, as her mother before her, and she was the mother of all women to come after her. She was Sar, the corn-goddess. She was Isthar who conquered death. She was Sheba and Cleopatra; she was Esther and Herodias. She was Mary the Madonna, and Mary the Magdalene, and Mary the sister of Martha, also she was Martha. And she was Brünnhilde and Guinevere, Iseult and Juliet, Héloïse and Nicolette. Yes, and she was Eve, she was Lilith, she was Astarte. She was eleven years old, and she was all women that had been, all women to be.

I sit in my cell now, while the flies hum in the drowsy summer afternoon, and I know that my time is short. Soon they will apparel me in the shirt without a collar. . . . But hush, my heart. The spirit is immortal. After the dark I shall live again, and there will be women. The future holds the little women for me in the lives I am yet to live. And though the stars drift, and the heavens lie, ever remains woman, resplendent, eternal, the one woman, as I, under all my masquerades and misadventures, am the one man, her mate.

7
The Parrot
Alfred Noyes
(1925)

H.P. Lovecraft complimented Howard on the publication of his Conan tale "Shadows in the Moonlight" in the April 1934 issue of *Weird Tales* magazine. Howard replied to Lovecraft in a June 1934 letter, writing, "Thanks for the kind things you said about my 'Shadows in the Moon-light'. (My original title was 'Iron Shadows in the Moon') I'm afraid I can't claim originality in regard to the parrot and his repetition of the god's invocation. I got the idea from a poem of Noyes', entitled, I believe, 'The Parrot.'" Howard then wrote down some of the passages for Lovecraft, adding that "the poem ends on what seems to me a powerful and shuddersome note." Howard then explained to Lovecraft that, "Noyes is one of my favorites," because, "I like the music of drums and wind-harps that throbs through so much of his poetry." The poem appeared in Noyes' book *Dick Turpin's Ride and Other Poems*, published in 1925, and sits on the Robert E. Howard bookshelf in Cross Plains.

When the king and his folk lay dead,
   And the murderous hordes had gone,
He gnawed through his cage and fled
   To the swallowing woods alone;
But, after an endless age,
   He was taken by a man once more;
And swung in a sturdier cage
   By a sun-bleached wine-house door.

And there, on a hot white noon,
   From his place on the blistered wall,
He whistled a dark old tune
   And called, as a ghost may call,
Farlo — Merillo — Rozace,
   With a chuckle of impish glee,
The words of the vanished race,
   That none knew now but he.

Farlo – Merillo – Geray!
   And the spell struck listeners heard
The tongue of the dead that day
   Talking again in a bird;
And his eyes were like blood-red stones,
   For round him the wise men drew,
And coaxed him with terrapin bones
   To tell the words he knew.

Sleek as a peach was his breast
   His long wings green as palms;
And, whiles, like a prince he'd jest,
   Then, beggar-like, whine for alms;
And, whiles, like a girl in flight
   He'd titter, then mimic a kiss,
And chuckle again with delight
   In that wicked old way of his.

He'd courtesy low, and he'd dance
   On his perch, and mockingly leer,
And stiffen himself and prance
   For the grey-beards listening there;
And once – O, dreadful and wild,
   In the blaze of that noonday sun;
He shrieked, like a frightened child,
   That into the dark had gone.

8
The Call of Cthulhu
H.P. Lovecraft
(1928)

Before the great letter exchange between Robert E. Howard and H.P. Lovecraft commenced, Howard was already a fan of Lovecraft's fiction. After first reading "The Call of Cthulhu" in the February 1928 issue of *Weird Tales* Magazine, Howard mailed a letter to the reader's forum, "The Eyrie." Published in the May 1928 issue, Howard wrote, "Mr. Lovecraft's latest story, *The Call of Cthulhu*, is indeed a masterpiece, which I am sure will live as one of the highest achievements of literature. Mr. Lovecraft holds a unique position in the literary world; he has grasped, to all intents, the worlds outside our paltry ken. His scope is unlimited and his range is cosmic. He has the rare gift of making the unreal seem very real and terrible, without lessening the sensation of horror attendant thereto. He touches peaks in his tales which no modern or ancient writer has ever hinted. Sentences and phrases leap suddenly at the reader, as if in utter blackness of solar darkness a door were suddenly flung open, whence flamed the red fire of Purgatory and through which might be momentarily glimpsed monstrous and nightmarish shapes. Herbert Spencer may have been right when he said that it was beyond the human mind to grasp the Unknowable, but Mr. Lovecraft is in a fair way of disproving that theory, I think. I await his next story with eager anticipation, knowing that whatever the subject may be, it will be handled with the skill and incredible vision which he has always shown." This was Howard's third yarn he considered a "masterpiece."

"Of such great powers or beings there may be conceivably a survival . . . a survival of a hugely remote period when . . . consciousness was manifested, perhaps, in shapes and forms long since withdrawn before the tide of advancing humanity . . . forms of which poetry and legend alone have caught a flying memory and called them gods, monsters, mythical beings of all sorts and kinds. . . ."
—*Algernon Blackwood.*

Found among the papers of the late Francis Wayland Thurston, of Boston:

1. The Horror in Clay.

The most merciful thing in the world, I think, is the inability of the human mind to correlate all its contents. We live on a placid island of ignorance in the midst of black seas of infinity, and it was not meant that we should voyage far. The sciences, each straining in its own direction, have hitherto harmed us little; but some day the piecing together of dissociated knowledge will open up such terrifying vistas of reality, and of our frightful position therein, that we shall either go mad from the revelation or flee from the deadly light into the peace and safety of a new dark age.

Theosophists have guessed at the awesome grandeur of the cosmic cycle wherein our world and human race form transient incidents. They have hinted at strange survivals in terms which would freeze the blood if not masked by a bland optimism. But it is not from them that there came the single glimpse of forbidden eons which chills me when I think of it and maddens me when I dream of it. That glimpse, like all dread glimpses of truth, flashed out from an accidental piecing together of separated things—in this case an old newspaper item and the notes of a dead professor. I hope that no one else will accomplish this piecing out; certainly, if I live, I shall never knowingly supply a link in so hideous a chain. I think that the professor, too, intended to keep silent regarding the part he knew, and that he would have destroyed his notes had not sudden death seized him.

My knowledge of the thing began in the winter of 1926–27 with the death of my granduncle George Gammell Angell, Professor Emeritus of Semitic Languages in Brown University, Providence, Rhode Island. Professor Angell was widely known as an authority on ancient inscriptions, and had frequently been resorted to by the heads of prominent museums; so that his passing at the age of ninety-two may be recalled by many. Locally, interest was intensified by the obscurity of the cause of death. The professor had been stricken whilst returning from the Newport boat; falling suddenly, as witnesses said, after having been jostled by a nautical-looking negro who had come from one of the queer dark courts on the precipitous hillside which formed a short cut from the waterfront to the deceased's home in Williams Street. Physicians were unable to find any visible disorder, but concluded after perplexed debate that some obscure lesion of the heart, induced by the brisk ascent of so steep a hill by so elderly a man, was responsible for the end. At the time I saw no reason to dissent from this dictum, but latterly I am inclined to wonder—and more than wonder.

As my granduncle's heir and executor, for he died a childless widower, I was expected to go over his papers with some thoroughness; and for that purpose moved his entire set of files and boxes to my quarters in Boston. Much of the material which I correlated will be later published by the American Archaeological Society, but there was one box which I found exceedingly puzzling, and which I felt much averse from shewing to other eyes. It had been locked, and I did not find the key till it occurred to me to examine the personal ring which the professor carried always in his pocket. Then indeed I succeeded in opening it, but when I did so seemed only to be confronted by a greater and more closely locked barrier. For what could be the meaning of the queer clay bas-relief and the disjointed jottings, ramblings, and cuttings which I found? Had my uncle, in his latter years, become credulous of the most superficial impostures? I resolved to search out the eccentric sculptor responsible for this apparent disturbance of an old man's peace of mind.

The bas-relief was a rough rectangle less than an inch thick and about five by six inches in area; obviously of modern origin. Its designs, however, were far from modern in atmosphere and suggestion; for although the vagaries of cubism and futurism are many and wild, they do not often reproduce that cryptic regularity which lurks in prehistoric writing. And writing of some kind the bulk of these designs seemed certainly to be; though my memory, despite much familiarity with the papers and collections of my uncle, failed in any way to identify this particular species, or even to hint at its remotest affiliations.

Above these apparent hieroglyphics was a figure of evidently pictorial intent, though its impressionistic execution forbade a very clear idea of its nature. It seemed to be a sort of monster, or symbol representing a monster, of a form which only a diseased fancy could conceive. If I say that my somewhat extravagant imagination yielded simultaneous pictures of an octopus, a dragon, and a human caricature, I shall not be unfaithful to the spirit of the thing. A pulpy, tentacled head surmounted a grotesque and scaly body with rudimentary wings; but it was the *general outline* of the whole which made it most shockingly frightful. Behind the figure was a vague suggestion of a Cyclopean architectural background.

The writing accompanying this oddity was, aside from a stack of press cuttings, in Professor Angell's most recent hand; and made no pretense to literary style. What seemed to be the main document was headed "*CTHULHU CULT*" in characters painstakingly printed to avoid the erroneous reading of a word so unheard-of. The manuscript was divided into two sections, the first of which was headed "1925—Dream and Dream Work of H. A. Wilcox, 7 Thomas St., Providence, R.I.," and the second, "Narrative of Inspector John R. Legrasse, 121 Bienville St., New Orleans, La., at 1908 A. A. S. Mtg.—Notes on Same, & Prof. Webb's Acct." The other manuscript papers were all brief notes, some of them accounts of the queer dreams of different persons, some of them citations from theosophical books and magazines (notably W. Scott-Elliot's *Atlantis and the Lost Lemuria*), and the rest comments on long-surviving secret societies and hidden cults, with references to passages in such mythological and anthropological source-books as Frazer's *Golden Bough* and Miss Murray's *Witch-Cult in Western Europe*. The cuttings largely alluded to outré mental illnesses and outbreaks of group folly or mania in the spring of 1925.

The first half of the principal manuscript told a very peculiar tale. It appears that on March 1st, 1925, a thin, dark young man of neurotic and excited aspect had called upon Professor Angell bearing the singular clay bas-relief, which was then exceedingly damp and fresh. His card bore the name of Henry Anthony Wilcox, and my uncle had recognized him as the youngest son of an excellent family slightly known to him, who had latterly been studying sculpture at the Rhode Island School of Design and living alone at the Fleur-de-Lys Building near that institution. Wilcox was a precocious youth of known genius but great eccentricity, and had from childhood excited attention through the strange stories and odd dreams he was in the habit of relating. He called himself "psychically hypersensitive", but the staid folk of the ancient commercial city dismissed him as merely "queer". Never mingling much with his kind, he had dropped gradually from social visibility, and was now known only to a small group of aesthetes from other towns. Even the Providence Art Club, anxious to preserve its conservatism, had found him quite hopeless.

On the occasion of the visit, ran the professor's manuscript, the sculptor abruptly asked for the benefit of his host's archaeological knowledge in identifying the hieroglyphics on the bas-relief. He spoke in a dreamy, stilted manner which suggested pose and alienated sympathy; and my uncle shewed some sharpness in replying, for the conspicuous freshness of the tablet implied kinship with anything but archaeology. Young Wilcox's rejoinder, which impressed my uncle enough to make him recall and record it verbatim, was of a fantastically poetic cast which must have typified his whole conversation, and which I have since found highly characteristic of him. He said, "It is new, indeed, for I made it last night in a dream of strange cities; and dreams are older than brooding Tyre, or the contemplative Sphinx, or garden-girdled Babylon."

It was then that he began that rambling tale which suddenly played upon a sleeping memory and won the fevered interest of my uncle. There had been a slight earthquake tremor the night before, the most considerable felt in New England for some years; and Wilcox's imagination had been keenly affected. Upon retiring, he had had an unprecedented dream of great Cyclopean cities of titan blocks and sky-flung monoliths, all dripping with green ooze and sinister with latent horror. Hieroglyphics had covered the walls and pillars, and from some undetermined point below had come a voice that was not a voice; a chaotic sensation which only fancy could transmute into sound, but which he attempted to render by the almost unpronounceable jumble of letters, "*Cthulhu fhtagn*".

This verbal jumble was the key to the recollection which excited and disturbed Professor Angell. He questioned the sculptor with scientific minuteness; and studied with almost frantic intensity the bas-relief on which the youth had found himself working, chilled and clad only in his night-clothes, when waking had stolen bewilderingly over him. My uncle blamed his old age, Wilcox afterward said, for his slowness in recognizing both hieroglyphics and pictorial design. Many of his questions seemed highly out-of-place to his visitor, especially those which tried to connect the latter with strange cults or societies; and Wilcox could not understand the repeated promises of silence which he was offered in exchange for an admission of membership in some widespread mystical or paganly religious body. When Professor Angell became convinced that the sculptor was indeed ignorant of any cult or system of cryptic lore, he besieged his visitor with demands for future reports of dreams. This bore regular fruit, for after the first interview the manuscript records daily calls of the young man, during which he related startling fragments of nocturnal imagery whose burden was always some terrible Cyclopean vista of dark and dripping stone, with a subterrene voice or intelligence shouting monotonously in enigmatical sense-impacts uninscribable save as gibberish. The two sounds most frequently repeated are those rendered by the letters "*Cthulhu*" and "*R'lyeh*".

On March 23rd, the manuscript continued, Wilcox failed to appear; and inquiries at his quarters revealed that he had been stricken with an obscure sort of fever and taken to the home of his family in Waterman Street. He had cried out in the night, arousing several other artists in the building, and had manifested since then only alternations of unconsciousness and delirium. My uncle at once telephoned the family, and from that time forward kept close watch of the case; calling often at the Thayer Street office of Dr. Tobey, whom he learned to be in charge. The youth's febrile mind, apparently, was dwelling on strange things; and the doctor shuddered now and then as he spoke of them. They included not only a repetition of what he had formerly dreamed, but touched wildly on a gigantic thing "miles high" which walked or lumbered about. He at no time fully described this object, but occasional frantic words, as repeated by Dr. Tobey, convinced the professor that it must be identical with the nameless monstrosity he had sought to depict in his dream-sculpture. Reference to this object, the doctor added, was invariably a prelude to the young man's subsidence into lethargy. His temperature, oddly enough, was not greatly above normal; but his whole condition was otherwise such as to suggest true fever rather than mental disorder.

On April 2nd at about 3 p.m. every trace of Wilcox's malady suddenly ceased. He sat upright in bed, astonished to find himself at home and completely ignorant of what had happened in dream or reality since the night of March 22nd. Pronounced well by his physician, he returned to his quarters in three days; but to Professor Angell he was of no further assistance. All traces of strange dreaming had vanished with his recovery, and my uncle kept no record of his night-thoughts after a week of pointless and irrelevant accounts of thoroughly usual visions.

Here the first part of the manuscript ended, but references to certain of the scattered notes gave me much material for thought—so much, in fact, that only the ingrained skepticism then forming my philosophy can account for my continued distrust of the artist. The notes in question were those descriptive of the dreams of various persons covering the same period as that in which young Wilcox had had his strange visitations. My uncle, it seems, had quickly instituted a prodigiously far-flung body of inquiries amongst nearly all the friends whom he could question without impertinence, asking for nightly reports of their dreams, and the dates of any notable visions for some time past. The reception of his request seems to have been varied; but he must, at the very least, have received more responses than any ordinary man could have handled without a secretary. This original correspondence was not preserved, but his notes formed a thorough and really significant digest. Average people in society and business— New England's traditional "salt of the earth"—gave an almost completely negative result, though scattered cases of uneasy but formless nocturnal impressions appear here and there, always between March 23d and April 2nd—the period of young Wilcox's delirium. Scientific men were little more affected, though four cases of vague description suggest fugitive glimpses of strange landscapes, and in one case there is mentioned a dread of something abnormal.

It was from the artists and poets that the pertinent answers came, and I know that panic would have broken loose had they been able to compare notes. As it was, lacking their original letters, I half suspected the compiler of having asked leading questions, or of having edited the correspondence in corroboration of what he had latently resolved to see. That is why I continued to feel that Wilcox, somehow cognizant of the old data which my uncle had possessed, had been imposing on the veteran scientist. These responses from aesthetes told a disturbing tale. From February 28th to April 2nd a large proportion of them had dreamed very bizarre things, the intensity of the dreams being immeasurably the stronger during the period of the sculptor's delirium. Over a fourth of those who reported anything, reported scenes and half-sounds not unlike those which Wilcox had described; and some of the dreamers confessed acute fear of the gigantic nameless thing visible toward the last. One case, which the note describes with emphasis, was very sad. The subject, a widely known architect with leanings toward theosophy and occultism, went violently insane on the date of young Wilcox's seizure, and expired several months later after incessant screamings to be saved from some escaped denizen of hell. Had my uncle referred to these cases by name instead of merely by number, I should have attempted some corroboration and personal investigation; but as it was, I succeeded in tracing down only a few. All of these, however, bore out the notes in full. I have often wondered if all the objects of the professor's questioning felt as puzzled as did this fraction. It is well that no explanation shall ever reach them.

The press cuttings, as I have intimated, touched on cases of panic, mania, and eccentricity during the given period. Professor Angell must have employed a cutting bureau, for the number of extracts was tremendous and the sources scattered throughout the globe. Here was a nocturnal suicide in London, where a lone sleeper had leaped from a window after a shocking cry. Here likewise a rambling letter to the editor of a paper in South America, where a fanatic deduces a dire future from visions he has seen. A dispatch from California describes a theosophist colony as donning white robes en masse for some "glorious fulfilment" which never arrives, whilst items from India speak guardedly of serious native unrest toward the end of March. Voodoo orgies multiply in Haiti, and African outposts report ominous mutterings. American officers in the Philippines find certain tribes bothersome about this time, and New York policemen are mobbed by hysterical Levantines on the night of March 22–23. The west of Ireland, too, is full of wild rumor and legendry, and a fantastic painter named Ardois-Bonnot hangs a blasphemous *Dream Landscape* in the Paris spring salon of 1926. And so numerous are the recorded troubles in insane asylums, that only a miracle can have stopped the medical fraternity from noting strange parallelisms and drawing mystified conclusions. A weird bunch of cuttings, all told; and I can at this date scarcely envisage the callous rationalism with which I set them aside. But I was then convinced that young Wilcox had known of the older matters mentioned by the professor.

2. The Tale of Inspector Legrasse.

The older matters which had made the sculptor's dream and bas-relief so significant to my uncle formed the subject of the second half of his long manuscript. Once before, it appears, Professor Angell had seen the hellish outlines of the nameless monstrosity, puzzled over the unknown hieroglyphics, and heard the ominous syllables which can be rendered only as "*Cthulhu*"; and all this in so stirring and horrible a connection that it is small wonder he pursued young Wilcox with queries and demands for data.

The earlier experience had come in 1908, seventeen years before, when the American Archaeological Society held its annual meeting in St. Louis. Professor Angell, as befitted one of his authority and attainments, had had a prominent part in all the deliberations; and was one of the first to be approached by the several outsiders who took advantage of the convocation to offer questions for correct answering and problems for expert solution.

The chief of these outsiders, and in a short time the focus of interest for the entire meeting, was a commonplace-looking middle-aged man who had travelled all the way from New Orleans for certain special information unobtainable from any local source. His name was John Raymond Legrasse, and he was by profession an Inspector of Police. With him he bore the subject of his visit, a grotesque, repulsive, and apparently very ancient stone statuette whose origin he was at a loss to determine.

It must not be fancied that Inspector Legrasse had the least interest in archaeology. On the contrary, his wish for enlightenment was prompted by purely professional considerations. The statuette, idol, fetish, or whatever it was, had been captured some months before in the wooded swamps south of New Orleans during a raid on a supposed voodoo meeting; and so singular and hideous were the rites connected with it, that the police could not but realize that they had stumbled on a dark cult totally unknown to them, and infinitely more diabolic than even the blackest of the African voodoo circles. Of its origin, apart from the erratic and unbelievable tales extorted from the captured members, absolutely nothing was to be discovered; hence the anxiety of the police for any antiquarian lore which might help them to place the frightful symbol, and through it track down the cult to its fountain-head.

Inspector Legrasse was scarcely prepared for the sensation which his offering created. One sight of the thing had been enough to throw the assembled men of science into a state of tense excitement, and they lost no time in crowding around him to gaze at the diminutive figure whose utter strangeness and air of genuinely abysmal antiquity hinted so potently at unopened and archaic vistas. No recognized school of sculpture had animated this terrible object, yet centuries and even thousands of years seemed recorded in its dim and greenish surface of unplaceable stone.

The figure, which was finally passed slowly from man to man for close and careful study, was between seven and eight inches in height, and of exquisitely artistic workmanship. It represented a monster of vaguely anthropoid outline, but with an octopus-like head whose face was a mass of feelers, a scaly, rubbery-looking body, prodigious claws on hind and fore feet, and long, narrow wings behind. This thing, which seemed instinct with a fearsome and unnatural malignancy, was of a somewhat bloated corpulence, and squatted evilly on a rectangular block or pedestal covered with undecipherable characters. The tips of the wings touched the back edge of the block, the seat occupied the centre, whilst the long, curved claws of the doubled-up, crouching hind legs gripped the front edge and extended a quarter of the way down toward the bottom of the pedestal. The cephalopod head was bent forward, so that the ends of the facial feelers brushed the backs of huge fore paws which clasped the croucher's elevated knees. The aspect of the whole was abnormally life-like, and the more subtly fearful because its source was so totally unknown. Its vast, awesome, and incalculable age was unmistakable; yet not one link did it shew with any known type of art belonging to civilization's youth—or indeed to any other time.

Totally separate and apart, its very material was a mystery; for the soapy, greenish-black stone with its golden or iridescent flecks and striations resembled nothing familiar to geology or mineralogy. The characters along the base were equally baffling; and no member present, despite a representtation of half the world's expert learning in this field, could form the least notion of even their remotest linguistic kinship. They, like the subject and material, belonged to something horribly remote and distinct from mankind as we know it; something frightfully suggestive of old and unhallowed cycles of life in which our world and our conceptions have no part.

And yet, as the members severally shook their heads and confessed defeat at the Inspector's problem, there was one man in that gathering who suspected a touch of bizarre familiarity in the monstrous shape and writing, and who presently told with some diffidence of the odd trifle he knew. This person was the late William Channing Webb, Professor of Anthropology in Princeton University, and an explorer of no slight note.

Professor Webb had been engaged, forty-eight years before, in a tour of Greenland and Iceland in search of some Runic inscriptions which he failed to unearth; and whilst high up on the West Greenland coast had encountered a singular tribe or cult of degenerate Eskimos whose religion, a curious form of devil-worship, chilled him with its deliberate bloodthirstiness and repulsiveness. It was a faith of which other Eskimos knew little, and which they mentioned only with shudders, saying that it had come down from horribly ancient eons before ever the world was made. Besides nameless rites and human sacrifices there were certain queer hereditary rituals addressed to a supreme elder devil or *tornasuk*; and of this Professor Webb had taken a careful phonetic copy from an aged *angekok* or wizard-priest, expressing the sounds in Roman letters as best he knew how. But just now of prime significance was the fetish which this cult had cherished, and around which they danced when the aurora leaped high over the ice cliffs. It was, the professor stated, a very crude bas-relief of stone, comprising a hideous picture and some cryptic writing. And so far as he could tell, it was a rough parallel in all essential features of the bestial thing now lying before the meeting.

These data, received with suspense and astonishment by the assembled members, proved doubly exciting to Inspector

Legrasse; and he began at once to ply his informant with questions. Having noted and copied an oral ritual among the swamp cult-worshippers his men had arrested, he besought the professor to remember as best he might the syllables taken down amongst the diabolist Esquimaux. There then followed an exhaustive comparison of details, and a moment of really awed silence when both detective and scientist agreed on the virtual identity of the phrase common to two hellish rituals so many worlds of distance apart. What, in substance, both the Esquimau wizards and the Louisiana swamp-priests had chanted to their kindred idols was something very like this—the word-divisions being guessed at from traditional breaks in the phrase as chanted aloud:

"Ph'nglui mglw'nafh Cthulhu R'lyeh wgah'nagl fhtagn."

Legrasse had one point in advance of Professor Webb, for several among his mongrel prisoners had repeated to him what older celebrants had told them the words meant. This text, as given, ran something like this:

"In his house at R'lyeh dead Cthulhu waits dreaming."

And now, in response to a general and urgent demand, Inspector Legrasse related as fully as possible his experience with the swamp worshippers; telling a story to which I could see my uncle attached profound significance. It savoured of the wildest dreams of myth-maker and theosophist, and disclosed an astonishing degree of cosmic imagination among such half-castes and pariahs as might be least expected to possess it.

On November 1st, 1907, there had come to the New Orleans police a frantic summons from the swamp and lagoon country to the south. The squatters there, mostly primitive but good-natured descendants of Lafitte's men, were in the grip of stark terror from an unknown thing which had stolen upon them in the night. It was voodoo, apparently, but voodoo of a more terrible sort than they had ever known; and some of their women and children had disappeared since the malevolent tom-tom had begun its incessant beating far within the black haunted woods where no dweller ventured. There were insane shouts and harrowing screams, soul-chilling chants and dancing devil-flames; and, the frightened messenger added, the people could stand it no more.

So a body of twenty police, filling two carriages and an automobile, had set out in the late afternoon with the shivering squatter as a guide. At the end of the passable road they alighted, and for miles splashed on in silence through the terrible cypress woods where day never came. Ugly roots and malignant hanging nooses of Spanish moss beset them, and now and then a pile of dank stones or fragment of a rotting wall intensified by its hint of morbid habitation a depression which every malformed tree and every fungous islet combined to create. At length the squatter settlement, a miserable huddle of huts, hove in sight; and hysterical dwellers ran out to cluster around the group of bobbing lanterns. The muffled beat of tom-toms was now faintly audible far, far ahead; and a curdling shriek came at infrequent intervals when the wind shifted. A reddish glare, too, seemed to filter through the pale undergrowth beyond endless avenues of forest night. Reluctant even to be left alone again, each one of the cowed squatters refused point-blank to advance another inch toward the scene of unholy worship, so Inspector Legrasse and his nineteen colleagues plunged on unguided into black arcades of horror that none of them had ever trod before.

The region now entered by the police was one of traditionally evil repute, substantially unknown and untraversed by white men. There were legends of a hidden lake unglimpsed by mortal sight, in which dwelt a huge, formless white polypous thing with luminous eyes; and squatters whispered that bat-winged devils flew up out of caverns in inner earth to worship it at midnight. They said it had been there before D'Iberville, before La Salle, before the Indians, and before even the wholesome beasts and birds of the woods. It was nightmare itself, and to see it was to die. But it made men dream, and so they knew enough to keep away. The present voodoo orgy was, indeed, on the merest fringe of this abhorred area, but that location was bad enough; hence perhaps the very place of the worship had terrified the squatters more than the shocking sounds and incidents.

Only poetry or madness could do justice to the noises heard by Legrasse's men as they ploughed on through the black morass toward the red glare and the muffled tom-toms. There are vocal qualities peculiar to men, and vocal qualities peculiar to beasts; and it is terrible to hear the one when the source should yield the other. Animal fury and orgiastic licence here whipped themselves to demoniac heights by howls and squawking ecstasies that tore and reverberated through those nighted woods like pestilential tempests from the gulfs of hell. Now and then the less organized ululation would cease, and from what seemed a well-drilled chorus of hoarse voices would rise in sing-song chant that hideous phrase or ritual:

"Ph'nglui mglw'nafh Cthulhu R'lyeh wgah'nagl fhtagn."

Then the men, having reached a spot where the trees were thinner, came suddenly in sight of the spectacle itself. Four of them reeled, one fainted, and two were shaken into a frantic cry which the mad cacophony of the orgy fortunately deadened. Legrasse dashed swamp water on the face of the fainting man, and all stood trembling and nearly hypnotized with horror.

In a natural glade of the swamp stood a grassy island of perhaps an acre's extent, clear of trees and tolerably dry. On this now leaped and twisted a more indescribable horde of human abnormality than any but a Sime or an Angarola could paint. Void of clothing, this hybrid spawn were braying, bellowing, and writhing about a monstrous ring-shaped bonfire; in the center of which, revealed by occasional rifts in the curtain of flame, stood a great granite monolith some eight feet in height; on top of which, incongruous with its diminutiveness, rested the noxious carven statuette. From a wide circle of ten scaffolds set up at regular intervals with the flame-girt monolith as a center hung, head downward, the oddly marred bodies of the helpless squatters who had disappeared. It was inside this circle that the ring of worshippers jumped and roared, the general direction of the mass motion being from left to right in endless Bacchanal between the ring of bodies and the ring of fire.

It may have been only imagination and it may have been only echoes which induced one of the men, an excitable Spaniard, to fancy he heard antiphonal responses to the ritual from some far and unillumined spot deeper within the wood of ancient legendry and horror. This man, Joseph D. Galvez, I later met and questioned; and he proved distractingly imaginative. He indeed went so far as to hint of the faint beating of great wings, and of a glimpse of shining eyes and a mountainous white bulk beyond the remotest trees—but I suppose he had been hearing too much native superstition.

Actually, the horrified pause of the men was of comparatively brief duration. Duty came first; and although there must have been nearly a hundred mongrel celebrants in the throng, the police relied on their firearms and plunged determinedly into the nauseous rout. For five minutes the resultant din and chaos were beyond description. Wild blows were struck, shots were fired, and escapes were made; but in the end Legrasse was able to count some forty-seven sullen prisoners, whom he forced to dress in haste and fall into line between two rows of policemen. Five of the worshippers lay dead, and two severely wounded ones were carried away on improvised stretchers by their fellow-prisoners. The image on the monolith, of course, was carefully removed and carried back by Legrasse.

Examined at headquarters after a trip of intense strain and weariness, the prisoners all proved to be men of a very low, mixed-blooded, and mentally aberrant type. Most were seamen, and a sprinkling of negroes and mulattoes, largely West Indians or Brava Portuguese from the Cape Verde Islands, gave a coloring of voodooism to the heterogeneous cult. But before many questions were asked, it became manifest that something far deeper and older than negro fetishism was involved. Degraded and ignorant as they were, the creatures held with surprising consistency to the central idea of their loathsome faith.

They worshipped, so they said, the Great Old Ones who lived ages before there were any men, and who came to the young world out of the sky. Those Old Ones were gone now, inside the earth and under the sea; but their dead bodies had told their secrets in dreams to the first men, who formed a cult which had never died. This was that cult, and the prisoners said it had always existed and always would exist, hidden in distant wastes and dark places all over the world until the time when the great priest Cthulhu, from his dark house in the mighty city of R'lyeh under the waters, should rise and bring the earth again beneath his sway. Some day he would call, when the stars were ready, and the secret cult would always be waiting to liberate him.

Meanwhile no more must be told. There was a secret which even torture could not extract. Mankind was not absolutely alone among the conscious things of earth, for shapes came out of the dark to visit the faithful few. But these were not the Great Old Ones. No man had ever seen the Old Ones. The carven idol was great Cthulhu, but none might say whether or not the others were precisely like him. No one could read the old writing now, but things were told by word of mouth. The chanted ritual was not the secret—that was never spoken aloud, only whispered. The chant meant only this: "In his house at R'lyeh dead Cthulhu waits dreaming."

Only two of the prisoners were found sane enough to be hanged, and the rest were committed to various institutions. All denied a part in the ritual murders, and averred that the killing had been done by Black-winged Ones which had come to them from their immemorial meeting-place in the haunted wood. But of those mysterious allies no coherent account could ever be gained. What the police did extract, came mainly from an immensely aged mestizo named Castro, who claimed to have sailed to strange ports and talked with undying leaders of the cult in the mountains of China.

Old Castro remembered bits of hideous legend that paled the speculations of theosophists and made man and the world seem recent and transient indeed. There had been eons when other Things ruled on the earth, and They had had great cities. Remains of Them, he said the deathless Chinamen had told him, were still to be found as Cyclopean stones on islands in the Pacific. They all died vast epochs of time before men came, but there were arts which could revive Them when the stars had come round again to the right positions in the cycle of eternity. They had, indeed, come themselves from the stars, and brought Their images with Them.

These Great Old Ones, Castro continued, were not composed altogether of flesh and blood. They had shape—for did not this star-fashioned image prove it?—but that shape was not made of matter. When the stars were right, They could plunge from world to world through the sky; but when the stars were wrong, They could not live. But although They no longer lived, They would never really die. They all lay in stone houses in Their great city of R'lyeh, preserved by the spells of mighty Cthulhu for a glorious resurrection when the stars and the earth might once more be ready for Them. But at that time some force from outside must serve to liberate Their bodies. The spells that preserved Them intact likewise prevented

Them from making an initial move, and They could only lie awake in the dark and think whilst uncounted millions of years rolled by. They knew all that was occurring in the universe, but Their mode of speech was transmitted thought. Even now They talked in Their tombs. When, after infinities of chaos, the first men came, the Great Old Ones spoke to the sensitive among them by molding their dreams; for only thus could Their language reach the fleshly minds of mammals.

Then, whispered Castro, those first men formed the cult around small idols which the Great Ones shewed them; idols brought in dim aeras from dark stars. That cult would never die till the stars came right again, and the secret priests would take great Cthulhu from His tomb to revive His subjects and resume His rule of earth. The time would be easy to know, for then mankind would have become as the Great Old Ones; free and wild and beyond good and evil, with laws and morals thrown aside and all men shouting and killing and reveling in joy. Then the liberated Old Ones would teach them new ways to shout and kill and revel and enjoy themselves, and all the earth would flame with a holocaust of ecstasy and freedom. Meanwhile the cult, by appropriate rites, must keep alive the memory of those ancient ways and shadow forth the prophecy of their return.

In the elder time chosen men had talked with the entombed Old Ones in dreams, but then something had happened. The great stone city R'lyeh, with its monoliths and sepulchers, had sunk beneath the waves; and the deep waters, full of the one primal mystery through which not even thought can pass, had cut off the spectral intercourse. But memory never died, and high-priests said that the city would rise again when the stars were right. Then came out of the earth the black spirits of earth, moldy and shadowy, and full of dim rumors picked up in caverns beneath forgotten sea-bottoms. But of them old Castro dared not speak much. He cut himself off hurriedly, and no amount of persuasion or subtlety could elicit more in this direction. The *size* of the Old Ones, too, he curiously declined to mention. Of the cult, he said that he thought the center lay amid the pathless deserts of Arabia, where Irem, the City of Pillars, dreams hidden and untouched. It was not allied to the European witch-cult, and was virtually unknown beyond its members. No book had ever really hinted of it, though the deathless Chinamen said that there were double meanings in the *Necronomicon* of the mad Arab Abdul Alhazred which the initiated might read as they chose, especially the much-discussed couplet:

"That is not dead which can eternal lie,
And with strange eons even death may die."

Legrasse, deeply impressed and not a little bewildered, had inquired in vain concerning the historic affiliations of the cult. Castro, apparently, had told the truth when he said that it was wholly secret. The authorities at Tulane University could shed no light upon either cult or image, and now the detective had come to the highest authorities in the country and met with no more than the Greenland tale of Professor Webb.

The feverish interest aroused at the meeting by Legrasse's tale, corroborated as it was by the statuette, is echoed in the subsequent correspondence of those who attended; although scant mention occurs in the formal publications of the society. Caution is the first care of those accustomed to face occasional charlatanry and imposture. Legrasse for some time lent the image to Professor Webb, but at the latter's death it was returned to him and remains in his possession, where I viewed it not long ago. It is truly a terrible thing, and unmistakably akin to the dream-sculpture of young Wilcox.

That my uncle was excited by the tale of the sculptor I did not wonder, for what thoughts must arise upon hearing, after a knowledge of what Legrasse had learned of the cult, of a sensitive young man who had *dreamed* not only the figure and exact hieroglyphics of the swamp-found image and the Greenland devil tablet, but had come in his dreams upon at least three of the precise words of the formula uttered alike by Esquimau diabolists and mongrel Louisianans? Professor Angell's instant start on an investigation of the utmost thoroughness was eminently natural; though privately I suspected young Wilcox of having heard of the cult in some indirect way, and of having invented a series of dreams to heighten and continue the mystery at my uncle's expense. The dream-narratives and cuttings collected by the professor were, of course, strong corroboration; but the rationalism of my mind and the extravagance of the whole subject led me to adopt what I thought the most sensible conclusions. So, after thoroughly studying the manuscript again and correlating the theosophical and anthropological notes with the cult narrative of Legrasse, I made a trip to Providence to see the sculptor and give him the rebuke I thought proper for so boldly imposing upon a learned and aged man.

Wilcox still lived alone in the Fleur-de-Lys Building in Thomas Street, a hideous Victorian imitation of seventeenth-century Breton architecture which flaunts its stuccoed front amidst the lovely colonial houses on the ancient hill, and under the very shadow of the finest Georgian steeple in America. I found him at work in his rooms, and at once conceded from the specimens scattered about that his genius is indeed profound and authentic. He will, I believe, some time be heard from as one of the great decadents; for he has crystallized in clay and will one day mirror in marble those nightmares and phantasies which Arthur Machen evokes in prose, and Clark Ashton Smith makes visible in verse and in painting.

Dark, frail, and somewhat unkempt in aspect, he turned languidly at my knock and asked me my business without rising. When I told him who I was, he displayed some interest; for my uncle had excited his curiosity in probing his strange dreams, yet had never explained the reason for the study. I did not enlarge his knowledge in this regard, but sought with some subtlety to draw him out.

In a short time I became convinced of his absolute sincerity, for he spoke of the dreams in a manner none could mistake. They and their subconscious residuum had influenced his art profoundly, and he shewed me a morbid statue whose contours almost made me shake with the potency of its black suggestion. He could not recall having seen the original of this thing except in his own dream bas-relief, but the outlines had formed themselves insensibly under his hands. It was, no doubt, the giant shape he had raved of in delirium. That he really knew nothing of the hidden cult, save from what my uncle's relentless catechism had let fall, he soon made clear; and again I strove to think of some way in which he could possibly have received the weird impressions.

He talked of his dreams in a strangely poetic fashion; making me see with terrible vividness the damp Cyclopean city of slimy green stone—whose *geometry*, he oddly said, was *all wrong*—and hear with frightened expectancy the ceaseless, half-mental calling from underground: "*Cthulhu fhtagn*", "*Cthulhu fhtagn.*"

These words had formed part of that dread ritual which told of dead Cthulhu's dream-vigil in his stone vault at R'lyeh, and I felt deeply moved despite my rational beliefs. Wilcox, I was sure, had heard of the cult in some casual way, and had soon forgotten it amidst the mass of his equally weird reading and imagining. Later, by virtue of its sheer impressiveness, it had found subconscious expression in dreams, in the bas-relief, and in the terrible statue I now beheld; so that his imposture upon my uncle had been a very innocent one. The youth was of a type, at once slightly affected and slightly ill-mannered, which I could never like; but I was willing enough now to admit both his genius and his honesty. I took leave of him amicably, and wish him all the success his talent promises.

The matter of the cult still remained to fascinate me, and at times I had visions of personal fame from researches into its origin and connections. I visited New Orleans, talked with Legrasse and others of that old-time raiding-party, saw the frightful image, and even questioned such of the mongrel prisoners as still survived. Old Castro, unfortunately, had been dead for some years. What I now heard so graphically at first-hand, though it was really no more than a detailed confirmation of what my uncle had written, excited me afresh; for I felt sure that I was on the track of a very real, very secret, and very ancient religion whose discovery would make me an anthropologist of note. My attitude was still one of absolute materialism, as I wish it still were, and I discounted with almost inexplicable perversity the coincidence of the dream notes and odd cuttings collected by Professor Angell.

One thing I began to suspect, and which I now fear I know, is that my uncle's death was far from natural. He fell on a narrow hill street leading up from an ancient waterfront swarming with foreign mongrels, after a careless push from a negro sailor. I did not forget the mixed blood and marine pursuits of the cult-members in Louisiana, and would not be surprised to learn of secret methods and poison needles as ruthless and as anciently known as the cryptic rites and beliefs. Legrasse and his men, it is true, have been let alone; but in Norway a certain seaman who saw things is dead. Might not the deeper inquiries of my uncle after encountering the sculptor's data have come to sinister ears? I think Professor Angell died because he knew too much, or because he was likely to learn too much. Whether I shall go as he did remains to be seen, for I have learned much now.

3. The Madness from the Sea.

If heaven ever wishes to grant me a boon, it will be a total effacing of the results of a mere chance which fixed my eye on a certain stray piece of shelf-paper. It was nothing on which I would naturally have stumbled in the course of my daily round, for it was an old number of an Australian journal, the *Sydney Bulletin* for April 18, 1925. It had escaped even the cutting bureau which had at the time of its issuance been avidly collecting material for my uncle's research.

I had largely given over my inquiries into what Professor Angell called the "Cthulhu Cult," and was visiting a learned friend in Paterson, New Jersey; the curator of a local museum and a mineralogist of note. Examining one day the reserve specimens roughly set on the storage shelves in a rear room of the museum, my eye was caught by an odd picture in one of the old papers spread beneath the stones. It was the *Sydney Bulletin* I have mentioned, for my friend has wide affiliations in all conceivable foreign parts; and the picture was a half-tone cut of a hideous stone image almost identical with that which Legrasse had found in the swamp.

Eagerly clearing the sheet of its precious contents, I scanned the item in detail; and was disappointed to find it of only moderate length. What it suggested, however, was of portentous significance to my flagging quest; and I carefully tore it out for immediate action. It read as follows:

MYSTERY DERELICT FOUND AT SEA

—

Vigilant Arrives With Helpless Armed New Zealand Yacht in Tow. One Survivor and Dead Man Found Aboard. Tale of Desperate Battle and Deaths at Sea. Rescued Seaman Refuses Particulars of Strange Experience. Odd Idol Found in His Possession. Inquiry to Follow.

—

The Morrison Co.'s freighter Vigilant, bound from Valparaiso, arrived this morning at its wharf in Darling Harbour, having in tow the battled and disabled but heavily armed steam yacht *Alert* of Dunedin, N. Z., which was sighted April 12th in S. Latitude 34° 21', W. Longitude 152° 17' with one living and one dead man aboard.

The *Vigilant* left Valparaiso March 25th, and on April 2nd was driven considerably south of her course by exceptionally heavy storms and monster waves. On April 12th the derelict was sighted; and though apparently deserted, was found upon boarding to contain one survivor in a half-delirious condition and one man who had evidently been dead for more than a week.

The living man was clutching a horrible stone idol of unknown origin, about a foot in height, regarding whose nature authorities at Sydney University, the Royal Society, and the Museum in College Street all profess complete bafflement, and which the survivor says he found in the cabin of the yacht, in a small carved shrine of common pattern.

This man, after recovering his senses, told an exceedingly strange story of piracy and slaughter. He is Gustaf Johansen, a Norwegian of some intelligence, and had been second mate of the two-masted schooner *Emma* of Auckland, which sailed for Callao February 20th with a complement of eleven men.

The *Emma*, he says, was delayed and thrown widely south of her course by the great storm of March 1st, and on March 22nd, in S. Latitude 49° 51′, W. Longitude 128° 34′, encountered the *Alert*, manned by a queer and evil-looking crew of Kanakas and half-castes. Being ordered peremptorily to turn back, Capt. Collins refused; whereupon the strange crew began to fire savagely and without warning upon the schooner with a peculiarly heavy battery of brass cannon forming part of the yacht's equipment. The Emma's men shewed fight, says the survivor, and though the schooner began to sink from shots beneath the waterline they managed to heave alongside their enemy and board her, grappling with the savage crew on the yacht's deck, and being forced to kill them all, the number being slightly superior, because of their particularly abhorrent and desperate though rather clumsy mode of fighting.

Three of the *Emma's* men, including Capt. Collins and

First Mate Green, were killed; and the remaining eight under Second Mate Johansen proceeded to navigate the captured yacht, going ahead in their original direction to see if any reason for their ordering back had existed.

The next day, it appears, they raised and landed on a small island, although none is known to exist in that part of the ocean; and six of the men somehow died ashore, though Johansen is queerly reticent about this part of his story, and speaks only of their falling into a rock chasm.

Later, it seems, he and one companion boarded the yacht and tried to manage her, but were beaten about by the storm of April 2nd.

From that time till his rescue on the 12th the man remembers little, and he does not even recall when William Briden, his companion, died. Briden's death reveals no apparent cause, and was probably due to excitement or exposure.

Cable advices from Dunedin report that the Alert was well known there as an island trader, and bore an evil reputation along the waterfront. It was owned by a curious group of halfcastes whose frequent meetings and night trips to the woods attracted no little curiosity; and it had set sail in great haste just after the storm and earth tremors of March 1st.

Our Auckland correspondent gives the Emma and her crew an excellent reputation, and Johansen is described as a sober and worthy man. The admiralty will institute an inquiry on the whole matter beginning tomorrow, at which every effort will be made to induce Johansen to speak more freely than he has done hitherto.

This was all, together with the picture of the hellish image; but what a train of ideas it started in my mind! Here were new treasuries of data on the Cthulhu Cult, and evidence that it had strange interests at sea as well as on land. What motive prompted the hybrid crew to order back the *Emma* as they sailed about with their hideous idol? What was the unknown island on which six of the *Emma's* crew had died, and about which the mate Johansen was so secretive? What had the vice-admiralty's investigation brought out, and what was known of the noxious cult in Dunedin? And most marvelous of all, what deep and more than natural linkage of dates was this which gave a malign and now undeniable significance to the various turns of events so carefully noted by my uncle?

March 1st—our February 28th according to the International Date Line—the earthquake and storm had come. From Dunedin the *Alert* and her noisome crew had darted eagerly forth as if imperiously summoned, and on the other side of the earth poets and artists had begun to dream of a strange, dank Cyclopean city whilst a young sculptor had molded in his sleep the form of the dreaded Cthulhu. March 23d the crew of the *Emma* landed on an unknown island and left six men dead; and on that date the dreams of sensitive men assumed a heightened vividness and darkened with dread of a giant monster's malign pursuit, whilst an architect had gone mad and a sculptor had lapsed suddenly into delirium! And what of this storm of April 2nd—the date on which all dreams of the dank city ceased, and Wilcox emerged unharmed from the bondage of strange fever? What of all this—and of those hints of old Castro about the sunken, star-born Old Ones and their coming reign; their faithful cult *and their mastery of dreams?* Was I tottering on the brink of cosmic horrors beyond man's power to bear? If so, they must be horrors of the mind alone, for in some way the second of April had put a stop to whatever monstrous menace had begun its siege of mankind's soul.

That evening, after a day of hurried cabling and arranging, I bade my host adieu and took a train for San Francisco. In less than a month I was in Dunedin; where, however, I found that little was known of the strange cult-members who had lingered in the old sea-taverns. Waterfront scum was far too common for special mention; though there was vague talk about one inland trip these mongrels had made, during which faint drumming and red flame were noted on the distant hills.

In Auckland I learned that Johansen had returned *with yellow hair turned white* after a perfunctory and inconclusive questioning at Sydney, and had thereafter sold his cottage in West Street and sailed with his wife to his old home in Oslo. Of his stirring experience he would tell his friends no more than he had told the admiralty officials, and all they could do was to give me his Oslo address.

After that I went to Sydney and talked profitlessly with seamen and members of the vice-admiralty court. I saw the *Alert*, now sold and in commercial use, at Circular Quay in Sydney Cove, but gained nothing from its non-committal bulk. The crouching image with its cuttlefish head, dragon body, scaly wings, and hieroglyphed pedestal, was preserved in the Museum at Hyde Park; and I studied it long and well, finding it a thing of balefully exquisite workmanship, and with the same utter mystery, terrible antiquity, and unearthly strangeness of material which I had noted in Legrasse's smaller specimen. Geologists, the curator told me, had found it a monstrous puzzle; for they vowed that the world held no rock like it. Then I thought with a shudder of what old Castro had told Legrasse about the primal Great Ones: "They had come from the stars, and had brought Their images with Them."

Shaken with such a mental revolution as I had never before known, I now resolved to visit Mate Johansen in Oslo. Sailing for London, I re-embarked at once for the Norwegian capital; and one autumn day landed at the trim wharves in the shadow of the Egeberg.

Johansen's address, I discovered, lay in the Old Town of King Harold Haardrada, which kept alive the name of Oslo during all the centuries that the greater city masqueraded as "Christiana." I made the brief trip by taxicab, and knocked with palpitant heart at the door of a neat and ancient building with plastered front. A sad-faced woman in black answered my summons, and I was stung with disappointment when she told me in halting English that Gustaf Johansen was no more.

He had not survived his return, said his wife, for the doings at sea in 1925 had broken him. He had told her no more than he had told the public, but had left a long manuscript—of "technical matters" as he said—written in English, evidently in order to safeguard her from the peril of casual perusal. During a walk through a narrow lane near the Gothenburg dock, a bundle of papers falling from an attic window had knocked him down. Two Lascar sailors at once helped him to his feet, but before the ambulance could reach him he was dead. Physicians found no adequate cause for the end, and laid it to heart trouble and a weakened constitution.

I now felt gnawing at my vitals that dark terror which will never leave me till I, too, am at rest; "accidentally" or otherwise. Persuading the widow that my connection with her husband's "technical matters" was sufficient to entitle me to his manuscript, I bore the document away and began to read it on the London boat.

It was a simple, rambling thing—a naive sailor's effort at a post-facto diary—and strove to recall day by day that last awful voyage. I cannot attempt to transcribe it verbatim in all its cloudiness and redundance, but I will tell its gist enough to shew why the sound of the water against the vessel's sides became so unendurable to me that I stopped my ears with cotton.

Johansen, thank God, did not know quite all, even though he saw the city and the Thing, but I shall never sleep calmly again when I think of the horrors that lurk ceaselessly behind life in time and in space, and of those unhallowed blasphemies from elder stars which dream beneath the sea, known and favored by a nightmare cult ready and eager to loose them on the world whenever another earthquake shall heave their monstrous stone city again to the sun and air.

Johansen's voyage had begun just as he told it to the vice-admiralty. The *Emma*, in ballast, had cleared Auckland on February 20th, and had felt the full force of that earthquake-born tempest which must have heaved up from the sea-bottom the horrors that filled men's dreams. Once more under control, the ship was making good progress when held up by the Alert on March 22nd, and I could feel the mate's regret as he wrote of her bombardment and sinking. Of the swarthy cult-fiends on the *Alert* he speaks with significant horror. There was some peculiarly abominable quality about them which made their destruction seem almost a duty, and Johansen shews ingenuous wonder at the charge of ruthlessness brought against his party during the proceedings of the court of inquiry. Then, driven ahead by curiosity in their captured yacht under Johansen's command, the men sight a great stone pillar sticking out of the sea, and in S. Latitude 47° 9', W. Longitude 126° 43' come upon a coast-line of mingled mud, ooze, and weedy Cyclopean masonry which can be nothing less than the tangible substance of earth's supreme terror—the nightmare corpse-city of R'lyeh, that was built in measureless eons behind history by the vast, loathsome shapes that seeped down from the dark stars. There lay great Cthulhu and his hordes, hidden in green slimy vaults and sending out at last, after cycles incalculable, the thoughts that spread fear to the dreams of the sensitive and called imperiously to the faithful to come on a pilgrimage of liberation and restoration. All this Johansen did not suspect, but God knows he soon saw enough!

I suppose that only a single mountain-top, the hideous monolith-crowned citadel whereon great Cthulhu was buried, actually emerged from the waters. When I think of the extent of all that may be brooding down there I almost wish to kill myself forthwith. Johansen and his men were awed by the cosmic majesty of this dripping Babylon of elder daemons, and must have guessed without guidance that it was nothing of this or of any sane planet. Awe at the unbelievable size of the greenish stone blocks, at the dizzying height of the great carven monolith, and at the stupefying identity of the colossal statues and bas-reliefs with the queer image found in the shrine on the *Alert*, is poignantly visible in every line of the mate's frightened description.

Without knowing what futurism is like, Johansen achieved something very close to it when he spoke of the city; for instead of describing any definite structure or building, he dwells only on broad impressions of vast angles and stone surfaces—surfaces too great to belong to any thing right or proper for this earth, and impious with horrible images and hieroglyphs. I mention his talk about *angles* because it suggests something Wilcox had told me of his awful dreams. He had said that the *geometry* of the dream-place he saw was abnormal, non-Euclidean, and loathsomely redolent of spheres and dimensions apart from ours. Now an unlettered seaman felt the same thing whilst gazing at the terrible reality.

Johansen and his men landed at a sloping mud-bank on this monstrous Acropolis, and clambered slipperily up over titan oozy blocks which could have been no mortal staircase. The very sun of heaven seemed distorted when viewed through the polarizing miasma welling out from this sea-soaked perversion, and twisted menace and suspense lurked leeringly in those crazily elusive angles of carven rock where a second glance shewed concavity after the first shewed convexity.

Something very like fright had come over all the explorers before anything more definite than rock and ooze and weed was seen. Each would have fled had he not feared the scorn of the others, and it was only half-heartedly that they searched—vainly, as it proved—for some portable souvenir to bear away.

It was Rodriguez the Portuguese who climbed up the foot of the monolith and shouted of what he had found. The rest followed him, and looked curiously at the immense carved door with the now familiar squid-dragon bas-relief. It was, Johansen said, like a great barn-door; and they all felt that it was a door because of the ornate lintel, threshold, and jambs around it, though they could not decide whether it lay flat like a trap-door or slantwise like an outside cellar-door. As Wilcox would have said, the geometry of the place was all wrong. One could not be sure that the sea and the ground were horizontal, hence the relative position of everything else seemed fantasmally variable.

Briden pushed at the stone in several places without result. Then Donovan felt over it delicately around the edge, pressing each point separately as he went. He climbed interminably along the grotesque stone molding—that is, one would call it climbing if the thing was not after all horizontal—and the men wondered how any door in the universe could be so vast. Then, very softly and slowly, the acre-great panel began to give inward at the top; and they saw that it was balanced.

Donovan slid or somehow propelled himself down or along the jamb and rejoined his fellows, and everyone watched the queer recession of the monstrously carven portal. In this phantasy of prismatic distortion it moved anomalously in a diagonal way, so that all the rules of matter and perspective seemed upset.

The aperture was black with a darkness almost material. That tenebrousness was indeed a *positive quality*; for it obscured such parts of the inner walls as ought to have been revealed, and actually burst forth like smoke from its eon-long imprisonment, visibly darkening the sun as it slunk away into the shrunken and gibbous sky on flapping membranous wings. The odor arising from the newly opened depths was intolerable, and at length the quick-eared Hawkins thought he heard a nasty, slopping sound down there. Everyone listened, and everyone was listening still when It lumbered slobberingly into sight and gropingly squeezed Its gelatinous green immensity through the black doorway into the tainted outside air of that poison city of madness.

Poor Johansen's handwriting almost gave out when he wrote of this. Of the six men who never reached the ship, he thinks two perished of pure fright in that accursed instant. The Thing cannot be described—there is no language for such abysms of shrieking and immemorial lunacy, such eldritch contradictions of all matter, force, and cosmic order. A mountain walked or stumbled. God! What wonder that across the earth a great architect went mad, and poor Wilcox raved with fever in that telepathic instant? The Thing of the idols, the green, sticky spawn of the stars, had awaked to claim his own. The stars were right again, and what an age-old cult had failed to do by design, a band of innocent sailors had done by accident. After vigintillions of years great Cthulhu was loose again, and ravening for delight.

Three men were swept up by the flabby claws before anybody turned. God rest them, if there be any rest in the universe. They were Donovan, Guerrera, and Ångstrom. Parker slipped as the other three were plunging frenziedly over endless vistas of green-crusted rock to the boat, and Johansen swears he was swallowed up by an angle of masonry which shouldn't have been there; an angle which was acute, but behaved as if it were obtuse. So only Briden and Johansen reached the boat, and pulled desperately for the *Alert* as the mountainous monstrosity flopped down the slimy stones and hesitated floundering at the edge of the water.

Steam had not been suffered to go down entirely, despite the departure of all hands for the shore; and it was the work of only a few moments of feverish rushing up and down between wheel and engines to get the *Alert* under way. Slowly, amidst the distorted horrors of that indescribable scene, she began to churn the lethal waters; whilst on the masonry of that charnel shore that was not of earth the titan Thing from the stars slavered and gibbered like Polypheme cursing the fleeing ship of Odysseus. Then, bolder than the storied Cyclops, great

Cthulhu slid greasily into the water and began to pursue with vast wave-raising strokes of cosmic potency. Briden looked back and went mad, laughing shrilly as he kept on laughing at intervals till death found him one night in the cabin whilst Johansen was wandering deliriously.

But Johansen had not given out yet. Knowing that the Thing could surely overtake the *Alert* until steam was fully up, he resolved on a desperate chance; and, setting the engine for full speed, ran lightning-like on deck and reversed the wheel. There was a mighty eddying and foaming in the noisome brine, and as the steam mounted higher and higher the brave Norwegian drove his vessel head on against the pursuing jelly which rose above the unclean froth like the stern of a daemon galleon. The awful squid-head with writhing feelers came nearly up to the bowsprit of the sturdy yacht, but Johansen drove on relentlessly.

There was a bursting as of an exploding bladder, a slushy nastiness as of a cloven sunfish, a stench as of a thousand opened graves, and a sound that the chronicler would not put on paper. For an instant the ship was befouled by an acrid and blinding green cloud, and then there was only a venomous seething astern; where—God in heaven!—the scattered plasticity of that nameless sky-spawn was nebulously *recombining* in its hateful original form, whilst its distance widened every second as the *Alert* gained impetus from its mounting steam.

That was all. After that Johansen only brooded over the idol in the cabin and attended to a few matters of food for himself and the laughing maniac by his side. He did not try to navigate after the first bold flight, for the reaction had taken something out of his soul. Then came the storm of April 2nd, and a gathering of the clouds about his consciousness. There is a sense of spectral whirling through liquid gulfs of infinity, of dizzying rides through reeling universes on a comet's tail, and of hysterical plunges from the pit to the moon and from the moon back again to the pit, all livened by a cachinnating chorus of the distorted, hilarious elder gods and the green, bat-winged mocking imps of Tartarus.

Out of that dream came rescue—the *Vigilant*, the vice-admiralty court, the streets of Dunedin, and the long voyage back home to the old house by the Egeberg. He could not tell—they would think him mad. He would write of what he knew before death came, but his wife must not guess. Death would be a boon if only it could blot out the memories.

That was the document I read, and now I have placed it in the tin box beside the bas-relief and the papers of Professor Angell. With it shall go this record of mine—this test of my own sanity, wherein is pieced together that which I hope may never be pieced together again. I have looked upon all that the universe has to hold of horror, and even the skies of spring and the flowers of summer must ever afterward be poison to me. But I do not think my life will be long. As my uncle went, as poor Johansen went, so I shall go. I know too much, and the cult still lives.

Cthulhu still lives, too, I suppose, again in that chasm of stone which has shielded him since the sun was young. His accursed city is sunken once more, for the *Vigilant* sailed over the spot after the April storm; but his ministers on earth still bellow and prance and slay around idol-capped monoliths in lonely places. He must have been trapped by the sinking whilst within his black abyss, or else the world would by now be screaming with fright and frenzy. Who knows the end? What has risen may sink, and what has sunk may rise. Loathsomeness waits and dreams in the deep, and decay spreads over the tottering cities of men. A time will come—but I must not and cannot think! Let me pray that, if I do not survive this manuscript, my executors may put caution before audacity and see that it meets no other eye.

9
Cravetheen the Harper
A. Leslie
(1928)

This poem appeared in the September 1928 issue of *Weird Tales* magazine. Robert E. Howard, at the time, was embracing his Celtic persona, so Leslie's poem no doubt struck a chord with Howard for this reason. In a letter to his fellow Celt, dated August of 1928, he wrote, "I have a rime in this month's *Weird Tales* which you might like, and tucked away in the back of the magazine is a real poem by Leslie – a better verse than I'll probably ever write." Howard's poem in the same issue was "The Harp of Alfred."

Cravetheen the Harper plays a ghostly tune,
When the earth is barred and speek-led
With silver o' the moon.
The fretted fires flow over him,
And from his moaning harp
Pour floods of singing moonlight
Keening high and sharp.

Cravetheen the Harper
Plays the harp that grieves,
And the souls of murdered women,
Like little rustling leaves,
Come and follow after,
Moaning in the storm,
But the harp of Cravetheen
Keeps him safe from harm.

When the ghost-strings murmur
Their feet must tread the tune,
When the earth is barred and speckled
With silver o' the moon.

Cravetheen the Harper
Comes not in the sun,
For his harp is voiceless
Till the day is done:
Leprechaun and banshee
Listen to the croon,
When the earth is barred and speckled
With silver o' the moon.

10
A Jest and a Vengeance
E. Hoffmann Price
(1929)

This short story by Price was published in the September 1929 issue of *Weird Tales* magazine. A letter appeared two months later (November 1929) in the reader's column, "The Eyrie," written by "Robert E. Howard, author of *The Shadow Kingdom*." Howard wrote, "I have just been reading the September *Weird Tales*, which blossomed out on the news stands today. I was especially taken with *A Jest and a Vengeance*, by E. Hoffmann Price. I've never been east of New Orleans, but as far as I am concerned Price has captured the true spirit of the East in his tales, just as Kipling did. His stories *breathe* the Orient. In this latest tale I note, as in all his others, that patterned background of beauty for which he is noted. The action is perfectly attuned to the thought of the tale and that thought goes deep. More, through the weaving runs a minor note of diabolical humor, tantalizing and enthralling."

A bullet flattened itself against the chiseled arabesques of the wall behind Sultan Schamas ad Din of Angor-lana, spattering him with bits of lead and splinters of marble.

"Maksoud is a notoriously wretched marksman," observed the sultan as he fingered the leaden slug which Amru, his white-haired wazir, had retrieved from the tiled floor. "Still, with enough trials—"

The sultan thrust his cushions a sword's length to the right, and moved just far enough to be secure against further rifle fire from the minaret of the neighboring mosque.

"With enough trials," resumed Schamas ad Din, "Maksoud may not have to wait for the British Resident to find a pretext to depose me."

"It might not have been the son of your brother," suggested Amru, as he moved the fuming nargileh to the sultan's new position, and offered him the carved jade stem. "There are several who have old grudges to settle."

"Undoubtedly," agreed the sultan. "But who else would fire from the mosque? And then miss such an easy mark!"

From afar came the throbbing of drums that muttered of revolt in the mountains.

"Rebels without and assassins within! A luxurious little coffin, this city which the Old Tiger and I built with our swords. Then with this infidel Resident, and Maksoud, who can't wait for me to be deposed—"

The sultan coiled the tube of the nargileh about his wrist and drank deeply of its white smoke. Then he achieved the smile he reserved for occasions demanding the higher justice.

"By Allah and by Abaddon and by the honor of my beard! Resident or no Resident, we will convince this Maksoud of his stupidity! Amru, call me that old bandit of an Ismeddin!"

"At once, *saidi*?" queried the old wazir, as he bowed.

"No. Tonight. He's doubtless asleep now, after a hard evening's discussion with some poorly guarded caravan."

The drumming in the mountains at last ceased. But late that night, long after the outposts at Djeb el Azhár had been doubled, there came another and a different drumming, this time from the palace itself: very low, giving rather the sense of a massive vibration rather than of sound. And this deep pulsing was picked up and relayed until it crept into those very mountains where the tribesmen sharpened their curved yataghans, stuffed their scarlet saddle-bags with grain, and awaited the signal to descend and plunder, certain that they would not be pursued beyond the Sultan's borders, and safe in the assurance that the Resident was but waiting for a pretext to depose Schamas ad Din.

To one who lived in those mountains, and understood the code, the deep-voiced, far-relayed drum spoke very clearly; so that, late as it was, Ismeddin emerged from his cave, belted on a jeweled scimitar that gleamed frostily against his tattered, greasy garments, and picked his way on foot along the hidden trails that led through the camps of the revolting tribesmen and to the plains below.

The darvish had heard the signal, and knew that the son of the Old Tiger was in need.

Ismeddin smiled as he heard the guttural chant of the rebels about their guard fires. But as he approached their outposts, he picked his way more warily, ceased smiling, muttered in his long beard something about the exceeding unfairness of having to contend with mounted sentries, and loosened the Ladder to Heaven in its scabbard . . .

Since the flat roof of the palace at Angor-lana was higher than any building in the city, the sultan was passably secure against marksmen addicted to royal targets, particularly in view of his being in an angle of the parapet that could not be reached from the minaret of the mosque. And thus it was that he reclined at ease in the shadow of a striped canopy, sipping Shirazi wine to his heart's content and his soul's damnation.

But peace and sultans are strangers. A captain of the guard clanked into the Presence, saluted, and made his report: "*Saidi*, the troops at Djeb el Azhár surprised and captured a detachment of the rebels. A ragged old man riding a stolen horse led the outpost commander—"

"Ismeddin, by the Power and by the Splendor!" interrupted the sultan. "Where are the prisoners? And Ismeddin?"

"In the hall of audience, *saidi*. Abdurrahman Khan, his son, and sixty of their followers."

"Very good, Ismail," exulted the sultan. "We will pass sentence at once. Announce me to the court."

The older lords of the court, stout, white-haired ruffians, companions of the Old Tiger, knew well what the Old Tiger's son contemplated when he appeared in the hall of audience. And the younger lords knew the tradition, and beamed in anticipation of old glories revived.

Each of the two chief executioners had three assistants, standing a pace to the left and three paces to the rear; and all were fingering the hilts of their two-handed swords.

There would be notable dismemberments, and a surprising scarcity of rebels long before evening prayer. As for Abdurrahman Khan—

Old Ismeddin, ragged and grimy among the glittering captains, smiled as he thought of an ancient score.

And then the Resident appeared to take his customary station at the left of the throne. He whispered in the sultan's ear; but not even the fan-bearers behind the throne could hear what he said.

The captains exulted at the great rage that flamed in the sultan's eyes as he rose from the dais. But the captains gaped stupidly when the sultan spoke.

"Take these sons of flat-nosed mothers back to their cells. I will deal with them later."

The court dispersed.

The lords and ministers escorted the sultan to his apartments. The brazen doors closed softly behind him, so that they did not see him hurl his turban to the floor, did not hear his scimitar clang against the tiles, rebound, and clatter into a corner. Nor did they hear the Resident, materialized at the height of the storm, expostulate: "But, your Majesty, you may have them hanged, you know—have all of them hanged, in public—roll of drums and all that. But one simply can't have these dismemberings and impalings, you know. Barbarous, and uncivilized, and all that."

Then the sultan, as he twice struck together his hands: "Amru, an order: release the rebels! And to each, his own horse and a robe of honor!"

The Resident endured the sultan's eye for a full moment, and admirably concealed his alarm. Then he left the Presence, conscious of duty well done, even if in the shadow of a bow-string with a running noose: enraged princes do forget themselves, and the sanctity of Residents.

But Schamas ad Din issued no further orders. He and his nargileh fumed and bubbled on the flat roof of the palace . . .

Then the calm voice of Ismeddin: "A thousand years, *saidi*."

"And to you, a thousand," returned the sultan, as he rose to greet his old friend.

The darvish declined the honor of sharing the sultan's seat.

"Hard rocks are my cushions, *saidi*," he protested, as he squatted, cross-legged, at the sultan's feet. But he accepted the stem of the nargileh and solemnly inhaled its white fumes.

Amru set out fresh wine and withdrew; for that grimy wanderer from the mountains was closer to the sultan even than an old and trusted wazir.

"I summoned you last night to help me devise a quiet and effective way of dealing with my brother's son. Need I say that since Maksoud is a friend of the Resident, I need help?"

"Therefore," replied the darvish, "you put me to the trouble of stealing by night through the lines of the mountaineers." Then, smiling a crooked smile, he continued, "And I am an old man, *saidi*—"

"And I," retorted the sultan, "am by this day's work an old woman! That dog of an infidel! That friend of the rebels! The white-haired companions of the Old Tiger pity the mockery that his son has become."

"It is indeed vain in these evil days to be a king," observed Ismeddin. "Yet even a sultan should have his vengeance. And even Residents have their limitations."

Ismeddin smiled thinly, and fingered the hilt of the Ladder to Heaven.

"It is beyond any sword, Ismeddin," mourned the sultan. "In the old days one rode out of the mountains with a troop of horse. But now a Resident stands behind my throne. Look what has happened to my old enemy the Rajah of Laera-kai, on whom be peace!"

The darvish shrugged his shoulders. "I was in the hall of audience. I saw and I heard. And we two are powerless. But, *inshallah*! There is yet much that can be done."

"Then let it be done—before I am deposed."

"You shall have your vengeance, *saidi*. There is one who is the master of vengeances. The Lord of the World, who sits dreaming in the ruins of Atlânaat."

The sultan shivered. "Why speak of Atlânaat? There is some slight merit in living long enough to be deposed and end one's days in Feringhistan, spending an annuity and being addressed as Majesty. Many have entered Atlânaat in hopes of wisdom and loot, and have left without even hope of forgetting what they have seen. Really, Ismeddin, that monstrous citadel was built by devils, and Shaitan's little sister dances there by moonlight."

"Devils?" retorted Ismeddin. "Built rather by pre-Adamite kings."

"As you will," conceded the sultan. "The distinction is purely academic. Yet the fact remains that sane men find less and less reason for visiting that fiend-haunted ruin. Once, a very long time ago, I saw a very little. But that was entirely too much. And that music, and that strange sweetness that drifts up from the depths . . ."

Again the sultan shivered.

"But I," countered Ismeddin, "have seen Atlânaat to its nethermost foundations. And there and there only lies your vengeance, and a jest such as the Old Tiger himself would have relished, if you can face the Lord of the World and his counsel."

The darvish leaped to his feet. "*Saidi*, the Old Tiger would not have hesitated."

"Done, by Allah and by my beard!" swore the sultan. "Yet I know any number of places I would rather visit, either by day or by night. Nevertheless—"

"Let it then be nevertheless, my lord!"

The sultan twice clapped his hands.

Amru reappeared, and received orders: two horses at the Ispahan Gate, an hour after evening prayer; horses meanly equipped and poorly caparisoned.

But before Amru could leave, Ismeddin interposed: "A moment, oh father of all wazirs!"

And then, to the sultan: "What is to be done must be done quickly. Let Maksoud meet us at Atlânaat, so that the wisdom of the Lord of the World will not have time to cool in our ears."

The sultan nodded, then spoke very briefly of four tongueless, black mamelukes, and of Maksoud who was to accompany them; and this cavalcade was to leave the city by a small gate which had no name.

An hour's ride from the Ispahan Gate brought Ismeddin and the sultan to the edge of the jungle in whose depths brooded the foundations of prodigious Atlânaat. They halted for a moment to gaze at the uncounted domes and minarets that towered high above the jungle and muttered secret words to the stars as they crept out one by one. Then Ismeddin took the lead, the sultan following in his trace.

How strange, pondered the sultan, that he should ride alone in the jungle, following a white blur that was the dirty *djellab* of an old man who was so entirely at home in unsavory places; and how much stranger yet that he should step from his throne to seek aid from a darvish who lived in a cavern and pitied the futility of kings.

Then the sultan thought of his vengeance, and wondered at the terrific words the Lord of the World would speak . . .

The darvish finally halted at the edge of a clearing. Before them loomed the incredible bulk of the outer walls of Atlânaat, walls that had for ages mocked the age-old trees that sought to reach their parapet.

"To our left, *saidi*," announced the darvish.

They skirted the wall until they came to a breach wide enough to admit four horsemen abreast.

"Those who enter through the gate are seriously in error," commented Ismeddin, as he picked his way among the gigantic blocks of rose granite that still lay in the breach. "There is a sculptured hand on the keystone of the arch . . ."

The moon had risen over the crests of the trees. Long shadows of columns shattered at mid-height marched across the broad, paved avenue that at the breach in the wall turned and led to the heart of the citadel.

"My lord," began Ismeddin, as the sultan cleared the last block of granite and drew up at his side, "we have not yet committed ourselves to anything."

"Conceivably," admitted the sultan, "the ride back to Angor-lana by moonlight would be pleasant. Yet Maksoud also would find it a pleasant ride. But tell me," continued Schamas ad Din, "what advantage there is in taking my vengeance here? It might be more odd and quaint than anything I might devise at home; but in the end, there would be the Resident—"

"Ah, but would there?" smiled Ismeddin. "The Lord of the World dreams strange things. However, if you wish—"

Ismeddin wheeled his horse about.

"Not at all!" countered the sultan. "To the finish, then. And as for this god and his playmate?"

"Even so, *saidi*."

The darvish led the way down the broad avenue. The sultan glanced once at the sculptured columns, shuddered, and found a glance sufficient. Then he smiled: for Maksoud would find Atlânaat not a bit more savory.

The avenue ended in a small court bounded by columns whose capitals were on friendly terms with a single sultry-glowing star that glared evilly . . . . At the base of each pillar was an ornately chiseled pedestal: On eleven of these pedestals, forming a crescent, were life-sized images of bearded men, sitting cross-legged. The head of each was bowed as in sleep; and each held in his left hand a curiously carved scepter.

The sultan started at the sound of hoofs clicking on the pavement behind them.

"Maksoud and his escort." And then, as the hoof-beats ceased: "They fancy this place no more than you do, *saidi.*"

The sultan scrutinized the cross-legged, bearded images. "Strangely life-like," he observed.

"No," contradicted Ismeddin. "Not *strangely* life-like. Rather it would be strange were they otherwise. Nevertheless, seek the girl and her sleeping master. She may tell you how to outwit the Resident and dispose very neatly of Maksoud. But"—Ismeddin glanced again at the disconcerting images—"she may offer a most unusual solution."

In the center of the court was a circular balustrade that guarded the brink of a pit along whose walls spiraled a gently sloping runway down which a man on horse or foot might easily make his way to the abysmal depths that mocked the single star overhead.

"Advance boldly," counseled the darvish, "down the center, not rashly close to the edge, nor timidly close to the wall. And in the meanwhile I will be here with Maksoud, awaiting your return."

"My return? You are optimistic."

"But with reason," countered Ismeddin. "I myself was once there; and I returned."

"If you are wrong, it will be the first time," conceded the sultan as he began his descent.

"Ismeddin," reflected the sultan, "is doubtless right. And yet I would rather be up there in the courtyard watching him pick his way down and out of sight and into this playground of Shaitan's little sister. Ismeddin would be quite in his element."

Darkness did not engulf him as quickly as he had expected. The blackness receded as he descended, and the broad, white tiles gleamed dully ahead of him, so that it was simple enough to keep to the middle of the spiral runway.

From far above came the click-click of horses' hoofs.

The sultan smiled grimly at the thought of Maksoud awaiting a doom that was to emerge from that black pit.

Down . . . down . . . turn after turn . . . until finally the sultan was as far beneath the court as the capitals of its encircling pillars were above it. Then came the scarcely perceptible thump-thump of a drum, and the thin wailing notes of a pipe. An overwhelming, poison sweetness breathed from the blackness and enfolded him.

"By Allah and by Abaddon!" said the sultan to himself, as he paused and half turned. "Vengeance is costly!"

He wiped his brow, and licked his lips; then resolutely advanced.

The spiraling path was curving in ever narrowing circles, vortex-like.

The perfume was now overwhelming.

At the bottom of the pit he found himself facing a low archway that opened into a vault pervaded by glowing vapors whose luminescence throbbed to the cadence of those muttering drums and wailing pipes.

Then a gong sounded once: thinly, as the rustle of silk rather than the resonance of bronze; and the rose-hued mists parted, revealing a girl whose Babylonic eyes gazed through and past him as though he were nebulous as the smoke-wisps of gauze that thinly veiled her loveliness.

A numbness crept over the sultan; all save those intent, sultry eyes was blotted out of existence.

Then she spoke. "Welcome, son of the Old Tiger. You have done well. But unaided you can go no farther."

The girl extended her slender arms and with serpentine passes and gestures stroked his forehead; and then, stepping to his left side, with her knuckles she rapped sharply here and there along his spine, making the lost magic of far-off Tibet, whereby men become gods, and gods become beasts.

Then in softly purring syllables she continued, "You can not cross the threshold to enter the presence of the Lord of the World. Try and see whether I am right."

The sultan sought to advance; but his feet were fixed to the tiles, and a heaviness that forbade all movement possessed him.

Again that soft rippling voice: "You have become as immobile as those eleven who were once kings. And with another pass I could weave about you that silence from the ancient mountains, from which you could not emerge until the end of all time . . ."

She faced him, regarded him intently, then continued: "But I shall restore you and make you more agile than the fancies of those who eat the plums that grow on the slopes of Mount Kaf."

Whereat she made passes and tapped him as she had done before.

"Now, Schamas ad Din, son of the Old Tiger, enter the presence of the Lord of the World."

The sultan advanced, marveling that he could not feel the touch of his feet on the floor. The sighing music ceased piping; and as the rose- and saffron-shot mists thinned and drew back and vanished, he found himself in a circular vault on whose domed ceiling glittered stars arranged in strange constellations; and the floor of the vault was not tiled, but strewn with powdered cinnabar. In the center of the vault was a low couch of grotesquely chiseled green basalt on which sat an old man whose head was bowed in sleep.

"Son of the Old Tiger," said the incredible girl at the sultan's side, "you are before the Lord of the World, he who built this prodigious citadel the day he completed the creation of this and all other worlds. He sleeps, and sleeping, dreams; and all things that seem to be are but the figments of his dream; and those things whereof he ceases to dream at that moment cease to be. For nothing is real, save it be the illusion of him who sits here dreaming."

"Then who are you?" queried the sultan.

The girl smiled, and patted the twining, jeweled blackness of her hair.

"I also am illusion, and his masterwork."

"Then if all this be a dream, who and what am I?"

"You too are but one of his fancies; and when he ceases to picture you—"

The sultan shuddered at the girl's gesture of dismissal; but he resumed, "Then if he were to awaken?"

"All things," replied the girl, "would revert to that which existed before he fell asleep. Even I would vanish, just as your dreams when you awaken from them become as nothing."

The girl smiled at the dazed sultan, and continued, "But I shall not and can not vanish, since he can not cease dreaming his most wondrous vision. Nor can he awaken, since I have made his sleep eternal. He ascribed to me all perfection; and thus I have the power which you perceived in my greeting of you. And more than that: it is I who cast a spell over him whose dream I am, so that through the boundless wastes of time he can not awaken; and I can even now whisper in his ear that which I wish him to dream, and straightway his visions create that which I desire."

"Then," deduced the sultan after a long pause, "you are greater than this Lord of the World whose fancy you are?"

The girl stared fixedly as a brooding fate. Then finally she spoke.

"There you have that which few men have ever known: that their illusion transcends and finally conquers them—even as this god is the toy of his own dream, and the prey of an old magic from Tibet."

The sultan gazed intently at the white-bearded Master of Illusion. Then he laughed softly at the simple answer to an insoluble riddle. For a dream, this girl was surprisingly human and reasonable ...

"It seems," began the sultan, "that this ancient Lord of the World endowed me with a touch of his own folly. For I have become the plaything of this mad kingdom which the Old Tiger and I dreamed twenty years ago as we sharpened our blades and rode out of the mountains. But not being a god, I may escape my doom."

"And how might that be?" queried the girl.

Her left eyebrow rose ever so slightly. She nodded approvingly at Schamas ad Din.

"You might," suggested the sultan, "whisper into his ear a thought I might whisper into yours."

"In a word, *saidi*," said the girl, "you wish that mad kingdom of yours made a bit more habitable for its ruler? You came seeking vengeance, and end by wanting to recast your entire fate? But that would be unreasonable; for then, in your own way, you would be greater than this very Lord of the World, since even he is subject to me, his dream."

"Wrong!" exclaimed the sultan. "By my beard, you are wrong! I seek but a jest and a vengeance, and let dreams go where they will. Such a vengeance as until a moment ago I had not contemplated or imagined."

"Even as I sought a vengeance and found a jest when I chanted this Dreamer to sleep. *Saidi*, you are a man after my own heart; and your fancy appeals to me. You please me exceedingly. And I think it could be arranged. Yet listen well: in the end you must leave me, and take your place among those who sit motionless in the courtyard above us. The hour is at hand; for there is one here of whom I have for some time been weary, and who will soon occupy the twelfth pedestal."

The girl paused, flung into a censer at the Dreamer's feet a handful of incense, and resumed as she turned to face Schamas ad Din, "But think well, Son of the Old Tiger. A lesser vengeance, and one such as you contemplated when you sought me, could be bought much more cheaply . . . Go back to the courtyard and ponder with clear sky over your head . For only that old rogue of an Ismeddin ever escaped the penalty . . ."

The girl smiled reminiscently and fondly, then continued, "And it is no jesting matter, this sitting cross-legged on a pedestal when I have tired of you. Nor would Maksoud find a cheaper vengeance at all pleasant."

Yet her eyes belied the discouragement her lips spoke. The sultan ceased comparing her to the women of Gurjestan and Tcherkess, for she was incomparable. Even his jest and his vengeance were trifling . . .

The sultan disengaged himself from her perfumed embrace.

"Ismeddin is waiting."

And Schamas ad Din ascended the winding incline, smiling and stroking his curled beard.

Ismeddin in the meanwhile had led Maksoud, still bound and gagged, and his escort of black mamelukes into the courtyard.

"Father of many little pigs," murmured the darvish, "our lord the Sultan has taken offense at your last display of wretched marksmanship. And since none of his own fancies were worthy of you, he is even now taking counsel with Abaddon of the Black Hands. I expect him any moment, well advised and smiling. So be assured against anything as commonplace as being sawed asunder between two planks."

The Africans had dismounted, and were taking from their packs all manner of implements, as well as cords, flasks of oil, charcoal, and a pair of small bellows. One of them set to work kindling a fire while the other three deftly fitted together mortised and tenoned pieces of dark, heavy wood, assembling a stout frame equipped with hooks, manacles, and shackles.

"It is difficult to say what form the master's fancy will take," resumed Ismeddin, as he approvingly regarded the executioners at their work. "But surely it will not be commonplace."

He picked up a keen, two-handed sword, tested its edge and balance.

"Very pretty. But you will have nothing to do with this."

Then, as he noted the four horses tethered to a column: "Ah! . . . now *that*, with certain variations, has real possibilities. You are quite substantial, Maksoud . . . but those horses are sturdy little beasts . . ."

Ismeddin stroked the neck of a savage Barbary stallion, and continued, "But then, that also is swift. At the best, it lasts but a little over a day, even with the nicest of workmanship," mused the old man.

Ismeddin deftly removed the gag from the prisoner's mouth.

"He can no more than banish me!" sputtered Maksoud. "The Resident would depose him were I not to return. Old ape . . . son of many pork-eating fathers . . . do you think all this parade of curious torments will kill *me* of fright? That is an old story. I myself once helped him—"

And Maksoud's laugh rang true.

"So?" Ismeddin smiled suavely. "Well, and I said that you would meet none of these commonplace things. But supposing . . . just sup- posing, as food for thought, that we were to let you down into that black pit. You have seen those who have played about these ruins—"

Ismeddin nodded to the black slaves, who advanced to remove the prisoner from his horse.

"Not *that, saidi*," implored Maksoud.

"That, and more than that. You have seen those who lost their way in these ruins. And you once laughed at what was left of one who finally did find his way out."

The executioners, skilled as they were at handling tormented wretches, kept their hold on Maksoud with difficulty.

And then the cool voice of the sultan, as he emerged from the pit: "Well, Ismeddin, couldn't you wait for me? I heard his howling long before I reached the surface."

"Mercy, O Magnificent! Not into that pit of Iblis!"

"The penalty of poor marksmanship, Maksoud," declared the sultan. "Had you practiced in private a few more days, I would not be here deciding your fate."

He smiled and stroked his beard.

"And so you fancied being sultan, did you?" resumed Schamas ad Din. "Those wild fancies are deplorable. Yussuf, here, has devised an entertainment worthy of your bungling; but he shall save it for another."

The chief of the black slaves looked up from his implements, and grinned.

"That pit, master . . . spare me that!"

"Well, and so be it, Maksoud . . . ungrateful son of my brother. But listen: I have devised a doom which will make that pit seem a childish game, and the companions of the pit pleasant playmates. For those whom these ruins have done to death and torment and madness have lived but a month or two of frenzy. But what I have devised—"

He paused, ignoring the prisoner and his pleas. The sultan's smile faded, and his features became drawn and thoughtful. He leaned against the balustrade, and stared at those eleven all too life-like figures squatting on their pedestals of chiseled stone.

The executioners were now supporting rather than holding fast the prisoner. And they themselves, hardened as they were to applying fire and steel, shifted uneasily, and licked their dry lips as they regarded the sultan. And when he turned, they dropped their eyes to avoid his eyes.

Still the sultan did not speak.

His presence was a smoldering doom.

Then a poison sweetness crept up from the mouth of the pit.

From its blacknesses emerged the figure of a bearded king, who solemnly advanced with measured steps, as to the cadence of a slowly beaten drum.

The tongueless executioners dropped their implements, and made horrible, choking grasps at speech.

But as if alone in a desert waste, the presence strode through the group. His robe brushed Maksoud as he passed toward the other side of the court, bearing in his left hand a strangely carved scepter, and with his right hand stroking his long, curled beard.

Straight across the moon-bathed tiles, and to the twelfth pedestal; and then with infinite care and deliberation, he seated himself cross-legged after the fashion of those eleven all too life-like images.

Very faintly came the sound of a distant gong: not resonant as bronze, but rather as the hissing of a serpent or the rustling of silk.

The sultan started. Then he looked Maksoud full in the eye, and smiled that terrific smile of his father, the Old Tiger.

"Maksoud," he began, "you sought to be king before your day, and forgot my friendship and favor. You could not wait for me to meet my doom on the highroads of Allah. And I shall now punish you by giving you—"

The prisoner choked and gasped.

"Not that, *saidi*—"

"By giving you," continued the sultan, "that which you sought, so that the fullness of possession shall corrode your soul worse than any torment could corrode your body. You shall sit on my lofty throne and publish the orders dictated by an infidel Resident. He shall thwart your vengeances. He shall make a mockery of you, the last remnant of the lordly estate of kings. You shall rule by words rather than by swords."

The sultan drew his scimitar.

"Your friends shall seek you with daggers in your gardens. Poison shall lurk in your food and in your thoughts. Bungling marksmen shall never quite attain the mark you will finally wish them to attain. Your enemies will pity you."

The scimitar flickered twice, and the stout cords fell from Maksoud's wrists and ankles.

"To horse, Maksoud, and ride to your throne!"

The sultan sheathed his blade, advanced a pace down the spiral pathway of darkness, then paused to listen to the hoofbeats of Maksoud's cavalcade.

Old Ismeddin leaned over the balustrade.

"A moment, *saidi*! Let your first whisper in the girl's ear ask for *two* British Residents in Angor-lana."

And with a courtly salaam to the master, Ismeddin disappeared among the ruins.

11
The Silver Key
H.P. Lovecraft
(1929)

Originally written in 1926 and submitted to *Weird Tales* magazine the following year, Editor Farnsworth Wright initially rejected the story. He later asked Lovecraft if he could read the story again; this time Wright accepted it for publication, and it appeared in the January 1929 issue of *Weird Tales*. According to Lovecraft scholar, S.T. Joshi, Wright later told Lovecraft that the readers of the magazine, "violently disliked" the story. Howard, however, saw something in the story that he liked, for as he later wrote Lovecraft, "I remember 'The Silver Key'—yet remember is hardly the word to use. I have constantly referred to that story in my meditations ever since I read it, years ago—have probably thought of it more than any other story that ever appeared in *Weird Tales*. There was something about it that struck deep. I read it aloud to Tevis Clyde Smith, some years ago, and he agreed with me as to its cosmic sweep."

When Randolph Carter was thirty he lost the key of the gate of dreams. Prior to that time he had made up for the prosiness of life by nightly excursions to strange and ancient cities beyond space, and lovely, unbelievable garden lands across ethereal seas; but as middle age hardened upon him he felt these liberties slipping away little by little, until at last he was cut off altogether. No more could his galleys sail up the river Oukranos past the gilded spires of Thran, or his elephant caravans tramp through perfumed jungles in Kled, where forgotten palaces with veined ivory columns sleep lovely and unbroken under the moon.

He had read much of things as they are, and talked with too many people. Well-meaning philosophers had taught him to look into the logical relations of things, and analyze the processes which shaped his thoughts and fancies. Wonder had gone away, and he had forgotten that all life is only a set of pictures in the brain, among which there is no difference betwixt those born of real things and those born of inward dreamings, and no cause to value the one above the other. Custom had dinned into his ears a superstitious reverence for that which tangibly and physically exists, and had made him secretly ashamed to dwell in visions. Wise men told him his simple fancies were inane and childish, and he believed it because he could see that they might easily be so. What he failed to recall was that the deeds of reality are just as inane and childish, and even more absurd because their actors persist in fancying them full of meaning and purpose as the blind cosmos grinds aimlessly on from nothing to something and from something back to nothing again, neither heeding nor knowing the wishes or existence of the minds that flicker for a second now and then in the darkness.

They had chained him down to things that are, and had then explained the workings of those things till mystery had gone out of the world. When he complained, and longed to escape into twilight realms where magic molded all the little vivid fragments and prized associations of his mind into vistas of breathless expectancy and unquenchable delight, they turned him instead toward the new-found prodigies of science, bidding him find wonder in the atom's vortex and mystery in the sky's dimensions. And when he had failed to find these boons in things whose laws are known and measurable, they told him he lacked imagination, and was immature because he preferred dream-illusions to the illusions of our physical creation.

So Carter had tried to do as others did, and pretended that the common events and emotions of earthy minds were more important than the fantasies of rare and delicate souls. He did not dissent when they told him that the animal pain of a stuck pig or dyspeptic ploughman in real life is a greater thing than the peerless beauty of Narath with its hundred carven gates and domes of chalcedony, which he dimly remembered from his dreams; and under their guidance he cultivated a painstaking sense of pity and tragedy.

Once in a while, though, he could not help seeing how shallow, fickle, and meaningless all human aspirations are, and how emptily our real impulses contrast with those pompous ideals we profess to hold. Then he would have recourse to the polite laughter they had taught him to use against the extravagance and artificiality of dreams; for he saw that the daily life of our world is every inch as extravagant and artificial, and far less worthy of respect because of its poverty in beauty and its silly reluctance to admit its own lack of reason and purpose. In this way he became a kind of humorist, for he did not see that even humor is empty in a mindless universe devoid of any true standard of consistency or inconsistency.

In the first days of his bondage he had turned to the gentle churchly faith endeared to him by the naive trust of his fathers, for thence stretched mystic avenues which seemed to promise escape from life. Only on closer view did he mark the starved fancy and beauty, the stale and prosy triteness, and the owlish gravity and grotesque claims of solid truth which reigned boresomely and overwhelmingly among most of its professors; or feel to the full the awkwardness with which it sought to keep alive as literal fact the outgrown fears and guesses of a primal race confronting the unknown. It wearied Carter to see how solemnly people tried to make earthly reality out of old myths which every step of their boasted science confuted, and this misplaced seriousness killed the attachment he might have kept for the ancient creeds had they been content to offer the sonorous rites and emotional outlets in their true guise of ethereal fantasy.

But when he came to study those who had thrown off the old myths, he found them even more ugly than those who had not. They did not know that beauty lies in harmony, and that loveliness of life has no standard amidst an aimless cosmos save only its harmony with the dreams and the feelings which have gone before and blindly molded our little spheres out of the rest of chaos. They did not see that good and evil and beauty and ugliness are only ornamental fruits of perspective, whose sole value lies in their linkage to what chance made our fathers think and feel, and whose finer details are different for every race and culture. Instead, they either denied these things altogether or transferred them to the crude, vague instincts which they shared with the beasts and peasants; so that their lives were dragged malodorously out in pain, ugliness, and disproportion, yet filled with a ludicrous pride at having escaped from something no more unsound than that which still held them. They had traded the false gods of fear and blind piety for those of license and anarchy.

Carter did not taste deeply of these modern freedoms; for their cheapness and squalor sickened a spirit loving beauty alone, while his reason rebelled at the flimsy logic with which their champions tried to gild brute impulse with a sacredness stripped from the idols they had discarded. He saw that most of them, in common with their cast-off priestcraft, could not escape from the delusion that life has a meaning apart from that which men dream into it; and could not lay aside the crude notion of ethics and obligations beyond those of beauty, even when all Nature shrieked of its unconsciousness and impersonal unmorality in the light of their scientific discoveries. Warped and bigoted with preconceived illusions of justice, freedom, and consistency, they cast off the old lore and the old ways with the old beliefs; nor ever stopped to think that that lore and those ways were the sole makers of their present thoughts and judgments, and the sole guides and standards in a meaningless universe without fixed aims or stable points of reference. Having lost these artificial settings, their lives grew void of direction and dramatic interest; till at length they strove to drown their ennui in bustle and pretended usefulness, noise and excitement, barbaric display and animal sensation. When these things palled, disappointed, or grew nauseous through revulsion, they cultivated irony and bitterness, and found fault with the social order. Never could they realize that their brute foundations were as shifting and contradictory as the gods of their elders, and that the satisfaction of one moment is the bane of the next. Calm, lasting beauty comes only in dream, and this solace the world had thrown away when in its worship of the real it threw away the secrets of childhood and innocence.

Amidst this chaos of hollowness and unrest Carter tried to live as befitted a man of keen thought and good heritage. With his dreams fading under the ridicule of the age he could not believe in anything, but the love of harmony kept him close to the ways of his race and station. He walked impassive through the cities of men, and sighed because no vista seemed fully real; because every flash of yellow sunlight on tall roofs and every glimpse of balustraded plazas in the first lamps of evening served only to remind him of dreams he had once known, and to make him homesick for ethereal lands he no longer knew how to find. Travel was only a mockery; and even the Great War stirred him but little, though he served from the first in the Foreign Legion of France. For a while he sought friends, but soon grew weary of the crudeness of their emotions, and the sameness and earthiness of their visions. He felt vaguely glad that all his relatives were distant and out of touch with him, for they could not have understood his mental life. That is, none but his grandfather and great-uncle Christopher could, and they were long dead.

Then he began once more the writing of books, which he had left off when dreams first failed him. But here, too, was there no satisfaction or fulfilment; for the touch of earth was upon his mind, and he could not think of lovely things as he had done of yore. Ironic humor dragged down all the twilight minarets he reared, and the earthy fear of improbability blasted all the delicate and amazing flowers in his faery gardens. The convention of assumed pity spilt mawkishness on his characters, while the myth of an important reality and significant human events and emotions debased all his high fantasy into thin-veiled allegory and cheap social satire. His new novels were successful as his old ones had never been; and because he knew how empty they must be to please an empty herd, he burned them and ceased his writing. They were very graceful novels, in which he urbanely laughed at the dreams he lightly sketched; but he saw that their sophistication had sapped all their life away.

It was after this that he cultivated deliberate illusion, and dabbled in the notions of the bizarre and the eccentric as an antidote for the commonplace. Most of these, however, soon shewed their poverty and barrenness; and he saw that the popular doctrines of occultism are as dry and inflexible as those of science, yet without even the slender palliative of truth to redeem them. Gross stupidity, falsehood, and muddled thinking are not dream; and form no escape from life to a mind trained above their level. So Carter bought stranger books and sought out deeper and more terrible men of fantastic erudition; delving into arcana of consciousness that few have trod, and learning things about the secret pits of life, legend, and immemorial antiquity which disturbed him ever afterward. He decided to live on a rarer plane, and furnished his Boston home to suit his changing moods; one room for each, hung in appropriate colors, furnished with befitting books and objects, and provided with sources of the proper sensations of light, heat, sound, taste, and odor.

Once he heard of a man in the South who was shunned and feared for the blasphemous things he read in prehistoric books and clay tablets smuggled from India and Arabia. Him he visited, living with him and sharing his studies for seven years, till horror overtook them one midnight in an unknown and archaic graveyard, and only one emerged where two had entered. Then he went back to Arkham, the terrible witch-haunted old town of his forefathers in New England, and had experiences in the dark, amidst the hoary willows and tottering gambrel roofs, which made him seal forever certain pages in the diary of a wild-minded ancestor. But these horrors took him only to the edge of reality, and were not of the true dream country he had known in youth; so that at fifty he despaired of any rest or contentment in a world grown too busy for beauty and too shrewd for dream.

Having perceived at last the hollowness and futility of real things, Carter spent his days in retirement, and in wistful disjointed memories of his dream-filled youth. He thought it rather silly that he bothered to keep on living at all, and got from a South American acquaintance a very curious liquid to take him to oblivion without suffering. Inertia and force of habit, however, caused him to defer action; and he lingered indecisively among thoughts of old times, taking down the strange hangings from his walls and refitting the house as it was in his early boyhood—purple panes, Victorian furniture, and all.

With the passage of time he became almost glad he had lingered, for his relics of youth and his cleavage from the world made life and sophistication seem very distant and unreal; so much so that a touch of magic and expectancy stole back into his nightly slumbers. For years those slumbers had known only such twisted reflections of every-day things as the commonest slumbers know, but now there returned a flicker of something stranger and wilder; something of vaguely awesome immanence which took the form of tensely clear pictures from his childhood days, and made him think of little inconsequential things he had long forgotten. He would often awake calling for his mother and grandfather, both in their graves a quarter of a century.

Then one night his grandfather reminded him of a key. The grey old scholar, as vivid as in life, spoke long and earnestly of their ancient line, and of the strange visions of the delicate and sensitive men who composed it. He spoke of the flame-eyed Crusader who learnt wild secrets of the Saracens that held him captive; and of the first Sir Randolph Carter who studied magic when Elizabeth was queen. He spoke, too, of that Edmund Carter who had just escaped hanging in the Salem witchcraft, and who had placed in an antique box a great silver key handed down from his ancestors. Before Carter awaked, the gentle visitant had told him where to find that box; that carved oak box of archaic wonder whose grotesque lid no hand had raised for two centuries.

In the dust and shadows of the great attic he found it, remote and forgotten at the back of a drawer in a tall chest. It was about a foot square, and its Gothic carvings were so fearful that he did not marvel no person since Edmund Carter had dared to open it. It gave forth no noise when shaken, but was mystic with the scent of unremembered spices. That it held a key was indeed only a dim legend, and Randolph Carter's father had never known such a box existed. It was bound in rusty iron, and no means was provided for working the formidable lock. Carter vaguely understood that he would find within it some key to the lost gate of dreams, but of where and how to use it his grandfather had told him nothing.

An old servant forced the carven lid, shaking as he did so at the hideous faces leering from the blackened wood, and at some unplaced familiarity. Inside, wrapped in a discolored parchment, was a huge key of tarnished silver covered with cryptical arabesques; but of any legible explanation there was none. The parchment was voluminous, and held only the strange hieroglyphs of an unknown tongue written with an antique reed. Carter recognized the characters as those he had seen on a certain papyrus scroll belonging to that terrible scholar of the South who had vanished one midnight in a nameless cemetery. The man had always shivered when he read this scroll, and Carter shivered now.

But he cleaned the key, and kept it by him nightly in its aromatic box of ancient oak. His dreams were meanwhile increaseing in vividness, and though shewing him none of the strange cities and incredible gardens of the old days, were assuming a definite cast whose purpose could not be mistaken. They were calling him back along the years, and with the mingled wills of all his fathers were pulling him toward some hidden and ancestral source. Then he knew he must go into the past and merge himself with old things, and day after day he thought of the hills to the north where haunted Arkham and the rushing Miskatonic and the lonely rustic homestead of his people lay.

In the brooding fire of autumn Carter took the old remembered way past graceful lines of rolling hill and stone-walled meadow, distant vale and hanging woodland, curving road and nestling farmstead, and the crystal windings of the Miskatonic, crossed here and there by rustic bridges of wood or stone. At one bend he saw the group of giant elms among which an ancestor had oddly vanished a century and a half before, and shuddered as the wind blew meaningly through them. Then there was the crumbling farmhouse of old Goody Fowler the witch, with its little evil windows and great roof sloping nearly to the ground on the north side. He speeded up his car as he passed it, and did not slacken till he had mounted the hill where his mother and her fathers before her were born, and where the old white house still looked proudly across the road at the breathlessly lovely panorama of rocky slope and verdant valley, with the distant spires of Kingsport on the horizon, and hints of the archaic, dream-laden sea in the farthest background.

Then came the steeper slope that held the old Carter place he had not seen in over forty years. Afternoon was far gone when he reached the foot, and at the bend half way up he paused to scan the outspread countryside golden and glorified in the slanting floods of magic poured out by a western sun. All the strangeness and expectancy of his recent dreams seemed present in this hushed and unearthly landscape, and he thought of the unknown solitudes of other planets as his eyes traced out the velvet and deserted lawns shining undulant between their tumbled walls, the clumps of faery forest setting off far lines of purple hills beyond hills, and the spectral wooded valley dipping down in shadow to dank hollows where trickling waters crooned and gurgled among swollen and distorted roots.

Something made him feel that motors did not belong in the realm he was seeking, so he left his car at the edge of the forest, and putting the great key in his coat pocket walked on up the hill. Woods now engulfed him utterly, though he knew the house was on a high knoll that cleared the trees except to the north. He wondered how it would look, for it had been left vacant and untended through his neglect since the death of his strange great-uncle Christopher thirty years before. In his boyhood he had reveled through long visits there, and had found weird marvels in the woods beyond the orchard.

Shadows thickened around him, for the night was near. Once a gap in the trees opened up to the right, so that he saw off across leagues of twilight meadow and spied the old Congregational steeple on Central Hill in Kingsport; pink with the last flush of day, the panes of the little round windows blazing with reflected fire. Then, when he was in deep shadow again, he recalled with a start that the glimpse must have come from childish memory alone, since the old white church had long been torn down to make room for the Congregational

Hospital. He had read of it with interest, for the paper had told about some strange burrows or passages found in the rocky hill beneath.

Through his puzzlement a voice piped, and he started again at its familiarity after long years. Old Benijah Corey had been his Uncle Christopher's hired man, and was aged even in those far-off times of his boyhood visits. Now he must be well over a hundred, but that piping voice could come from no one else. He could distinguish no words, yet the tone was haunting and unmistakable. To think that "Old Benijy" should still be alive!

"Mister Randy! Mister Randy! Whar be ye? D'ye want to skeer yer Aunt Marthy plumb to death? Hain't she tuld ye to keep nigh the place in the arternoon an' git back afur dark? Randy! Ran-dee! . . . He's the beatin'est boy fer runnin' off in the woods I ever see; haff the time a-settin' moonin' raound that snake-den in the upper timber-lot! . . . Hey, yew, Ran-dee!"

Randolph Carter stopped in the pitch darkness and rubbed his hand across his eyes. Something was queer. He had been somewhere he ought not to be; had strayed very far away to places where he had not belonged, and was now inexcusably late. He had not noticed the time on the Kingsport steeple, though he could easily have made it out with his pocket telescope; but he knew his lateness was something very strange and unprecedented. He was not sure he had his little telescope with him, and put his hand in his blouse pocket to see. No, it was not there, but there was the big silver key he had found in a box somewhere. Uncle Chris had told him something odd once about an old unopened box with a key in it, but Aunt Martha had stopped the story abruptly, saying it was no kind of thing to tell a child whose head was already too full of queer fancies. He tried to recall just where he had found the key, but something seemed very confused. He guessed it was in the attic at home in Boston, and dimly remembered bribing Parks with half his week's allowance to help him open the box and keep quiet about it; but when he remembered this, the face of Parks came up very strangely, as if the wrinkles of long years had fallen upon the brisk little Cockney.

"Ran-dee! Ran-dee! Hi! Hi! Randy!"

A swaying lantern came around the black bend, and old Benijah pounced on the silent and bewildered form of the pilgrim.

"Durn ye, boy, so thar ye be! Ain't ye got a tongue in yer head, that ye can't answer a body? I ben callin' this haff hour, an' ye must a heerd me long ago! Dun't ye know yer Aunt Marthy's all a-fidget over yer bein' off arter dark? Wait till I tell yer Uncle Chris when he gits hum! Ye'd orta know these here woods ain't no fitten place to be traipsin' this hour! They's things abroad what dun't do nobody no good, as my gran'sir' knowed afur me. Come, Mister Randy, or Hannah wun't keep supper no longer!"

So Randolph Carter was marched up the road where wondering stars glimmered through high autumn boughs. And dogs barked as the yellow light of small-paned windows shone out at the farther turn, and the Pleiades twinkled across the open knoll where a great gambrel roof stood black against the dim west. Aunt Martha was in the doorway, and did not scold too hard when Benijah shoved the truant in. She knew Uncle Chris well enough to expect such things of the Carter blood. Randolph did not shew his key, but ate his supper in silence and protested only when bedtime came. He sometimes dreamed better when awake, and he wanted to use that key.

In the morning Randolph was up early, and would have run off to the upper timber-lot if Uncle Chris had not caught him and forced him into his chair by the breakfast table. He looked impatiently around the low-pitched room with the rag carpet and exposed beams and corner-posts, and smiled only when the orchard boughs scratched at the leaded panes of the rear window. The trees and the hills were close to him, and formed the gates of that timeless realm which was his true country.

Then, when he was free, he felt in his blouse pocket for the key; and being reassured, skipped off across the orchard to the rise beyond, where the wooded hill climbed again to heights above even the treeless knoll. The floor of the forest was mossy and mysterious, and great lichened rocks rose vaguely here and there in the dim light like Druid monoliths among the swollen and twisted trunks of a sacred grove. Once in his ascent Randolph crossed a rushing stream whose falls a little way off sang runic incantations to the lurking fauns and aegipans and dryads.

Then he came to the strange cave in the forest slope, the dreaded "snake-den" which country folk shunned, and away from which Benijah had warned him again and again. It was deep; far deeper than anyone but Randolph suspected, for the boy had found a fissure in the farthermost black corner that led to a loftier grotto beyond—a haunting sepulchral place whose granite walls held a curious illusion of conscious artifice. On this occasion he crawled in as usual, lighting his way with matches filched from the sitting-room match-safe, and edging through the final crevice with an eagerness hard to explain even to himself. He could not tell why he approached the farther wall so confidently, or why he instinctively drew forth the great silver key as he did so. But on he went, and when he danced back to the house that night he offered no excuses for his lateness, nor heeded in the least the reproofs he gained for ignoring the noontide dinner-horn altogether.

Now it is agreed by all the distant relatives of Randolph Carter that something occurred to heighten his imagination in his tenth year. His cousin, Ernest B. Aspinwall, Esq., of Chicago, is fully ten years his senior; and distinctly recalls a change in the boy after the autumn of 1883. Randolph had looked on scenes of fantasy that few others can ever have beheld, and stranger still were some of the qualities which he shewed in relation to very mundane things. He seemed, in fine, to have picked up an odd gift of prophecy; and reacted unusually to things which, though at the time without meaning, were later found to justify the singular impressions. In subsequent decades as new inventions, new names, and new events appeared one by one in the book of history, people would now and then recall wonderingly how Carter had years before let fall some careless word of undoubted connection with what was then far in the future. He did not himself understand these words, or know why certain things made him feel certain emotions; but fancied that some unremembered dream must be responsible. It was as early as 1897 that he turned pale when some traveler mentioned the French town of Belloy-en-Santerre, and friends remembered it when he was almost mortally wounded there in 1916, while serving with the Foreign Legion in the Great War.

Carter's relatives talk much of these things because he has lately disappeared. His little old servant Parks, who for years bore patiently with his vagaries, last saw him on the morning he drove off alone in his car with a key he had recently found. Parks had helped him get the key from the old box containing it, and had felt strangely affected by the grotesque carvings on the box, and by some other odd quality he could not name. When Carter left, he had said he was going to visit his old ancestral country around Arkham.

Half way up Elm Mountain, on the way to the ruins of the old Carter place, they found his motor set carefully by the roadside; and in it was a box of fragrant wood with carvings that frightened the countrymen who stumbled on it. The box held only a queer parchment whose characters no linguist or palaeographer has been able to decipher or identify. Rain had long effaced any possible footprints, though Boston investigators had something to say about evidences of disturbances among the fallen timbers of the Carter place. It was, they averred, as though someone had groped about the ruins at no distant period. A common white handkerchief found among forest rocks on the hillside beyond can not be identified as belonging to the missing man.

There is talk of apportioning Randolph Carter's estate among his heirs, but I shall stand firmly against this course because I do not believe he is dead. There are twists of time and space, of vision and reality, which only a dreamer can divine; and from what I know of Carter I think he has merely found a way to traverse these mazes. Whether or not he will ever come back, I cannot say. He wanted the lands of dream he had lost, and yearned for the days of his childhood. Then he found a key, and I somehow believe he was able to use it to strange advantage.

I shall ask him when I see him, for I expect to meet him shortly in a certain dream-city we both used to haunt. It is rumored in Ulthar, beyond the river Skai, that a new king reigns on the opal throne in Ilek-Vad, that fabulous town of turrets atop the hollow cliffs of glass overlooking the twilight sea wherein the bearded and finny Gnorri build their singular labyrinths, and I believe I know how to interpret this rumor. Certainly, I look forward impatiently to the sight of that great silver key, for in its cryptical arabesques there may stand symbolized all the aims and mysteries of a blindly impersonal cosmos.

Robert E. Howard's

12
Thirsty Blades
Otis Adelbert Kline & E. Hoffmann Price
(1930)

Robert E. Howard regularly hunted down copies of *Weird Tales* magazine, usually at a newsstand in Brownwood, whether he had a story in it or not. On occasion, when he liked a particular story, he sent a letter to *Weird Tales* magazine's reader forum, "The Eyrie." Referring to the appearance of "Thirsty Blades" in the February 1930 issue, Howard's wrote to the editor, and his letter was published in the April issue. Howard wrote, "'Thirsty Blades' is fine. It moves like a cavalry charge, with an incessant clashing of steel that stirs the blood. Gigantic shadows from the outer gulfs fall across the actors of the drama, yet the sense of realism is skillfully retained." In a few years, Kline became Howard's literary agent, and E. Hoffmann Price became the only other *Weird Tales* author to ever meet Howard.

The side entrance to the *caravanserai* was closed. Well then, back down the alley, and around the corner to the main gate. But when Rankin turned to retrace his steps, he saw that it might be a long way from there to any other place. For to his right and left were blank walls; at his back, a closed gate; and in front, a crescent of drawn blades was closing in on him.

Behind the six advancing swordsmen rode their commander. He reined in his Barbary stallion, stroked his beard—henna red, as Rankin could see plainly in the white moonlight—and settled back to enjoy the spectacle.

"Click-click-click!" mocked the hammer of Rankin's .45 as it fell on a succession of empty chambers.

The red-bearded chief smiled. And Rankin knew that more than his own carelessness was responsible for the unloading of that revolver. Someone had worked fast and skillfully as Rankin reclined in the *souk* that afternoon, smoking a *narghileh*, sipping bitter Abyssinian coffee, and pondering on how to extricate the lady Azizah from the peril that was descending from the mountains of Kurdistan.

Shoulder to shoulder the assailants advanced. Their steps were deliberate, now that they were certain rather than hopeful that the .45 had not been reloaded. Six lean swordsmen from the desert, grim phantoms whose curved blades gleamed frostily in the moonlight; curved scimitars whose drawing cut shears from shoulder to hip with one swift stroke.

Rankin drew his scimitar, cursed the disguise that had forbidden his favorite saber, and came on guard. The six paused a moment in their advance. *One* of them, they knew, must close with their prey, while the other five hacked him to pieces. And the sentence of that *one* was written; for their victim's frenzy would not be tempered with any hope of escape. *One* of them was even now a dead man...

One ... two ... three paces ...

Rankin dropped his point and laughed.

The line wavered. It takes courage to assault a madman.

A long, fierce lunge, and a deadly swift flicker of steel; and Rankin withdrew from the mêlée, on guard again. That sudden assault from beyond probable striking-distance had caught them off balance; *one* of them was even now a dead man, shorn half asunder.

Then they closed in. Rankin's footwork saved him, and during that instant of grace, his blade again hit deep as he evaded the charge.

"*Mashallah*"! gasped the red-bearded chief as he spurred his horse a pace forward.

There were only four to continue the attack, but their assault would be a reckless whirlwind of steel. No more sidestepping or retreating for Rankin.

"—hacked to pieces in some side street of Tekrit—" flashed through his mind. Ismeddin the Darvish was right.

And then he saw the chief draw his blade.

"Horse and foot! Christ, if I could only get *him*!" prayed Rankin.

Time had ceased. He remembered how very slowly a swift blade approaches when one is in the last extremity. He could parry, cut, retreat, parry again, cut—and then the chief on horse would cut him down. But there was plenty of time...

Then something on the wall behind Rankin cast its shadow over him: attack from the rear.

"They are thorough in Tekrit!" flashed through his mind as the very end of that interminable instant came in an irresistibly flailing mill of blades.

Clack-clack-click! And a silent stroke that bit flesh. Clack-clack—

"Halt!" roared the chief from his Barbary horse.

His upraised blade swept down. In response to his signal, something soft and clinging dropped from the wall and enveloped Rankin. Snared in a net!

The three surviving footmen sheathed their blades, seized Rankin, now firmly enmeshed in the silken net, shouldered him, and followed their chief.

"Well," reflected Rankin, as he resigned himself to captiveity, "if I'm hacked to pieces at all, it probably won't be in a side street... I wonder if Ismeddin foresaw *this*?

"And this only the 11th of Nisan...two more like this, and I'll be in good training for that black swordsman in the vault...

"They expected me—just staring at that girl had nothing to do with it," Rankin assured himself by way of minimizing the folly of having stared too intently into the eyes of the veiled woman who had that afternoon appraised him from the height of her glittering litter.

But Rankin knew that there was a direct connection between the sanguinary combat of a few moments ago, and the exchange of glances between him and the veiled girl whose gorgeously adorned litter had followed the red-bearded dignitary through the *souk*. There was but one conclusion: the girl had called the redbeard's attention to Rankin.

Well, and so be it then! For those were the eyes of Azizah who so often had accompanied Suleiman Baalshem in that haunting, recurring dream that for twenty years had driven Rankin the length and breadth of Asia, and across all the lands of Islam. He was attaining his goal, even if only to meet the thirsty blades whereof Ismeddin had spoken.

The chief of his assailants, then, must be the Shareef, Sayyid Yussuf, the girl's uncle and guardian. In which case, all the better: at least Rankin was not in the hands of the devil-worshipers who had been filtering out of Kurdistan to celebrate their dreadful *sabbat* in that ravine two days' ride from Tekrit . . . and thus and thus Rankin speculated . . . with never a passer-by to intrude on the unreality of it all.

The chief at last drew up before a massive, iron-studded gate that was firmly hinged to the heavy masonry jamb and wall. He thumped the brazen lock-plate with the pommel of his scimitar. The door opened without a challenge from the porter within. The redbeard dismounted and signaled his men-at-arms to release Rankin from his silken web.

At the end of a long, narrow passage, they turned into a courtyard where fountains sprayed mistily in the moonlight. Rankin's captors released their grip on his arms; and one of them presented Rankin's scimitar, hilt foremost.

Rankin accepted the blade and glanced sharply about him. More combat?

The chief smiled. "You are among friends, Saidi Rankin."

"Your playmates didn't look so friendly," retorted Rankin.

"I am Absál, the son of our lord the Shareef," continued the redbeard, "and my six playmates were only to assure me of your identity. There are others on the same mission that leads you to Tekrit. Anyway, before I could signal Silat up there on the wall with his net, three of my men were out of action."

"One should," agreed Rankin, "always be sure of a stranger's identity. But what if they had cut me into many small pieces?"

Absál shrugged. "*Wallah!* That would have been deplorable, of course. But it would have proved to my entire satisfaction that you are not the man for the venture I have in mind. As it is—"

"As it is, saidi," interrupted Rankin, "you think that perhaps I may be fit to meet the Black Presence in the vault on the night of the 14th of Nisan?"

"*Inshallah!*" evaded Absál. "If it please God. And our lord the Shareef has a good deal to say about that."

A gong clanged. The heavy drapes that masked the horseshoe arch in the left wall of the courtyard parted, revealing a long, narrow room at whose farther end was a dais on which sat a white-bearded, hook-nosed man: Absál's father, the Shareef.

They paused in the archway to bow, and offer the peace.

"*Wa'salaam aleikum!*" responded the Shareef. And then, after scrutinizing Rankin with his hard, piercing eyes: "So this is the stout swordsman of the tradition?"

"Even so, father," replied Absál.

The old man twice clapped his hands. There was a rustling behind the curtains at the Shareef's right, and the tinkle of anklets. The curtains parted slightly, and Rankin again looked into the smoldering, Saracenic eyes of the veiled lady of the market-place.

"Is this the man?" queried the Shareef, half turning to catch the eye of the girl in the doorway.

"This is indeed the man, uncle."

"Very well," he acknowledged. And then, to Rankin: "If you are the man, what is your hidden name?"

"Abdemon."

"Again, very well," agreed the Shareef. "Now tell me, Abdemon, how it was that Suleiman Baalshem could not keep his promise to you; and why, through all these dusty centuries, the word of Suleiman has been in the power of Shaitan the Damned."

"A neighboring king," began Rankin, "proposed a riddle that Suleiman could not solve. Therefore he swore by his beard that if I, Abdemon, a captain of his guard, would solve the riddle, he would give me his daughter, who was the granddaughter of the sultan of Egypt. Suleiman, the Lord of the Name, swore by his beard and by his right hand, but he failed to add, '*Inshallah*! If it so please God.' And Allah punished Suleiman for his impiety by giving Iblis, prince of djinn, full power over the promise of Suleiman for a whole day. And during that day of power, Iblis abducted my bride-to-be, so that Suleiman could not keep the oath he had sworn. Yet in the end Allah relented, and granted that after the march of centuries Suleiman would finally be able to keep his promise: provided that Abdemon in one of his incarnations would meet Iblis, sword to sword, and defeat him. And thus, bound by my oath to Suleiman and bound by my love for this girl who was almost mine, I have marched across the centuries, from one failure to another, to meet Iblis, the Dark Presence, in the vault, on the night of the 14th of Nisan: the first full moon of spring.

"In those days they called her Neferte, but now she is called Azizah," continued Rankin. "And on nights of the full moon she lies as one dead; her heartbeat is stopped, and her breath is imperceptible."

"Well said," agreed the Shareef. "Now for the final proof: give me the seal."

"What seal?" countered Rankin.

"The leaden seal from the shattered urn."

Rankin started at this glib mention of the seal his father had given him nearly twenty years ago, and wondered how the Shareef could know of the incident.

"That I can not do," declared Rankin. "It is the leaden impression of the seal of Suleiman Baalshem, who commanded that no hands other than my own should touch it."

The old man nodded and smiled.

"I was aware also of that. So hold it in your own hands that I may examine it."

Rankin produced a small leather bag suspended from a chain passed around his neck. Opening the bag, he took therefrom a small disk of lead, and held it up for the Shareef to examine.

The Shareef and his son bowed low.

"*Bismillahi rahmani raheem!*" they exclaimed. "Praise to God, Lord of the Worlds! It is truly the seal of Suleiman Baalshem."

"But tell me," continued the Shareef, "who told you that you would find your destiny in Tekrit?"

"Ismeddin the Darvish interpreted the dreams which have haunted me since I was a boy, and told me how I could release your brother's daughter from the blackness that clouds her senses on nights of the full moon, when the power of Iblis the Damned is at its height," replied Rankin. The Shareef frowned at the mention of Ismeddin.

"So that old ruffian and heretic sent you to Tekrit? Did he by any chance speak of the dooms that over-take meddlers who roam about here in search of adventure?"

"At great length, *saidi*," responded Rankin, "even as he explained that due to various misunderstandings you two have had regarding some horses, he could scarcely appear in person to present me to you. But I came, nevertheless. Is it not written," quoted Rankin, "*There is no shield to turn aside the spear cast of Destiny: gold, glory, silver, each avail not?*"

"Spoken like a true believer," agreed the Shareef. And then, sharply, "Testify!"

"*La illaha ilia allah—*" began Rankin, and paused.

The sequence was familiar as his own name, but Rankin was not truly a Moslem, and one can not testify falsely when the word of Suleiman and its fulfillment lie in one's hands.

"*Wa Muhammad er-rasul allahi!*" recited the red-bearded chief. "I have testified in his place. And let us consider that this infidel has testified that Muhammad is the prophet of God as well as that there is no God but Allah. For if he can wear the seal of Suleiman Baalshem without harm, it makes little difference what he testifies. For Allah is wise, all-knowing," concluded Sayyid Absál sonorously.

"There is something in what you say," conceded the Shareef. "Still, am I to entrust the welfare of my brother's daughter to the hands of an infidel? And an infidel sent by that bandit of an Ismeddin!"

"But," protested the redbeard, "didn't he prove himself? He is the stout swordsman of the tradition, Abdemon whose skill was the delight of Suleiman, ages ago, and whose sword must give the word of Suleiman its only chance of fulfilment. And he has the seal—"

"Mummeries to fool true believers!" growled the Shareef. "Tonight is but the 11th of Nisan. I will look into this fellow's story, and on the 12th I will either let him carry out his plan, or else—"

The old man nodded significantly at the stalwart African at his left, who was toying with the hilt of a ponderous two-handed sword.

The Shareef clapped his hands. "Show this unbeliever every consideration," he directed, as two slaves approached at his signal. "But on your lives, keep him locked up."

"The swords," thought Rankin, as his escort led him to a cell, "may quench their thirst unless Ismeddin is closer than he seems."

Just before he passed out of ear-shot, he caught the faint tinkle of anklets, but he dared not turn back for even a glance at Azizah, who once had almost been his.

Zantut, servant of Iblis and high priest of the devil-worshipers who had come down from the mountains of Kurdistan, sat in an upper room of the caravanserai just across the street from that selected by Rankin the day before. Two lamps flared ruddily at each side of the Master, casting a flickering light on the parchment scroll he studied. Zantut muttered to himself as he spelled out, line by line, the fine, intricate characters of the manuscript.

At times he would raise his eyes from his work, glance sharply to either side, and at the door of the room, which he was facing. At last he addressed the adept who squatted, cross-legged, in a shadowy corner where he fed grains of sandalwood to a censer that fumed before the silver image of a peacock.

"Humayd, what time is it?"

"Well past midnight, *saidi*. The sentries have been changed three times since sunset."

"And still no report!" muttered Zantut as he stroked his black beard. Then, to Humayd: "Sound recall."

The adept drew from behind the pedestal of the silver peacock a small drum, carefully tuned it, and with knuckles and the heel of his hand beat a curious, broken rhythm. The drum emitted a surprising volume of sound for its size; yet so low-pitched was its hollow chug-chug-thump that it barely disturbed the silence of that late hour.

Scarcely had Humayd set aside the drum when there came at the door a tapping that mimicked the cadence of the recall.

"Enter!" commanded Zantut. And then, recognizing the newcomer, "What luck, Saoud?"

"Less than none, *saidi*. I waited at the entrance of the *caravanserai* across the street until my legs were knotted with cramps. And this"—he flashed from beneath his *djellab* a keen, curved blade—"is all too clean."

Zantut scrutinized him gravely.

"You slept!" snapped the Master.

"Not in that corner of perdition, *saidi*. And I reported while that drum was still warm."

"Granted!" admitted Zantut.

And then came another sequence of taps at the door.

"Enter and report!" commanded Zantut.

"Weariness and waste of time, saidi," announced the latest arrival. "As you ordered, I had a word with the guards posted at the city gates. My purse is somewhat lighter, but to no purpose."

And the purport of each of the succeeding scouts was similar. Rankin had evaded them all. Then, after an interval, came the last scout.

"I saw a man on horse, followed by three on foot, *saidi*," he began. "They carried a burden that might very well have been a man. The horseman halted at the house of the Shareef Yussuf, where he and his followers entered."

"Ah! . . . could it have been the Shareef's son, Absál?"

"It could. He had a red beard, and was very tall and lean."

"Sayyid Absál himself! Then what, Ismail!"

"Someone of the party had been wounded. I followed blood splashes on the paving until I came to a side street close to the *caravanserai* of this madman we are seeking. In a blind street I saw three men lying where they had fallen. They had no further use for the swords they still clutched. But before I could investigate, a party of armed men approached to pick up the dead."

"Then what?" demanded Zantut.

"I gathered from their remarks that an additional corpse would be easily enough handled. And I didn't wish to arouse suspicion by loitering."

"Very good, Ismail," replied Zantut. "It seems that our enemy is in good hands: either dead or imprisoned. That saves us considerable annoyance. Being strangers, we could not handle an assassination as safely or effectively as the son of our Lord the Shareef."

"But why," queried one of the adepts, "should Sayyid Absál have killed or captured this madman, Rankin?"

"Iblis alone can say. Power and praise to Thousand-Eyed Malik Taûs!"

"Praise and power to him!" intoned the assembled adepts in unison as they made with their left hands a curious fleeting gesture.

"It may be," continued Zantut, "that the Shareef or Sayyid Absál doubted that Rankin is indeed the Elect, the reincarnated Abdemon who alone can thwart Iblis on the 14th of Nisan. Which is all the better; for then one of us can very easily approach the Shareef claiming to be the Elect, get possession of the lady Azizah on the pretext of breaking the spell that clouds her senses on nights of the full moon, and then seek the hidden vault. But it is late. Humayd, stand guard while we sleep."

Humayd took his post, scimitar in hand.

Zantut set aside his scrolls and stretched out on his divan. The adepts extinguished the flaring lamps and lay down on the thick rug at the foot of the Master's couch.

"Well," thought Rankin, as he surveyed his cell by the light of the jailer's torch as the barred door clanged shut, "I've been in worse holes than this."

Odors were present, and vermin also; but by no means as plentiful or as unbearable as, for instance, they had been in the dungeons of the Emir's palace in Boukhara. And the air was almost fresh. In the course of a few years of adventure, one at times sleeps on a worse bed than the stone bench that ran along the wall of the cell.

"And Ismeddin," reflected Rankin, "is doubtless on the job. All the worse for Iblis and his friends!"

The very absence of any sign of Ismeddin seemed to Rankin to be certain proof that the wily old darvish was busily at work against the followers of Iblis, who was worshiped in Kurdistan as Malik Taûs, the Lord Peacock. Rankin had heard tales the length and breadth of Kurdistan, telling of the outrageous feats and resourcefulness of that unusual hermit who divided his time between the walls of his cavern and the palaces of princes: that is, when not engaged in the single-handed looting of caravans.

Then, like any seasoned campaigner, Rankin sought and found the soft spots of the stone bench, and stretched out for as much sleep as the night afforded. But that sleep was to have its interruption.

A pebble clicked against the wall at Rankin's side; and then another.

"Ismeddin, by God!" was Rankin's first thought as he raised himself on his elbow and looked up at the tiny, barred window through which filtered the moon's dazzling whiteness.

Then, lest a repetition of the signal attract the attention of the sentry posted somewhere in the hall leading to the door of the cell, Rankin intoned the sonorous first lines of the Sura of the Brightness, as any piously inclined prisoner might do in resigning himself to captivity:

> "*By the noonday brightness, and by the night when it darkeneth!*
> *Thy Lord hath not forsaken thee, neither hath he been displeased.*"

The pebbles ceased.

But the hand thrust in between the bars of the window was certainly not the grimy talon of Ismeddin. The slender white fingers released a scrap of paper that fluttered a moment in the moonlight, then, passing out of the beam, settled to the floor where in the darkness Rankin could just distinguish it.

"*Truly the future shall be better for thee than the Past,*" concluded Rankin. "*And thy Lord shall be gracious, and thou satisfied.*"

The jeweled fingers gestured ever so slightly, paused a moment, and disappeared.

Rankin curbed his impatience and contented himself with staring at the scarcely perceptible blotch that was the note from his unknown friend.

Very faintly from the hall came the snore of the sentry.

"My devoutness was wasted," thought Rankin, as he arose to get the note. "Still, a bit of piety is never out of order."

Rankin struck a match. One sufficed, for the note was brief:

Bismillahi! Neferte to Abdemon, greeting! The darvish, Ismeddin, will spring the bars
of your cell and release you on the night of the 12th of Nissan. Ride and overtake us at the oasis of al Akra.

The night of the twelfth . . . two days of hard riding . . . well, that would not be so bad . . . so let Ismeddin do the worrying for the next few hours . . .

On the evening of the 12th, the porter admitted seven darvishes seeking audience of the Shareef shortly before the sunset prayer.

"Prayer and the Peace upon you, Cousin of the Prophet," saluted Zantut as he bowed low before the white-bearded Shareef. "My companions and I have ridden day and night from the north of Kurdistan in our haste to fulfill an ancient prophecy. It is written—"

Zantut paused and turned to the adept at his left: "Humayd, tell the Cousin of the Prophet, our Lord the Shareef, of your vision."

"Three nights, ago," began Humayd, after receiving the Shareef's permission to speak, "I was sitting in contemplation of holy things, when suddenly a great light appeared in my cave. A tall stranger whose face and garments shone like the noonday sun stood there before me.

"'Rise at once, Abdemon,' he said, 'and with your pious companions seek the house of the Shareef, Sayyid Yussuf—'

"'A thousand pardons,' I replied, 'but I am Humayd, a darvish, and not Abdemon.'

"'You are wrong,' said the glittering stranger; 'not Humayd, but Abdemon, who in a former life were favored by our lord, Suleiman Baalshem, who promised you his daughter, Neferte. But that promise, as you know, Suleiman could not keep, on account of Allah's wrath at his impiety. But Allah, the Merciful, the Compassionate, has relented; and on the 14th of Nisan, the first full moon of spring, you must take Neferte, who in this life is the lady Azizah, the niece of our lord the Shareef, to the Valley of Djinn, and there perform the ritual which will lift the curse from her life. And then Suleiman's promise to you in an earlier life can be fulfilled. Finally, there is a great treasure which Suleiman left awaiting this day; one third of it is yours, and the rest is for the pious Shareef.'

"Then there came an intolerable brightness which blinded me; and when I could again see, the Presence had vanished. I sought my instructor the holy Zantut; and behold, we are here," concluded Humayd.

"So there is also a treasure?" queried the Shareef.

"Even so, saidi. Just as Humayd has said."

"What of the seal?" asked the Shareef.

Humayd drew from a small pouch suspended at his throat a leaden seal.

"The seal of Suleiman Baalshem," admitted the Shareef. "And then, Ishtitad!" he commanded. "Testify!"

"*La illaha illa allah*," intoned Humayd. "*Wa Muhammad er-rasul allahi.*"

"At least we have a true believer this time," reflected the Shareef. Then, to his son: "Was I not right in imprisoning the infidel you brought before me?"

"Not entirely," protested Sayyid Absál. "The *kaffir* is a great swordsman, even as the prophecy said. And one of these men is a liar, for one of the leaden seals must be false."

"My lord," interposed Zantut, "is it not more likely that a true believer should have the seal of Suleiman Baalshem than an unbeliever?"

"That goes without saying," agreed the Shareef.

"But," protested Sayyid Absál, "who are we to know what is acceptable to Allah, and to whom he would entrust the seal of Suleiman? Is this fellow Humayd a fighting man? Let him meet my six best retainers in a side street," challenged Sayyid Absál, "and if he can prove himself in that way, I will agree."

"Son," reproved the Shareef, "it seems to me that you have no more to agree than to disagree."

"Well," retorted Sayyid Absál, "and has this pious Zantut by any chance dazzled you with his tale of great treasure? The tradition speaks of the promise of Suleiman, and the health of our cousin, Azizah, and not of chests of treasure."

"My lord," interrupted Zantut, "is it not also possible that this infidel impostor said nothing about the treasure so that he could keep it all for himself?"

"Even so," assented the Shareef.

"Now by Allah and by my beard!" thundered Sayyid Absál. "The issue is evaded! What of the stout swordsman of the tradition?"

"Humayd," replied Zantut, "is a great swordsman, even if he has not distinguished himself in street brawling in Tekrit."

"Then if he is such a swordsman, let him meet this *kaffir* in single combat, and may Allah judge between them!" demanded Sayyid Absál.

"That," conceded the Shareef, "would be fair."

Humayd's confusion did not escape Sayyid Absál. But the triumph was fleeting.

"My lord," protested Zantut, "need we put a revelation from Allah to the trial of combat? Would that be an auspicious beginning, making the favored of Allah prove himself against an infidel?"

"Assuredly not," agreed the Shareef.

"Allah, and again, by Allah!" stormed Sayyid Absál. "My uncle's daughter identified this unbeliever as the stout swordsman of her visions. Let her at least identify this holy darvish."

"That also would be well," admitted Zantut. "But my lord knows as well as I do what value to set on the fancy of a woman. She saw him sitting in the *souk*, smoking, and he pleased her. Is that to be taken against the revelations of an angel to a devout and holy man?"

Zantut paused, stroked his beard, and continued: "Cousin of the Prophet, I am a peacemaker. I would not for the very treasure of Suleiman cause contention between you and your son. My disciple may have been deceived; or what he saw might have been a snare of Iblis. And lest injustice be done, let this *kaffir* accompany us; and if Humayd fails in the ritual, then let the *kaffir* prove himself. Thus we will have twice the chance of dissolving the curse that clouds the life of your brother's daughter."

"Done, by Allah and by my beard!" exclaimed the Shareef. "Wise and holy man, none but Suleiman himself has equal wisdom."

The Shareef twice clapped his hands.

"Fresh camels for Zantut and his followers," he commanded. "A litter for the lady Azizah. Then get the infidel swordsman, well bound, and put him in a litter."

With a lordly gesture, the Shareef dismissed Zantut and his companions.

An hour after sunset, ten swift *meharis* filed past the sentries at the Isfayan Gate. Two of them bore between them a richly adorned *takht rawan*; and a third carried a litter of ordinary design. The other seven camels were ridden by the darvishes who but a short while before had been dismissed by the Shareef.

A one-eyed hunch-backed beggar squatted at the gate, whining to Allah and all passers-by for alms.

"The Lord will provide," growled Zantut from the height of his *mehari*.

"Son of a flat-nosed mother," muttered the beggar as he adjusted the patch over his right eye, "you would be amazed if you knew what the Lord will provide for you!"

He stroked his long beard, and grinned evilly.

"Alms, in the name of Allah, alms!" he whined, the stout savagery of his expression changing swiftly to one more in keeping with his position as he noted the approach of a tall slave in a striped *kaftán*.

The slave tossed him a coin, glanced quickly about him, then stooped and muttered in the mendicant's ear.

"What's this?" demanded the beggar. "Released? How, and by whom?"

"My lord the Shareef ordered it. Both the infidel and the lady Azizah left just a short while ago."

"Left?"

"Yes. With the darvish Zantut and his pious companions."

"Father of seven hundred pigs!" stormed the beggar. "Son of calamity! Where is the Shareef?"

"In his reception hall, *saidi*," replied the slave respectfully.

"Alms, for the love of Allah!" whined the beggar for the benefit of a passer-by. And then to the slave, in an undertone: "Very well, Musa. I shall remember this."

And with a surprisingly jaunty gait, the hunchback strode down the main street of Tekrit, and then, turning down a side alley, bore directly toward the great house of the Shareef. But instead of waiting to be announced, the beggar thrust the porter aside, stalked down the hall, across the courtyard, and into the Shareef's presence.

"Old man," demanded the Shareef, "who admitted you?"

"I admitted myself, *saidi*," replied the beggar. "And as soon as your men withdraw," he continued, indicating the porter and two slaves who were advancing to seize him, "I will say more."

The Shareef gasped, turned the color of an old saddle; then, meeting for a moment the grimy wanderer's fierce eye, relented. The man was obviously mad, reflected the Shareef; some saint or holy man whose wits were in Allah's keeping.

"I will see him, Kasim," he said, dismissing with a gesture the astonished porter and his companions.

"Now, old man, what is it?"

"Prayer, and the Peace, Cousin of the Prophet!" began the hunchback, "I have come to make a wager."

"And what would you wager, holy man?"

The Shareef was now quite convinced, from the intruder's wild manner, unkempt beard, and one glittering eye, that this was indeed a wandering saint.

"My head against your two best horses, saidi. Have them saddled, saidi, and when we are well beyond the city walls, I will propose the wager."

"By Allah," muttered the Shareef, "but he is mad!"

"My lord," resumed the beggar, "I am unarmed, and an old man. I repeat my wager: my head against two good horses."

"So be it," agreed the Shareef, as he clapped his hands. "Horses and arms at once, Kasim!"

"Allah upon you, my lord, but you wish to win this very good head of mine?"

"Holy stranger," replied the Shareef, "leave your prayer with this house; and if you lose your wager, you may keep your head."

"Of what use are my prayers, *saidi*, seeing that the servant of Satan the Damned this very day beguiled you? Where is the daughter of your brother, on whom be peace?"

"On the way to the Valley of Djinn, with Zantut the darvish and his pious companions."

"And what of the infidel, Rankin?" next demanded the beggar.

"The *kaffir* rides with them. But who are you, reverend saint?" wondered the Shareef; for there was something strangely familiar about this madman.

"I am as much a saint as Zantut is a darvish. It is you who are stark mad, and not I," declared the beggar.

"Even so," agreed the Shareef. "But what do you mean?"

"Wait until we are well without the city walls, and in the desert which has seen all things. Wait until we have seen what we are to see—"

Kasim entered and bowed to the Shareef.

"In readiness, *saidi*," he announced.

The beggar followed the Shareef to the main entrance, where a groom with two mares, saddled and richly caparisoned, awaited them.

"*Wallah!*" ejaculated the beggar, "but my lord wagers heavily against one cracked head. Each a Saklawiyah-Jidraniyah—"

He bowed low as he pronounced the race and strain of the matchless beasts; and then, "To horse, *saidi!*"

"You are strangely familiar with noble horses," observed the Shareef.

The grimy hunchback smiled crookedly.

"To the Isfayan Gate, *saidi*," he suggested, as the Shareef took the lead.

At the gate the sentries challenged them, but recognizing Sayyid Yussuf, permitted them to pass.

The beggar muttered a few words to the sentry.

"I have kept it safely, *saidi*," replied the sentry, as he unbuckled from his waist a belt and scimitar which he handed the beggar.

"I ride unarmed. Sayyid Yussuf, be kind enough to carry my sword."

"Allah, and again, by Allah!" marveled the Shareef as he accepted the blade, and noted the sentry's respectful address. "Saint or beggar, or both...but who are you, old man?"

"You would be amazed, my lord," was the evasive reply. "Ride on yet a way. Let me lead."

This time the Shareef followed in the wanderer's trace. And as he rode, he fingered the hilt of the beggar's scimitar, and wondered at the cool, unblinking sapphires that adorned the pommel, and the cunning workmanship of the embroidered belt.

"Let us halt here, *saidi*," requested the beggar after half an hour's brisk ride.

They dismounted beside a low, half-crumbled, white-washed cupola that loomed spectrally in the moonlight: the ruined tomb of a forgotten saint. They made their salaam to the unknown occupant of the holy place.

"For a beggar," began the Shareef, "you are armed like a prince. And I wonder whether you are mad as you pretend to be."

"And for a cousin of the Prophet," replied the beggar, "I wonder if you are as wise as you ought to be."

The moon was masked by a thin wisp of cloud. A cool, chilling breeze crept across the desert.

"Kneel here, three paces before me, *saidi*," murmured the beggar. "Kneel facing me, with this ghost of a wind at your left . . . and let this ghost of a moon bear witness to the truth that lies hidden in these sands . . . Let it bear witness to my wager: my head against those two *asil* mares . . . With my own sword strike off my head, *saidi*," crooned the beggar, "if what you see be not the truth as Allah, the Merciful, the Compassionate, sees it . . . and the truth, my lord, is that Iblis the Damned has beguiled you . . .

"Look, *saidi*," chanted the beggar, as he gathered handfuls of sand and let it trickle between his fingers. "Look at this sand which is the dust of unremembered kings and the dust of forgotten slaves . . . look at this sand over which kings and slaves have marched, endless procession, ages without end . . ."

The beggar's gesture of scooping sand lengthened until his hands swept in an arc from the ground to the full extent of his arm. The cool breeze caught the fine dust, blowing it into little clouds that whisked and whirled uncannily.

"And that moon, *saidi*, that pale moon who hides her face behind a veil, *saidi* . . . let her bear witness, for she has seen all things and knows all things . . ."

As the beggar chanted, the breeze centered in a vortex between him and the Shareef.

"Look closely, *saidi* . . . these sands bear witness, and this dust bears witness...and this moon also, who knows all things . . ."

Faster and yet faster the old man flung sand before him; yet slower and still more slowly he chanted in murmuring monotone, like the maddening pulse of a necromancer's drum.

Sayyid Yussuf stared fixedly into the veil of ever moving, ever present, living dust . . . for the dust lived, and danced in tiny figures before him . . . He shuddered . . .

"And now you see that which there is to see," chanted the beggar. "Now you see the peril into which you sent Azizah . . . they file into the black pit of the Lord of the Black Hands . . . and Abdemon whom you denied is bound, and can not save her . . . it is written in this dust, saidi . . . it is written on these sands . . . and this moon bears witness, this moon who knows all that is to be . . . for that which is to be is one with that which has been, O cousin of the Prophet . . ."

The beggar abruptly ceased chanting, and clapped his hands sharply.

"*Wallah!*" gasped the Shareef, blinking. "By my beard!"

He trembled violently at that which had left the beggar's swiftly weaving hands to dance in the tiny whirlwinds before him.

"That sign with the left hand, old man—"

"Just as I said. But it has not yet happened—"

"Not yet?"

The Shareef vaulted to the saddle.

"No. But wait a moment. We have time. Your horses are fast."

The beggar drew from somewhere in the ragged folds of his dirty *djellab* a slender tube the length of his forearm.

"Strike light, *saidi!*" he commanded.

The Shareef fumbled with flint and steel.

"The fire of your pistol will do!" snapped the beggar. The Shareef fired. Then the sputtering of a fuse, and a shower of sparks, and three red stars hung high above them, flamed ruddily for half a minute, and vanished.

"The *Feringhi* troops used them to signal," explained the beggar. "I stole a box of them at Beirut."

"Ah!" And the Shareef frowned. "Old man, whom are you signaling? On your head—"

He leveled his pistol.

"Peace upon you, my lord," grinned the beggar. "I am signaling a detachment of the guard to follow us as fast as their horses can travel."

"*You*, signal the guard? Now, by Allah, but this is too much! Who are you?" demanded the Shareef.

The beggar readjusted his turban; reached with his right hand into his *djellab* and over his left shoulder, dragging forth a large leather pouch; jerked, the patch from his right eye; stretched himself, clutching skyward with his grimy talons;

and then stood before the astonished Shareef, straight as a lance, fierce-eyed as a bird of prey.

"I am Ismeddin! Whose head you swore you would have. As it is, I keep my head, and, *inshallah*, those two *asil* mares," exulted the darvish.

"By Allah and by Abaddon!" gasped Sayyid Yussuf. "Old thief, you dared venture into Tekrit at the risk of your head?"

"Even so, my lord. For the promise of Suleiman has waited all these centuries for fulfilment. And the infidel Rankin, who was once Abdemon, could not have accomplished his mission single-handed. But now, to horse! Those sons of Iblis the Damned are mounted on your swiftest *meharis*."

The Shareef snorted.

"Follow me!"

Their mounts stretched out in an extended gallop.

"*Wallah!*" exulted Ismeddin, as he drew up beside the Shareef's mare. "She flies! And to think that I overlooked her when I raided your camp at Deir el Zor . . . had your men but snored a moment longer . . . but give me my sword, *saidi* . . . we have hot work ahead of us . . ."

Ismeddin leaned forward in the saddle, caught the scimitar the Shareef tossed him, and buckled the belt about his waist.

Biban ul Djinni they called that desolate, narrow valley: the Valley of the Djinn. But these bearded strangers out of northern Kurdistan eagerly sought that avoided citadel where their dark monarch sat dreaming of ancient days before Suleiman learned the Word of Power; for this was the eve of the 14th of Nisan, when they could make secure for their lord forever after the triumph of that one day wherein he held absolute power over the word of Suleiman.

Ten *meharis* filed down an avenue dimly outlined by the stumps of shattered columns. They picked their way slowly, for the full moon had not yet risen to illuminate the desolation. Finally, at the end of the avenue, they halted. The seven *soi-*

disant darvishes dismounted and gathered about the kneeling *meharis* that bore the rich *tahkt rawan*. Zantut parted the curtains and by the light of a torch looked in.

"As I expected," he announced, "she is in a trance. Ibrahaim, stand guard," he commanded. "And keep an eye on the infidel, Rankin. The rest of you, follow me."

Zantut, followed by his adepts, turned toward the black-tiled circular court at the extremity of the avenue up which they had ridden.

"Look, master! There it is, just as it was written!" exclaimed one of the adepts as he pointed out to Zantut a copper image that gleamed dully on its basalt pedestal.

"There is where Iblis sits dreaming of those broad, rich days before Suleiman—may wild hogs defile his grave!—learned the Word of Power. Stand by, brethren!" commanded Zantut.

They formed in a crescent before the image.

Zantut advanced, bearing in each hand a torch which he planted at either side of the image. Then, taking from his belt a small copper mallet, he tapped the image in various spots, each tap sounding a different note; and as he tapped, he listened carefully. Over and over he tapped, here and there; then finally announced, "The third arm; the second hand; the fourth head."

Three stepped forward, each grasping one of the members named by Zantut.

"Ready?" demanded Zantut.

"Ready, master," they replied.

"Now!" exclaimed the master.

And as each adept twisted the member he grasped, the copper image, pedestal and all, swung noiselessly aside.

"Follow me!" directed Zantut.

The dark-robed devotees of Iblis, torch in hand, filed after the master, stepping in unison down the smooth, black stairs.

"The Sura of the Darkness!" commanded Zantut. "One . . . Two . . . Three!"

In deep, resonant tones they chanted as they advanced into the abysmal blacknesses of the vault, swaying their torches in cadence:

"Lord of many brazen hells,
Lord of the Painted Fan,
Prince of the Outer Marches,
Prince of the Borderland,
Iblis, 'tis Thee that we adore,
Just and logical God!"

Flight after flight they marched, chanting as they descended into the depths, until finally, arriving at the foot of the winding stairs, they halted at the entrance of a great hall whose floor was paved with tiles of lapis lazuli.

The master halted and lifted his left arm. His followers ceased chanting and, following Zantut's example, removed their shoes before entering the sanctuary of Iblis.

"Lord and Master," intoned Zantut as he made a swift gesture with his left hand, "we Thy faithful servants bring Thee reverence and worship."

Then, with heads bowed and arms crossed, Zantut and his followers advanced across the blue tiles toward the Presence that sat cross-legged on a lofty dais at the farther end of the hall. When within five paces of the dais, all except Zantut halted, and kneeling, formed a semicircle.

Zantut advanced to the first step, knelt, and carefully scrutinized the approach to the high place. With his finger tips he caressed the polished stones.

"The holy place has not been defiled," he announced. "The dust of the weary centuries has not been disturbed. The Master sits dreaming of the Night of Power; and his sleep has not been broken."

Then, raising his head and lifting up his arms, Zantut gazed full at the Presence. "Hail, Iblis, Lord of the Outer

Darkness, Malik Taûs, Prince of the Painted Fan!" he saluted, and bowed his head once more to the paving.

"Servants of Iblis," he announced, "you may lift up your eyes and gaze at your Prince."

They contemplated their Prince, stared in wonder at the onyx blackness of his lean, aquiline features: the predatory nose and hard mouth of one whose iron soul has experienced everything save submission. But the eyes were sightless and blank.

"He breathes," murmured an adept.

"That is but the final trace of life the conqueror could not quite extinguish," explained Zantut. "And it is that trace which we must fan into full flame tonight. At each former meeting, Abdemon has failed; and this is his last chance. And we know best what this last chance is worth!

"Talaat! Saoud! Ismail! Go up and get the girl, and Abdemon also. And tell Ibrahaim that when the comrades from Azerbaijan arrive, they are to descend at once. The hour is close at hand."

"Harkening and obedience, *saidi*," replied Talaat, bowing first to the Dark Presence on the throne, and then to Zantut.

From the dim shadows of the hall, Zantut and the two remaining adepts dragged forth a great block of chiseled porphyry, which they slid readily enough across the polished tiles to a position exactly in front of the throne. Zantut then plucked from five of the tiles the pentagonal silver plates with which they were inlaid, uncovering orifices that led to unplumbed depths beneath that subterranean hall. An adept, standing by, presented with ceremonious gestures a small glazed flask which Zantut with gestures equally formal accepted. As he un-stoppered the flask, acrid, resinous, violet-colored fumes rose from its mouth. The adepts knelt as Zantut paced about the ominous block of porphyry, pausing at each of the five holes in the floor to pour into the depths a portion of the fuming contents of the flask.

Then a faint humming was heard, which in a few moments became a steady throbbing as of a slowly beaten drum: and tall, slender threads of violet flame rose from the openings in the floor.

At Zantut's signal, the torches were extinguished.

"They are here, Master," whispered the adept at the right of the altar.

Zantut turned to face the entrance of the hall.

The acolytes were bringing in the veiled Azizah, and Rankin, securely bound.

"Lay them on the altar," commanded Zantut.

The deep resonance of a brazen gong rang down the succession of winding stairways, and rolled and thundered in the vaulted holy of holies.

"The hour is at hand," proclaimed Zantut solemnly. And then, to those who had carried Azizah and Rankin into the sanctuary: "The brethren from Azerbaijan are late. Did you see any signs of them?"

"Yes, *saidi*. And Ibrahaim up there is watching the star of our Lord very closely so as to withhold the final signal until the very last moment. He will strike two warning taps. And then the third, to let you know that the moment has arrived. But they heard the first stroke, and are riding hard to get here in time."

"Very good," acknowledged Zantut, as he stripped from Azizah the silken gauze that enfolded her. "This time our Lord will not be bothered with bungling swordsmen... Unbeliever, would it not have been better to have stayed in *Feringhistan* where you belong?"

To which Rankin, bound and gagged, could reply with neither word nor gesture.

"Ismeddin," thought Rankin, as he saw an acolyte kneel at Zantut's feet and present a long knife and a whetstone, "for once was wrong . . . That butcher's tool is no thirsty sword . . ."

Again the solemn, brazen resonance of the gong rolled and surged through the vaulted sanctuary.

"Number two," reflected Rankin. "Thank God she's unconscious..."

As the note of the gong died, there came from above the clank of arms and the tinkle of accouterments, and the measured tread of feet descending the winding stairways.

"Ismeddin and the guard!" exulted Rankin.

And then he heard the measured cadence of voices chanting in an unknown tongue.

"The brethren from Azerbaijan!" shouted the assembled adepts.

And Zantut, with statuesquely formal gestures, stroked the blade of his long knife against the whetstone, with each steely caress pausing to intone a sentence in a language that was forgotten when the last stone of that sanctuary of devil-worship was laid and awfully cemented into place.

The brethren from Azerbaijan, still chanting, were filing into the hall, and grouping themselves in a crescent about the sacrificial stone.

Through the coolness of the desert's windswept night and through the sultry flame of its day rode Ismeddin and the Shareef, with but an occasional rest to share with their horses a handful of parched corn. But as the sun set on the eve of the 14th of Nisan, Ismeddin reined in the *asil* mare.

"Slowly, uncle. We must let those sons of confusion get into their underground rendezvous with Satan. They are eight...eight at least—"

"And doubtless, Hajj Ismeddin," laughed' the Shareef, "you are an old man—"

"Praise be to Allah," agreed the darvish, "my days have been many—"

"And pious also," scoffed the Shareef. "But what is your plan, *Haaji*?"

"The sentry at the entrance must be silenced without disturbance. As for the rest . . . six or seven to one is not so bad . . . *Inshallah*! but I have a surprise for them. Hot fires for Satan's wings, *saidi*!

"To our left front, an hour's easy ride from here, is Biban ul Djinni, in which the home of Malik Taûs is buried," continued Ismeddin as he scanned the horizon.

Dusk came swiftly on the heels of sunset. The Shareef followed the dirty white blotch that was Ismeddin's *djellab,* and wondered what strange device the darvish had in mind. For while Ismeddin had signaled the captain of the guard, he had not given him a chance, even with the hardest riding, to overtake them. The encounter would surely be against odds.

From afar they heard the sonorous clang of a gong. The lower edge of the first full moon of spring had just cleared the horizon. Filing down Biban ul Djinni was a caravan of camels and horses, bearing at a steady gait toward a duster of shattered columns whose stumps towered skyward. As the light of the rising moon grew stronger, they could pick out the figure of a warder on guard in the center of a circular courtyard.

"Worse and worse yet!" exclaimed Ismeddin, as the Shareef drew up beside him. "Though I more than half expected as much. About forty of those sons of Satan . . . You and I might have taken those seven by surprise—"

"Well, why not wait for the guard, *Haaji*?" demanded the Shareef.

"Too late!" snapped Ismeddin. "You heard that gong? A warning signal. That caravan arrived just in time for the sacrifice. You and I must stop it."

"*Wallah*! But the odds are great . . . Still—"

The Shareef drew his scimitar.

"After my own heart, *saidi*!" exclaimed the darvish.

"But rash. Let them first get under ground—"

"But how about the sentry?" demanded the Shareef. "He'll give the alarm."

"On the contrary, uncle. Look!"

Ismeddin produced from his capacious wallet a small, glittering object: the effigy of a peacock carved of silver.

"Malik Taûs! The damnation of Allah upon him!" exclaimed the Shareef as he recognized the symbol of the devil-worshipers.

"Follow me!" commanded Ismeddin, as he spurred his weary horse flown the steep side of the valley.

They rode boldly now, making no attempt at concealment. The warder standing watch in the center of the ruined courtyard was taking an observation with his astrolabe, following the course of a star that flamed bloodily overhead. Then he set aside his instrument and smote a brazen gong whose golden sheen they could plainly see in the white moonlight. The solemn, vibrant note rolled dreadfully across the valley. The tall figure of doom once more turned his astrolabe on the star whose altitude he was reading.

Ismeddin leaned forward in the saddle, chirping and muttering to his exhausted beast.

"Allah, what a horseman!" gasped the Shareef as he saw the *asil* mare, true to her breeding, stretch out again at a full gallop.

They clattered up the broad avenue, clearing fragments of monstrous columns at a bound, Ismeddin shouting in a language unknown to the Shareef.

The warder started, and turned to face them.

"Hurry, *saidi*! The moment is almost here." And then: "The sign and the symbol!"

Ismeddin extended the silver image of the peacock, and in response to the warder's muttered formula, replied in that same obscure tongue.

The warder bowed, gestured toward the cavernous entrance to the vault, and turned to resume his observations . .

The Shareef's blade flickered in the moonlight.

Ismeddin seized one of the torches that flared smokily at each side of the copper image, and plunged into the depths, three steps at a time.

"Snick-snick-snick!" whispered the slender knife as Zantut continued the ceremonial whetting.

"Christ on the mountain tops!" despaired Rankin. "Sharpen that knife and be done with it!"

Rankin sighed, and relaxed as the diabolical whisper of steel against stone ceased, and Zantut, pacing about the altar, passed his hands and knife through each of the five streamers of violet flame. The Dark Prince would this time be victorious without even stepping from his throne. And this was the last chance . . .

From the depths came the ever-increasing volume of a beaten drum.

"Abaddon in the darkness beats his black drum triumphantly!" intoned Zantut. And then he uttered a word of command, at which the assembled devil-worshipers knelt about the altar.

Zantut, knife in hand, stepped forward.

"Malik Taûs, Lord and Master, accept the sacrifice that Thy servants offer!" he intoned, timing his words so that the last syllable would be coincident with the final stroke of the gong. "Malik Taûs, the Night of Power is at hand. Malik Taûs, the broad moon rises—"

"Halt!" commanded a voice that rang like sword against sword.

Zantut whirled about, knife in hand.

The adepts leaped to their feet.

Ismeddin, sword in one hand, torch in the other, stood in the entrance. Following him came the Shareef.

"Holy darvish! Oh, son of many pigs!" roared the Shareef, and opened fire with his pistol. But the old man's rage was too much for his aim.

"Steady, uncle!" snapped Ismeddin. "You'll hit the girl!"

Zantut and his followers charged, swords drawn.

Ismeddin dashed his blade to the floor, drew from his *djellab* a slim tube the length of his forearm, and touched it with his torch.

The fuse sputtered . . . and then a cascade of sparks and flame.

"There is neither might nor majesty save in Allah, the Merciful, the Compassionate!" thundered Ismeddin. "Out, sons of calamity!"

And as he sprayed the devil-worshipers with his torrent of flame, he side-stepped to his right, flanking the howling, smoking, milling company of adepts, driving them toward the entrance of the vault.

The devil-worshipers bolted, Zantut leading.

The Shareef opened fire with his pistol. Ismeddin tossed aside the dead signal rocket and retrieved his blade.

"*Allah Akbar!*" roared the Shareef as he dropped his emptied pistol, drew his sword, and carved his way into the fugitives, cutting them down as they fought their way up the stairs.

Above the confusion and uproar of the slaughter, Ismeddin heard the clank of arms and the clatter of hoofs in the courtyard, far above them.

"If that's the guard," observed Ismeddin, as he paused to wipe on his *djellab* the blood-drenched grip of his scimitar, "all is well. But if it's reinforcements for these sons of flat-nosed mothers, they'll regain their wits . . . Drive hard, uncle!"

And the two graybeards resumed the pursuit, slashing and hacking as they took the steps three at a leap.

"*Bismillah!*" exclaimed the Shareef, as he paused for breath. And then, listening to the increasing uproar from the courtyard: "Mamoun and the guard are at it!"

"*Wallah!* But he made good time," agreed Ismeddin. "Do you blame me for stealing a few horses like those, Cousin of the Prophet?"

"Not after a night like this," panted the Shareef.

"And now," resumed Ismeddin, "let us attend to our work downstairs. Much is to be done, and there is little time."

They retraced their steps, picking their way among the devil-worshipers that lay on the slippery stairs.

"Seven . . . eight," counted Ismeddin as he led the way, "nine . . . of a disease, how did I miss you?"

The old man's blade drove home.

"Nine . . . ten . . . eleven," continued the darvish. "And now, when we release Saidi Rankin, we will see some fighting. The Father of Lies must step from his black throne and meet Abdemon, sword to sword. And if Abdemon defeats him, the promise of Suleiman will at last be kept."

"But he is a *kaffir!*" protested the Shareef. "And my brother's daughter—"

"Be that as it may. If Saidi Rankin wins, it will only be because it so pleases Allah. Would you rather leave her spirit in the hands of Shaitan the Damned? Give me a hand, here," directed Ismeddin, as they halted at the black altar on which the prisoners lay bound.

Together they pushed the massive block a dozen paces from the throne, then cut the cords that bound Rankin, and removed from between his teeth the piece of wood with which he had been gagged.

"Ismeddin!" gasped Rankin as he stretched his numbed limbs. "How much of this did you foresee?"

"All of it, *saidi*," smiled the darvish. "Except the final outcome. And that, *inshallah*, depends on your sword."

Rankin leaped to the tiled floor and flexed his cramped legs. He stared in wonder at the unveiled features of Azizah. "Allah, and again, by Allah! Neferte . . . after all these centuries . . . Then give me a sword!"

"Presently, my lord, presently." And then, to the Shareef: "*Kaffir* or true believer, she is his . . . for even Satan's fortune can not last forever."

Whereupon Ismeddin with a piece of chalk traced on the floor a circle some ten paces in diameter; and at three of the four cardinal points of the compass he inscribed a curious symbol, and several characters in the ancient Kufic script. Then from his knapsack he took a small box whose contents, a fine, reddish powder, he poured evenly in a circle that inclosed the first circle drawn in chalk, except for a yard-long gap precisely in front of the dark stranger's throne.

"Saidi Rankin—Abdemon, as tonight you are—take your post," commanded the darvish. "Just a pace from the inner circumference, and facing that dark mocker on his lofty throne. Will you use my sword, or that of our lord, the Shareef?"

"Yours will bring me luck, Haaj Ismeddin," replied Rankin. "Though all swords are alike tonight," he concluded, as with a final glance at the sleeping loveliness on the porphyry block, he turned to belt Ismeddin's scimitar to his waist.

"No scabbards tonight," directed the darvish. "Take only the blade."

As Rankin took his post, Ismeddin advanced to the foot of the dais. Extending his arms, Ismeddin began his invocation:

"Father of Mockeries, Master of Deceptions," he intoned, "the dusty centuries are weary of your dominion. The word of Suleiman seeks its fulfilment, and the servant of Suleiman awaits your awakening. Dark Prince, Black Lord, the circle of your destiny has been drawn, and a doom awaits you with a sword."

The darvish advanced a step of the ascent to the dais.

"I know your hidden name, and I can speak it to your ruin," continued the darvish; and thus, step by step, he ascended. But on the last step, instead of speaking aloud, he leaned forward and whispered in the ear of the Dark Prince.

"Harkening and obedience," growled the Presence. And like a doom that marches down the corridors of the world, he strode down the steps of his dais and entered the circle, facing Rankin.

As he crossed the inner circumference, Ismeddin drew at the fourth cardinal point characters and symbols resembling those at the other three; and with a remnant of the red powder, he completed the outer circle. And all the while the Dark Presence stared at Rankin and beyond him cool and unconcerned, scorning even to smile his scorn.

Ismeddin then struck light to the circle of powder. A tall, unwavering green flame crept along the circumference, until Rankin and his opponent were enclosed in a waist-high wall of fire: and this incredible flame emitted an overpowering sweetness that made Rankin's senses reel.

He saw nebulous forms gathering behind the Dark Prince, and crowding against the wall of flame. They muttered to each other, and with their left hands made curious signs. Then, from a great distance, Rankin heard the thump-thump of a drum, and the solemn voice of Ismeddin:

"Abdemon, friend of Suleiman; and you, Iblis, bound to human form, stand in this circle which is neither earth nor high heaven, nor the house of everlasting fire: and this circle but one of you may leave."

A pause; and then Ismeddin's command: "Strike!"

The drum resumed its savage muttering; and the opponents, swords advanced, circled warily, each seeking an opening in the other's guard. Then swift as thought came a relentless whirlwind of steel that bore Rankin back, step by step. The green flames singed his kaftan. Rankin halted, flat-footed, parrying and returning, cut for cut. And from without the circle of quivering, leaping flame the little drum muttered fiercely the song of doom which old Ismeddin's knuckles and finger tips coaxed from its head of serpent hide.

"In four lives you have failed!" taunted the Dark Prince as he paused in his attack, and relaxed, point lowered.

Rankin's blade wavered—groped—then sheared swiftly down and back in a drawing cut to the adversary's forearm.

"You improve with practice!" mocked the Dark Prince as Rankin's blade cut only the poison sweetness of the heavy air. "If you only had another life—"

Then he fell back before Rankin's renewed attack.

Clack-clack-click! Blade against blade, whirling, circling, yielding a step, gaining a step, traversing, dodging: parry, return, and cut again—an endless, deadly mill. The Dark Prince ceased smiling, and his breath came too fast for mockery. But Rankin's tough arm ached to the very shoulder from the merciless, biting assault of steel upon steel. And his head whirled from the everlasting mutter of the snakeskin drum...

The figures crowding against the wall of green flame became more distinct. Their mumbled words became more plain. At times Rankin caught a word, and was glad that he could not understand all...

Steel against steel... strength against strength... but ages of cunning against the wits of one short life: for only the body of that terrific adversary was human.

The tall flames were diminishing. With them would perish the last chance. Those who had crossed the Border to aid their Prince crowded against the barrier that would soon give way. Rankin wondered if Suleiman's shadowy presence was behind him; but he dared not glance back for even an instant.

The Dark Prince stood fast in the center of the circle, secure in his faultless defense. Rankin knew that when he had exhausted himself against that flashing barrier of steel, the enemy would resume his deadly assault. Six to one in a side street... that was easy... but this thirsty blade would soon drink deep . . . Rankin's arm was numb, and his parry against those biting swift returns was ragged. Just one slip—and that would be any moment now . . .

The enemy's eye shifted ever so slightly. He measured the height of the diminishing green flame, and smiled again.

Then Rankin cut to the head. The adversary parried, and the hungry blade flamed swiftly in return—

Rankin could not parry. But stretched out in a full lunge, he passed beneath the shearing steel, and drove home with his point—

The green flame flickered and died.

Rankin, still clutching his blade, lurched forward on his face as the Dark Prince crumpled in a heap on the tiles. But before the blackness descended, Rankin caught a glimpse of the shadowy figure of a bearded king who bowed and extended his arm in salutation. And this time the smiling loveliness of the girl at his side was not obscured by any veil . . .

A strong hand gripped Rankin's shoulder, pulled him back to his knees, and lifted him to his feet.

"*Wallah!*" marveled the Shareef. "*Kaffir* or not, he is the father of all swordsmen! I knew that his
head would be clipped off. And then he stretched out and impaled that son of confusion . . . Look! That stroke sheared off a bit of his turban. Allah, and again, by Allah!"

"Then give him his prize, *saidi*," replied Ismeddin. And to Azizah, who sat upright and wondering on the polished black sacrificial stone: "You need no veil, *ya bint!* After all these dusty centuries, you are his."

Ismeddin turned to the Shareef: "As for me, *saidi*, I will be content with but one of those *asil* mares you wagered against my cracked head."

"So be it," laughed the Shareef, as he led the way up the blood-drenched stairs. "Though doubtless you will steal the other in due course!"

Robert E. Howard's

13
The Rats in the Walls
H. P. Lovecraft
(1930)

This is the story that commenced the famous correspondence between Robert E. Howard and H.P. Lovecraft. First published in *Weird Tales* in March of 1924 and reprinted in the June 1930 issue of the magazine, it is the latter that Howard read and for which, after finishing, he wrote a letter to editor Farnsworth Wright inquiring about Lovecraft's use of language at the end of the story. Howard pointed out to Wright that at the end of the story, "Mr. Lovecraft has his character speaking Gaelic instead of Cymric." Lovecraft had cribbed the ancient language phrasing from Fiona Macleod's "The Sin-Eater" (1895). In a 1923 letter to Frank Belknap Long, Lovecraft wrote, "The only objection to the phrase is that it's Gaelic instead of Cymric as the south-of-England locate demands. But as with anthropology—details don't count. Nobody will ever stop to note the difference." Robert E. Howard, however, did take notice. Still, despite noting the issue, Howard also wrote how much he enjoyed the yarn. "I have long looked forward to reading Mr. Lovecraft's 'The Rats in the Walls,'" Howard began, "and it certainly comes up to all expectations. I was amazed by the sweep of his imagination—not so much because of the extent of his reachings into the realms of imagination, which though cosmic enough in his story, he has exceeded in other tales, to my mind, but because of the strange and unthinkable by-path into which he was wandered in this tale." Even regarding the ending, Howard effulgently wrote, "The climax of the story alone puts Mr. Lovecraft in a class by himself; undoubtedly he must have the most unusual and wonderfully constructed brain of any man in the world. He alone can paint pictures in shadows and make them terrifically real."

On July 16, 1923, I moved into Exham Priory after the last workman had finished his labors. The restoration had been a stupendous task, for little had remained of the deserted pile but a shell-like ruin; yet because it had been the seat of my ancestors I let no expense deter me. The place had not been inhabited since the reign of James the First, when a tragedy of intensely hideous, though largely unexplained, nature had struck down the master, five of his children, and several servants; and driven forth under a cloud of suspicion and terror the third son, my lineal progenitor and the only survivor of the abhorred line.

With this sole heir denounced as a murderer, the estate had reverted to the crown, nor had the accused man made any attempt to exculpate himself or regain his property. Shaken by some horror greater than that of conscience or the law, and expressing only a frantic wish to exclude the ancient edifice from his sight and memory, Walter de la Poer, eleventh Baron Exham, fled to Virginia and there founded the family which by the next century had become known as Delapore.

Exham Priory had remained untenanted, though later allotted to the estates of the Norrys family and much studied because of its peculiarly composite architecture; an architecture involving Gothic towers resting on a Saxon or Romanesque substructure, whose foundation in turn was of a still earlier order or blend of orders—Roman, and even Druidic or native Cymric, if legends speak truly. This foundation was a very singular thing, being merged on one side with the solid limestone of the precipice from whose brink the priory overlooked a desolate valley three miles west of the village of Anchester.

Architects and antiquarians loved to examine this strange relic of forgotten centuries, but the country folk hated it. They had hated it hundreds of years before, when my ancestors lived there, and they hated it now, with the moss and mould of abandonment on it. I had not been a day in Anchester before I knew I came of an accursed house. And this week workmen have blown up Exham Priory, and are busy obliterating the traces of its foundations.

The bare statistics of my ancestry I had always known, together with the fact that my first American forbear had come to the colonies under a strange cloud. Of details, however, I had been kept wholly ignorant through the policy of reticence always maintained by the Delapores. Unlike our planter neighbors, we seldom boasted of crusading ancestors or other mediaeval and Renaissance heroes; nor was any kind of tradition handed down except what may have been recorded in the sealed envelope left before the Civil War by every squire to his eldest son for posthumous opening. The glories we cherished were those achieved since the migration; the glories of a proud and honorable, if somewhat reserved and unsocial Virginia line.

During the war our fortunes were extinguished and our whole existence changed by the burning of Carfax, our home on the banks of the James. My grandfather, advanced in years, had perished in that incendiary outrage, and with him the envelope that bound us all to the past. I can recall that fire today as I saw it then at the age of seven, with the Federal soldiers shouting, the women screaming, and the negroes howling and praying. My father was in the army, defending Richmond, and after many formalities my mother and I were passed through the lines to join him.

When the war ended we all moved north, whence my mother had come; and I grew to manhood, middle age, and ultimate wealth as a stolid Yankee. Neither my father nor I ever knew what our hereditary envelope had contained, and as I merged into the greyness of Massachusetts business life I lost all interest in the mysteries which evidently lurked far back in my family tree. Had I suspected their nature, how gladly I would have left Exham Priory to its moss, bats, and cobwebs!

My father died in 1904, but without any message to leave me, or to my only child, Alfred, a motherless boy of ten. It was this boy who reversed the order of family information; for although I could give him only jesting conjectures about the past, he wrote me of some very interesting ancestral legends when the late war took him to England in 1917 as an aviation officer. Apparently the Delapores had a colorful and perhaps sinister history, for a friend of my son's, Captain Edward Norrys of the Royal Flying Corps, dwelt near the family seat at Anchester and related some peasant superstitions which few novelists could equal for wildness and incredibility. Norrys himself, of course, did not take them seriously; but they amused my son and made good material for his letters to me. It was this legendry which definitely turned my attention to my transatlantic heritage, and made me resolve to purchase and restore the family seat which Norrys shewed to Alfred in its picturesque desertion, and offered to get for him at a surprisingly reasonable figure, since his own uncle was the present owner.

I bought Exham Priory in 1918, but was almost immediately distracted from my plans of restoration by the return of my son as a maimed invalid. During the two years that he lived I thought of nothing but his care, having even placed my business under the direction of partners.

In 1921, as I found myself bereaved and aimless, a retired manufacturer no longer young, I resolved to divert my remaining years with my new possession. Visiting Anchester in December, I was entertained by Captain Norrys, a plump, amiable young man who had thought much of my son, and secured his assistance in gathering plans and anecdotes to guide in the coming restoration. Exham Priory itself I saw without emotion, a jumble of tottering mediaeval ruins covered with lichens and honeycombed with rooks' nests, perched perilously upon a precipice, and denuded of floors or other interior features save the stone walls of the separate towers.

As I gradually recovered the image of the edifice as it had been when my ancestor left it over three centuries before, I began to hire workmen for the reconstruction. In every case I was forced to go outside the immediate locality, for the Anchester villagers had an almost unbelievable fear and hatred of the place. This sentiment was so great that it was sometimes communicated to the outside laborers, causing numerous desertions; whilst its scope appeared to include both the priory and its ancient family.

My son had told me that he was somewhat avoided during his visits because he was a de la Poer, and I now found myself subtly ostracized for a like reason until I convinced the peasants how little I knew of my heritage. Even then they sullenly disliked me, so that I had to collect most of the village traditions through the mediation of Norrys. What the people could not forgive, perhaps, was that I had come to restore a symbol so abhorrent to them; for, rationally or not, they viewed Exham Priory as nothing less than a haunt of fiends and werewolves.

Piecing together the tales which Norrys collected for me, and supplementing them with the accounts of several savants who had studied the ruins, I deduced that Exham Priory stood on the site of a prehistoric temple; a Druidical or ante-Druidical thing which must have been contemporary with Stonehenge. That indescribable rites had been celebrated there, few doubted; and there were unpleasant tales of the transference of these rites into the Cybele-worship which the Romans had introduced.

Inscriptions still visible in the sub-cellar bore such unmistakable letters as "DIV . . . OPS . . . MAGNA. MAT . . ." sign of the Magna Mater whose dark worship was once vainly forbidden to Roman citizens. Anchester had been the camp of the third Augustan legion, as many remains attest, and it was said that the temple of Cybele was splendid and thronged with worshippers who performed nameless ceremonies at the bidding of a Phrygian priest. Tales added that the fall of the old religion did not end the orgies at the temple, but that the priests lived on in the new faith without real change. Likewise was it said that the rites did not vanish with the Roman power, and that certain among the Saxons added to what remained of the temple, and gave it the essential outline it subsequently preserved, making it the center of a cult feared through half the heptarchy. About 1000 A.D. the place is mentioned in a chronicle as being a substantial stone priory housing a strange and powerful monastic order and surrounded by extensive gardens which needed no walls to exclude a frightened populace. It was never destroyed by the Danes, though after the Norman Conquest it must have declined tremendously; since there was no impediment when Henry the Third granted the site to my ancestor, Gilbert de la Poer, First Baron Exham, in 1261.

Of my family before this date there is no evil report, but something strange must have happened then. In one chronicle there is a reference to a de la Poer as "cursed of God" in 1307, whilst village legendry had nothing but evil and frantic fear to tell of the castle that went up on the foundations of the old temple and priory. The fireside tales were of the most grisly description, all the ghastlier because of their frightened reticence and cloudy evasiveness. They represented my ancestors as a race of hereditary daemons beside whom Gilles de Retz and the Marquis de Sade would seem the veriest tyros, and hinted whisperingly at their responsibility for the occasional disappearance of villagers through several generations.

The worst characters, apparently, were the barons and their direct heirs; at least, most was whispered about these. If of healthier inclinations, it was said, an heir would early and mysteriously die to make way for another more typical scion. There seemed to be an inner cult in the family, presided over by the head of the house, and sometimes closed except to a few members. Temperament rather than ancestry was evidently the basis of this cult, for it was entered by several who married into the family. Lady Margaret Trevor from Cornwall, wife of Godfrey, the second son of the fifth baron, became a favorite bane of children all over the countryside, and the daemon heroine of a particularly horrible old ballad not yet extinct near the Welsh border. Preserved in balladry, too, though not illustrating the same point, is the hideous tale of Lady Mary de la Poer, who shortly after her marriage to the Earl of Shrewsfield was killed by him and his mother, both of the slayers being absolved and blessed by the priest to whom they confessed what they dared not repeat to the world.

These myths and ballads, typical as they were of crude superstition, repelled me greatly. Their persistence, and their application to so long a line of my ancestors, were especially annoying; whilst the imputations of monstrous habits proved unpleasantly reminiscent of the one known scandal of my immediate forbears—the case of my cousin, young Randolph Delapore of Carfax, who went among the negroes and became a voodoo priest after he returned from the Mexican War.

I was much less disturbed by the vaguer tales of wails and howlings in the barren, windswept valley beneath the limestone cliff; of the graveyard stenches after the spring rains; of the floundering, squealing white thing on which Sir John Clave's horse had trod one night in a lonely field; and of the servant who had gone mad at what he saw in the priory in the full light of day. These things were hackneyed spectral lore, and I was at that time a pronounced sceptic. The accounts of vanished peasants were less to be dismissed, though not especially significant in view of mediaeval custom. Prying curiosity meant death, and more than one severed head had been publicly shewn on the bastions—now effaced—around Exham Priory.

A few of the tales were exceedingly picturesque, and made me wish I had learnt more of comparative mythology in my youth. There was, for instance, the belief that a legion of bat-winged devils kept witches' sabbath each night at the priory—a legion whose sustenance might explain the disproportionate abundance of coarse vegetables harvested in the vast gardens. And, most vivid of all, there was the dramatic epic of the rats—the scampering army of obscene vermin which had burst forth from the castle three months after the tragedy that doomed it to desertion—the lean, filthy, ravenous army which had swept all before it and devoured fowl, cats, dogs, hogs, sheep, and even two hapless human beings before its fury was spent. Around that unforgettable rodent army a whole separate cycle of myths revolves, for it scattered among the village homes and brought curses and horrors in its train.

Such was the lore that assailed me as I pushed to completion, with an elderly obstinacy, the work of restoring my ancestral home. It must not be imagined for a moment that these tales formed my principal psychological environment. On the other hand, I was constantly praised and encouraged by Captain Norrys and the antiquarians who surrounded and aided me. When the task was done, over two years after its commencement, I viewed the great rooms, wainscotted walls, vaulted ceilings, mullioned windows, and broad staircases with a pride which fully compensated for the prodigious expense of the restoration.

Every attribute of the Middle Ages was cunningly reproduced, and the new parts blended perfectly with the original walls and foundations. The seat of my fathers was complete, and I looked forward to redeeming at last the local fame of the line which ended in me. I would reside here permanently, and prove that a de la Poer (for I had adopted again the original spelling of the name) need not be a fiend. My comfort was perhaps augmented by the fact that, although Exham Priory was mediaevally fitted, its interior was in truth wholly new and free from old vermin and old ghosts alike.

As I have said, I moved in on July 16, 1923. My household consisted of seven servants and nine cats, of which latter species I am particularly fond. My eldest cat, "Nigger-Man," was seven years old and had come with me from my home in Bolton, Massachusetts; the others I had accumulated whilst living with Captain Norrys' family during the restoration of the priory.

For five days our routine proceeded with the utmost placidity, my time being spent mostly in the codification of old family data. I had now obtained some very circumstantial accounts of the final tragedy and flight of Walter de la Poer, which I conceived to be the probable contents of the hereditary paper lost in the fire at Carfax. It appeared that my ancestor was accused with much reason of having killed all the other members of his household, except four servant confederates, in their sleep, about two weeks after a shocking discovery which changed his whole demeanor, but which, except by implication, he disclosed to no one save perhaps the servants who assisted him and afterward fled beyond reach.

This deliberate slaughter, which included a father, three brothers, and two sisters, was largely condoned by the villagers, and so slackly treated by the law that its perpetrator escaped honored, unharmed, and undisguised to Virginia; the general whispered sentiment being that he had purged the land of an immemorial curse. What discovery had prompted an act so terrible, I could scarcely even conjecture. Walter de la Poer must have known for years the sinister tales about his family, so that this material could have given him no fresh impulse. Had he, then, witnessed some appalling ancient rite, or stumbled upon some frightful and revealing symbol in the priory or its vicinity? He was reputed to have been a shy, gentle youth in England. In Virginia he seemed not so much hard or bitter as harassed and apprehensive. He was spoken of in the diary of another gentleman-adventurer, Francis Harley of Bellview, as a man of unexampled justice, honor, and delicacy.

On July 22 occurred the first incident which, though lightly dismissed at the time, takes on a preternatural significance in relation to later events. It was so simple as to be almost negligible, and could not possibly have been noticed under the circumstances; for it must be recalled that since I was in a building practically fresh and new except for the walls, and surrounded by a well-balanced staff of servitors, apprehension would have been absurd despite the locality.

What I afterward remembered is merely this—that my old black cat, whose moods I know so well, was undoubtedly alert and anxious to an extent wholly out of keeping with his natural character. He roved from room to room, restless and disturbed, and sniffed constantly about the walls which formed part of the old Gothic structure. I realize how trite this sounds—like the inevitable dog in the ghost story, which always growls before his master sees the sheeted figure—yet I cannot consistently suppress it.

The following day a servant complained of restlessness among all the cats in the house. He came to me in my study, a lofty west room on the second story, with groined arches, black oak paneling, and a triple Gothic window overlooking the limestone cliff and desolate valley; and even as he spoke I saw the jetty form of Nigger-Man creeping along the west wall and scratching at the new panels which overlaid the ancient stone.

I told the man that there must be some singular odor or emanation from the old stonework, imperceptible to human senses, but affecting the delicate organs of cats even through the new woodwork. This I truly believed, and when the fellow suggested the presence of mice or rats, I mentioned that there had been no rats there for three hundred years, and that even the field mice of the surrounding country could hardly be found in these high walls, where they had never been known to stray. That afternoon I called on Captain Norrys, and he assured me that it would be quite incredible for field mice to infest the priory in such a sudden and unprecedented fashion.

That night, dispensing as usual with a valet, I retired in the west tower chamber which I had chosen as my own, reached from the study by a stone staircase and short gallery—the former partly ancient, the latter entirely restored. This room was circular, very high, and without wainscotting, being hung with arras which I had myself chosen in London.

Seeing that Nigger-Man was with me, I shut the heavy Gothic door and retired by the light of the electric bulbs which so cleverly counterfeited candles, finally switching off the light and sinking on the carved and canopied four-poster, with the venerable cat in his accustomed place across my feet. I did not draw the curtains, but gazed out at the narrow north window which I faced. There was a suspicion of aurora in the sky, and the delicate traceries of the window were pleasantly silhouetted.

At some time I must have fallen quietly asleep, for I recall a distinct sense of leaving strange dreams, when the cat started violently from his placid position. I saw him in the faint auroral glow, head strained forward, fore feet on my ankles, and hind feet stretched behind. He was looking intensely at a point on the wall somewhat west of the window, a point which to my eye had nothing to mark it, but toward which all my attention was now directed.

And as I watched, I knew that Nigger-Man was not vainly excited. Whether the arras actually moved I cannot say. I think it did, very slightly. But what I can swear to is that behind it I heard a low, distinct scurrying as of rats or mice. In a moment the cat had jumped bodily on the screening tapestry, bringing the affected section to the floor with his weight, and exposing a damp, ancient wall of stone; patched here and there by the restorers, and devoid of any trace of rodent prowlers.

Nigger-Man raced up and down the floor by this part of the wall, clawing the fallen arras and seemingly trying at times to insert a paw between the wall and the oaken floor. He found nothing, and after a time returned wearily to his place across my feet. I had not moved, but I did not sleep again that night.

In the morning I questioned all the servants, and found that none of them had noticed anything unusual, save that the cook remembered the actions of a cat which had rested on her windowsill. This cat had howled at some unknown hour of the night, awaking the cook in time for her to see him dart purposefully out of the open door down the stairs. I drowsed away the noontime, and in the afternoon called again on Capt. Norrys, who became exceedingly interested in what I told him. The odd incidents—so slight yet so curious—appealed to his sense of the picturesque, and elicited from him a number of reminiscences of local ghostly lore. We were genuinely perplexed at the presence of rats, and Norrys lent me some traps and Paris green, which I had the servants place in strategic localities when I returned.

I retired early, being very sleepy, but was harassed by dreams of the most horrible sort. I seemed to be looking down from an immense height upon a twilit grotto, knee-deep with filth, where a white-bearded daemon swineherd drove about with his staff a flock of fungous, flabby beasts whose appearance filled me with unutterable loathing. Then, as the swineherd paused and nodded over his task, a mighty swarm of rats rained down on the stinking abyss and fell to devouring beasts and man alike.

From this terrific vision I was abruptly awaked by the motions of Nigger-Man, who had been sleeping as usual across my feet. This time I did not have to question the source of his snarls and hisses, and of the fear which made him sink his claws into my ankle, unconscious of their effect; for on every side of the chamber the walls were alive with nauseous sound—the verminous slithering of ravenous, gigantic rats. There was now no aurora to shew the state of the arras—the fallen section of which had been replaced—but I was not too frightened to switch on the light.

As the bulbs leapt into radiance I saw a hideous shaking all over the tapestry, causing the somewhat peculiar designs to execute a singular dance of death. This motion disappeared almost at once, and the sound with it. Springing out of bed, I poked at the arras with the long handle of a warming-pan that rested near, and lifted one section to see what lay beneath. There was nothing but the patched stone wall, and even the cat had lost his tense realization of abnormal presences. When I examined the circular trap that had been placed in the room, I found all of the openings sprung, though no trace remained of what had been caught and had escaped.

Further sleep was out of the question, so, lighting a candle, I opened the door and went out in the gallery toward the stairs to my study, Nigger-Man following at my heels. Before we had reached the stone steps, however, the cat darted ahead of me and vanished down the ancient flight. As I descended the stairs myself, I became suddenly aware of sounds in the great room below; sounds of a nature which could not be mistaken.

The oak-paneled walls were alive with rats, scampering and milling, whilst Nigger-Man was racing about with the fury of a baffled hunter. Reaching the bottom, I switched on the light, which did not this time cause the noise to subside. The rats continued their riot, stampeding with such force and distinctness that I could finally assign to their motions a definite direction. These creatures, in numbers apparently inexhaustible, were engaged in one stupendous migration from inconceivable heights to some depth conceivably, or inconceivably, below.

I now heard steps in the corridor, and in another moment two servants pushed open the massive door. They were searching the house for some unknown source of disturbance which had thrown all the cats into a snarling panic and caused them to plunge precipitately down several flights of stairs and squat, yowling, before the closed door to the sub-cellar. I asked them if they had heard the rats, but they replied in the negative. And when I turned to call their attention to the sounds in the panels, I realized that the noise had ceased.

With the two men, I went down to the door of the sub-cellar, but found the cats already dispersed. Later I resolved to explore the crypt below, but for the present I merely made a round of the traps. All were sprung, yet all were tenantless. Satisfying myself that no one had heard the rats save the felines and me, I sat in my study till morning; thinking profoundly, and recalling every scrap of legend I had unearthed concerning the building I inhabited.

I slept some in the forenoon, leaning back in the one comfortable library chair which my mediaeval plan of furnishing could not banish. Later I telephoned to Captain Norrys, who came over and helped me explore the sub-cellar.

Absolutely nothing untoward was found, although we could not repress a thrill at the knowledge that this vault was built by Roman hands. Every low arch and massive pillar was Roman—not the debased Romanesque of the bungling Saxons, but the severe and harmonious classicism of the age of the Caesars; indeed, the walls abounded with inscriptions familiar to the antiquarians who had repeatedly explored the place—things like "P.GETAE. PROP . . . TEMP . . . DONA . . ." and "L. PRAEC . . . VS . . . PONTIFI . . . ATYS . . ."

The reference to Atys made me shiver, for I had read Catullus and knew something of the hideous rites of the Eastern god, whose worship was so mixed with that of Cybele. Norrys and I, by the light of lanterns, tried to interpret the odd and nearly effaced designs on certain irregularly rectangular blocks of stone generally held to be altars, but could make nothing of them. We remembered that one pattern, a sort of rayed sun, was held by students to imply a non-Roman origin, suggesting that these altars had merely been adopted by the Roman priests from some older and perhaps aboriginal temple on the same site. On one of these blocks were some brown stains which made me wonder. The largest, in the center of the room, had certain features on the upper surface which indicated its connection with fire—probably burnt offerings.

Such were the sights in that crypt before whose door the cats had howled, and where Norrys and I now determined to pass the night. Couches were brought down by the servants, who were told not to mind any nocturnal actions of the cats, and Nigger-Man was admitted as much for help as for companionship. We decided to keep the great oak door—a modern replica with slits for ventilation—tightly closed; and, with this attended to, we retired with lanterns still burning to await whatever might occur.

The vault was very deep in the foundations of the priory, and undoubtedly far down on the face of the beetling limestone cliff overlooking the waste valley. That it had been the goal of the scuffling and unexplainable rats I could not doubt, though why, I could not tell. As we lay there expectantly, I found my vigil occasionally mixed with half-formed dreams from which the uneasy motions of the cat across my feet would rouse me. These dreams were not wholesome, but horribly like the one I had had the night before. I saw again the twilit grotto, and the swineherd with his unmentionable fungous beasts wallowing in filth, and as I looked at these things they seemed nearer and more distinct—so distinct that I could almost observe their features. Then I did observe the flabby features of one of them—and awaked with such a scream that Nigger-Man started up, whilst Captain Norrys, who had not slept, laughed considerably. Norrys might have laughed more—or perhaps less—had he known what it was that made me scream. But I did not remember myself till later. Ultimate horror often paralyses memory in a merciful way.

Norrys waked me when the phenomena began. Out of the same frightful dream I was called by his gentle shaking and his urging to listen to the cats. Indeed, there was much to listen to, for beyond the closed door at the head of the stone steps was a veritable nightmare of feline yelling and clawing, whilst Nigger-Man, unmindful of his kindred outside, was running excitedly around the bare stone walls, in which I heard the same babel of scurrying rats that had troubled me the night before.

An acute terror now rose within me, for here were anomalies which nothing normal could well explain. These rats, if not the creatures of a madness which I shared with the cats alone, must be burrowing and sliding in Roman walls I had thought to be of solid limestone blocks . . . unless perhaps the action of water through more than seventeen centuries had eaten winding tunnels which rodent bodies had worn clear and ample. . . . But even so, the spectral horror was no less; for if these were living vermin why did not Norrys hear their disgusting commotion? Why did he urge me to watch Nigger-Man and listen to the cats outside, and why did he guess wildly and vaguely at what could have aroused them?

By the time I had managed to tell him, as rationally as I could, what I thought I was hearing, my ears gave me the last fading impression of the scurrying; which had retreated *still downward*, far underneath this deepest of sub-cellars till it seemed as if the whole cliff below were riddled with questing rats. Norrys was not as skeptical as I had anticipated, but instead seemed profoundly moved. He motioned to me to notice that the cats at the door had ceased their clamor, as if giving up the rats for lost; whilst Nigger-Man had a burst of renewed restlessness, and was clawing frantically around the bottom of the large stone altar in the center of the room, which was nearer Norrys' couch than mine.

My fear of the unknown was at this point very great. Something astounding had occurred, and I saw that Captain Norrys, a younger, stouter, and presumably more naturally materialistic man, was affected fully as much as myself—perhaps because of his lifelong and intimate familiarity with local legend. We could for the moment do nothing but watch the old black cat as he pawed with decreasing fervour at the base of the altar, occasionally looking up and mewing to me in that persuasive manner which he used when he wished me to perform some favour for him.

Norrys now took a lantern close to the altar and examined the place where Nigger-Man was pawing; silently kneeling and scraping away the lichens of centuries which joined the massive pre-Roman block to the tessellated floor. He did not find anything, and was about to abandon his effort when I noticed a trivial circumstance which made me shudder, even though it implied nothing more than I had already imagined.

I told him of it, and we both looked at its almost imperceptible manifestation with the fixedness of fascinated discovery and acknowledgment. It was only this—that the flame of the lantern set down near the altar was slightly but certainly flickering from a draught of air which it had not before received, and which came indubitably from the crevice between floor and altar where Norrys was scraping away the lichens.

We spent the rest of the night in the brilliantly lighted study, nervously discussing what we should do next. The discovery that some vault deeper than the deepest known masonry of the Romans underlay this accursed pile—some vault unsuspected by the curious antiquarians of three centuries—would have been sufficient to excite us without any background of the sinister. As it was, the fascination became twofold; and we paused in doubt whether to abandon our search and quit the priory forever in superstitious caution, or to gratify our sense of adventure and brave whatever horrors might await us in the unknown depths. By morning we had compromised, and decided to go to London to gather a group of archaeologists and scientific men fit to cope with the mystery. It should be mentioned that before leaving the sub-cellar we had vainly tried to move the central altar which we now recognized as the gate to a new pit of nameless fear. What secret would open the gate, wiser men than we would have to find.

During many days in London Captain Norrys and I presented our facts, conjectures, and legendary anecdotes to five eminent authorities, all men who could be trusted to respect any family disclosures which future explorations might develop. We found most of them little disposed to scoff, but instead intensely interested and sincerely sympathetic. It is hardly necessary to name them all, but I may say that they included Sir William Brinton, whose excavations in the Troad excited most of the world in their day. As we all took the train for Anchester I felt myself poised on the brink of frightful revelations, a sensation symbolized by the air of mourning among the many Americans at the unexpected death of the President on the other side of the world.

On the evening of August 7th we reached Exham Priory, where the servants assured me that nothing unusual had occurred. The cats, even old Nigger-Man, had been perfectly placid; and not a trap in the house had been sprung. We were to begin exploring on the following day, awaiting which I assigned well-appointed rooms to all my guests.

I myself retired in my own tower chamber, with Nigger-Man across my feet. Sleep came quickly, but hideous dreams assailed me. There was a vision of a Roman feast like that of Trimalchio, with a horror in a covered platter. Then came that damnable, recurrent thing about the swineherd and his filthy drove in the twilit grotto. Yet when I awoke it was full daylight, with normal sounds in the house below. The rats, living or spectral, had not troubled me; and Nigger-Man was quietly asleep. On going down, I found that the same tranquility had prevailed elsewhere; a condition which one of the assembled savants—a fellow named Thornton, devoted to the psychic—rather absurdly laid to the fact that I had now been shewn the thing which certain forces had wished to shew me.

All was now ready, and at 11 a.m. our entire group of seven men, bearing powerful electric searchlights and implements of excavation, went down to the sub-cellar and bolted the door behind us. Nigger-Man was with us, for the investigators found no occasion to despise his excitability, and were indeed anxious that he be present in case of obscure rodent manifestations. We noted the Roman inscriptions and unknown altar designs only briefly, for three of the savants had already seen them, and all knew their characteristics. Prime attention was paid to the momentous central altar, and within an hour Sir William Brinton had caused it to tilt backward, balanced by some unknown species of counterweight.

There now lay revealed such a horror as would have overwhelmed us had we not been prepared. Through a nearly square opening in the tiled floor, sprawling on a flight of stone steps so prodigiously worn that it was little more than an inclined plane at the center, was a ghastly array of human or semi-human bones. Those which retained their collocation as skeletons shewed attitudes of panic fear, and over all were the marks of rodent gnawing. The skulls denoted nothing short of utter idiocy, cretinism, or primitive semi-apedom.

Above the hellishly littered steps arched a descending passage seemingly chiseled from the solid rock, and conducting a current of air. This current was not a sudden and noxious rush as from a closed vault, but a cool breeze with something of freshness in it. We did not pause long, but shiveringly began to clear a passage down the steps. It was then that Sir William, examining the hewn walls, made the odd observation that the passage, according to the direction of the strokes, must have been chiseled *from beneath.*

I must be very deliberate now, and choose my words.

After ploughing down a few steps amidst the gnawed bones we saw that there was light ahead; not any mystic phosphorescence, but a filtered daylight which could not come except from unknown fissures in the cliff that overlooked the waste valley. That such fissures had escaped notice from outside was hardly remarkable, for not only is the valley wholly uninhabited, but the cliff is so high and beetling that only an aeronaut could study its face in detail. A few steps more, and our breaths were literally snatched from us by what we saw; so literally that Thornton, the psychic investigator, actually fainted in the arms of the dazed man who stood behind him. Norrys, his plump face utterly white and flabby, simply cried out inarticulately; whilst I think that what I did was to gasp or hiss, and cover my eyes.

The man behind me—the only one of the party older than I—croaked the hackneyed "My God!" in the most cracked voice I ever heard. Of seven cultivated men, only Sir William Brinton retained his composure; a thing more to his credit because he led the party and must have seen the sight first.

It was a twilit grotto of enormous height, stretching away farther than any eye could see; a subterranean world of limitless mystery and horrible suggestion. There were buildings and other architectural remains—in one terrified glance I saw a weird pattern of tumuli, a savage circle of monoliths, a low-domed Roman ruin, a sprawling Saxon pile, and an early English edifice of wood—but all these were dwarfed by the ghoulish spectacle presented by the general surface of the ground. For yards about the steps extended an insane tangle of human bones, or bones at least as human as those on the steps. Like a foamy sea they stretched, some fallen apart, but others wholly or partly articulated as skeletons; these latter invariably in postures of daemoniac frenzy, either fighting off some menace or clutching other forms with cannibal intent.

When Dr. Trask, the anthropologist, stooped to classify the skulls, he found a degraded mixture which utterly baffled him. They were mostly lower than the Piltdown man in the scale of evolution, but in every case definitely human. Many were of higher grade, and a very few were the skulls of supremely and sensitively developed types. All the bones were gnawed, mostly by rats, but somewhat by others of the half-human drove. Mixed with them were many tiny bones of rats—fallen members of the lethal army which closed the ancient epic.

I wonder that any man among us lived and kept his sanity through that hideous day of discovery. Not Hoffmann or Huysmans could conceive a scene more wildly incredible, more frenetically repellent, or more Gothically grotesque than the twilit grotto through which we seven staggered; each stumbling on revelation after revelation, and trying to keep for the nonce from thinking of the events which must have taken place there three hundred years, or a thousand, or two thousand, or ten thousand years ago. It was the antechamber of hell, and poor Thornton fainted again when Trask told him that some of the skeleton things must have descended as quadrupeds through the last twenty or more generations.

Horror piled on horror as we began to interpret the architectural remains. The quadruped things—with their occasional recruits from the biped class—had been kept in stone pens, out of which they must have broken in their last delirium of hunger or rat-fear. There had been great herds of them, evidently fattened on the coarse vegetables whose remains could be found as a sort of poisonous ensilage at the bottom of huge stone bins older than Rome. I knew now why my ancestors had had such excessive gardens—would to heaven I could forget! The purpose of the herds I did not have to ask.

Sir William, standing with his searchlight in the Roman ruin, translated aloud the most shocking ritual I have ever known; and told of the diet of the antediluvian cult which the priests of Cybele found and mingled with their own. Norrys, used as he was to the trenches, could not walk straight when he came out of the English building. It was a butcher shop and kitchen—he had expected that—but it was too much to see familiar English implements in such a place, and to read familiar English graffiti there, some as recent as 1610. I could not go in that building—that building whose daemon activities were stopped only by the dagger of my ancestor Walter de la Poer.

What I did venture to enter was the low Saxon building, whose oaken door had fallen, and there I found a terrible row of ten stone cells with rusty bars. Three had tenants, all skeletons of high grade, and on the bony forefinger of one I found a seal ring with my own coat-of-arms. Sir William found a vault with far older cells below the Roman chapel, but these cells were empty. Below them was a low crypt with cases of formally arranged bones, some of them bearing terrible parallel inscriptions carved in Latin, Greek, and the tongue of Phrygia.

Meanwhile, Dr. Trask had opened one of the prehistoric tumuli, and brought to light skulls which were slightly more human than a gorilla's, and which bore indescribable ideographic carvings. Through all this horror my cat stalked unperturbed. Once I saw him monstrously perched atop a mountain of bones, and wondered at the secrets that might lie behind his yellow eyes.

Having grasped to some slight degree the frightful revelations of this twilit area—an area so hideously foreshadowed by my recurrent dream—we turned to that apparently boundless depth of midnight cavern where no ray of light from the cliff could penetrate. We shall never know what sightless Stygian worlds yawn beyond the little distance we went, for it was decided that such secrets are not good for mankind. But there was plenty to engross us close at hand, for we had not gone far before the searchlights shewed that accursed infinity of pits in which the rats had feasted, and whose sudden lack of replenishment had driven the ravenous rodent army first to turn on the living herds of starving things, and then to burst forth from the priory in that historic orgy of devastation which the peasants will never forget.

God! those carrion black pits of sawed, picked bones and opened skulls! Those nightmare chasms choked with the pithecanthropoid, Celtic, Roman, and English bones of countless unhallowed centuries! Some of them were full, and none can say how deep they had once been. Others were still bottomless to our searchlights, and peopled by unnamable fancies. What, I thought, of the hapless rats that stumbled into such traps amidst the blackness of their quests in this grisly Tartarus?

Once my foot slipped near a horribly yawning brink, and I had a moment of ecstatic fear. I must have been musing a long time, for I could not see any of the party but the plump Captain Norrys. Then there came a sound from that inky, boundless, farther distance that I thought I knew; and I saw my old black cat dart past me like a winged Egyptian god, straight into the illimitable gulf of the unknown. But I was not far behind, for there was no doubt after another second. It was the eldritch scurrying of those fiend-born rats, always questing for new horrors, and determined to lead me on even unto those grinning caverns of earth's center where Nyarlathotep, the mad faceless god, howls blindly to the piping of two amorphous idiot flute-players.

My searchlight expired, but still I ran. I heard voices, and yowls, and echoes, but above all there gently rose that impious, insidious scurrying; gently rising, rising, as a stiff bloated corpse gently rises above an oily river that flows under endless onyx bridges to a black, putrid sea.

Something bumped into me—something soft and plump. It must have been the rats; the viscous, gelatinous, ravenous army that feast on the dead and the living. . . . Why shouldn't rats eat a de la Poer as a de la Poer eats forbidden things? . . . The war ate my boy, damn them all . . . and the Yanks ate Carfax with flames and burnt Grandsire Delapore and the secret . . . No, no, I tell you, I am not that daemon swineherd in the twilit grotto! It was *not* Edward Norrys' fat face on that flabby, fungous thing! Who says I am a de la Poer? He lived, but my boy died! . . . Shall a Norrys hold the lands of a de la Poer? . . . It's voodoo, I tell you . . . that spotted snake . . . Curse you, Thornton, I'll teach you to faint at what my family do! . . . 'Sblood, thou stinkard, I'll learn ye how to gust . . . wolde ye swynke me thilke wys? . . . *Magna Mater! Magna Mater! . . . Atys . . . Dia ad aghaidh 's ad aodann . . . agus bas dunach ort! Dhonas 's dholas ort, agus leat-sa! . . . Ungl . . . ungl . . . rrrlh . . . chchch . . .*

That is what they say I said when they found me in the blackness after three hours; found me crouching in the blackness over the plump, half-eaten body of Capt. Norrys, with my own cat leaping and tearing at my throat. Now they have blown up Exham Priory, taken my Nigger-Man away from me, and shut me into this barred room at Hanwell with fearful whispers about my heredity and experiences. Thornton is in the next room, but they prevent me from talking to him. They are trying, too, to suppress most of the facts concerning the priory. When I speak of poor Norrys they accuse me of a hideous thing, but they must know that I did not do it. They must know it was the rats; the slithering, scurrying rats whose scampering will never let me sleep; the daemon rats that race behind the padding in this room and beckon me down to greater horrors than I have ever known; the rats they can never hear; the rats, the rats in the walls!

14
Teotíhuacán
Alice l'Anson
(1931)

Robert E. Howard was so taken with this poem in the November 1930 issue of *Weird Tales*, that he wrote a letter to "The Eyrie." In his letter, published in the January 1931 issue, Howard wrote, "I was particularly fascinated by the poem by Alice l'Anson in the latest issue. The writer must surely live in Mexico, for I believe that only one familiar with that ancient land could so reflect the slumbering soul of prehistoric Aztec-land as she has done. There is a difference in a poem written on some subject by one afar off and a poem written on the same subject by one familiar with the very heart of that subject. I have put it very clumsily, but *Teotihuacan* breathes the cultural essence, spirit and soul of Mexico." Alice l'Anson, born on January 25, 1872, in San Francisco, California, published five poems in *Weird Tales* magazine (and one in *Oriental Stories*) of which this was the first. She did indeed live in Mexico at the time of her writings, but sadly died there of heart failure on June 5, 1931. She was only 58 years of age.

I sing of pagan rites that long ago
Ruled the great city lying far below
The twin volcanoes' hoary bridge of snow—
    I sing the Song of Teotíhuacán!

Deep is the womb of Time in which I see
The drama of a dead idolatry!—
I hear old voices chanting now in me
    The mystic Song of Teotíhuacán!

Robert E. Howard's

"The red dawn shimmers on Tezcoco lake,
O City of the Priests, awake, awake!
It is another Feast Day of the Snake,
    The Serpent God of Teotíhuacán!

"Behold the flaming signal in the skies!
The dawn is led!—today a victim dies!
Ohear, Ohear his agonizing cries,
    Great Serpent God of Teotíhuacán!

"Upon the stone his writhing form is laid—
His blood spurts redly from the 'itxli' blade—
With his dripping heart an offering is made,
    To the mighty God of Teotíhuacán!"

Shadow of centuries! still they grow apace
While Mystery hovers o'er the solemn place
Whose ruins whisper in this year of grace:
    "Where is the God of Teotíhuacán?"

O Souls that cross again the yawning deep
While round these monuments the lizards creep,
I feel your ghostly contact as you keep
    Your vigils in old Teotíhuacán!

O Spirit Guardians of this grim terrain,
Has Karma bound us with the selfsame chain?
Did I, too, worship at that gory fane
    Long years agone . . . in Teotíhuacán?

15
Doom Around the Corner
Wilfred Blanch Talman
(1931)

Wilfred Blanch Talman was a friend of H.P. Lovecraft's, and it was the latter who suggested Robert E. Howard as a potential author for Talman's magazine, *The Texaco Star,* for which Howard wrote, "The Ghost of Camp Colorado," published in the April 1931 issue. One question regarding close relations with Lovecraft is how much editing or writing/rewriting Lovecraft did for his friend's stories. According to pulp scholar, Will Murray, writing in *Crypt of Cthulhu* #11, there is scant evidence to suggest that Lovecraft had a hand in editing this Talman story. If he did, Murray states it was most likely limited to some light editing with minor additions. After the story was published in the November 1931 issue of *Weird Tales* magazine, Howard sent a letter to Talman writing, "I believe, though, of all your stories, I like 'Doom Around the Corner,' though this statement is in no way meant to depreciate the rest of your tales. This story is the sort that especially appeals to me—subject matter, style and development. It possesses unusual realism and convincingness, and is free from the artificial sort of conversation so often dragged into tales in order to conform to certain vague literary conventions. I've noticed this freedom and ease in your other stories. All in all, 'Doom Around the Corner' is one of the most perfect short stories I've read in a long time."

All of Mr. Thomas Drumlin's acquaintances, had he possessed any, would have said that he was in a rut. Drumlin even had some suspicion of it himself, and so, even if the only persons with whom he came in contact refrained from calling it to his attention because they were in a rut themselves, he did not think them remiss for not warning him.

The chief reason for Drumlin being in a rut was his latent curiosity. Perhaps it was because he was lazy, or perchance it was only because he had such a vicarious imagination that his curiosity remained latent until the night that he heard the spirit singing.

In the dusty back room of a factory tucked away in a corner of New York City, Drumlin found little to be curious about except the sums of certain columns of figures that confronted him daily as he sat on a high stool. Any questions that did occur to his mind about how objects changed in appearance, or why it became dark at night, or why it rained on certain days and not on others could be easily solved by Drumlin in his imagination, without recourse to natural science. There was little need, he felt, for sticking one's nose into a book, or running from one end of the earth to another when the fairies and genii that he had been taught to believe in during a more adventurous childhood could be regarded as the agents of nearly everything that happened.

So that when he climbed own from his stool late every afternoon to follow hundreds of others like himself into a cavern where stuffy trains ran underground and under rivers, it is not to be wondered at that Drumlin, not being at all inquisitive about transportation problems or the sources of motive power, thought (if, indeed, he bothered to consider it) that the subway coach in which he clung to a strap was a chariot drawn by some red-eyed underworld dragon.

He always took the same route from the subway to his furnished room—four hundred and twenty steps straight ahead to the grocery store on the corner, and then one hundred and two paces, turning to the right when he had left the store, to the door of the house where he lived. Drumlin had gone home by another route once, but it was twenty-nine steps further, and no grocery store along the way.

There was another corner just a few paces beyond his door, but Drumlin had never seen around it. To go that far out of his way had never occurred to him, and he must have known that around the corner would be only another street, probably just like the one he lived on, and people walking to and fro in the course of business or pleasure. One corner in a city was to him the same as another.

Touching a match to his diminutive gas stove, Drumlin each night would prepare himself a little supper, wash his dishes, and perhaps straighten up a few things about the room that his landlady had neglected. Then he would sit before his one narrow window, opening to the rear of the house, and gaze out—not because there was much to see outside, or anything he cared to look at, but because looking out of a window seemed to allow greater breadth for meditation.

Then Drumlin's eyes would grow wide with thought, and he would conjure up, without effort, pictures of elves and witches and strange demons that he believed were part of the very world he lived in. Since he rarely spoke to any one except about matters concerning the business represented by the dusty back room, no one had ever argued with Drumlin that these things were not part of the everyday world, and so he never considered the fact that perhaps others did not think so. Drumlin thought not only of the good fairies and the helpful little people, but also of ghouls and specters and werewolves, for even he knew that the world was a balance of good and evil principles.

This was another reason why he never had ventured around the corner. For all he knew, the next street might be peopled with evil spirits. Since he never had seen evidence of any but good genii on his own street, it stood to reason, without the thought ever crossing his mind, that it was better to remain among the good than to venture into something about which he was not in the least curious and which might be harmful. He really cared not in the slightest what might be around the corner until he heard the spirit music, and so he never missed the thrill of exploration until the music called it to his attention.

Of course Mr. Thomas Drumlin, knowing all that he did about fairies and ghosts, never bothered to read anything to learn more about them. He practically ceased reading when he was a youth. He thought he knew what each elf and ghost looked like—even knew how they talked. That is how he recognized the spirit music when first he heard it. He had never met or spoke to a leprechaun or brownie or pixy because he considered himself only one of the lesser beings that the genii served, and as such not entitled to see or converse with them. The big, successful men of the world, Drumlin considered, must confer with good fairies every day, and the very evil men commune with witches and vampires.

Whether it was winter or summer, Drumlin sat by his window and thought—though exactly what his thoughts were at all times we may never know—until it was the hour for bed. And then in the morning he would rise and make some breakfast, go to sit on his stool in the dusty back room, and the day would start all over again.

As a matter of fact, Drumlin's subconscious attitude about the evil that might be around the corner was correct, for he lived on the edge of a settlement of swarthy foreigners who were not the most law-abiding of the city's population, according to the records of the near-by police station. They were continually making merry and becoming drunk and fighting, though Drumlin knew nothing of it except for certain sounds that welled up from between the houses that he could see off beyond his window. When the window was closed he heard no sounds, and when the casement was open it is to be assumed that he was so engrossed with his musings that they were not apparent to him.

On one particular summer evening, however, when the sun had long disappeared and when Drumlin was chin in hand at the window-sill as usual, with his mind wondering in the distance where the stars were beginning to come out, a certain rhythmical cadence intruded upon his thoughts. In some way it appeared to parallel the course of his thinking at the time and almost without realizing, Drumlin found himself listening.

The music floated up from one of the dingy brick canyons beyond his window, and consisted of the twanging of a stringed instrument accompanied by several voices not so musical. They were repeating, again and again, a refrain that Drumlin seemed to recognize, and emphasizing the end of the line with vigorous stamping of the feet. Gradually, as his consciousness focused upon it, Drumlin realized that the singing was in the language of the little people.

Olla huula, huula hei!
Olla huula, huula hei!

The refrain continued for some time, the shuffling and stamping leading Drumlin to believe that the persons to whom the voices belonged were dancing clumsily in a circle. Suddenly the singing and twanging stopped and, although Drumlin listened for a long time, it was not resumed. The spot from which it had come was far beneath his sight.

Though the words of the singers could have no translation in worldly language, Drumlin understood them as an invitation to join the singers in rites of some sort. His heart thumped at the thought that at last some of the little people were calling him to speak with them. His curiosity was stirred as to whether these were elves or demons, for Drumlin knew that good and evil spirits speak the same language at times, yet he went to bed and tossed wakefully for a long time without once thinking of venturing around the corner.

The next night, because he had been slow in adding his columns of figures during the day, Mr. Thomas Drumlin arrived home much later than usual, and the stars were already out before he filled his kettle with water for washing the dishes and placed it over the gas flame. Just then there came through the open window the sound of a twanging instrument, voices singing and feet stamping.

Olla huula, huula hei!

Drumlin stood still for many minutes, not daring to move lest he might lose some note of the repeated invitation. Presently he realized that if he was to answer the spirit music that called him, he must do so before the notes died away. And standing there, with his tea-kettle singing on the stove, Mr. Thomas Drumlin at last conceived the idea of going downstairs and around the corner.

Something seemed to restrain him when first he attempted to move, but he wrenched away and, holding his breath so that he might lose none of the refrain that he could barely hear after he had shut the door of his room, Drumlin tiptoed down the stairs. As he stepped out on the street he wondered that his feet were so light and ethereal, but the twanging and singing were louder now, and the little people were stamping harder than ever.

Then, as Mr. Thomas Drumlin turned the corner around which he had never seen before, the shouting and stamping rose into a final crescendo—*Olla huula, huula HEI!*—and stopped, and there was Drumlin, around the corner, with no voices calling him, and nothing but the same old hum of the city to guide him to the little people.

Just what happened after that concerned Drumlin in a far different way. Part of it is a matter of record which, if people were to take the same attitude that he did, might prove that genii and fairies do cause some of the things that happen.

There is on record, for instance, the fact that Patrolman Moriarity telephoned to his station house to say that he had found a little, middle-aged man wandering near his call-box on a certain corner apparently suffering from loss of memory, and the fact that he called a few minutes later to tell his superior that the man had disappeared. There is also a slip of paper on which the medical examiner wrote, several hours later, of finding one Thomas Drumlin dead on arrival after a tea-kettle had boiled over and extinguished a gas flame.

Nothing was ever committed to writing, however, about Patrolman Moriarity's remark to the medical examiner that Mr. Thomas Drumlin, lying before his stove at the time, was the same individual that he had found groping in the darkness on a near-by corner, or about the medical examiner's reply to Patrolman Moriarity that the latter must have been mistaken and have an imagination that played tricks with him.

But it somehow occurred to Patrolman Moriarity, with his Celtic background of supernaturalism, that something other than Drumlin's worldly body was on that corner just after the little bookkeeper had drawn his last breath. Patrolman Moriarity confided his information to Mr. Drumlin's landlady, whose ancestry was similar to his, and who told of having heard occasionally strange, unearthly sounds of revelry from regions behind the house. Putting two and two together, the pair listened one night and heard a voice that the landlady swears was Mr. Thomas Drumlin's singing much louder than a number of others, as a group of invisible persons apparently stamped around in a circle to the twanging of instrument strings.

Robert E. Howard's

16
The Return of the Sorcerer
By Clark Ashton Smith
(1931)

Clark Ashton Smith published "The Return of the Sorcerer" in the premier issue of *Strange Tales of Mystery and Terror* in September of 1931. The story is one of the earliest to tie into H.P. Lovecraft's Cthulhu yarns because of its mention of the dreaded *Necronomicon*. Robert E. Howard had yet to be published in *Strange Tales*, but he was evidently reading the magazine attempting to get a feel for the type of stories included in the new magazine as compared to his main market, *Weird Tales*. He wrote a letter to *Strange Tales'* editor praising the story, and in a letter to H.P. Lovecraft in October of the following year, Howard mentioned this story. "That he," as Howard wrote, "is capable of writing straight horror-stuff is evidenced by such tales as 'The Return of the Sorcerer' in *Strange Tales*, which was, as I wrote the editor, one of the most intolerably hideous stories I ever read—in other words, a sheer masterpiece." Finally, Howard later wrote to Clark Ashton Smith directly and told him, "I envy you your knack of making the fantastic seem real. I particularly remember your remarkable 'Return of the Sorcerer' in *Strange Tales*. That was no story for one with weak nerves. The horror you evoked was almost unbearable. I have read . . . it is the honest truth that my hair stood up when I read that story. Poe never wrote anything that congealed my blood like that did. I wrote the editor to that effect."

I had been out of work for several months, and my savings were perilously near the vanishing point. Therefore I was naturally elated when I received from John Carnby a favorable answer inviting me to present my qualifications in person. Carnby had advertised for a secretary, stipulating that all applicants must offer a preliminary statement of their capacities by letter; and I had written in response to the advertisement.

Carnby, no doubt, was a scholarly recluse who felt averse to contact with a long waiting-list of strangers; and he had chosen this manner of weeding out beforehand many, if not all, of those who were ineligible. He had specified his requirements fully and succinctly, and these were of such nature as to bar even the average well-educated person. A knowledge of Arabic was necessary, among other things; and luckily I had acquired a certain degree of scholarship in this unusual tongue.

I found the address, of whose location I had formed only a vague idea, at the end of a hilltop avenue in the suburbs of Oakland. It was a large, two-story house, over-shaded by ancient oaks and dark with a mantling of unchecked ivy, among hedges of unpruned privet and shrubbery that had gone wild for many years. It was separated from its neighbors by a vacant, weed-grown lot on one side and a tangle of vines and trees on the other, surrounding the black ruins of a burnt mansion.

Even apart from its air of long neglect, there was something drear and dismal about the place—something that inhered in the ivy-blurred outlines of the house, in the furtive, shadowy windows, and the very forms of the misshapen oaks and oddly sprawling shrubbery. Somehow, my elation became a trifle less exuberant, as I entered the grounds and followed an unswept path to the front door.

When I found myself in the presence of John Carnby, my jubilation was still somewhat further diminished; though I could not have given a tangible reason for the premonitory chill, the dull, somber feeling of alarm that I experienced, and the leaden sinking of my spirits. Perhaps it was the dark library in which he received me as much as the man himself—a room whose musty shadows could never have been wholly dissipated by sun or lamplight. Indeed, it must have been this; for John Carnby himself was very much the sort of person I had pictured him to be.

He had all the earmarks of the lonely scholar who has devoted patient years to some line of erudite research. He was thin and bent, with a massive forehead and a mane of grizzled hair; and the pallor of the library was on his hollow, clean-shaven cheeks. But coupled with this, there was a nerve-shattered air, a fearful shrinking that was more than the normal shyness of a recluse, and an unceasing apprehensiveness that betrayed itself in every glance of his dark-ringed, feverish eyes and every movement of his bony hands. In all likelihood his health had been seriously impaired by over-application; and I could not help but wonder at the nature of the studies that had made him a tremulous wreck But there was something about him—perhaps the width of his bowed shoulders and the bold aquilinity of his facial outlines—which gave the impression of great former strength and a vigor not yet wholly exhausted.

His voice was unexpectedly deep and sonorous.

"I think you will do, Mr. Ogden," he said, after a few formal questions, most of which related to my linguistic knowledge, and in particular my mastery of Arabic. "Your labors will not be very heavy; but I want someone who can be on hand at any time required. Therefore you must live with me. I can give you a comfortable room, and I guarantee that my cooking will not poison you. I often work at night; and I hope you will not find the irregular hours too disagreeable."

No doubt I should have been overjoyed at this assurance that the secretarial position was to be mine. Instead, I was aware of a dim, unreasoning reluctance and an obscure forewarning of evil as I thanked John Carnby and told him that I was ready to move in whenever he desired.

He appeared to be greatly pleased; and the queer apprehensiveness went out of his manner for a moment.

"Come immediately—this very afternoon, if you can," he said. "I shall be very glad to have you and the sooner the better. I have been living entirely alone for some time; and I must confess that the solitude is beginning to pall upon me. Also, I have been retarded in my labors for lack of the proper help. My brother used to live with me and assist me, but he has gone away on a long trip."

I returned to my downtown lodgings, paid my rent with the last few dollars that remained to me, packed my belongings, and in less than an hour was back at my new employer's home. He assigned me a room on the second floor, which, though unaired and dusty, was more than luxurious in comparison with the hall-bedroom that failing funds had compelled me to inhabit for some time past. Then he took me to his own study, which was on the same floor, at the further end of the hall. Here, he explained to me, most of my future work would be done.

I could hardly restrain an exclamation of surprise as I viewed the interior of this chamber. It was very much as I should have imagined the den of some old sorcerer to be. There were tables strewn with archaic instruments of doubtful use, with astrological charts, with skulls and alembics and crystals, with censers such as are used in the Catholic Church, and volumes bound in worm-eaten leather with verdigris-mottled clasps. In one corner stood the skeleton of a large ape; in another, a human skeleton; and overhead a stuffed crocodile was suspended.

There were cases overpiled with books, and even a cursory glance at the titles showed me that they formed a singularly comprehensive collection of ancient and modern works on demonology and the black arts. There were some weird paintings and etchings on the walls, dealing with kindred themes; and the whole atmosphere of the room exhaled a medley of half-forgotten superstitions. Ordinarily I would have smiled it confronted with such things; but somehow, in this lonely, dismal house, beside the neurotic, hag-ridden Carnby, it was difficult for me to repress an actual shudder.

On one of the tables, contrasting incongruously with this melange of medievalism and Satanism, there stood a typewriter, surrounded with piles of disorderly manuscript. At one end of the room there was a small, curtained alcove with a bed in which Carnby slept. At the end opposite the alcove, between the human and simian skeletons, I perceived a locked cupboard that was set in the wall.

Carnby had noted my surprise, and was watching me with a keen, analytic expression which I found impossible to fathom. He began to speak, in explanatory tones.

"I have made a life-study of demonism and sorcery," he declared. "It is a fascinating field, and one that is singularly neglected. I am now preparing a monograph, in which I am trying to correlate the magical practices and demon-worship of every known age and people. Your labors, at least for a while, will consist in typing and arranging the voluminous preliminary notes which I have made, and in helping me to track down other references and correspondences. Your knowledge of Arabic will be invaluable to me, for I am none too well-grounded in this language myself, and I am depending for certain essential data on a copy of the Necronomicon in the original Arabic text. I have reason to think that there are certain omissions and erroneous renderings in the Latin version of Olaus Wormius."

I had heard of this rare, well-high fabulous volume, but had never seen it. The book was supposed to contain the ultimate secrets of evil and forbidden knowledge; and, moreover, the original text, written by the mad Arab, Abdul Alhazred, was said to be unprocurable. I wondered how it had come into Carnby's possession.

"I'll show you the volume after dinner," Carnby went on. "You will doubtless be able to elucidate one or two passages that have long puzzled me."

The evening meal, cooked and served by my employer himself, was a welcome change from cheap restaurant fare. Carnby seemed to have lost a good deal of his nervousness. He was very talkative, and even began to exhibit a certain scholarly gaiety after we had shared a bottle of mellow Sauterne. Still, with no manifest reason, I was troubled by intimations and forebodings which I could neither analyze nor trace to their rightful source.

We returned to the study, and Carnby brought out from a locked drawer the volume of which he had spoken. It was enormously old, and was bound in ebony covers arabesqued with silver and set with darkly glowing garnets. When I opened the yellowing pages, I drew back with involuntary revulsion at the odor which arose from them — an odor that was more than suggestive of physical decay, as if the book had lain among corpses in some forgotten graveyard and had taken on the taint of dissolution.

Carnby's eyes were burning with a fevered light as he took the old manuscript from my hands and turned to a page near the middle. He indicated a certain passage with his lean forefinger.

"Tell me what you make of this," he said, in a tense, excited whisper.

I deciphered the paragraph, slowly and with some difficulty, and wrote down a rough English version with the pad and pencil which Caraby offered me. Then, at his request, I read it aloud:

"It is verily known by few, but is nevertheless no attestable fact, that the will of a dead sorcerer hath power upon his own body and can raise it up from the tomb and perform therewith whatever action was unfulfilled in life. And such resurrections are invariably for the doing of malevolent deeds and for the detriment of other's. Most readily can the corpse be animated if all its members have remained intact; and yet there are cases in which the excelling will of the wizard hath reared up from death the sundered pieces of a body hewn in many fragments, and hath caused them to serve his end, either separately or in a temporary reunion. But in every instance, after the action hath been completed, the body lapseth into its former state."

Of course, all this was errant gibberish. Probably it was the strange, unhealthy look of utter absorption with which my employer listened, more than that damnable passage from the Necronomicon, which caused my nervousness and made me start violently when, toward the end of my reading, I heard an indescribable slithering noise in the hall outside. But when I finished the paragraph and looked up at Carnby, I was more startled by the expression of stark, staring fear which his features had assumed—an expression as of one who is haunted by some hellish phantom. Somehow, I got the feeling that he was listening to that odd noise in the hallway rather than to my translation of Abdul Alhazred.

"The house is full of rats," he explained, as he caught my inquiring glance. "I have never been able to get rid of them, with all my efforts."

The noise, which still continued, was that which a rat might make in dragging some object slowly along the floor. It seemed to draw closer, to approach the door of Carnby's room, and then, after an intermission, it began to move again and receded. My employer's agitation was marked; he listened with fearful intentness and seemed to follow the progress of the sound with a terror that mounted as it drew near and decreased a little with its recession.

"I am very nervous," he said. "I have worked too hard lately, and this is the result. Even a little noise upsets me."

The sound had now died away somewhere in the house. Carnby appeared to recover himself in a measure.

"Will you please re-read your translation?" he requested. "I want to follow it very carefully, word by word."

I obeyed. He listened with the same look of unholy absorption as before, and this time we were not interrupted by any noises in the hallway. Carnby's face grew paler, as if the last remnant of blood had been drained from it, when I read the final sentences; and the fire in his hollow eyes was like phosphorescence in a deep vault.

"That is a most remarkable passage," he commented. "I was doubtful about its meaning, with my imperfect Arabic; and I have found that the passage is wholly omitted in the Latin of Olaus Wormius. Thank you for your scholarly rendering. You have certainly cleared it up for me."

His tone was dry and formal, as if he were repressing himself and holding back a world of unsurmisable thoughts and emotions. Somehow I felt that Carnby was more nervous and upset than ever, and also that my rendering from the Necronomicon had in some mysterious manner contributed to his perturbation. He wore a ghastly brooding expression, as if his mind were busy with some unwelcome and forbidden theme.

However, seeming to collect himself, he asked me to translate another passage. This turned out to be a singular incantatory formula for the exorcism of the dead, with a ritual that involved the use of rare Arabian spices and the proper intoning of at least a hundred names of ghouls and demons. I copied it all out for Carnby, who studied it for a long time with a rapt eagerness that was more than scholarly.

"That, too," he observed, "is not in Olaus Wormius." After perusing it again, he folded the paper carefully and put it away in the same drawer from which he had taken the Necronomicon.

That evening was one of the strangest I have ever spent. As we sat for hour after hour discussing renditions from that unhallowed volume, I came to know more and more definitely that my employer was mortally afraid of something; that he dreaded being alone and was keeping me with him on this account rather than for any other reason. Always he seemed to be waiting and listening with a painful, tortured expectation, and I saw that he gave only a mechanical awareness to much that was said. Among the weird appurtenances of the room, in that atmosphere of unmanifested evil, of untold horror, the rational part of my mind began to succumb slowly to a recrudescence of dark ancestral fears. A scorner of such things in my normal moments. I was now ready to believe in the most baleful creations of superstitious fancy. No doubt, by some process of mental contagion, I had caught the hidden terror from which Carnby suffered.

By no word or syllable, however, did the man admit the actual feelings that were evident in his demeanor, but he spoke repeatedly of a nervous ailment. More than once, during our discussion, he sought to imply that his interest in the supernatural and the Satanic was wholly intellectual, that he, like myself, was without personal belief in such things. Yet I knew infallibly that his implications were false; that he was driven and obsessed by a real faith in all that he pretended to view with scientific detachment, and had doubtless been a victim to some imaginary horror entailed by his occult researches. But my intuition afforded me no clue to the actual nature of this horror.

There was no repetition of the sounds that had been so disturbing to my employer. We must have sat till after midnight with the writings of the mad Arab open before us. At last Carnby seemed to realize the lateness of the hour.

"I fear I have kept you up too long," he said apologetically. "You must go and get some sleep. I am selfish, and I forget that such hours are not habitual to others, as they are to me."

I made the formal denial of his self-impeachment which courtesy required, said good night, and sought my own chamber with a feeling of intense relief. It seemed to me that I would leave behind me in Carnby's room all the shadowy fear and oppression to which I had been subjected.

Only one light was burning in the long passage. It was near Carnby's door; and my own door at the further end, close to the stair-head, was in deep shadow. As I groped for the knob, I heard a noise behind me, and turned to see in the gloom a small, indistinct body that sprang from the hall landing to the top stair, disappearing from view. I was horribly startled; for even in that vague, fleeting glimpse, the thing was much too pale for a rat and its form was not at all suggestive of an animal. I could not have sworn what it was, but the outlines had seemed unmentionably monstrous. I stood trembling violently in every limb, and heard on the stairs a singular bumping sound like the fall of an object rolling downward from step to step. The sound was repeated at regular intervals, and finally ceased.

If the safety of the soul and body had depended upon it, I could not have turned on the stair-light; nor could I have gone to the top steps to ascertain the agency of that unnatural bumping. Anyone else, it might seem, would have done this. Instead, after a moment of virtual petrification, I entered my room, locked the door, and went to bed in a turmoil of unresolved doubt and equivocal terror. I left the light burning; and I lay awake for hours, expecting momentarily a recurrence of that abominable sound. But the house was as silent as a morgue, and I heard nothing. At length, in spite of my anticipations to the contrary, I fell asleep and did not awaken till after many sodden, dreamless hours.

It was ten o'clock, as my watch informed me. I wondered whether my employer had left me undisturbed through thoughtfulness, or had not arisen himself. I dressed and went downstairs, to find him waiting at the breakfast table. He was paler and more tremulous than ever, as if he had slept badly.

"I hope the rats didn't annoy you too much," he remarked, after a preliminary greeting. "Something really must be done about them."

"I didn't notice them at all," I replied. Somehow, it was utterly impossible for me to mention the queer, ambiguous thing which I had seen and heard on retiring the night before. Doubtless I had been mistaken; doubtless it had been merely a rat after all, dragging something down the stairs. I tried to forget the hideously repeated noise and the momentary flash of unthinkable outlines in the gloom.

My employer eyed me with uncanny sharpness, as if he sought to penetrate my inmost mind. Breakfast was a dismal affair; and the day that followed was no less dreary. Carnby isolated himself till the middle of the afternoon, and I was left to my own devices in the well-supplied but conventional library downstairs. What Carnby was doing alone in his room I could not surmise; but I thought more than once that I heard the faint, monotonous intonations of a solemn voice. Horror-breeding hints and noisome intuitions invaded my brain. More and more the atmosphere of that house enveloped and stifled me with poisonous, miasmal mystery; and I felt everywhere the invisible brooding of malignant incubi.

It was almost a relief when my employer summoned me to his study. Entering, I noticed that the air was full of a pungent, aromatic smell and was touched by the vanishing coils of a blue vapor, as if from the burning of Oriental gums and spices in the church censors. An Ispahan rug had been moved from its position near the wall to the center of the room, but was not sufficient to cover entirely a curving violet mark that suggested the drawing of a magic circle on the floor. No doubt Carnby had been performing some sort of incantation; and I thought of the awesome formula I had translated at his request.

However, he did not offer any explanation of what he had been doing. His manner had changed remarkably and was more controlled and confident than at any former time. In a fashion almost business-like he laid before me a pile of manuscript which he wanted me to type for him. The familiar click of the keys aided me somewhat in dismissing any apprehensions of vague evil, and I could almost smile at the recherché and terrific information comprised in my employer's notes, which dealt mainly with formulae for the acquisition of unlawful power. But still, beneath my reassurance, there was a vague, lingering disquietude.

Evening came; and after our meal we returned again to the study. There was a tenseness in Carnby's manner now, as if he were eagerly awaiting the result of some hidden test. I went on with my work; but some of his emotion communicated itself to me, and ever and anon I caught myself in an attitude of strained listening.

At last, above the click of the keys, I heard the peculiar slithering in the hall. Carnby had heard it, too, and his confident look utterly vanished, giving place to the most pitiable fear.

The sound drew nearer and was followed by a dull, dragging noise, and then by more sounds of an unidentifiable slithering and scuttling nature that varied in loudness. The hall was seemingly full of them, as if a whole army of rats were hauling some carrion booty along the floor. And yet no rodent or number of rodents could have made such sounds, or could have moved anything so heavy as the object which came behind the rest. There was something in the character of those noises, something without name or definition, which caused a slowly creeping chill to invade my spine.

"Good Lord! What is all that racket?" I cried.

"The rats! I tell you it is only the rats!" Carnby's voice was a high, hysterical shriek.

A moment later, there came an unmistakable knocking on the door, near the sill. At the same time I heard a heavy thudding in the locked cupboard at the further end of the room. Caraby had been standing erect, but now he sank limply into a chair. His features were ashen, and his look was almost maniacal with fright.

The nightmare doubt and tension became unbearable and I ran to the door and flung it open, in spite of a frantic remonstrance from my employer. I had no idea what I should find as I stepped across the sill into the dim-lit hall.

When I looked down and saw the thing on which I had almost trodden, my feeling was one of sick amazement and actual nausea. It was a human hand which had been severed at the wrist—a bony, bluish hand like that of a week-old corpse, with garden-mold on the fingers and under the long nails. *The damnable thing had moved!* It had drawn back to avoid me, and was crawling along the passage somewhat in the manner of a crab. And following it with my gaze, I saw that there were other things beyond it, one of which I recognized as a man's foot and another as a forearm. I dared not look at the rest. All were moving slowly, hideously away in a charnel procession, and I cannot describe the fashion in which they moved. Their individual vitality horrifying beyond endurance. It was more than the vitality of life, yet the air was laden with a carrion taint. I averted my eyes and stepped back into Carnby's room, closing the door behind me with a shaking hand. Carnby was at my side with the key, which he turned in the lock with palsy-stricken fingers that had become as feeble as those of an old man.

"You saw them?" he asked in a dry, quavering whisper.

"In God's name, what does it all mean?" I cried.

Carnby went back to his chair, tottering a little with weakness. His lineaments were agonized by the gnawing of some inward horror, and he shook visibly like an ague patient. I sat down in a chair beside him, and he began to stammer forth his unbelievable confession, half incoherently, with inconsequential mouthings and many breaks and pauses:

"He is stronger than I am—even in death, even with his body dismembered by the surgeon's knife and saw that I used. I thought he could not return after that—after I had buried the portions in a dozen different places, in the cellar, beneath the shrubs, at the foot of the ivy-vines. But the Necronomicon is right . . . and Helman Carnby knew it. He warned me before I killed him, he told me he could return—*even in that condition.*

"But I did not believe him. I hated Helman, and he hated me, too. He had attained to higher power and knowledge and was more favored by the Dark Ones than I. That was why I killed him—my own twin-brother, and my brother in the service of Satan and of Those who were before Satan. We had studied together for many years. We had celebrated the Black Mass together and we were attended by the same familiars. But Helman Carnby had gone deeper into the occult, into the forbidden, where I could not follow him. I feared him, and I could not endure his supremacy.

"It is more than a week—it is ten days since I did the deed. But Helman—or some part of him—has returned every night . . . God! His accursed hands crawling on the floor! His feet, his arms, the segments of his legs, climbing the stairs in some unmentionable way to haunt me! . . . Christ! His awful, bloody torso lying in wait. I tell you, his hands have come even by day to tap and fumble at my door . . . and I have stumbled over his arms in the dark.

"'Oh, God! I shall go mad with the awfulness of it. But he wants me to go mad, he wants to torture me till my brain gives way. That is why he haunts me in this piece-meal fashion. He could end it all any time with the demoniacal power that is his. He could re-knit his sundered limbs and body and slay me as I slew him.

"How carefully I buried the parts, with what infinite forethought! And how useless it was! I buried the saw and knife, too, at the farther end of the garden, as far away as possible from his evil, itching hands. But I did not bury the head with the other pieces—I kept it in that cupboard at the end of my room. Sometimes I have heard it moving there, as you heard it a little while ago . . . But he does not need the head, his will is elsewhere, and can work intelligently through all his members.

"Of course, I locked all the doors and windows at night when I found that he was coming back . . . But it made no difference. And I have tried to exorcize him with the appropriate incantations—with all those that I knew. Today I tried that sovereign formula from the Necronomicon which you translated for me. I got you here to translate it. Also, I could no longer bear to be alone and I thought that it might help if there were someone else in the house. That formula was my last hope. I thought it would hold him—it is a most ancient and most dreadful incantation. But, as you have seen, it is useless . . ."

His voice trailed off in a broken mumble, and he sat staring before him with sightless, intolerable eyes in which I saw the beginning flare of madness. I could say nothing—the confession he had made was so ineffably atrocious. The moral shock, and the ghastly supernatural horror, had almost stupefied me. My sensibilities were stunned; and it was not till I had begun to recover that I felt the irresistible surge of a flood of loathing for the man beside me.

I rose to my feet. The house had grown very silent, as if the macabre and charnel army of beleaguerment had now retired to its various graves. Carnby had left the key in the lock; and I went to the door and turned it quickly.

"Are you leaving? Don't go," Carnby begged in a voice that was tremulous with alarm, as I stood with my hand on the door-knob.

"Yes, I am going," I said coldly. "I am resigning my position right now; and I intend to pack my belongings and leave your house with as little delay as possible."

I opened the door and went out, refusing to listen to the arguments and pleadings and protestations he had begun to babble. For the nonce, I preferred to face whatever might lurk in the gloomy passage, no matter how loathsome and terrifying, rather than endure any longer the society of John Carnby.

The hall was empty; but I shuddered with repulsion at the memory of what I had seen, as I hastened to my room. I think I should have screamed aloud at the least sound or movement in the shadows.

I began to pack my valise with a feeling of the most frantic urgency and compulsion. It seemed to me that I could not escape soon enough from that house of abominable secrets, over which hung an atmosphere of smothering menace. I made mistakes in my haste, I stumbled over chairs, and my brain and fingers grew numb with a paralyzing dread.

I had almost finished my task, when I heard the sound of slow measured footsteps coming up the stairs. I knew that it was not Carnby, for he had locked himself immediately in his room when I had left; and I felt sure that nothing could have tempted him to emerge. Anyway, he could hardly have gone downstairs without my hearing him.

The footsteps came to the top landing and went past my door along the hall, with that same dead monotonous repetition, regular as the movement of a machine. Certainly it was not the soft, nervous tread of John Carnby.

Who, then, could it be? My blood stood still in my veins; I dared not finish the speculation that arose in my mind.

The steps paused; and I knew that they had reached the door of Carnby's room. There followed an interval in which I could scarcely breathe; and then I heard an awful crashing and shattering noise, and above it the soaring scream of a man in the uttermost extremity of fear.

I was powerless to move, as if an unseen iron hand had reached forth to restrain me; and I have no idea how long I waited and listened. The scream had fallen away in a swift silence; and I heard nothing now, except a low, peculiar, recurrent sound which my brain refused to identify.

It was not my own volition, but a stronger will than mine, which drew me forth at last and impelled me down the hall to Carnby's study. I felt the presence of that will as an overpowering, superhuman thing—a demoniac force, a malign mesmerism.

The door of the study had been broken in and was hanging by one hinge. It was splintered as by the impact of more than mortal strength. A light was still burning in the room, and the unmentionable sound I had been hearing ceased as I neared the threshold. It was followed by an evil, utter stillness.

Again I paused, and could go no further. But, this time, it was something other than the hellish, all-pervading magnetism that petrified my limbs and arrested me before the sill. Peering into the room, in the narrow space that was framed by the doorway and lit by an unseen lamp, I saw one end of the Oriental rug, and the gruesome outlines of a monstrous, unmoving shadow that fell beyond it on the floor. Huge, elongated, misshapen, the shadow was seemingly cast by the arms and torso of a naked man who stooped forward with a surgeon's saw in his hand. Its monstrosity lay in this: though the shoulders, chest, abdomen and arms were all clearly distinguishable, the shadow was headless and appeared to terminate in an abruptly severed neck. It was impossible, considering the relative position, for the head to have been concealed from sight through any manner of foreshortening.

I waited, powerless to enter or withdraw. The blood had flowed back upon my heart in an ice-thick tide, and thought was frozen in my brain. An interval of termless horror, and then, from the hidden end of Carnby's room, from the direction of the locked cupboard, there came a fearsome and violent crash, and the sound of splintering wood and whining hinges, followed by the sinister, dismal thud of an unknown object striking the floor.

Again there was silence—a silence as of consummated Evil brooding above its unnamable triumph. The shadow had not stirred. There was a hideous contemplation in its attitude, and the saw was still held in its poising hand, as if above a completed task.

Another interval, and then, without warning, I witnessed the awful and unexplainable *disintegration* of the shadow, which seemed to break gently and easily into many different shadows ere it faded from view. I hesitate to describe the manner, or specify the places, in which this singular disrupttion, this manifold cleavage, occurred. Simultaneously, I heard the muffled clatter of a metallic implement on the Persian rug, and a sound that was not that of a single body but of many bodies falling.

Once more there was silence—a silence as of some nocturnal cemetery, when grave-diggers and ghouls are done with their macabre toil, and the dead alone remain.

Drawn by that baleful mesmerism, like a somnambulist led by an unseen demon, I entered the room, I knew with a loathly prescience the sight that awaited me beyond the sill—the *double* heap of human segments, some of them fresh and bloody, and others already blue with beginning putrefaction and marked with earth-stains, that were mingled in abhorrent confusion on the rug.

A reddened knife and saw were protruding from the pile; and a little to one side, between the rug and the open cupboard with its shattered door, there reposed a human head that was fronting the other remnants in an upright posture. It was in the same condition of incipient decay as the body to which it had belonged; but I swear that I saw the fading of a malignant exultation from its features as I entered. Even with the marks of corruption upon them, the lineaments bore a manifest likeness of John Carnby, and plainly they could belong only to a twin brother.

The frightful inferences that smothered my brain with their black and clammy cloud are not to be written here. The horror which I beheld—and the greater horror which I surmised—would have put to shame hell's foulest enormities in their frozen pits. There was but one mitigation and one mercy: I was compelled to gaze only for a few instants on that intolerable scene. Then, all at once, I felt that something had withdrawn from the room; the malign spell was broken, the overpowering volition that had held me captive was gone. It had released me now, even as it had released the dismembered corpse of Helman Carnby. I was free to go; and I fled from the ghastly chamber and ran headlong through an unlit house and into the outer darkness of the night.

Robert E. Howard's

17
The Little Gods Wait
Donald Wandrei
(1932)

Donald Wandrei's poem "The Little Gods Wait," published in the July 1932 issue of *Weird Tales*, appeared in the same issue as Robert E. Howard's classic tale, "The Dark Man." In his July 13, 1932 letter to H.P. Lovecraft, Howard wrote, "I was much taken with Wandrei's recent poem, 'The Little Gods Wait.' It had a distinctly Celtic flavor; so much so that I would not have believed that anyone besides an Irishman could have written it. I have always highly admired Wandrei's work, and I believe I like that poem better than anything else of his I ever read." The first writer to emulate Lovecraft, Wandrei, along with August Derleth, created Arkham House, which published Howard's first collection from *Weird Tales* magazine: *Skull-Face and Others* (1946).

The little gods wait in the heart of the mountains,
  The little gods dream an apocalyptic dream;
The little gods sleep by faëry's phantom fountains,
  The little gods hide where the fen-fires gleam.

Their elders have promised them a day of returning,
  When post-historic revels will utfetter them,
When skies turn to flame in a universe burning,
  And ashes consume what the elders condemn.

The little gods then will tremble and waken
  And rub out the granules of sleep from their eyes;
When death has been captured and time overtaken
  The little gods will answer their elders and rise.

Robert E. Howard's

The little gods will walk from hill and from highlands,
   And four-dimension vaults revolve and open wide;
They will spew from the sea and climb from sunken islands,
   From time-gulfs and planes of space they will glide.

The little gods wait in the heart of the mountains,
   The little gods dream their apocalyptic dream;
They sleep a long sleep by faëry's phantom fountains,
   And they hide in eery lands where the fen-fires gleam.

18
The Last of Placide's Wife
Kirk Mashburn
(1932)

Born in Meridian, Mississippi and six years older than Robert E. Howard, Wallace Kirkpatrick Mashburn, Jr. was an insurance salesman in Houston, Texas, who had a brief career as an author for *Weird Tales* magazine. His first published story, "The Sword of Jean Lafitte," appeared in the December 1927 issue, and his last story, "The Toad Idol," appeared in the September 1935 issue. In between, the first of two stories about Nita Duboin, "Placide's Wife," was published in the November 1931 issue, while the second story featured here, appeared in the September 1932 issue. In a letter to Kirk Mashburn, dated that same month, Howard wrote, "Just a line (and rather belated too,) to congratulate you on 'The Last of Placide's Wife.' It's a splendid story; you have the knack of making the impossible convincing, which is the true test of a weird story writer." It should also be noted that Mashburn wrote a letter in defense of Howard against Robert Bloch's scathing comments about his most popular character, Conan, that were published in the March 1935 issue's readers forum, "The Eyrie."

It must have been a fierce and bloody fight. I heard excited talk of it as soon as I stepped from the train in Labranch. My duties as district highway engineer had brought me there before, and nearly every one in the little town knew who I was. But they are folk shy in the presence of strangers, most of them, in that rural, almost isolated section. I was an outsider, and sensed something of their talk kept apart from me as such.

I heard only that there had been a wild fight, the night before, between the sheriff's men and a gang of murderous gispies—though particulars were more than vague about the gipsies. On the island in the fork of Labranch Bayou, they said it was; and that roused my interest at once. For it was there the highway department was building a difficult stretch of road no contractor had cared to undertake. I hurried to the island, and what I found in the road camp brought me back at once to town.

I had been told—almost the only definite information I had got—that I would find young Delacroix, the timekeeper and camp clerk, at the only hotel in Labranch. I located his room, and entered in a considerable temper, when he opened to my knock.

"Come in—sit down," Delacroix greeted me pleasantly, waving to a chair and himself slumped casually upon the bed. His gesture embraced a bottle of whiskey, half empty, that sat upon a table handy to his reach. "Have a drink?"

"No, I won't have a drink!" I snapped. "Is everybody else drunk, too? I went out to the job, and found two teams idling around, and a half-dozen Cajun and nigger laborers sitting stupidly on stumps—no engineer, no foreman, no timekeeper—nobody!"

"I guess so," Delacroix agreed vaguely, pouring himself a drink. I was by now thoroughly exasperated.

"You guess so!" I exploded. "You're like those Cajun laborers, for all your two years at the university! The total information I got out of them was where to find you. They wouldn't even tell me where the foreman was. Nor Gregory." The latter was the department's section engineer.

"They don't know where Gregory and the foreman are—but you'll never see *them* again," Delacroix informed mildly, after he had swallowed his drink. Then, with sudden force—"Have a drink and keep quiet—or just keep quiet—and I'll tell you about it. *Sit down!*"

Startled, I obeyed without thinking, dropping into the chair behind me. As I was on the point of rising and rescuing my dignity, Delacroix's words caught my attention. Forgetting my anger, I sat and listened.

This is the meat of what I heard:

Old man Landry [Delacroix began] had a son who was attacked, one evening after sunset, while he was hunting in the woods of Labranch Island. They found what was left of him the next day, a small wound in his throat, and his body drained of blood. Well! Right away, everybody said that Placide's wife did it—the wife of Placide Duboin buried one night a dozen years ago, because he thought he had killed her. But Nita, his wife, came out of her grave, an undead thing who preyed on the living after sundown. Placide was her first victim.

This dead-alive woman, who lay like a corpse in her grave during each day, rose and walked abroad at night between sunset and dawn, seeking living victims to quench her thirst for blood. Old Landry's son was one of the first to fall her prey, nearly eleven years ago. They found him the next day, and buried him with a stake through his heart. So he did not lie where Nita left him, to arise the next night with his own terrible craving for blood—to be from then on, another such thing as she.

Oh? No, I am not drunk; not yet, at any rate. I am trying to tell you what became of Gregory, and why the road camp is almost empty. Do you want to listen, or not?

Well, anyway, Nita, and those who feel into her clutches and became like her, could not get off that island between the forks of Labranch Bayou, and island some six to eight miles wide, by nearly fifteen miles long. (Vampires and werewolves, you understand, can not cross running water.)

It is across this island that we have been building the new highway. One night, not very long ago, while I was telling Gregory the story of Placide's wife, there was a knock on the door. And who do you suppose was there? Placide's wife, herself! She pretended otherwise, naturally, but I recognized her and called to old Landry, who had hoped to meet her, and been prepared for the meeting, ever since his son's death. He carried a gun loaded with silver bullets blessed by the priest, the only kind that can kill a vampire. But Nita ran to the woods before Landry came up, and I kept him from following. In the forest, with her pack around her, she would have made short work of the old man.

It had become the main thing in Landry's life, to even up with Nita on account of his son. He finally got so impatient that he went into the woods alone, one evening, hoping to put a silver bullet into Nita. Doubtless he was a little crazy on the subject. And it turned out that Nita got him! At least, we found he had gone, and he did not come back.

Gregory was sort of skeptical, and didn't much believe the story I told him about Placide's wife. He insisted Nita was nothing but one of a band of gipsy thieves and murderers. He was a special deputy sheriff, Gregory, so he could carry a gun, on account of our payroll and things like that, and he was pretty mad, you understand, about old many Landry. He was already disgusted because it was hard for us to get men who were not afraid of Nita and would stay in our camp on the island at night, and they would come straggling in late every morning. So Gregory got most of our men together the next morning and gave them guns; then sent word to the sheriff here in Labranch, that he was going into the swamps and round up the "gipsies". Ha! I was one of those who went.

We went clear down to where the swamp begins at the end of the island on the bay, without seeing any sign of anybody except two trappers we ran across, men we knew. Nobody expected to find Nita, except Gregory. The men began to get uneasy, late in the afternoon, and decided to turn back before sundown caught us away from camp. Gregory didn't like it, but what was he going to do? The men told him he could stay if he wanted, but they were going back. Gregory used some language

I wish I could remember—me, I never can say what I want to when I'm mad!—but he turned back with the rest.

Sundown found us a good mile away from camp, deep in the woods. We still could count on nearly an hour of daylight, and Gregory sneered at the men's uneasiness because the sun had set. But everybody *else* was uneasy, some more than others. The woods were thick, and in the fading light of late day, dim and shadowy. Except for the noise we made ourselves, the forest was still and quiet. But it was an uncomfortable quiet, as if the trees all around us hid things that watched, and waited their own time to show themselves. So!

Suddenly, amid startled exclamations, we stopped in our tracks. Anybody would have stopped! I think we all saw the gleaming shape that barred our way, at the same moment. In a little cleared space ahead of us stood a slender figure, a woman whose body gleamed in the red light of sunset like a statue carved from smooth old ivory. She was completely nude, except that the light breeze wrapped the ends of her shining black hair (which hung like a dark cloak almost to the backs of her knees), carelessly about her hips. Her face was the most beautiful I have ever seen on a woman. Beautiful, that is, except for the evil in her bright eyes, and the cruelty in the smile of her scarlet lips.

But there was nothing beautiful about her to us—we knew that here was the thing we had hunted—that we had met at least with Placide's wife!

Nita stood, with that mocking smile, looking at us from between narrowed lids that slanted upward, a little, at the corners. She seemed careless, and amused, but I saw her nostrils twitch from where I stood. Like any other wild, naked thing of the woods! Her eyes opened suddenly wide, and they blazed with the same light I have seen in a cat's when she pounced upon a mouse. She waved one slim hand toward us in a swift, fierce gesture.

The woods were suddenly alive. Silent, grinning figures, some clad and some as naked as she, sprang at us from among the trees. Without waiting for a word from Gregory, our men blazed away, with shotguns and pistols. Gregory himself aimed squarely at Nita, and I saw his shotgun spit fire. Nita stood straining forward on her toes, watching as her pack closed with us, her lips drawn tightly back from her sharp, pointed teeth. I saw her laugh, horribly, as Gregory shot at her; then she sprang at him. He pumped buckshot from his gun at close range, but she merely gurgled with that horrible laughter, and leaped at him. After that, I was too busy with a shock-headed and foul-smelling old devil who flung himself on me, to bother with Gregory and Nita.

Nita's band numbered about the same as ours, but they had the strength of oxen. The thing with which I fought, for all his blazing red eyes and dripping mouth, looked like only a scrawny old man. But his hands were iron, and I was helpless in his grip. It seemed that I was tangled in a web, and my arms and legs would not move as I wanted them to, after the old man glared into my eyes. It was like a nightmare, when you try to scream, to run, and can not. Unable to do more than stare ahead, with my eyes popping in fright, I felt the awful, reeking mouth of that ancient horror drooling upon my neck. Dimly, I heard Nita screaming, felt the cold lips draw back from my flesh. Nita's voice kept on, sounding as if she moved swiftly from one place to another. All about was a snarling, as of hungry beasts driven from their kills; then everything swam in blackness.

My head cleared, after a minute, and I realized that I was being carried along through the forest, thrown over the shoulder of that old creature who stank, and who had fought me. I said he was old and scrawny; but he carried me as easily as a ten-pound sack of meal. We went through the woods as fast as a horse trots, the trampling of many feet keeping pace with us. I twisted my head about, trying to see.

We went through a dim open space; I twisted enough to look ahead of the dirty old one who carried me, and saw Nita, with Gregory slung on her back, leading the way as easily as though she ran unburdened. Around and behind, the hell-pack ran with us. Each of them carried a man, and some of them seemed to be carrying double. All flitted through the woods, silently and lightly as dark shadows.

On we went, and I knew our direction more by instinct than otherwise, toward the southern end of the island, where the dank woods blend into the swamp that becomes a marsh, lying along the Gulf.

Soon we were in the swamp. Often I heard the suck of soggy earth that clutched at hurrying feet; once scummy water splashed into my down-hung face, as the pack pattered through a shallow pool of smelly, stagnant water. All this time, until we finally came to a stop, I lay quietly over that old one's shoulder. His arms were about my legs like bands of steel, but not even the thought of struggle or escape came into my queerly dulled brain.

When the troop finally halted, I dimly saw that we were in the middle of a large piece of dry land, slightly higher than the swamp around it, and almost clear of trees. The old pig who carried me let me slip head first to the ground. Thanks to the soft ground, and none to him, my neck was not broken; it was bad enough at that.

I sat up and looked around that place. Other men, no doubt also dropped like sacks of onions, were lying on the ground, or sitting looking stupid, like me. A few were getting groggily to their feet. Not much showed plainly in the dark, but there were other figures with eyes gleaming like wolves', standing over those on the ground, or getting in the way of the few who tottered on their feet. All of these with glowing eyes were half stretching their hands toward the ones they stood by, and at the same thing, all looking eagerly at something near where I sat. I looked to see what it was they stared at so, and saw that Nita was standing there. Her eyes were glowing like yellow coals, and she had one hand out to steady Gregory on his feet. Then she waved her other hand lazily toward a clump of bushes, and the shadows with eyes pulled the figures upon the ground to their feet, and prodded them in that direction.

All at once, the knoll began to glow with a dim bluish light, like a wet match in the dark. It came from nowhere, you understand, and did not seem to light the swamp beyond the wide knoll. The light grew stronger, while my dirty old one pushed me along with the rest.

Nita led toward a covert of bushes almost in the middle of the knoll. Within these bushes, the blue light glowed stronger than anywhere else. Nita parted the growth and stepped through, leading Gregory. We pushed and jostled our way behind her.

We scrambled through into a circular open place, in the center of which was a low mount of earth. Nita urged Gregory toward the mound, and gently forced him to sit. She herself leaped lightly up, and turned to face the rest of us, her body gleaming now like a silver column in the blue light. My old one pushed me closer, and the others crowded around. Nita looked us over carefully for a moment, before she spoke.

"There are two more than we are," she said, evidently talking for the benefit of her pack. "I will keep the man I have taken"—she motioned toward Gregory—"and also those other two—" She paused and leaned slightly forward, as the place hummed with angry murmurs and snarls of protest. Her eyes blazed from her narrowed lid, and she snarled back at them.

"Pigs and cattle! I say that three are mine! I am first among you, the mother of the pack, and I claim the right." Her gaze rested on me. "I will take that one," she said, pointing. The smelly old creature who had my arm tightened his grip until his hard, skinny fingers sank into my flesh.

"No!" he screeched; "I caught this one, and I keep him."

"Durand has two: take that one from him." The old one followed the point of her finger, and observed a wolf-eyed one who held fast to a pair of our men. They were two young fellows out of our grubbing gang; and though they stood as quietly as terrified sheep in the clutch of the one Nita called Durand, they were both husky, full-blooded youngsters. My *sale vieux* peered at hem, both so much larger and stronger than I, and grinned. Slobbering as he grinned, he pushed me toward Nita, and with a little squeal of satisfaction ran and pounced upon the nearest of the grubbers.

Nita coolly claimed a third captive, and the pack started to hustle the rest of our men out of the circular enclosure with a sudden eagerness. Nita halted them with a sharp word.

"Wait!" she called, her hand upraised. The pack paused. "Remember," Nita continued, "there is a new one among us, who must have a grave that he can not dig himself . . . Let the newcomers dig his—*and their own!*—before you . . . drink . . ." Then she waved them away.

Most of the dullness that had numbed my wits cleared, with the transfer of that old thing's attention from me, and I suddenly observed one that I had not before noticed. I saw old Landry (he whom we have come to avenge!) pushing from the place as eagerly as any of Nita's crew. One knotted hand gripped a staring, white-faced figure—a man he had worked beside, a few days before—that he regarded with greedy, blazing eyes! Landry was the recruit to whom Nita had referred!

The place was left bare of all except Nita and us three she had claimed: Gregory, myself, and a youngish fellow named Alcide Breaux. Nita bent and smiled into Gregory's eyes.

"I leave you for a little while," she told him; and it amused me, even then, because she said it as if it was something for Greg to regret. She stared into his eyes a moment more, and added, "Wait here, quietly, until I come back."

Stepping lithely down, she came over to me, a mocking smile upon her lips.

"So, *M'sieu'* Delacroix! We meet again!" She waited for me to answer, but I only stared at her, trying to put my finger on something that puzzled me.

"This time, you can not call for old Landry to come with his silver bullets—as you did another time, when I knocked at your door in the road camp! This little talk is different, yes?"

That was it! Her talk. Queer, is it not, how trifles occupy the mind at such times?

"Yes," I said; "*your* talk is a whole lot different: the last time I heard you, your English, it was not so good."

"Aha, *M'sieu le Cajun*," she mocked, "your own is rather queer!" She smiled indulgently, and explained, "I am speaking my own language, the language spoken in the high mountains in a country far beyond the sea. You understand it because I will it, and it seems to you that I speak a familiar tongue."

I shrugged, because I could think of nothing to say. Nita touched my chin with the tip of her finger, which was cold as the hand of Death. I bent my head under her touch, so that I looked full into her eyes, that seemed to have points of flame dancing in their depths. Once more I began to feel dull and numb, and my wits grew sluggish. It was an effort to think, to concentrate. Nita lightly flipped my chin as she took away her finger.

"You amuse me—a very little, but still you amuse me," I heard her mocking voice in a kind of daze. "I think I shall leave you until later, and take this other oaf. Go sit upon my—" Whatever she was about to say, she checked it, and finished, "Go sit with Gregory."

With no thought to do otherwise, I went and sat down where she told me. Then I saw she was staring into Breaux's face as she had into mine; but her smile was a terrible and ghoulish thing, while her eyes were like flaming pools of fire.

"Come!" she commanded, in a husky, quivering whisper. Obediently, though with a fleeting spasm of despair twitching his face, Breaux followed. He moved too slowly for Nita's liking, for she seized his arm and drew him with feverish eagerness across the clearing. Into the screening bushes she pulled him. Nita fairly panted as she pushed poor Alcide through the growth, and I thought dully, that her red mouth drooled. It is horrible when I think of it now; but I looked on without interest, then, as the bushes closed behind them, and Nita and Alcide . . . were gone . . .

How long Gregory and I sat there alone, I have no idea. Neither of us spoke, and time seemed to stand still. It would have been too much effort to talk or move, or even lie back to rest. We kept motionless, I think, and waited; nothing at all mattered, until Nita suddenly came back and smiled down on us.

The fire had left her eyes, and she seemed younger, and *refreshed* . . . There was a smile of exhilaration on her beautiful red lips, redder now than before. I saw the tip of her tongue lick over those lips with satisfaction. Poor Alcide!

Nita dropped lazily down between us, smiling first at Gregory, then at me. "Don't be so dull-witted!" she reproved. She must have had some deliberate intention of lifting the spell that kept us so listless; for my brain cleared with her words, and I straightened as I sat. So did Gregory. Nita leaned toward him.

"Ah, that is better!" she breathed. "It has been long since any one except stupid, clod-like men, little better than brute beasts, came to this place." She reached out a hand, put it softly upon Greg's knee, her eyes half closed, smoldering with a fire different from the fierce light that had flamed in them earlier in the evening. "There are other good things besides food and drink—warm, salty drinks! This body of mine is still a woman's . . . Is it not fair?"

God, she was beautiful! There was reason for Gregory to lean toward her, biting his lips—even though he knew, now, what sort of thing she was. Nita had said that she came from a far land: her old-ivory skin, with its hint of underlying olive tint, and the upward slant of her eyes at the corners, told that she spoke the truth. The shameless creature lay back and laughed with brazen delight at Gregory's open fascination.

"Do you find me beautiful?" she demanded naïvely. Sitting up quickly, she eagerly asked, "Do you like beautiful things?"

Gregory stared at her without answering, but there was something in his silence that seemed to please Nita as well as words. "Will you come to me willingly, Gregory, rather than as that one of your men I—had—tonight, without my arms and love to make—what happened—a caress and a promise of future delight in me? Will you take a love no mortal woman could give?"

Suddenly she struck the earth with one small hand. "Do you know what this is?" she demanded. Without waiting for answer, she told us. "It is where I lie and rest during the day—is it not in a good place, here in the heart of this swamp? No trappers or hunters come so far, and you will be safe with me." She laughed, with sudden malicious merriment.

"Old Placide, that dear husband of mine, showed me this place! There was a gipsy peddler who wanted both me and Placide's money: the money he got for his land when oil was found on it, before I came to Labranch and married him. The money was buried near out house, but Placide was frightened of the peddler, and dug it up, and brought it here where he knew no one would ever come to look for it. I spied him when he did it, and followed him here. Afterward, I remembered this place. His money is there now, at the head of my earthen couch!" She laughed gleefully again, but sobered quickly. She leaned toward Gregory, and her voice was vibrant with passion. Gregory half raised his hands, and her pale body writhed into his arms. I stared, you can imagine, with my mouth open: I was astonished at Nita, but I was ashamed of Gregory. I was thinking of poor Alcide, you understand!

Then, in a flash, I comprehended. Nita's wild mood fixed her interest on him, and Gregory played up to her, so she would not notice me. He was forcing himself to hold her close, swallowing his disgust to bend his head to those unclean red lips—so I might slip out and escape!

As Greg seized Nita in a sudden fierce grip that I thought was fine acting, I crept on hands and knees behind her back, toward that place through which she took Alcide. Creeping through the bushes, I came on something that caused me to jerk upright, scratching my face on the twigs around me. I looked down into the dead, staring face of Alcide, and shivered all over as I made the cross. Behind me was the mound in the darkness, with a glow like phosphorous hanging around it and around two dark forms, so close together that they were like one . . .

Not until that minute did I fully realize the awful nightmare of that place and the things that lived there. All my life I had heard tales of vampires and werewolves; I had listened to stories of Placide's wife, and how men had gone into this same swamp, and had not come back. True, I wondered, and I had been careful to keep in camp after sundown, since we had been on the island. But the tales had been tales, and this was something else. I felt the little silver medal hung on a cord around my neck, and whispered to all the saints I could remember. Heh! You can believe *that!*

Very carefully, I poked my head out and looked around. There was not much of a moon, and all I could see, at first, was those other mounds that covered the flat knoll. The bluish glow that had lighted up the place when we first came had died away; but there was that sort of phosphorous haze about some of the mounds, and I gradually made out some dark objects lying or hunkered upon on all of them. In most cases, there were two of them on each mound—one lying across the other.

In a flash, I knew what those dark shapes were! One of each pair was a man of our party; the other was the thing that owned the mound . . . It was horrible, I tell you! Those devils were lying there on our poor fellows, still and quiet, like dogs that have gorged on too much meat. Piff-f!

I remember that I didn't have time to get sick at the stomach. You comprehend, I wanted to be going, to get away from there and bring back help to Gregory. The way we had come was mostly over a dry path through the swamp; I wondered if I could slip across the knoll and get back the same way. I started to find out, crawling on hands and knees, and holding my breath to keep from making a sound.

One of the mounds was close by, but I crawled past it without anything happening. After going a little further, I saw that, whichever way I turned, there was nothing for it but to creep between two more. I went forward inch by inch, cold sweat running down into my eyes. But the things lying on the mounds kept lying there. They were so close together that I had to crawl near enough to see that the mounds were heaps of turned-up raw clods; there was an open hole to the side of them. Dully, I wondered how much trouble it was for the things to pull the dirt in on top of them, when they crawled in their holes at sun-up . . . My heart stood still when the one on my right made a noise in its throat, and moved a little. But it was quiet, after that, and I crept on.

There was not much farther to go until I would be on the path through the swamp. One more heap of raw clods I had to pass; but there was a clump of those low bushes near it, that would hide as I passed. I reached the bushes, when a low squeaking noise made me sink flat on my stomach. I listened, my ears strained like my nerves, and heard it again—it seemed to come from over my head. I looked up. The white skeleton of a dead cypress stood on the other side of that grave the bushes grew by. Hanging to the lowest limb of the dead tree was a black something that looked like a bat—only it couldn't be. But it was! A bat as big as one of those buzzards, hanging there by its feet, and making overgrown squeaks, as bats do in their sleep.

I went around the bushes, hugging the ground. I had that bat all figured out you understand—there had been only *one* black splotch on those clods under the dead cypress!

The bat was too much on my mind. I didn't notice where I was going. Something moved, out there ahead of me. I had run right onto another one of those vampire nests—two glowing eyes glared into mine, and great wolf-thing—that I knew was *no* wolf!—rose up from on the other side of a hole, not twenty feet away!

The wolf snarled; I could see the gleam of its teeth in the dim moonlight. I knew that I was caught, that I had to run for it. There was no use in waiting there for that thing to come slobbering at my throat. The swamp was right ahead of me. I jumped up and dashed for it; and that wolf howled and dashed after me!

Never did I go anywhere as fast as I went from that place. The howls of the wolf behind me roused the knoll; a dozen howls answered, as if that many of the vampires took up the chase in the form of wolves. I had no thought of path, now; but plunged in blind fear through the swamp. Once more I felt of the little silver medal of the Virgin hung around my neck; I felt it while I called silently on all the saints I could remember.

The wolf panted at my heels, and only my terrible fright kept me ahead of it for so long. It was bound to catch me—I could almost feel its hot breath on my back. I whirled, just as the beast put on an extra spurt, to spring at my shoulders. What good my bare hands could have done against that slavering terror, I can not imagine; but I threw them out, instinctively.

Something strange happened. One clenched hand had torn the blessed little medal from its cord around my neck. That was pure accident; and it was also accident that I cast that medal straight into the open maw of the mad beast as it sprang at me. For one terrible instant I felt the hot stinking breath of the thing in my face. Then it dropped down, bucking and making choking noises in its throat.

Whether the holiness of the little medal had anything to do with it, or whether it was a plain case of the wolf-thing choking on it, I neither knew nor cared. The main thing was for me to go on while the going was good; and I did.

Suddenly out of the darkness behind me came a furious squeaking, and something beat at my head, scratching my cheek. It was a great bat, like the one I had seen hanging to the dead cypress; and another joined it. Their little eyes blazed like red fires of hate, and the wings that beat at me were as heavy as a man's arms. They beat me down on my knees in the mud. The howling of the vampire wolves from the knoll came closer and closer through the swamp.

Without thinking, I dug handfuls of the soft mud at my knees, flinging the slimy stuff into the squeaking faces of the monster bats. It seemed to annoy them, for they squeaked furiously and darted up out of reach. I used the second before they swooped back, to spring to my feet and stagger on. Then they were on me again, their heavy wings battering at my head, the claws on the wings scratching my face until the blood ran down onto my neck. A great, fire-eyed owl swooped suddenly down and joined the bats. The werewolves were so close that I saw their dark forms, their flaming eyes; and there were other dark shapes running with them, like men, but with eyes that blazed like theirs.

I felt the clinging mud beneath my feet go thin, become water that wet my ankles. I could go no further; the heavy wings pounded at my head, and I slipped and fell sprawling. Half choked with slimy water, I lay as I fell, lifting my head only to clear my nose and mouth. The water slowly crawled against my chin. Too exhausted to get up, or even to move or put my arms over my head to keep off those terrible wings, I waited without hope for an awful end.

Nothing happened. The wolves came dashing up, so close that I heard their panting, between yelps and snarling growls. Turning over on one elbow, I looked back and wondered. There were the wolves, whimpering and slavering, nor more than a couple of yards from y feet; and the red-eyed things in the shapes of men snarled there with them. In the air a half-dozen of the bats whirled and squeaked, and a pair of huge black owls with fiery eyes like saucers whirled with them. But none of the swooping things passed over my head; one of the whining pack sprang at me!

Suddenly I knew what held them back. Years and years before, some one had sunk what was hoped to be an oil well, on this part of the island. The well came in, flowing nothing but salt water, and was left there without even the casing being pulled. After all these years, a little water still flows occasionally from that old well, and seeps through the swamp of the bayou. I lay in water that flowed, however shallow and sluggish—*and those vampires could not cross or enter running water, nor even fly about it!*

As long as I lay there I was safe! But I could not lie there until morning sent the devil pack scampering to its holes, because of Gregory. I must get back to him before it was too late. I knew that old well was not far from the fork of the bayou nearest Labranch. The things that whined for my blood could not follow except by scampering all the way around the head of that blessed water. Perhaps I could them to the bayou bank. Well, I would try! So!

I staggered to my feet, shaking my fist at the things like men and wolves that yowled their helpless hate at me, and at those other things that hooted and Squeaked, swooping above them through the trees.

I had my breath back now, was no longer weak and panting. Splashing out of the water, I started for the bayou as fast as my legs would take me. The thirsting things behind me yelped and raced off to round the old well, and so come at me again. God, how I ran! And thanked heaven as I ran, that there was not much except solid ground under my feet, so far, nor much undergrowth to slow my pace.

On I went, until I began to pant for breath again. Hope of reaching the bayou rose, for I knew it could not be much farther away, and I had not yet heard any more of the howling devils on my track. Just as I was about to slow down and take it easier, I heard them again, yelping in the distance but coming like the rush of wind. One I staggered; on to the bayou. I could sense the nearness of the saving stream, now. Two hundred yards ahead through the darkness . . . a hundred . . .

Silently, without warning, the bats swarmed out of the swamp at my back. They came in a cloud, great devil owls with the monster bats, swooping, beating again at my head. I struggled on, on . . .

The wolves came up; close behind them padded the things like men with eyes of fire. There were so many that they were in one another's way; and that was all that saved me from being torn to pieces at once. The great bats beat me with their wings, and tore at my face with hooked claws. One of the men vampires seized my wrist. This time, I knew that my end had surely come. It was horrible to die like that, and with the bayou so near—horrible to die an unclean death from which I would rise up to be one of those things that howled for my blood! I went made for a moment, and fought with such fury that I held them off a little longer, screaming as I fought. And then—even in my madness, I heard what it was that made those snarling things fall back and stand quivering, listening: I had screamed—*and the cries of many men answered from near by in the swamp!*

Even while we stood frozen, those friends and I together, points of light showed faintly, moving through the trees. Lights—lanterns!—and the voices of *men!*

"Help!" I cried. "This way—help!"

Again my cry was answered; and some one fired three shots, as if they were a signal. Farther off, the baying of hounds sounded, and three rapid, answering shots.

The things around me, all but one of the werewolves, turned and rushed to meet the men who were running up with lights. The lone beast sprang in to finish me, but I fought so desperately, now that help was near, that it could not get at my throat. It knocked me from my feet, and we rolled and fought on the ground. I knew there could be but one end to this business; but shots rang out from close at hand, and yelps and howls mingled with shouts and curses of men. There was something—something of surprize and fear and pain—in the howls that made the beast leave off its slashing at me. It sprang back, bristling, its red eyes glaring madder than ever. Suddenly it let out one howl of its own, and raced to join the pack.

Staggering to my feet, I saw that a made fight was on, there among the trees. Dark figures blazed away with guns that spit fire in the murk; others stabbed at wolf and bat and red-eyed vampires in the shapes of men, with pointed wooden stakes. Every time a gun roared, there would be a shriek of agony, and a bat-thing would fall thudding to the ground; a wolf would spring high into the air, yowling its hate; or a thing like a man with blazing eyes would scream and fall writhing.

But the guns were few, and the men with stakes were not having things all their own way. Some of them fell, and I don't like to remember it. The vampires greatly outnumbered the others, you understand. But the baying of hounds came nearer and nearer. The gods themselves burst into view, furious and eager to join the fight. They rushed in—and yelped with sudden terror when they found what things they had to fight. Here were creatures no dogs could stand against. The poor beasts turned and fled!

But other men followed the dogs; and two of these had guns that joined the few already roaring. Now the odds changed; and suddenly something else happened. Except for maybe a dozen that were lying still on the ground—there were *no* vampires! The bats shot off through the trees; wolves streaked into the bushes; the things that looked like men faded into a gust of wind that swept away into the swamp!

I stumbled forward, and some one came to meet me. It was Sheriff Desarde.

"Hey, you, Delacroix!" he cried, "what's happened down here? Where's Gregory and the rest of your fellows?" Somebody had a canteen of water, and handed it to me. I gulped half of it down my dry throat before I started urging the sheriff toward that knoll where I had left Gregory with Nita. Tired as I was, I thought I could guide the sheriff and his men back over the way I had escaped, and I was in a hurry to go. I told Desarde what had taken place, in as few words as possible, and we set off at double time.

"They'll know we're coming, and not all of them were here," I warned the sheriff Desarde was confident.

"I was in Baton Rouge this morning," he told me as we went, "and Legendre"—Rene Legendre is his chief deputy, you understand—"didn't know what to do when Gregory's men came in with his note about old Jules Landry's disappearance, and saying he was going to go into the swamp and round up the 'gipsies.' I got back to town just before another man came in from your camp, saying you fellows hadn't come back. It was seven o'clock then, and I knew what had happened—I was a grown man when Placide Duboin married that Nita, and I know as much about her as anybody!

"I got a gunsmith to jerk the lead out of enough bullets for a half-dozen guns, and put silver in them, instead. That was all we had time to wait for; so I gave the rest of them some poles I had, already sharpened, ready to stake out some pole beans I'm growing; we took them by the church and wet them plenty, in the font of holy water . . . I got a pint flask of holy water on my hip, too."

You can believe me, I was glad the sheriff was born in this country, and had more sense about some things than men who thought they were a lot smarter—Gregory, for instance! So!

We came to the knoll, all right; and a lot quicker than I had been in getting away. The place was dark, but we could see red eyes glaring at us out of the blackness. The vampires were there waiting for us, ready to fight for their nest.

"Gregory!" Desarde shouted; "where are you?" There was no answer, either then or when the sheriff yelled again, louder. We hesitated, and Desarde called for all the men with lanterns to bring them to the front. Then something swept down at us, and sharp claws raked my face. The sheriff cursed and fired at something that slashed at his own head. It was like a signal; the fight was on.

Something snarled and rushed at me. There was a lantern on the ground in back of me, and I recognized, with satisfaction, the old devil who had brought me to the knoll in the first place. I had one of the stakes Desarde had brought, and it was pointed like a toothpick. I jabbed the old one in the stomach with it. He howled and hopped back, but started for me again.

"Aho, *sales vieux!*" I told him; "You want a better one, I see—well, take it!" And I drove it at his breast with all my strength. Uh-h! Did you ever drive a sharp pole into anybody's chest, vampire or otherwise? Neither did I, until then, but you comprehend that it was not nice . . . the way he *crunched!*

(Wait till I get a drink on that! You—? Oh, very well then! You never pushed a sharp pole into anything that crunched and squalled!)

Well! That old fellow flopped own like a bundle of rags. I pulled my stake out of him and jabbed up at a bat's stomach. It squealed and wheeled away. Snarling and growling things fought all over the place. The lanterns on the ground made just enough light to see a little; some of them were overturned and broken.

A wolfish shape sprang snarling into my face. I jabbed at it with my pole and missed, and then I was down. Desarde's gun roared, and the *loup-garou* went limp on top of me. I pushed it off and scrambled up. The sheriff was blazing away only whenever he was sure of a hit; he had none of the silver bullets to waste. Suddenly the fight died away. There was nothing there for us to fight! As before, the vampire pack had melted into the forest.

"Now," I reminded, "we find Gregory—and Nita!"

Desarde called a half-dozen men to bring lanterns, and told the rest to hurry and surround the knoll, and be on the lookout for a return of the pack. I rushed to the mound where I had left Nita and Gregory, the sheriff and the men with lanterns running with me. Not sure of what to expect, but in fear that Nita had run into the swamp with her pack, I pushed through the bushes.

Whatever I thought to find, it was not what the lanterns at my back showed. Gregory was on his knees, holding tight to Nita, who struggled and fought in his arms like a wild thing. Silent, panting, she clawed at his face, and he hunched his chin tight on her shoulder to protect himself from her sharp teeth.

"Quit fighting," Gregory pleaded, "these are my friends, and they won't hurt you."

"Let me go, fool!" Nita screamed at him. "*Let me go!*"

Why she was not able to fade from his arms and whisk herself way, what had passed between her and Gregory that may have made her powerless in his arms, I do not know. But

Gregory held tight to her, though she screamed now and fought like a mad thing. Desarde brushed past me.

"Let her loose, Greg!" the sheriff cried—"Move out of the way and I'll quiet her with a silver bullet."

Nita screamed louder; the howls of her pack ranged in closer. Gregory jerked his head around at us, unmindful that Nita seized the opportunity to bite savagely at his exposed neck.

"No!" he cried, in startled alarm. "She's mine from now on—I'll take care of her, and you won't have to worry about her, now. Go away and let us alone!"

What do you know about that? I thought Gregory was playing up to Nita so she wouldn't watch me, and I could get away—and he meant it, all along! He had actually fallen for that bloodsucking *thing!* He put his body between her and Desarde, and managed to stagger to his feet with her kicking in his arms.

The sheriff thought Gregory was crazy. So did I, as far as that goes, and I think so, now—no man could take a vampire in his arms and keep sane! Desarde was afraid to fire at Nita, for fear of hurting Gregory. He seemed to have a sudden idea; for I saw him grab at his hip pocket.

"Let's see what this'll do!" he muttered, pulling out the flask of holy water. "I can sprinkle this on both of them."

He slopped the water from the uncorked bottle on the pair, wetting Gregory as much as Nita. Greg started away with her, taking long steps and not seeming to mind the water; but she shrieked and howled, twisting as if Desarde had poured acid on her.

"Close in!" the sheriff cried to us. "Take her away from him and let's finish this!"

Gregory heard him, and began to run toward the swamp with Nita. Desarde started to jump after him. Then, without any warning, Nita's pack burst onto the knoll from out of the woods, and hell broke loose again. Howling, snarling and squeaking, fiends like wolves and bats and men flung themselves upon us, and between us and the poor fool who carried the mistress of them all.

We were hard pressed for a minute, and two of our men went down and never got up. Poor fellows! But heavy odds were with us in point of numbers, since we had killed at least a dozen in the first two fights; and there were still a few silver bullets in the guns. The vampires gave way, and then we realized that they were really beaten, and only fought to keep us away from Gregory and Nita.

We punched and jabbed with the sharpened stakes; now and then a gun blazed, whenever a sure shot offered. The blackness of the swamp was beginning to take on a gray tinge. Under the threat of dawn, the howls of the things became uneasy. We pushed on after Gregory with less resistance. The light grew, and we could see him staggering along ahead. Nita sagged limp and dangling in his arms.

The things swirling around us, just out of reach, began to change their snarls to whimpers. Two of them ran up to Gregory, fluttering around him like two frightened old women. He shook them off and tottered on. On toward the banks of the bayou, that showed through the grayness, not far away.

There was a sudden silence around us, for a moment. Snarls and whimpers hushed. Then, as if at a signal, the vampire pack whirled and raced away behind us.

Understanding flashed through my brain; and it was queer how I felt a little touch of pity for those things. They could not face the sun and scampered away to their holes, where we would find them with our stakes before another night...

Gregory stood swaying, facing us with his back to the bayou. We came slowly closer, seeing that his face was drawn and weary. He carried dead weight that must have felt like lead in his arms; Nita hung limp, moaning.

"Get back!" Gregory demanded hoarsely. "You can't shoot me, and I won't let you touch her. I'm too tired for it, but if you come closer, I'll jump in the bayou and try to swim across with her—if I drown, it'll be the same as if you murdered me."

Desarde stepped slowly forward, empty hands outstretched, intending to try reasoning with him. Gregory misunderstood, turned to jump, even while the sheriff cried to him to wait. Nita jerked suddenly to life, shrieking as she saw the water under them.

"No!" she screamed. For a fraction of a second, while Gregory tottered on the bank, she bit and clawed, and fought to tear his arms away. Desarde ran toward them, and we with him. But we were too late. Nita gave one last awful scream of fear, as Gregory toppled with her to the water . . .

There was a blinding flash, a blue-white sheet of flame that burned up the air we breathed. It burned to the back of our eyeballs. For long minutes we stood there, arms across our eyes, blinded, and afraid to move. Finally that passed, and we could see again. But there was nothing upon the surface of the bayou; the black water flowed on as it always had: creeping darkly toward the bay. What happened, or how, I don't pretend to know. Nor why. But all my life I've heard it said, *vampires can cross no flowing water!* Gregory had tried to take Nita . . . And that flame; and they were gone . . .

God! Let's have a drink!

I am interested in folklore, and had listened to Delacroix more for that reason than any other. Otherwise, I can not explain why my patience burst bounds no sooner.

"I don't want a drink, and you've already had too many." I was angry, and let him have in straight. "I heard talk in the town about a wild fight the sheriff's posse had with a gang of gipsies on the island; and then you waste my time with a version that would make Munchausen green with envy."

Delacroix laughed shortly. "You don't expect the people who know the truth to tell it to outsiders, do you? And be called crazy, or liars like you're calling me?"

"Anyway," I retorted, "you'd better sober up and be on the job in the morning. If your past record wasn't unusually good, I'd fire you now!"

"Oh!" Delacroix exclaimed innocently, "I forgot to tell you: When we went back to the knoll to take care of what was left to do, I hung back and did some private digging of my own! Old Placide's money was there, just as Nita said . . ."

Reaching into a pocket, he drew out a wallet. As he carelessly flipped the contents with his thumb, a sheaf of old currency showed for a minute, like the open corner of a fan. The bills were faded and dirty, and their size proved them of old-fashioned issue. Old and soiled they may have been, but the four numerals in their corners seemed very vivid to my startled eyes.

"Just a tin box and a little oilskin-wrapped pack of greenbacks," Delacroix observed. "But *big* ones! *So!* The only reason I'm here is because I can't get a train to New Orleans for a couple more hours . . .

"You better have a drink before you go? All right! Whether you do, or whether you don't"—he looked up, his grin taking the malice from his parting shot—"you take your job and go hop in the bayou—and see what happens to *you!*"

19
Death
Wilfred Blanch Talman
(1932)

This poem appeared in the March 1932 issue of *Weird Tales* magazine. Talman, who was a friend of H.P. Lovecraft, communicated with Howard and asked him to author something for the magazine Talman was editing, *The Texaco Star*. Howard sent him his only non-fiction piece ever published, "The Ghost of Camp Colorado," which appeared in the April 1931 issue of Talman's magazine and was then reprinted in *Frontier Times* in their June 1931 issue. Talman occasionally wrote for *Weird Tales*, and after this poem appeared, Howard wrote to him saying, "I was much taken with your recent poem in *Weird Tales*. It's difficult to capture a completed thought in so short a verse, but you seem to have succeeded admirably. I hope to see more of your work soon."

A stately ship stands in the offing now,
  Out past the reef where broken waves are drumming,
Her sails lit up with sun, bright gilded prow,
  And rigging taut through which the breeze is humming.
  Some day another ship is coming;
No breath of wind shall whisper through her spars,
  And I, through phantom sails, shall view the stars.

Robert E. Howard's

20
The Isle of the Torturers
Clark Ashton Smith
(1933)

"The Isle of the Torturers" first appeared in the March 1933 issue of *Weird Tales* magazine. It was the second in Smith's "Zothique Cycle" of short stories, the first being "Empire of the Necromancers" published in the September 1932 issue of *Weird Tales*. "The Isle of the Tortur-ers" was published in the same issue as Robert E. Howard's popular Conan short story, "The Tower of the Elephant." Fellow *Weird Tales* author Donald Wandrei wrote to Howard praising his story, and Howard, in a return letter dated February 21, 1933, wrote, "I appreciate your kind comments regarding my *Weird Tales* stories; though I'm afraid 'The Tower of the Elephant' won't stack up very highly against Smith's magnificent 'Isle of Tortures.'" Although the editor and many Howard fans would no doubt disagree, here is the yarn that Howard thought surpassed his own.

Between the sun's departure and return, the Silver Death had fallen upon Yoros. Its advent, however, had been foretold in many prophecies, both immemorial and recent. Astrologers had said that this mysterious malady, heretofore unknown on earth, would descend from the great star, Achernar, which presided balefully over all the lands of the southern continent of Zothique; and having sealed the flesh of a myriad men with its bright, metallic pallor, the plague would still go onward in time and space, borne by the dim currents of ether to other worlds.

Dire was the Silver Death; and none knew the secret of its contagion or the cure. Swift as the desert wind, it came into Yoros from the devastated realm of Tasuun, overtaking the very messengers who ran by night to give warning of its nearness. Those who were smitten felt an icy, freezing cold, an instant rigor, as if the outermost gulf had breathed upon them. Their faces and bodies whitened strangely, gleaming with a wan luster, and became stiff as long-dead corpses, all in an interim of minutes.

In the streets of Silpon and Siloar, and in Faraad, the capital of Yoros, the plague passed like an eery, glittering light from countenance to countenance under the golden lamps; and the victims fell where they were stricken; and the deathly brightness remained upon them.

The loud, tumultuous public carnivals were stifled by its passing, and the merry-makers were frozen in frolic attitudes. In proud mansions, the wine-flushed revelers grew pale amid their garish feasts, and reclined in their opulent chairs, still holding the half-emptied cups with rigid fingers. Merchants lay in their counting-houses on the heaped coins they had begun to reckon; and thieves, entering later, were unable to depart with their booty. Diggers died in the half completed graves they had dug for others; but no one came to dispute their possession.

There was no time to flee from the strange, inevitable scourge. Dreadfully and quickly, beneath the clear stars, it breathed upon Yoros; and few were they who awakened from slumber at dawn. Fulbra, the young king of Yoros, who had but newly suceeeded to the throne, was virtually a ruler without a people.

Fulbra had spent the night of the plague's advent on a high tower of his palace above Faraad: an observatory tower, equipped with astronomical appliances. A great heaviness had lain on his heart, and his thoughts were dulled with an opiate despair; but sleep was remote from his eye-lids. He knew the many predictions that foretold the Silver Death; and moreover he had read its imminent coming in the stars, with the aid of the old astrologer and sorcerer, Vemdeez. This latter knowledge he and Vemdeez had not cared to promulgate, knowing full well that the doom of Yoros was a thing decreed from all time by infinite destiny; and that no man could evade the doom, unless it were written that he should die in another way than this.

Now Vemdeez had cast the horoscope of Fulbra; and though he found therein certain ambiguities that his science could not resolve, it was nevertheless written plainly that the king would not die in Yoros. Where he would die, and in what manner, were alike doubtful. But Vemdeez, who had served Altath the father of Fulbra, and was no less devoted to the new ruler, had wrought by means of his magical art an enchanted ring that would protect Fulbra from the Silver Death in all times and places.

The ring was made of a strange. red metal, darker than ruddy gold or copper, and was set with a black and oblong gem, not known to terrestrial lapidaries, that gave forth eternally a strong aromatic perfume. The sorcerer told Fulbra never to remove the ring from the middle finger on which he wore it— not even in lands afar from Yoros and in days after the passing of the Silver Death: for if once the plague had breathed upon Fulbra, he would bear its subtle contagion always in his flesh; and the contagion would assume its wonted virulence with the ring's removal. But Vemdeez did not tell the origin of the red metal and the dark gem, nor the price at which the protective magic had been purchased.

With a sad heart, Fulbra had accepted the ring and had worn it; and so it was that the Silver Death blew over him in the night and harmed him not. But waiting anxiously on the high tower, and watching the golden lights of Faraad rather than the white, implacable stars, he felt a light, passing chillness that belonged not to the summer air. And even as it passed the gay noises of the city ceased; and the moaning lutes faltered strangely and expired. A stillness crept on the carnival; and some of the lamps went out and were not re-lit. In the palace beneath him there was also silence; and he heard no more the laughter of his courtiers and chamberlains. And Vemdeez came not, as was his custom, to join Fulbra on the tower at midnight. So Fulbra knew himself for a realmless king; and the grief that he still felt for the noble Altath was swollen by a great sorrow for his perished people.

Hour by hour he sat motionless, too sorrowful for tears. The stars changed above him; and Achernar glared dovm perpetually like the bright, cruel eye of a mocking demon; and the heavy balsam of the black-jewelled ring arose to his nostrils and seemed to stifle him. And once the thought occurred to Fulbra, to cast the ring away and die as his people had died. But his despair was too heavy upon him even for this; and so, at length, the dawn came slowly in heavens pale as the Silver Death, and found him still on the tower.

In the dawn, King Fulbra rose and descended the coiled stairs of porphyry into his palace. And midway on the stairs he saw the fallen corpse of the old sorcerer Vemdeez, who had died even as he climbed to join his master. The wrinkled face of Vemdeez was like polished metal, and was whiter than his beard and hair; and his open eyes, which had been dark as sapphires, were frosted with the plague. Then, grieving greatly for the death of Vemdeez, whom he had loved, as a fosterfather, the king went slowly on. And in the suites and halls below, he found the bodies of his courtiers and servants and guardsmen. And none remained alive, excepting three slaves who warded the green, brazen portals of the lower vaults, far beneath the palace.

Now Fulbra bethought him of the counsel of Vemdeez, who had urged him to flee from Yoros and to seek shelter in the southern isle of Cyntrom, which paid tribute to the kings of Yoros. And though he had no heart for this, nor for any course of action, Fulbra bade the three remaining slaves to gather food and such other supplies as were necessary for a voyage of some length, and to carry them aboard a royal barge of ebony that was moored at the palace porticoes on the river Voum.

Then, embarking with the slaves, he took the helm of the barge, and directed the slaves to unfurl the broad amber sail. And past the stately city of Faraad, whose streets were thronged with the silvery dead, they sailed on the widening jasper estuary of the Voum, and into the amaranth-colored gulf of the Indaskian Sea.

A favorable wind was behind them, blowing from the north over desolate Tasuun and Yoros, even as the Silver Death had blown in the night. And idly beside them, on the Voum, there floated seaward many vessels whose crews and captains had all died of the plague. And Faraad was still as a necropolis of old time; and nothing stirred on the estuary shores, excepting the plumy, fan-shapen palms that swayed southward in the freshening wind. And soon the green strand of Yoros receded, gathering to itself the blueness and the dreams of distance.

Creaming with a winy foam, full of strange murmurous voices and vague tales of exotic things, the halcyon sea was about the voyagers now beneath the high-lifting summer sun. But the sea's enchanted voices and its long languorous, immeasurable cradling could not soothe the sorrow of Fulbra; and in his heart a despair abided, black as the gem that was set in the red ring of Vemdeez.

Howbeit, he held the great helm of the ebon barge, and steered as straightly as he could by the sun toward Cyntrom. The amber sail was taut with the favoring wind; and the barge sped onward all that day, cleaving the amaranth waters with its dark prow that reared in the carven form of an ebony goddess. And when the night came with familiar austral stars, Fulbra was able to correct such errors as he had made in reckoning the course.

For many days they flew southward; and the sun lowered a little in its circling behind them; and new stars climbed and clustered at evening about the black goddess of the prow. And

Fulbra, who had once sailed to the isle of Cymtrom in boyhood days with his father Altath, thought to see ere long the lifting of its shores of camphor and sandalwood from the winy deep. But in his heart there was no gladness; and often now he was blinded by wild tears, remembering that other voyage with Altath.

Then, suddenly and at high noon, there fell an airless cabin, and the waters became as purple glass about the barge. The sky changed to a dome of beaten copper, arching close and low; and as if by some evil wizardry, the dome darkened with untimely night, and a tempest rose like the gathered breath of mighty devils and shaped the sea into vast ridges, and abysmal valleys. The mast of ebony snapped like a reed in the wind, and the sail was torn asunder, and the helpless vessel pitched headlong in the dark troughs and was hurled upward through veils of blinding foam to the giddy summits of the billows.

Fulbra clung to the useless helm, and the slaves, at his command, took shelter in the forward cabin. For countless hours they were borne onward at the will of the mad hurricane; and Fulbra could see naught in the lowering gloom, except the pale crests of the beetling waves; and he could tell no longer the direction of their course.

Then, in that lurid dusk, he beheld at intervals another vessel that rode the storm-driven sea, not far from the barge. He thought that the vessel was a galley such as might be used by merchants that voyaged among the southern isles, trading for incense and plumes and vermilion; but its oars were mostly broken, and the toppled mast and sail hung forward on the prow.

For a time the ships drove on together; till Fulbra saw, in a rifting of the gloom, the sharp and somber crags of an unknown shore, with sharper towers that lifted palely above them. He could not turn the helm; and the barge and its companion vessel were carried toward the looming rocks, till Fulbra thought that they would crash thereon. But, as if by some enchantment, even as it had risen, the sea fell abruptly in a windless calm; and quiet sunlight poured from a clearing sky; and the barge was left on a broad crescent of ochr-yellow sand between the crags and the lulling waters, with the galley beside it.

Dazed and marveling, Fulbra leaned on the helm, while his slaves crept timidly forth from the cabin, and men began to appear on the decks of the galley. And the king was about to hail these men, some of whom were dressed as humble sailors and others in the fashion of rich merchants. But he heard a laughter of strange voices, high and shrill and somehow evil, that seemed to fall from above; and looking up he saw that many people were descending a sort of stairway in the cliffs that enclosed the beach.

The people drew near, thronging about the barge and the galley. They wore fantastic turbans of blood-red, and were clad in closely fitting robes of vulturine black. Their faces and hands were yellow as saffron; their small and slaty eyes were set obliquely beneath lashless lids; and their thin lips, which smiled eternally, were crooked. as the blades of scimitars.

They bore sinister and wicked-looking weapons, in the form of saw-toothed swords and doubled-headed spears. Some of them bowed low before Fulbra and addressed him obsequiously, staring upon him all the while with an unblinking gaze that he could not fathom. Their speech was no less alien than their aspect; it was full of sharp and hissing sounds; and neither the king nor his slaves could comprehend it. But Fulbra bespoke the people courteously, in the mild and mellow-flowing tongue of Yoros, and inquired the name of this land whereon the barge had been cast by the tempest.

Certain of the people seemed to understand him, for a light came in their slaty eyes at his question; and one of them answered brokenly in the language of Yoros, saying that the land was the Isle of Uccastrog, Then, with something of covert evil in his smile, this person added that all shipwrecked mariners and seafarers would receive a goodly welcome from Ildrac, the king of the Isle.

At this, the heart of Fulbra sank within him; for he had heard numerous tales of Uccastrog in bygone years; and the tales were not such as would reassure a stranded traveler. Uccastrog, which lay far to the east of Cyntrom, was commonly known as the Isle of the Torturers; and men said that all who landed upon it unaware, or were cast thither by the seas, were imprisoned by the inhabitants and were subjected later to unending curious tortures whose infliction formed the chief delight of these cruel beings. No man, it was rumored, had ever escaped from Uccastrog; but many had lingered for years in its dungeons and hellish torture chambers, kept alive for the pleasure of King Ildrac and his followers. Also, it was believed that the Torturers were great magicians who could raise mighty storms with their enchantments, and could cause vessels to be carried far from the maritime routes, and then fling them ashore upon Uccastrog.

Seeing that the yellow people were all about the barge, and that no escape was possible, Fulbra asked them to take him at once before King Ildrac. To Ildrac he would announce his name and royal rank; and it seemed to him, in his simplicity, that one king, even though cruel-hearted, would scarcely torture another or keep him captive. Also, it might be that the inhabitants of Uccastrog had been somewhat maligned by the tales of travelers.

So Fulbra and his slaves were surrounded by certain of the throng and were led toward the palace of Ildrac, whose high, sharp towers crowned the crags beyond the beach, rising above those clustered abodes in which the island people dwelt. And while they were climbing the hewn steps in the cliff, Fulbra heard a loud outcry below and a clashing of steel against steel; and looking back, he saw that the crew of the stranded galley had drawn their swords and were fighting the islanders. But being outnumbered greatly, their resistance was borne down by the swarming Torturers; and most of them were taken alive. And Fulbra's heart misgave him sorely at this sight; and more and nore did he mistrust the yellow people.

Soon he came into the presence of Ildrac, who sat on a lofty brazen chair in a vast hall of the palace. Ildrac was taller by half a head than any of his followers; and his features were like a mask of evil wrought from some pale, gilded metal; and he was clad in vestments of a strange hue, like sea-purple brightened with fresh-flowing blood. About him were many guardsmen, armed with terrible scythe-like weapons; and the sullen, slant-eyed girls of the palace, in skirts of vermilion and breast-cups of lazuli, went to and fro among huge basaltic columns. About the hall stood numerous engineries of wood and stone and metal such as Fulbra had never beheld, and having a formidable aspect with their heavy chains, their beds of iron teeth and their cords and pulleys of fish-skin.

The young king of Yoros went forward with a royal and fearless bearing, and addressed Ildrac, who sat motionless and eyed him with a level, unwinking gaze. And Fulbra told Ildrac his name and station, and the calamity that had caused him to flee from Yoros; and he mentioned also his urgent desire to reach the Isle of Cyntrom.

"It is a long voyage to Cyntrom," said Ildrac, with a subtle smile. "Also, it is not our custom to permit guests to depart without having fully tasted the hospitality of the Isle of Uccastrog. Therefore, King Fulbra, I must beg you to curb your impatience. We have much to show you here, and many diversions to offer. My chamberlains will now conduct you to a room befitting your royal rank. But first I must ask you to leave with me the sword that you carry at your side; for swords are often sharp—and I do not wish my guests to suffer injury by their own hands."

So Fulbra's sword was taken from him by one of the palace guardsmen; and a small ruby-hilted dagger that he carried was also removed. Then several of the guards, hemming him in with their scythed weapons, led him from the hall and by many corridors and downward flights of stairs into the soft rock beneath the palace. And he knew not whither his three slaves were taken, or what disposition was made of the captured crew of the galley. And soon he passed from the daylight into cavernous halls illumed by sulfur-colored flames in copper cressets; and all around him, in hidden chambers, he heard the sound of dismal moans and loud, maniacal howlings that seemed to beat and die upon adamantine doors.

In one of these halls, Fulbra and his guardsnen met a young girl, fairer and less sullen of aspect than the others; and Fulbra thought that the girl smiled upon him compassionately as he went by; and it seemed that she murmured faintly in the language of Yoros: "Take heart, King Fulbra, for there is one who would help you." And her words apparently, were not heeded or understood by the guards, who knew only the harsh and hissing tongue of Uccastrog.

After descending many stairs, they came to a ponderous door of bronze; and the door was unlocked by one of the guards, and Fulbra was compelled to enter; and the door clanged dolorously behind him.

The chamber into which he had been thrust was walled on three sides with the dark stone of the island, and was walled on the fourth with heavy, unbreakable glass. Beyond the glass he saw the blue-green, glimmering waters of the undersea, lit by the hanging cressets of the chamber; and in the waters were great devil-fish whose tentacles writhed along the wall; and huge pythonomorphs with fabulous golden coils receding in the gloom; and the floating corpses of men that stared in upon him with eyeballs from which the lids had been excised.

There was a couch in one corner of the dungeon, close to the wall of glass; and food and drink had been supplied for Fulbra in vessels of wood. The king laid himself down, weary and hopeless, without tasting the food. Then, lying with close-shut eyes while the dead men and sea-monsters peered in upon him by the glare of the cressets, he strove to forget his griefs and the dolorous doom that impended. And through his clouding terror and sorrow, he seemed to see the comely face of the girl who had smiled upon him compassionately, and who, alone of all that he had met in Uccastrog, had spoken to him with words of kindness. The face returned ever and anon, with a soft haunting, a gentle sorcery; and Fulbra felt, for the first time in many suns, the dim stirring of his buried youth and the vague, obscure desire of life. So, after a while, he slept; and the face of the girl came still before him in his dreams.

The cressets burned above him with undiminished flames when he awakened; and the sea beyond the wall of glass was thronged with the same monsters as before, or with others of like kind. But amid the floating corpses he now beheld the flayed bodies of his own slaves, who, after being tortured by the island people, had been cast forth into the submarine cavern that adjoined his dungeon, so that he might see them on awakening.

He sickened with new horror at the sight; but even as he stared at the dead faces, the door of bronze swung open with a sullen grinding, and his guards entered. Seeing that he had not consumed the food and water provided for him, they forced him to eat and drink a little, menacing him with their broad, crooked blades till he complied. And then they led him from the dungeon and took him before King Ildrac, in the great hall of tortures.

Fulbra saw, by the level golden light through the palace windows and the long shadows of the columns and machines of torment, that the time was early dawn. The hall was crowded with the Torturers and their women; and many seemed to look on while others, of both sexes, busied themselves with ominous preparations. And Fulbra saw that a tall brazen statue, with cruel and demonian visage, like some implacable god of the underworld, was now standing at the right hand of Ildrac where he sat aloft on his brazen chair.

Fulbra was thrust forward by his guards, and Ildrac greeted him briefly, with a wily smile that preceded the words and lingered after them. And when Ildrac had spoken, the brazen image also began to speak, addressing Fulbra in the language of Yoros, with strident and metallic tones, and telling him with full and minute circumstance the various infernal tortures to which he was to be subjected on that day.

When the statue had done speaking, Fulbra heard a soft whisper in his ear, and saw beside him the fair girl whom he had previously met in the nether corridors. And the girl, seemingly unheeded by the Torturers, said to him: "Be courageous, and endure bravely all that is inflicted; for I shall effect your release before another day, if this be possible."

Fulbra was cheered by the girl's assurance; and it seemed to him that she was fairer to look upon than before; and he thought that her eyes regarded him tenderly; and the twin desires of love and life were strangely resurrected in his heart, to fortify him against the tortures of Ildrac.

Of that which was done to Fulbra for the wicked pleasure of King Ildrac and his people, it were not well to speak fully. For the islanders of Uccastrog had designed innumerable torments, curious and subtle, wherewith to harry and excruciate the five senses; and they could harry the brain itself, driving it to extremes more terrible than madness; and could take away the dearest treasures of memory and leave unutterable foulness in their place.

On that day, however, they did not torture Fulbra to the uttermost. But they racked his ears with cacophonous sounds; with evil flutes that chilled the blood and curdled it upon his heart; with deep drums that seemed to ache in all his tissues; and thin tabors that wrenched his very bones. Then they compelled him to breathe the mounting fumes of braziers wherein the dried gall of dragons and the adipocere of dead cannibals were burned together with a fetid wood. Then, when the fire had died down, they freshened it with the oil of vampire-bats; and Fulbra swooned, unable to bear the fetor any longer.

Later, they stripped away his kingly vestments and fastened about his body a silken girdle that had been freshly dipt in an acid corrosive only to human flesh; and the acid ate slowly, fretting his skin with infinite pangs.

Then, after removing the girdle lest it slay him, the Torturers brought in certain creatures that had the shape of ell-long serpents, but were covered from head to tail with sable hairs like those of a caterpillar. And these creatures twined themselves tightly about the arms and legs of Fulbra; and though he fought wildly in his revulsion, he could not loosen them with his hands; and the hairs that covered their constringent coils began to pierce his limbs like a million tiny needles, till he screamed with the agony. And when his breath failed him and he could scream no longer, the baby serpents were induced to relinquish their hold by a languorous piping of which the islanders knew the secret. They dropped away and left him; but the mark of their coils was imprinted redly about his limbs; and around his body there burned the raw branding of the girdle.

King Ildrac and his people looked on with a dreadful gloating; for in such things they took their joy, and strove to pacify an implacable obscure desire. But seeing now that Fulbra could endure no more, and wishing to wreak their will upon him for many future days, they took him back to his dungeon.

Lying sick with remembered horror, feverish with pain, he longed not for the clemency of death, but hoped for the coming of the girl to release him as she had promised. The long hours passed with a half-delirious tedium; and the cressets, whose flames had been changed to crimson, appeared to fill his eyes with flowing blood; and the dead men and the sea-monsters swam as if in blood beyond the wall of glass. And the girl came not; and Fulbra had begun to despair. Then, at last, he heard the door open gently and not with the harsh clangor that had proclaimed the entrance of his guards.

Turning, he saw the girl, who stole swiftly to his couch with a lifted fingertip, enjoining silence. She told him with soft whispers that her plan had failed; but surely on the following night she would be able to drug the guards and obtain the keys of the outer gates; and Fulbra could escape from the palace to a hidden cove in which a boat with water and provisions lay ready for his use. She prayed him to endure for another day the torments of Ildrac; and to this, perforce, he consented. And he thought that the girl loved him; for tenderly she caressed his feverous brow, and rubbed his torture-burning limbs with a soothing ointment. He deemed that her eyes were soft with a compassion that was more than pity. So Fulbra believed the girl and trusted her, and took heart against the horror of the coming day. Her name, it seemed, was Ilvaa; and her mother was a woman of Yoros who had married one of the evil islanders, choosing this repugnant union as an alternative to the flaying-knives of Ildrac.

Too soon the girl went away, pleading the great danger of discovery, and closed the door softly upon Fulbra. And after a while the king slept; and Ilvaa returned to him amid the delirious abominations of his dreams, and sustained him against the terror of strange hells.

At dawn the guards came with their hooked weapons, and led him again before Ildrac. And again the brazen, demoniac statue, in a strident voice, announced the fearful ordeals that he was to undergo. And this time he saw that other captives, including the crew and merchants of the galley, were also awaiting the malefic ministrations of the Torturers in the vast hall.

Once more in the throng of watchers the girl Ilvaa pressed

close to him, unreprimanded by his guards, and murmured words of comfort; so that Fulbra was enheartened against the enormities foretold by the brazen oracular image. And indeed a bold and hopeful heart was required to endure the ordeals of that day . . .

Among other things less goodly to be mentioned, the Torturers held before Fulbra a mirror of strange wizardry, wherein his own face was reflected as if seen after death. The rigid features, as he gazed upon them, became marked with the green and bluish marbling of corruption; and the withering flesh fell in on the sharp bones, and displayed the visible fretting of the worm. Hearing meanwhile the dolorous groans and agonizing cries of his fellow-captives all about the hall, he beheld other faces, dead, swollen, lidless, and flayed, that seemed to approach him from behind and to throng about his own face in the mirror. Their looks were dank and dripping, like the hair of corpses recovered from the sea; and sea-weed was mingled with the locks. Then, turning at a cold and clammy touch, he found that these faces were no illusion but the actual reflection of cadavers drawn from the under-sea by a malign sorcery, that had entered the hall of Ildrac like living men and were peering over his shoulder.

His own slaves, with flesh that the sea-things had gnawed even to the bone, were among them. And the slaves came toward him with glaring eyes that saw only the voidness of death. And beneath the sorcerous control of Ildrac, their evilly animated corpses began to assail Fulbra, clawing at his face and raiment with half-eaten fingers. And Fulbra, faint with loathing, struggled against his dead slaves, who knew not the voice of their master and were deaf as the wheels and racks of torment used by Ildrac . . .

Anon the drowned and dripping corpses went away; and Fulbra was stripped by the Torturers and was laid supine on the palace floor, with iron rings that bound him closely to the flags at knee and wrist, at elbow and ankle. Then they brought in the disinterred body of a woman, nearly eaten, in which a myriad maggots swarmed on the uncovered bones and tatters of dark corruption; and this body they placed on the right hand of Fulbra. And also they fetched the carrion of a black goat that was newly touched with beginning decay; and they laid it down beside him on the left hand. Then, across Fulbra, from right to left, the hungry maggots crawled in a long and undulant wave . . .

After the consummation of this torture, there came many others that were equally ingenious and atrocious, and were well designed for the delectation of King Ildrac and his people. And Fulbra endured the tortures valiantly, upheld by the thought of Ilvaa.

Vainly, however, on the night that followed this day, he waited in his dungeon for the girl. The cressets burned with a bloodier crimson; and new corpses were among the flayed and floating dead in the sea-cavern; and strange double-bodied serpents of the nether deep arose with an endless squirming; and their horned heads appeared to bloat immeasurably against the crystal wall. Yet the girl Ilvaa came not to free him as she had promised; and the night passed. But though despair resumed its old dominion in the heart of Fulbra, and terror came with talons steeped in fresh venom, he refused to doubt Ilvaa, telling himself that she had been delayed or prevented by some unforeseen mishap.

At dawn of the third day, he was again taken before Ildrac. The brazen image, announcing the ordeals of the day, told him that he was to be bound on a wheel of adamant; and, lying on the wheel, was to drink a drugged wine that would steal away his royal memories for ever, and would conduct his naked soul on a long pilgrimage through monstrous and infamous hells before bringing it back to the hall of Ildrac and the broken body on the wheel.

Then certain women of the Torturers, laughing obscenely, came forward and bound King Fulbra to the adamantine wheel with thongs of dragon-gut. And after they had done this, the girl Ilvaa, smiling with the shameless exultation of open cruelty, appeared before Fulbra and stood close beside him, holding a golden cup that contained the drugged wine. She mocked him for his folly and credulity in trusting her promises; and the other women and the male Torturers, even to Ildrac on his brazen seat, laughed loudly and evilly at Fulbra, and praised Ilvaa for the perfidy she had practised upon him.

So Fulbra's heart grew sick with a darker despair then any he had yet known, The brief, piteous love that had been born amid sorrow and agony perished within him, leaving but ashes steeped in gall. Yet, gazing at Ilvaa with sad eyes, he uttered no word of reproach. He wished to live no longer; and yearning for a swift death, he bethought him of the wizard ring of Vemdeez and of that which Vemdeez had said would follow its removal from his finger. He still wore the ring. which the Torturers had deemed a bauble of small value. But his hands were bound tightly to the wheel, and he could not remove it. So, with a bitter cunning, knowing full well that the islanders would not take away the ring if he should offer it to them, he feigned a sudden madness and cried wildly:

"Steal my memories, if ye will, with your accursed wine—and send me through a thousand hells and bring me back again to Uccastrog: but take not the ring that I wear on my middle finger; for it is more precious to me than many kingdoms or the pale breasts of love."

Hearing this, King Ildrac rose from his brazen seat; and bidding IIvaa to delay the administration of the wine, he came forward and inspected curiously the ring of Vemdeez, which gleamed darkly, set with its rayless gem, on Fulbra's finger. And all the while, Fulbra cried out against him in a frenzy, as if fearing that he would take the ring.

So Ildrac, deeming that he could plague the prisoner thereby and could heighten his suffering a little, did the very thing for which Fulbra had planned. And the ring came easily from the shrunken finger; and Ildrac, wishing to mock the royal captive, placed it on his own middle digit.

Then, while Ildrac regarded the captive with a more deeply graven smile of evil on the pale, gilded mask of his face, there came to King Fulbra of Yoros the dreadful and longed-for thing. The Silver Death, that had slept so long in his body beneath the magical abeyance of the ring of Vemdeez, was made manifest even as he hung on the adamantine wheel. His limbs stiffened with another rigor than that of agony; and his face shone brightly with the coming of the Death; and so he died.

Then, to Ilvaa and to many of the Torturers who stood wondering about the wheel, the chill and instant contagion of the Silver Death was communicated. They fell even where they had stood; and the pestilence remained like a glittering light on the faces and the hands of the men and shone forth from the nude bodies of the women. And the plague passed along the immense hall; and the other captives of King Ildrac were released thereby from their various torments; and the Torturers found surcease from the dire longing that they could assuage only through the pain of their fellowmen. And through all the palace, and throughout the Isle of Uccastrog, the Death flew swiftly, visible in those upon whom it had breathed, but otherwise unseen and inpalpable.

But Ilrac, wearing the ring of Vemdeez, was immune. And guessing not the reason for his immunity, he beheld with consternation the doom that had overtaken his followers, and watched in stupefaction the freeing of his victims. Then, fearful of some inimic sorcery, he rushed from the hall; and standing in the early sun on a palace-terrace above the sea, he tore the ring of Vemdeez from his finger and hurled it to the foamy billows far below, deeming in his terror that the ring was perhaps the source or agent of the unknown hostile magic.

So Ildrac, in his turn, when all the others had fallen, was smitten by the Silver Death; and its peace descended upon him where he lay in his robes of blood-brightened purple, with features shining palely to the unclouded sun. And oblivion claimed the Isle of Uccastrog; and the Torturers were one with the tortured.

Robert E. Howard's

21
Ismeddin and the Holy Carpet
E. Hoffmann Price
(1933)

This novelette was originally published in *The Magic Carpet Magazine*, January 1933. The magazine was an off-shoot of *Weird Tales* magazine, and was also edited by Farnsworth Wright. The premier issue was published in October 1930 under the name *Oriental Stories*, and after a six-month hiatus in 1932, this issue was the first to be published under the new name, *The Magic Carpet Magazine*. After reading the new issue, Howard, wrote in a letter to the magazine, "As usual, Price turned in a fine job with 'Ismeddin and the Holy Carpet.' Ismeddin is my favorite Oriental character, worthy to take his place beside Sinbad and the Kalif Haroun."

"Ismeddin," said the Sultan of Bir el Asad to the white-bearded darwish who scorned the cushions of the diwan and sat on the sand-strewn floor of the private reception hall, "there is a mad inglesi, Captain Rankin, who is bent on stealing the Holy Carpet from the shrine of that Persian heretic, Imam Ismail, may Allah not bless him!"

"The fool will probably be torn to pieces by the brethren of the monastery, or if he escapes their hands, the Amir will have him flayed alive," observed Ismeddin the Darwish. "But what's that to us?"

"In the old days," replied the Sultan, "it would have been nothing but good riddance. But now—well, times have changed. His Excellency the British Resident—"

The Sultan spat ostentatiously to cleanse his mouth of the contamination of the last phrase.

"The Resident will have a great deal of explaining ahead of him when his superiors hear of the captain's adventure. You see, Sir John issued a permit for Captain Rankin to excavate in the ruins just outside our walls, and carry on with the various idiocies so dear to these infidel pork-eaters, may Allah blacken them! And if Captain Rankin's hide is nailed to the door of Imam Ismail's shrine, the noble British government will demand Sir John's hide for not having kept him from stirring up trouble and losing his very valuable head."

"But supposing that Captain Rankin does steal the Holy Carpet?" asked the darwish. "He's a clever fellow, and he might succeed. What then?"

"Worse and worse!" replied the Sultan. "Those wild men of Kuh-i-Atesh will pour down out of the hills and loot the British mining concessions by way of reprisal. And there will be demonstrations in any number of places where the infidel hoof is planted on Moslem necks. Then after enough towns here and there have been shelled by British artillery, Sir John's successor would quarter a couple of regiments here, and all but depose me. Shaytan rip him open, he's bad enough, but there could be worse Residents! And so I've got to help the infidel out of this mess."

"Well," submitted Ismeddin, "why doesn't Sir John send him to the coast under guard? That would dispose of him in a hurry."

"Allah and again, by Allah! So he would, *ya* Ismeddin! So he would, if he could. But he can't. Captain Rankin disappeared last night on his way from the Residency, and Sir John's guard has been combing the town for him ever since.

"The scientist and archeologist vanished. I told Sir John to watch that fellow. I knew that his diggings and prowlings were a mask for something. I've heard of Rankin's doings in the secret service, and his roaming about, disguised as a true believer. And once they get into that habit, there's only one way of curing them."

The Sultan's swift gesture indicated that the executioner's two-handed sword was the infallible cure.

"But Sir John laughed. And now he's driving me mad, asking me to devise some way of stopping the theft, and saving Sir John's residential hide.

"That's why I called you. Keep Captain Rankin from plundering the shrine of Imam Ismail, and see that he gets back with his head on his shoulders—though a head that full of idiocy would serve as well in almost any position. Those *Feringhi* fools and their custom of collecting ancient carpets!"

"My lord," said the darwish as the Sultan paused for breath, "I once saw that carpet as I looked in through the door of the monastery of the Holy Brethren. It's about the length of two boys and the width of three men, and very worn. But it is a wonder, and a coolness to the eyes. Looking at it is like listening to exalting music. In the entire world there is not its like or equal. It is woven of moonbeams, and the smiles of Turki dancing girls. Still—"

Ismeddin felt his neck for a moment, just about where a scimitar stroke would separate head and shoulders, and made a grimace. "Still, this Rankin is doubtless a fool. And Sir John's another, asking you to cover all the ground between here and Kuh-i-Atesh, and bag the captain before he gets into mischief.

"I saw him, some ten years ago, in uniform. But when he's in disguise, his own men don't recognize him. The chances are that he will steal the Holy Carpet—"

The darwish paused to stroke his beard, and smiled as at an ancient jest.

"In fact, ya sidi, there is no way to stop him: except shooting him in his tracks, which you forbid."

Then the darwish rose and took un-ceremonious leave of the Sultan.

That evening Ismeddin called on Sir John at the Residency.

The Resident listened attentively to Ismeddin's plan, and registered but one protest.

"But we simply can't have Captain Rankin lashed to a camel's back and carried back here by those—" Sir John coughed, and continued, "By those Pious Companions of His Majesty the Sultan's late father. A certain propriety must be observed, if you get what I mean."

"Entirely so, Your Excellency," assured the darwish in English, which he could speak whenever he chose. "I understand perfectly that his Britannic Majesty's subjects must be treated with deference, even if they are engaged, so to speak, in—"

Ismeddin's command of English faltered for a moment, and Sir John hoped that for propriety's sake the darwish wouldn't select the word that he seemed on the point of pronouncing; although desperation had driven the Resident to the point of being able gracefully to ignore breaches of etiquette.

"—engaged in prying into the mysteries of the dancing darwishes," continued Ismeddin. "His Majesty the Sultan insisted that I use diplomacy, and as soon as I find Captain Rankin, convince him that his course is causing you great embarrassment.

"Just so, Sir John. Quite," concluded Ismeddin gravely.

Ismeddin's mimicry of Sir John's speech was obvious enough to goad the Resident to the verge of apoplexy; but he knew that the wily old scoundrel was the key to a ticklish situation, and controlled his flaming desire to have the darwish soundly flogged.

It was a relief when Ismeddin made inquiry as to whether Captain Rankin wrote the Arabic script as well as he spoke the language.

Ismeddin, upon learning that the talented captain could write half a dozen styles of script with uncommon elegance, announced his intention of then and there starting on the trail, and left the Residency.

"Well," reflected Sir John, "that old beggar may turn the trick for the Sultan's sake. And I'll probably pay for his services with several uncomfortable moments before I see the last of this Holy Carpet affair."

Then, as he watched Ismeddin striding on foot through the Isfayan Gate, past the sentries, "Some one would do very well to double the guards about his stables. That fellow won't be on foot very long."

Sir John was right: although, urged by some unusual whim, it was Ismeddin's own horse that he mounted.

The cloak of the darwish covers diverse possibilities, ranging from the Rufai who mortify the body with hot irons and knives, to the well-fed Melewi in their substantial monasteries, seeking oneness with Allah by pious meditation and the contemplation of divine harmony. The darwish may wander through the Moslem world alone, on foot, and in rags, with no possessions save his beggar's bowl, his knowledge of magic and medicine, and his reputation for loving nothing but books and study; or he may ride about on a blooded mare, followed by a handful of retainers, and bristling with weapons and arrogance.

A disgraced prime minister or ruined governor may seek the path to heaven, in the guise of the darwish; and the idler, vagabond or scoundrel may rely on that same cloak of eccentricity to carry him safe and harmless. He may pray, or not, just as he elects. And whenever he is in difficulties, his real or feigned madness will win him tolerance, fear, and respect. The darwish, in short, is the privileged adventurer of the Orient, and may be anything from a saint to a cutthroat.

And thus Ismeddin the Darwish rode into the mountains, this time not to loot a pack train, but to prevent the theft of the Holy Carpet that hung before the tomb of the Imam Ismail in the monastery of the Dancing Darwishes of fanatical Kuh-i-Atesh. Ismeddin's heart was not in his work, for he would have preferred being Captain Rankin's ally rather than adversary.

"Allah sift me!" exclaimed Ismeddin as he took the trail. "That *Feringhi* dog, Sir John, is becoming the pest of my life.

Shaytan blacken him, but I'll make him sweat for a moment before he gets any good news I'll bring him!"

As he rode, Ismeddin plotted the details of the nebulous plan he had conceived. With one short cut and another, he reduced whatever lead Captain Rankin had gained by his earlier start; for with his acquaintance with obscure mountain trails, the darwish could afford to give heavy odds.

Whether Rankin would travel as a beggar, an itinerant physician, or as a darwish, Ismeddin would not hazard a guess. But he was certain that Rankin would look the part, act the part, and, in the more odoriferous roles, smell the part he played; Rankin was one of those rare Europeans who had perfectly mastered not only the guttural sounds of Oriental languages, but also the thousand intricacies of ritual that guide the East through its daily life: so that Ismeddin's only hope would be to trip his adversary on an obscure point that even that master had overlooked. The darwish knew that he had to probe very deeply through Rankin's years of acquired Oriental thoughts and touch an instinct that would infallibly infallibly reveal the Englishman. And this done, he had to employ the betraying gesture in such a way as to dissuade Rankin from his quest, and at the same time, not actually expose the audacious captain to a certain and sanguinary doom in forbidden Kuh-i-Atesh, a city as holy now as it had been in the old, pre-Moslem days.

But before Rankin was tripped, he must first be recognized.

Ismeddin's scouting through the hills was circuitous in the extreme; and thus toward the end of the second day, he was riding, for the time being, away from his ultimate goal. The rumors he had collected and sifted totaled exactly nothing at all, except the news that one Abdullah ibn Yusuf, a pious and learned scribe, had passed through Wadi el Ghorab, on his way north.

Even if this pious and learned person were indeed Captain Rankin, there would be no virtue in overtaking him on the road, for accosting him in the marketplace of Kuh-i-Atesh would be a much more effective way of bluffing the talented infidel. And as the darwish made his camp that night in a cave known by him from old times, he was still at a loss as to the best approach.

To expose Rankin as an infidel would be futile. If he failed, he would only strengthen Rankin's position; if he succeeded, his victim would have no chance to retreat from his perilous venture. And a threat of exposure as an unbeliever would certainly be ignored by Rankin, who had in Mekka survived denunciation as an impostor. And thus and thus Ismeddin pondered until sleep found him in his cave.

Several hours later, Shaykh Hussayn, the chief of the Companions, woke the darwish from his light sleep. He fanned the embers of the dying fire, as Ismeddin wrote, and sealed the writing with a signet depending from a cord about his neck.

"Ride back to Bir el Asad," directed the darwish, "and give this to the Sultan. And remember, keep the Companions under cover while waiting for further word from me. Above all, don't let them amuse themselves by looting any villages."

"How about pack trains?" inquired Shaykh Hussayn gravely.

"Shaytan blacken thee, and no pack trains either! Now ride, and I will do likewise," replied Ismeddin as he mounted his horse.

The chief of the Companions took the trail toward Bir el Asad, and Ismeddin rode northward in the direction of Kuh-i-Atesh.

A public scribe sat in the marketplace of Kuh-i-Atesh, acting as secretary to all who had petitions to present to the Amir, or letters to write to distant friends and relatives.

"Write to my brother in Herat," demanded a tall, fierce Afghan of the Durani clan. "He is ill, and not expected to live much longer. I am returning as soon as I have completed my business in this den of thieves."

"Very well," agreed the scribe. "What shall I say?"

"What shall you say?" growled the Afghan. "God, by God, by the Very God, you're a letter-writers, aren't you? Jackass, do you expect me to tell you what to write?"

A hunchbacked ancient beggar, wooden bowl clutched in his grimy talons, pushed his way into the front rank of the circle about the scribe.

"With your permission, O scribe! Say on behalf of this man, *'From the percussion of the grave and from the interrogation of the grave, may Allah, the Merciful, the Compassionate, deliver thee! I, they brother'*—what's your name, O Afghan?— Achmed?—*'send thee greeting, and after, say that I will shortly leave Kuh-i-Atesh to return to Herat, if it so please Allah.'* Write thus, O scribe!"

The Afghan's teeth flashed in a broad smile.

"Allah grant that thy kindness never grow less! *There* is a letter that sounds like a letter!"

The scribe began writing in fine *naskh* script.

"*Wallah!* There is a letter that will do you credit. Let me see it before you seal it," demanded the beggar.

He wiped his fingers on his greasy djellab, took the paper by its margin, and scrutinized it carefully. With his index finger he followed the script, spelling out each word as he read it. And then he nodded his approbation.

"Very good. May your brother prosper, and his health improve!"

Then, as the scribe attended to the correspondence of his next client, the beggar studied him as closely as he had the Afghan's letter. One eye, or rather, the lack of one, was concealed by a patch; but the other was keen and piercing.

The beggar had roamed about the city since morning, crying for alms, and prying and poking about the taverns and the market-places and coffee-houses; but nothing had attracted his attention until he saw the scribe sitting on a rug nearly twice as long as it was wide. When he learned that the scribe was the pious and learned Abdullah ibn Yusuf, the beggar's interest quickened.

"A man concealing his true mission," reflected the beggar, "builds for himself a complete background and history. Now if this fellow were truly the scribe he claims to be, the gossip of Wadi el Ghorab and the other villages he passed through would not all be unanimous in remembering that Abdullah ibn Yusuf hails from al Yemen. Some few would have insisted that he was from Damascus, or Cairo..."

Ismeddin the One-Eye Beggar noted that the rug on which the scribe sat was old and thin, and woven in the days of his father's grandfather: its deep reds and solemn greens, the intricate perfection of its pattern, its very dimensions and proportions had a vague significance to Ismeddin.

"This may not be Captain Rankin, but this is a part that he might play..."

The scribe was doing a good business. In addition to his harvest of coppers and small silver coins, he reaped the day's crop of gossip, and the hope, and fear, and jest, and misery that stalked between the lines he wrote at the dictation of his clients.

The correspondents by proxy had for the moment given the scribe a breathing spell. He yawned, stretched himself, and set aside the tile with its ink-saturated mass of silken threads that served as an inkwell.

Ismeddin approached and squatted on the ground before the scribe.

"*Ya*, Abdullah," he began, "may Allah prosper you! Thy generosity is my evening meal!"

The scribe tossed a copper coin into the ever-yawning bowl.

"Allah requite thee, O scribe!" acknowledged Ismeddin.

Then, hearing the tramp of feet and the sound of arms carried by men marching in cadence, he turned, and saw a squad of soldiers escorting a prisoner to the public square. Following them came an executioner and his assistants.

"Some one is going to die an unpleasant death," observed Ismeddin. "Judging by the implements that black fellow is carrying, it will be uncommonly savage."

"God alone is wise, all-knowing!" ejaculated the scribe, with an indifferent shrug of the shoulders.

Ismeddin's keen eyes caught not a trace of the compassion or horror that even the most calloused infidel would betray at the sight of a man marching to a lingering barbarous doom. Nevertheless, there was something strikingly familiar about those eyes, and that nose.

"He goes to a savage doom," repeated Ismeddin. "For a trifling offense."

Then, staring fixedly at the scribe with his hard, glittering eye, "Captain Rankin, *he* goes to a feast compared with what you are facing."

"You call me by a strange name, O Grandfather," replied the scribe. "Possibly you mistake Abdullah ibn Yusuf for some one else?"

But for all his calmness, Captain Rankin knew then and there that he was in exceeding peril; and he knew also that the hunchback had penetrated his disguise.

"There is no mistaking Captain Rankin," answered Ismeddin. "And to steal the Holy Carpet is a hazardous enterprise . . . cease fingering the butt of that pistol . . . shooting an old beggar would by no means further your cause."

"I reached for a purse, not a pistol," liked Rankin. "And you suppose that you go with me to the Amir, to tell him that I am planning to loot the shrine of Imam Ismail."

The *darwish* smiled is recognition of an equal well met.

"What would that get me? The Amir would doubt that you are an infidel, and wouldn't believe that you were foolhardy enough to attempt such a mad feat. He would have me beaten, and you would go on with your scheme. By no means, *sidi* Rankin! I prefer to wait until you have committed yourself far enough to make my knowledge acceptable as truth."

"This," thought Rankin, "is no fanatic, but a blackmailer."

And then, to Ismeddin, "And how would you gain by exposing me?"

"A better chance to steal the Holy Carpet myself!" replied the *darwish*.

"Here are a hundred *tomans*," countered Rankin, producing a heavy purse. "And at the completion of my mission, another hundred, for your good will."

"I take refuge in Allah!" ejaculated Ismeddin piously, declining the purse. "I am seeking the Holy Carpet, and not a bribe!"

"But," protested Rankin, "we can't both take it. And if we work against each other, we may both end by being sawed asunder between two planks."

"Let us cast lots then," proposed Ismeddin, "so that one of us will withdraw and leave the other a clear field."

"Better yet," replied Rankin, "let us make a wager: whoever shall hold the other's life in his hands and yet refrain from exposing his rival, that one shall take the carpet. And the loser, for his good will, shall have from the winner a purse of a hundred *tomans*."

"Make it a thousand," said the beggar, whom Rankin had by this time appraised as no more a beggar than he, Ranking, was a scribe.

"Five hundred, and my blessing, Old Man!"

"Done, by Allah!" agreed Ismeddin. And then, as he picked up his wooden bowl, "I am starting on this quest this very hour. And since I knew you for Captain Rankin, it is but fair that you know that I am Ismeddin, and that I am neither hunch-backed nor one-eyed. *Was salaam!*"

Whereupon Ismeddin the Darwish limped toward the Herati Gate, crying to all true believers for alms.

"Ismeddin no more wants the Holy Carpet than I want ball-bearing eyeteeth," reflected Rankin. "And five hundred *tomans* is much more than he can get for my tanned hide, so he'll not betray me, though he'll not betray me, though he'll probably waylay me on the road from here and take both the carpet and the purse. And that's fa chance I'll have to take . . ."

Rankin picked up the implements of his adopted profession and sough *caravanserai* where he kept his baggage and stabled his mule.

That afternoon, Rankin wandered about the bazaar, making sundry purchases. The horse and arms he left in charge of a venerable retired soldier—or brigand, Rankin couldn't decide just which—whose hut was just outside the city wall, not far from the Herati Gate. Despite several flasks of potent *'araki* which the old fellow drank like water, Rankin's friendly inquisitiveness failed to uncover the grizzled raider's history and background, or to spur him to boastfulness. That, and the promise of a second purse, payable when Rankin returned to claim his property, gave excellent assurance of fidelity and discretion.

Late that night, Abdullah the Scribe mingled with the crowd that followed an outbound caravan past the city gate to wish it a safe trip, and a prosperous return. But the scribe was not with those who returned when the caravan had passed beyond earshot of the well-wishers.

The next morning, when the gates opened, a brother of the order of dancing darwishes picked himself up from the dust where he had slept, performed the ritual of morning prayer, and entered the city. Rankin's following in the trace of the caravan for several hours, and then marching back to the city, after assuming the costume of dancing darwish, had made him convincingly travel-stained and weary: and the sentries enjoyed their fill of gossip from Damascus, with which the wandering brother regaled them before he sought the monastery.

It was mid-afternoon of the day when the wandering brother from Damascus entered the city that the Amir of Kuh-i-Atesh sat beneath a striped awning on the flat roof of his palace, sipping Shirazi wine to his heart's content and his soul's damnation.

He thrust aside the freshly replenished glass and pointed toward the city gate.

"*Mashallah!*" he exclaimed. "What's that?"

Footmen armed with staves which they plied lustily were beating aside the crowd as they shouted, "Gang way, O uncle! Make way for the Holy Darwish, Ismeddin! Careful there, *ya bint!* The pious pilgrim, Ismeddin! Gang Way! Watch yourself, grandfather!"

Following the footmen, and filing through the Herati Gate, just past the guard, came eight camels, richly caparisoned and splendid with silken halters and silver bells. They bore on their backs musicians who alternately played Chinese and Hindustani music.

"*Wallahi! Yallahi! Billahi!*" swore the Amir, as the wailing notes of pipes and the clang of gongs and the thump-thump-thump of kettle-drums mingled with the shouts of the footmen. "Look at that ragged loafer mounted like a prince on a blooded mare! Bring him in right away, Mansur."

Four horsemen arranged in a square were now clearing the Herati Gate, mounted on trim, spirited desert horses. Each carried in his hand a lance: and on the four lance-heads they supported a canopy of crimson brocade splashed with gold, and decked with clusters of plumes.

Beneath the canopy, astride a bay mare with gilded hoofs, rode Ismeddin, arrayed in a ragged *djellab* and a turban even more disreputable. With one grimy talon he reined in the mare; and with the other he stroked his long beard, and half smiled to himself.

"Make way!" shouted the footmen. "Gang way for Ismeddin!"

Ismeddin dipped into his embroidered saddlebags and scattered handfuls of silver coins to the right and left, raining largess on the loafers and beggars that crowded the city entrance.

As the procession approached the palace, the footmen arranged themselves in two groups at the entrance. The musicians, still playing, countermarched; and Ismeddin's mare, stung by her rider's savage spurs, leaped with a great bound from beneath the canopy toward the entrance of the palace, where Ismeddin's strong hand on the curb reined her back on her haunches.

Ismeddin dismounted and tossed the reins to a groom.

His retinue and their beasts were taken in charge by the Amir's steward.

"My lord," announced Ismeddin as he was presented to the Amir in the reception hall, "I sought you empty-handed. But it pleased Allah that on the long march from Kabul I inherited various possessions."

"Allah alone is Wise, All-Knowing!" exclaimed the Amir piously. "I have heard of your heritages before."

"And therefore," continued Ismeddin, "I am presenting to you the various beasts and trappings I acquired on the road that led me to the shadow of your magnificence."

"There is lavishness for you!" acknowledged the Amir.

"Rather say that the splendor of my lord's presence is better than horses and goods," countered Ismeddin.

And thus they exchanged compliments and gifts.

Coffee was served, and bread, and lamb grilled on skewers, and stews and pilau.

"*El hamdu lilahi!*" exclaimed the darwish as he stuffed home the last morsel of food. And then, "*Ya* Amir, I am a man of honor, and in the old days I ate your break and salt; therefore I give you fair warning."

"There is neither might nor majesty save in Allah, the Great, the Glorious," intoned the Amir gravely. "But what might this warning be, *ya* Ismeddin?"

"Your city is favored by the presence of the shrine of the Imam Ismail, may Allah be pleased with him, and with the dancing darwishes who guard it. I have come from afar to seek the Holy Carpet that hangs before the tomb of Imam Ismail."

"Allah, by Allah, and again, by Allah!" swore the Amir. "Is it possible that you demand the Holy Carpet as a present?"

"No, my lord," replied the darwish. "I have come to steal it. And having eaten your bread and salt, I am bound in honor to declare my intention, so that you may be warned."

The Amir smiles, and stroked his beard for a moment. Then he struck his hands thrice together. An officer of the household advance to the foot of the Amir's dais.

"Harkening and obedience, my lord!"

"You, Mansur," directed the Amir, "will give to Ismeddin a horse from my stables, and a brocaded robe, and a purse of a thousand pieces. And let Qasim give him ten cakes of bread, a measure of wine, a quarter of dressed meat, each day that Ismeddin is with us. Also detail ten slaves to wait on him as long as he honors us with his presence."

The Amir paused a moment, and then continued, "And you, Zayd, post a company of the guard about the monastery of the holy brethren. Draw a line skirting its walls at a distance of twenty paces. As for this Ismeddin, the guard will shoot him in his tracks if so much as the nail of his great toe or the tip of his little finger crosses the line."

Then, to Ismeddin: "See how I esteem your company. I have made the stealing a long task, ever for one of your skill. Therefore take it if you can, and it is yours."

"Do you give me your word that if I can escape beyond three days' ride, it will be mine, and that you will not hold it against me, or demand reprisal of whoever gives me protection?"

"Even so, and let these be witnesses!" agreed the Amir, indicating the officers of the guard and the lords of the court.

That night, the secret wine-bibbers and the public coffee-drinkers marveled over their bubbling pipes at the mad darwish who had proclaimed his intention of looting the shrine.

The dancing darwishes were aghast at the blasphemy, and reassured by the presence of the guard, and the broad white streak of lime that marked the deadline that Ismeddin would have to cross in the face of rifle fire. They heard the mounted sentries riding their beats along the city wall, against which the monastery was built, and were further assured that the audacious looter could not climb from the wall into the monastery. And there was one among the brethren, a new arrival from the college of dancing darwishes in Damascus who was likewise assured by the guard the Amir had posted. This holy brother's assurance, however, was mixed with wonder at Ismeddin's brazen announcement.

"Ismeddin is certainly bent on winning the loser's purse," said Rankin to himself. "There's absolutely nothing to be done in the way of refraining from exposing him! Unless he does the impossible and passes the sentries, so that I can nab him in the act of taking the carpet . . . I wonder if he's allowed for my getting into the monastery at all, much less entering before they posted a guard!"

On the whole, Rankin felt that even though Ismeddin's demonstration might mask a subtle plan for looting the shrine, he, Rankin, had the advantage, since it would manifestly be easier to leave the monastery than to enter under the eyes of the guard. The theft of the carpet was, after all, nothing compared to observing the daily routine of the order of dancing darwishes, and carrying his life exposed to keen eyes ready to note the slightest false gesture, or word spoken out of character.

Ismeddin spent the following day wandering about the city, loitering in the *souk*, smoking and drinking coffee, and basking in the wondering stares of the populace, ever last man of whom had heard of his mad quest. And since madmen are favored of Allah, their infirmity being a sign of especial holiness, the darwish was received as a saint by the hanger-ons of the coffee shops, and the upstairs rooms where true believers, following the Amir's example, drank themselves drunk with wine and *'araki*, in defiance of the Prophet's precepts.

That afternoon, not long before sunset, Ismeddin approached the monastery and took his place at the plainly marked deadline, twenty paces before the wall, and in front of the entrance. He could look in through the arched doorway, and see, at the farther end of the hall, the Holy Carpet handing before the shrine of Imam Ismail, magnificent in the dim shadows, and shimmering silkily where bands of late sunlight crept through the barred windows and marched across its surface.

"*Ya Allah!*" gasped Ismeddin as he saw the splendor of that web of enchantment, rippling ever so slightly in the breeze that stirred the sunbaked plaza between the monastery and the Herati Gate.

Then Ismeddin set about with his preparation to beguile the guard.

The captain of the troops barked a command. The rifles of the guard came to the ready.

"Beware, *ya* Ismeddin!" warned the captain. "Cross that line, and we fire."

"Wait until I cross the line," replied Ismeddin. "It is not forbidden that I look at the Holy Carpet. And of an evening it pleases me to play at a curious game I learned in Yemen."

At the command of their captain, all save the two sentries on post along the whitewash line retired to the guard house that had been erected at the entrance of the monastery.

Ismeddin unslung from his back a knapsack, and seated himself on the ground within a hair's breadth of the deadline. Then he took from the knapsack a tiny drum, and with his finger tips and knuckles beat a curious rhythm.

"*Aywah! Aywah! Aywah!*" he changed. "Verily, O soldiers, I have learned odd feats in Hindustan—"

"You said al Yemen a moment ago, grandfather!" shouted one of the soldiers.

"See and judge for yourselves, O soldiers! *Aywah! Aywah! Aywah!* Yes, by God, O soldiers, I will show you a strange feat from Hindustan! Give me a copper coin, O soldiers, and watch this most entertaining feat!"

As he spoke, he reached into the capacious pack and withdrew a slim want no thicker than the reed of a scribe, and about as long as his forearm: a quaint little wand with a grotesque image of ivory mounted at one end, to give it the semblance of a tiny scepter or mace.

Long shadows were stretching out across the plaza, and the fierce glare of day was being cut off by the bulk of the city walls and the tall minarets of the adjoining mosque.

"Watch with all your eyes, O soldiers!"

"By Allah, O Captain!" continued Ismeddin, "your men may not fire, since our lord the Amir said nothing about my little staff. Now watch me remove it."

"Better not, uncle," muttered the sentry as he passed. "That father of many pigs would order us to fire if your little finger cross the line. I'll kick your staff to you the next time I pass."

"Captain," shouted Ismeddin, "is it truly forbidden that I reach across for my staff? Even just one little reach? I am an old man—"

"We warned you, O Ismeddin!"

"Then I am warned! So look with all your eyes, O soldiers, and see a most curious feat. *Aywah! Aywah! Aywah!* A most curious feat!"

As Ismeddin chanted his litany, he began making passes and gestures.

"*Mashallah!*" exclaimed the sentry. "It's moving."

Even as he spoke, the head of the little scepter rose a hand's breadth, halted, remained for an instant, its butt resting on the earth, head wavering from side to side. Then it rose another span toward the vertical, and yet again, until finally it stood as erect as a soldier on parade.

"O little staff," chanted Ismeddin, "take a pace forward, little staff. Old Ismeddin can't reach across to get you. Take another pace, little staff—" In cadence to his chant and weaving gestures, the rod pirouetted toward him, a span at a time; paused, nodded, dipped, steadied itself, bounded this time half its length; reached the line, then very slowly sank forward until its ivory head touched the ground.

"See, the little staff is a true believer!" pattered Ismeddin.

"*Ya sidi!*" shouted the guard. "*Kamaan! Kamaan!*"

"No more tonight, O soldiers," declared Ismeddin, as he gathered up the coins and twists of tobacco and pieces of bread the guard had tossed him. "I live by your generosity, O soldiers! For I have sworn not to eat the Amir's bread until I have stolen the Holy Carpet!"

"Does the old jackass think his jugglery will make our vigilance relax?" wondered the captain. "Is this that crafty Ismeddin who's going to steal the Holy Carpet? . . ."

Ismeddin in the meanwhile had thrust his miniature scepter into his pack and joined a group of the faithful who were going to the mosque to pray.

To each of the slaves that the Amir had given him, Ismeddin that evening assigned a sufficiency of tedious, trivial tasks that would keep him out of earshot. As they burnished the scimitar, the trappings of the bay mare, and the daggers that usually bristled from Ismeddin's belt, and went on all manner of errands, the darwish reclined on his cushions, drinking coffee and smoking the pipe the Amir had provided.

The two who trimmed the pipe and replenished the tiny coffee-cup were gray-bearded, leathery fellows more accustomed to sword hilts and rifle butts than coffee-pots and charcoal-tongs: in a word, they weren't slaves at all, but a pair of the Old Tiger's picked raiders, the advance guard of the Companions that Ismeddin had rescued from the limbo of peaceful, Resident-ridden Bir el Asad and posted in the hills to await developments.

At every turn they contrived to upset the coffee-pot and spill its steaming, aromatic liquid into the hearth, or fumble the tongs and scatter burning charcoal over the rug at Ismeddin's feet every time the pipe received the slightest attention.

"O sons of several dogs!" roared Ismeddin. "Allah curse each of your fathers!"

If the palace walls had ears, the assurances of the coffee-slave and his protestations of this penitence effectively drowned the words that Ismeddin spat out between the curses and revilings he heaped on his awkward attendants.

And as the coffee-brewer loudly begged pardon, and dodged the pot hurled by the irate darwish, the *chiboukjji*, trimming the pipe, for once failed to drop a live coal, and spoke in low, rapid syllables.

"We don't know where the infidel dog is hiding. We heard that one of the brethren from Aleppo, or Trebizond, or some such place, came to the monastery just the other day."

"Find out more. But do nothing to betray *Sidi* Rankin, if it's he who has palmed himself off as a dancing darwish. And tell the Companions to patrol the hills closely. Any day, now . . ."

They sat late at chess that night, Ismeddin and the Amir.

Thrice in succession the Amir just succeeded in checkmating the darwish, and was consequently in an amiable mood, and admired Ismeddin more than ordinarily.

"*Wallah!*" exclaimed Ismeddin. "Played like the Amir Timur. Up to the last, I had that game in my hand."

"Why speak of chess?" said the Amir. "Stealing the Holy Carpet is much more important! After all, you didn't come all this distance to beat me at chess."

The Amir beamed graciously.

"Come now, as one coffee companion to another, forget this stupid idea of taking the carpet. *Billahi!* You're a smart fellow, and an uncommonly good chess-player. How about taking a post as prime minister? Adburrahman Khan has overstepped himself recently, and he's all ready for the bowstring . . . only he doesn't know it. Suppose you take his position?"

"I take refuge with Allah!" protested the darwish. "I am an old man, too late in life for a high position. Still, since you put it that way, you could do me a favor—"

The darwish paused a moment, abashed at his presumption in suggesting some favor other than the one offered.

"Out with it, Ismeddin. Anything except the Holy Carpet."

"Well, since you insist . . . You know, the secretaries of your court, and some of the brethren of the monastery, are reputed to be the finest scribes in this part of the world. Will my lord arrange a completion in the more elegant scripts, and then let the decision go in my favor?"

Ismeddin grinned, and winked.

"*Wallahi!* Nothing simpler," agreed the Amir. "And if you can impose on some one by being proclaimed the first scribe of my court, I'll draw the proclamation now, and arrange the competition tomorrow. And in a way, a love of learning is better than high position. I envy the darwish, roaming about the world—"

"Voyaging," quoted Ismeddin pompously, "is victory."

"Even so," agreed the Amri. And then, quoting just as ponderously, *"But while in leaving home, one learns life, yet a journey is a bit of Jehannum!"*

And on the heels of that profound declaration, the Amir dictated an order for the competition in writing, followed by a proclamation announcing Ismeddin the Darwish as winner and chief scribe of the court.

For several days Ismeddin dallied about, riding through the city, scattering alms among the beggars, strutting through the *souk*, and carpeting about with his mountebank tricks for the benefit of the troops posted before the shrine of Imam Ismail.

"*Ya sidi,*" said Ismeddin's pipe attendant as he trimmed the pipe, "I hear that the newcomer from Damascus is distinguished for his piety and learning. I bribed a porter to let me take his place and help carry a load of meal and some dressed meal broke wide open—by accident, you understand—and I insisted on helping sweep it up. Luckily, I got a look at the brother from Damascus. He has deep-set eyes, and brows that rise to points in the middle, just as you described Abdullah the Scribe.

"And tonight they will hold a ceremony, dancing themselves into ecstasy and then into a stupor. Then, as they lie in a trance, communing with Allah, this newcomer will take the Holy Carpet—"

"Shaytan rip thee open, why didn't you take it?" demanded Ismeddin. "You were in the monastery."

"In the monastery, with the muzzles of two rifles prodding me as I swept up the spilled meal," explained the pipe slave.

"Fair enough. By the way, Selim, have you ever seen such elegant writing?" asked the darwish irrelevantly.

"Never," admitted Selim. "But what has that to do with the Holy Carpet?"

"That," explained the darwish, "remains to be seen. Suffice it to say that even I couldn't have written such elegant *diwani*, and *kufi*, and *naskh*, and *ta'alik*, and such intricate *jeresi*."

Ismeddin folded the manuscript and stuffed it into his wallet.

"Listen carefully. Have a horse waiting for me at the Herati Gate. Let there be another once close to the monastery, ridden aimlessly about by one of the Companions, so that if need be, I can mount behind him instead of running to the gate."

As Ismeddin approached the deadline, the guard hailed him joyously. "Will the little staff march in and take the Holy Carpet?"

"Sing us the one about the forty daughters of the Sultan—"

"No, tell us about Sitti Zobeide and the woodcutter."

"How about Abou Nowas and his wife's five lovers, O grandfather?"

"Sons of pigs, and eaters of pork!" retorted Ismeddin. "Allah sift me if I ever tell you another story, or sing another song, or perform any more juggleries for you. Tonight I have come to steal the Holy Carpet."

From within the monastery came the sound of pipes, and the eight-stringed *'oudh*, and the mutter of drums. The dancing darwishes were beginning their ritual of whirling.

The guard howled with good-natured derision. Sentry duty to keep this ancient madman out of the monastery was almost as good as unlimited looting.

"But before I steal the Holy Carpet, I will perform one more curious feat."

Ismeddin took from his knapsack half a dozen rods as long as his forearm and somewhat thicker than his thumb. These he planted in the ground, several feet apart, along the deadline.

"Tell me, O soldiers, have you ever been in *Feringhistan*?" he demanded as he fixed the last rod in place.

"No, by Allah!"

"Is it true that they eat pork?" asked one.

"And drink blood?" wondered another.

"And worship the images of three gods?" asked yet another.

"All that and more," replied Ismeddin. "But they have most amusing spectacles. In Damascus I stole these unusual sticks from the infidel oppressors of true believers."

The darwish indicated the upright rods: railroad signal flares, borrowed from the mining concessions in Bir el Asad.

Then Ismeddin produced several small red boxes, likewise the property of the British engineers, and scattered the contents, a grayish, glistening powder, along the deadline. Box after box he emptied until he had a continuous train that extended several paces on each side of the center of the line he dared not cross. This done, Ismeddin struck light to the signal flares, which flamed up with a fierce, consuming redness.

Three musicians approached from out of the darkness behind Ismeddin.

"Where have you been?" he roared. "When we're through here, I'll have you flogged! Take your places and begin playing!"

The musicians seated themselves behind Ismeddin, and unslung small brazen trumpets they wore suspended from their belts. Ismeddin, back to his musicians, made a gesture with the tiny ivory-headed scepter, and extended it at arm's length to his right front.

Ismeddin's wand flashed down.

The three musicians as one set their small brazen horns to their lips. The clear notes drowned the music coming from the monastery, where the brethren were well into the second phase of the ritual, whirling themselves into a trance. The blare of those brazen trumpets rang like the voice of a drunken god and wrenched the hearts of the listeners like daggers thrust home and fiercely twisted. And Ismeddin sang in sonorous Arabic that rolled and thundered like the voice of doom.

The guard stared at that little group of musicians, half blinded by the flares, and enthralled by that son that would carry across a battlefield. But they did not know that only two of the three trumpeters were sounding off; and that the third, for all his cheeks being inflated to bursting, was making not a sound, watching, instead, for Ismeddin's next move.

The red flares were dying. One was dead—no, not quite. For as the fire flickered up once more, it set light to a fuse that hissed and sputtered swiftly toward the train of ash-gray powder.

Ismeddin closed his eyes, and bowed his head.

And then came a terrible, dazzling flash like the full blaze of uncounted noonday suns.

As Ismeddin leaped to his feet and dashed through the heavy wall of smoke that rolled forward from the explosion of that heavy charge of photographer's flashlight powder, the hitherto silent trumpeter picked up the chant where Ismeddin had left off.

The guard was stone-blind from the terrific flame they had faced with un-averted eyes. But they heard a great voice singing to the nerve-searching blare of brass, and believed that Ismeddin was still with his musicians.

The whirling darwishes, a full dozen or more of them, lay scattered about the hall, drunk with the divine ecstasy of having attained Oneness with Allah. Ismeddin laughed triumphantly as he leaped forward and snatched from its silver pegs the rug that hung before the tomb of Imam Ismail.

From without still came the blare of the brazen horns.

But Ismeddin knew that any instant the guard would emerge from its beguilement: so he swiftly folded the carpet into a compact bundle, drew his pistol, and dashed for the door.

The guard of a sudden though of the Amir's sanguinary fancies, and of Ismeddin's sleight of hand. Panic-stricken, they milled about, groping in the impenetrable blackness that clouded their eyes.

From the monastery came the yells of the *shaykh*, and of the musicians who had played for the participants of the ceremony.

A bolt clicked home. A rifle barked. The captain roared orders which no one understood in the confusion. And the brethren who had not danced themselves into a stupor emerged from their cells behind the hall.

"The Holy Carpet is gone! Stop him!" shrieked the *shaykh*.

Ismeddin, followed by his musicians, ran across the plaza, crouched low and zigzagging to avoid the fusillade that poured after them. And with a hail of bullets whistling over their heads, they gained the Herati gate.

Ismeddin let drive with his pistol before the sentry at the gate could bring his rifle to the ready, and dropped him in his tracks. A dozen bounds brought him to the clump of trees where horses and a groom awaited.

Ismeddin and his musicians were getting a comfortable lead on the pursuit.

"*Ya sidi*," said the groom as he reined his horse to a walk, "just for a minute I came near mounting up and taking to the hills. Lucky you got there when you did."

"How so, Aieed?" demanded Ismeddin. "You had that thick wall between you and the rifle fire from in front of the monastery."

"That's not it at all, *sidi*," explained the groom. "I saw that flash. It looked like all Jehannum breaking out! *Wallah*! What a flame!"

"That's when I ran for the carpet," interposed Ismeddin.

"You made good time, then. For the next thing I knew, there was shooting and shouting, and a general riot. Then I looked about me, and up there on the wall I saw a horse without a rider, and a man going over the wall. I couldn't see whether he dropped, or climbed own."

"I was about to ride over to him—I thought it was you—when I heard the clatter of hoofs, and saw him charge out of the clump of trees he'd landed in.

"Just then you tore through the gate, with bullets kicking up dust all around you, and you shot the sentry's head loose from his chin. *Ya* Allah! If I hadn't waited—"

"But you did wait, *el hamdu lilahi!*"

The darwish frowned a moment, and stroked his beard. "What manner of man was this, Aieed?"

"I don't know, sidi. I got a glimpse of him on the wall, and it seemed that he wore a tall hat like the Brethren. But before he mounted his horse, he stumbled through the underbrush. I couldn't understand what he said, except a word or two—"

"And what was that?" asked Ismeddin.

"He spoke like the *Feringhi* engineers when they play that game of an evening. You know, when they poke sticks at little balls on a table, one who misses the ball says '*Damn*' and the other says '*Tough luck, Old Man.*'"

The darwish laughed.

"Captain Rankin, by Allah! Scared out at the last minute, he went over the side. Thought they were firing at him. But what was he doing on the wall? He should have stayed in the monastery if—But maybe he wasn't ready yet to take the Holy Carpet."

"God alone is wise and all-knowing!" interjected Aieed. "And those *Feringhi* are all madmen."

To which Ismeddin agreed, and the horses having somewhat regained their wind, the darwish resumed the gallop.

They rode steadily for an hour or more. And as they rode, Ismeddin chanted the son about the forty daughters of the Sultan. He patted the carpet slung across the pommel of the saddle, and laughed.

"The one certain way of keeping *Sidi* Rankin from stealing the Holy Carpet. Me, prime minister in Kuh-i-Atesh! With a world dripped with loot, and the son of the Old Tiger needing me to keep Sir John in his place!"

Ismeddin reined his horse to a walk. He whistled a low noted in ascending scale. In answer came the same thrilling, quavering whistle.

"Ho, there, Hussayn! Bring out some fresh horses!" he commanded.

"Ready and waiting!" replied a voice from the darkness. "Are you far enough ahead for a pot of coffee? I'll send 'Amru back a way to watch the road."

Ismeddin dismounted, tossing the reins to Shayk Hussayn. Then he unslung the burden from the pommel of his saddle, and dropped it to the ground by the smoldering fire. As Aieed fanned the coals to life, Ismeddin unrolled the precious carpet.

"*Ya* Allah!" exclaimed the darwish.

By the light of the glowing coals, Ismeddin recognized the very carpet on which Abdullah the Scribe had sat in the market-place of Kuh-i-Atesh. He examined the rug, peering at it from end to end to assure himself that his eyes were not deceiving him. But there was no mistake; it was the very rug, and no other.

"That infidel hung the false carpet beneath the true one, so that the theft wouldn't be noticed for several hours, or a day, perhaps. The brethren are so accustomed to seeing it that as long as something—almost anything that looks like a rug—hung there before the shrine, they suspected nothing."

"I take refuge from Satan!" exclaimed Shaykh Hussayn. He looked Ismeddin over from head to foot, and from foot o head. "Allah give me another twenty years to marvel at the first time Ismeddin was outwitted!"

"Allah grant you forth more!" retorted Ismeddin. "But not to marvel at Captain Rankin. As long as the Amir's troops think we have the carpet, the infidel can make good his escape."

Aieed the groom let out a fresh horse. Ismeddin swallowed his coffee, and leaped to the saddle.

"Mount up and follow me!" he commanded. "I'm going to find Rankin!"

Ismeddin's search for Rankin appeared to be a hopeless task; but the darwish knew the hills, and immediately made his disposition of the Companions. He ordered them to ride out in pairs and fours, cutting across country where none but seasoned mountaineers could pick their way, and patrolling the passes leading in every direction from Kuh-i-Atesh. Ismeddin himself took charge of the southwestern quarter of the field, Rankin's most logical route, with a detachment of the Companions covering the ground as only ex-brigands could.

Rankin *could* get through; but the odds were against him.

For three days they patrolled. At times Ismeddin heard the distant crackle of rifles and pistol fire, and the drumming of hoofs; and then, later, one of the Companions would report an engagement with a patrol of the Amir's troops on their way back to Kuh-i-Atesh. But still there was no sign of Rankin.

"Shaytan rip me open!" exclaimed the darwish, as he received negative reports from every quarter. "He couldn't have gotten beyond the limits of the ground we've covered. He must be between our patrols and the walls of Kuh-i-Atesh. So we'll close in."

The morning of the following day proved the worth of Ismeddin's decision.

The old darwish was riding along the narrow trail leading toward the ruins of a village sacked and looted several years previously by a band of raiding Kurds. In the distance, approaching the ruins, Ismeddin saw a man on foot, carrying a bundle on his back.

The wanderer was reeling, and his course zigzagged drunkenly. He stumbled, pitched forward on his face, lay there sprawled in the sunbaked dust. Then he laboriously rose to his knees, and with the aid of his staff, he lifted himself to his feet and resumed his staggering march.

There was something about the shape of the wanderer's burden that spurred Ismeddin to action. He urged his horse off the trail, and down the steep slope toward the wanderer. As he descended, Ismeddin signaled his followers to halt and take cover.

"Ho, there, *Sidi* Rankin!" he hailed.

For Rankin indeed it was, or what remained of him. By some unbelievable volition, he marched on when by all reason he should long since have dropped by the trail, with the vultures to administer the last rites, and a Sixteenth Century Persian carpet to serve as a shroud. His face was gashed and caked with dirt, and his long darwish cloak was slashed and tattered and stained with dried blood.

"Ho, there, *Sidi* Rankin!" repeated Ismeddin.

Rankin halted. With painful deliberation he unslung his bundle, laid it carefully on a rock, and drew the blade whose hilt peeped over his shoulder. Then he advanced at a brisk double-time, scimitar at the port.

Ismeddin marveled at that slashed, gory wreck of a man that had reeled and tottered just a moment ago, and now advanced with the agility of a tiger.

The darwish drew his blade, and crouched low in the saddle to meet the charge. The bay mare snorted and pawed at the smell of slaughter that the wind blew from the enemy.

At the instant of closing, Rankin shifted his attack from Ismeddin's right, where his blade would have full reach, to the left, where the darwish would have to cut over his horse's neck. Ismeddin wheeled just in time to evade Rankin's sweeping but; and as he wheeled, Ismeddin's scimitar flamed in a dazzling arc.

Ranking's blade rang against the rocks a dozen feet away.

Ismeddin dived out of the saddle, bearing Ranking to the ground.

"Take it easy, idiot!" growled the darwish. "I'm Ismeddin."

Ranking struggled vainly for a moment in Ismeddin's strong grasp. His strength and courage had left him with his blade. He glared for a moment at this enemy, and then recognized the ancient beggar who had accosted him as he played scribe in the market-place of Kuh-i-Atesh.

"It's your turn, Ismeddin. I got six of them on the way out here. You're the only one who had sense enough to disarm me."

The darwish helped Rankin to his feet, and supported him for a moment as he regained his balance. Then he took from his saddle-bags a cake of bread, and dates, and unslung a skin of water.

"Here, eat!"

But before Rankin could accept the food and drink, Ismeddin remembered that his mission was not complete, and withdrew the water and bread.

"*Ya*, Allah!" he exclaimed. "This interfering with honest looting is dirty business! Before there is bread and salt between us, there is this matter of a wager you made with an old man in the *souk*."

Ranking caught a flicker of steel in the background, halfway up the wall of the ravine, and marveled that Ismeddin would parley when he could take the carpet without further discussion. The remark about settling the wager before there was bread and salt between them had a sinister implication; yet the darwish thus far had shown no intention of resorting to force.

"Well then," said Rankin, as he took from the belt beneath his cloak two heavy purses, "here is the loser's portion, as we agreed. And as much more if you and your men will escort me to Mosul. Take it, and let me eat."

"*Wallah!*" exclaimed the darwish. "To refuse you food is painful. But you forget the wager: *Whoever shall hold the others life in his hands and yet refrain from exposing his rival, that one shall take the carpet. And the loser, for his good will, shall have from the winter a purse of five hundred tomans.*

"Now at what time between this moment and the day that we made our wager did your hold the life of Ismeddin in your hands?"

"Not once," acknowledged Rankin. "But—"

"Then by that sign," interrupted Ismeddin, "the Holy Carpet is mine, for I knew that you were in the monastery, and I refrained from denouncing you. One word from me, and your hide would even now be nailed to the city gate, and in their eagerness they would have flayed your before they killed you, and this you know well."

As he spoke, Ismeddin unslung a bundle lashed to the pommel of his saddle, and unrolled a rug.

"This is the carpet which you left in place of the one I sought. There is proof that in sparing your life, I gave you the chance to take the real, and leave me the substitute!"

At these words Rankin's spirit revived, instead of dying before his battered, hacked body: for with followers at his back, Ismeddin offered proof and invited argument instead of seizing what he could take.

"Not so fast there, Ismeddin, not so fast!" exclaimed Rankin exultantly. "Prove first that you held my life in your hands, instead of showing that you arrived some moments after I had succeeded! How do you think that I came to be accepted as a brother of the order of dancing darwishes? On what point of ritual could you have exposed me when the brethren themselves did not suspect me? Had you known enough about the mysteries of the order to betray me, you yourself would have entered as I did."

The darwish smiled and stroked his beard.

"But a wager is a wager, you still admit?"

"Granted," assented Rankin. "Then prove that my life was in your hands."

Ismeddin drew from his belt a scrap of paper.

"Here it is. Look at it!"

Ranking examined the fine *naskh* script, and the elegant *ta'alik*.

"Nothing but my own handwriting."

"Nothing but your death warrant, had I used it!" retorted Ismeddin. "The script that an infidel imposter submitted in a competition at the Amir's command."

Ranking laughed good-humoredly.

"Absurd! The *shaykh* himself complimented me on it."

"But supposing, *Sidi* Rankin," resumed Ismeddin, "that I had called to the Amir's attention that the triple dots over *sheen* and the double dots over *qaf* and beneath *yé* were made from *left* to *right*, according to the *Feringhi* direction of writing, even though the characters themselves were faultlessly made as we make them, from right to left. Your instinct betrayed you, and you never thought to make the right-hand dot first when you wrote, and you can plainly see how your reed moved in making them.

"One word to the Amir—but to say more is insulting."

"You saw that in the *souk,* when you read the letter I wrote for the Afghan, before we made our wager," raged Rankin, contending for more than your life he had so boldly risked. "And then you went to the Amir and announced your mission, so that it was impossible from the outset for me to betray you."

The darwish smiled; but he retreated a pace.

"Only a fool or an *inglesi* would wager without being certain in advance of the outcome; particularly when he adds to his oath the word of an *inglesi*. You wagered recklessly, not I. And who but yourself proposed the wager?

"You could have told the captain of the guard that I would blind his men with an explosion of flashlight powder, and take the carpet while they were sightless?" mocked Ismeddin.

Rankin turned and seized the Holy Carpet. His laugh was high-pitched and cackling.

"My life hung on three dots? What if I had mispronounced the password? What if they had seen me taking the carpet? What of the sentries patrolling the wall while you make your juggleries down there in the courtyard?"

Rankin's laughter froze Ismeddin.

The darwish signaled with his arm, and whistled a shrill note. Here and there from behind rocks and clumps of shrubbery along the slope appeared the heads of the Companions. The click of cocking pieces and the ring of bolts snapped home mingled strangely with Rankin's terrible laughter.

"Let them fire!" cried Rankin as he shouldered the rug. "And be damned to your three dots!"

Rankin strode along the trail at a brisk march, carpet balanced on his shoulder.

Ismeddin stared for a moment, reached again for the skin of water and cake of bread. But again he remembered that he served the Sultan, and not himself: and the darwish shouted a command.

The Companions swooped down on Rankin like falcons striking their prey.

The darwish mounted his horse, and took the trail toward Bir el Asad.

"Serving kings is a dirty business," he growled.

But as he rode, his frown was replaced by a smile, for Ismeddin contemplated the payment he would exact of Sir John.

Shortly after the morning prayer, Shams ud Din the Sultan sat beneath the glittering canopy of this throne of state. The captains of the guard and the officers of the court filed into the throne room and took their posts about the dais. Sir John Lindsay occupied his customary post at the Sultan's left.

The great gong rolled and thundered, formally announcing that the Sultan's Presence was for his people.

A *wazir* approached the dais. But his petition was not presented.

There was a clatter of hoofs in the courtyard. A horseman charged into the hall of audience, followed by a second. At the very foot of the dais they reined in their foaming horse. Both dismounted. And Ismeddin, tossing the reins to the grimy, bandaged survivor of hard fighting in the hills who served as groom, leaped up the steps to the throne.

"*Ana dakhilak, ya sultan!*" he cried. "Under your protection, O King!"

"You have our protection, *ya* Ismeddin," responded the Sultan: and then, remembering the old days when hard-pressed riders sought him, "Turn out the guard!"

"Never mind the guard!" said the darwish. "They're a day's march behind me!"

The Sultan's brows rose in saracenic arches.

Sir John twice opened his mouth to speak, and twice decided it was too late. Sir John had a premonition of evil: for with the Sultan's being startled into granting protection, no matter what devil's mess was following in the trace of the wily darwish, the Sultan was bound by his word to protect Ismeddin to the uttermost.

Ismeddin grinned, and stroked his beard. As he eyed Sir John, his grin widened.

"*Ya sultan*," he announced, "Captain Rankin will not steal the Holy Carpet."

Sir John sighed deeply, and ceased looking as though he could bite a rifle-barrel in half.

"Is this the truth?" demanded the Sultan.

"By your life and by your beard!" affirmed the darwish. "This is the very truth of the One True God. I have done that which you commanded, and Rankin is safe, though corroded by the treachery of man."

But the Sultan suspected something that should not be revealed in public: so he signaled his *wazir* to dismiss the court.

And as the hall of audience was cleared of all save Ismeddin and his groom, and the Resident, the Sultan said, "O subtle serpent, for what villainy have you tricked me into giving you protection? For the sake of what thievery and what slaying have you made a fool of me?

"Let it pass this time, but by your life, I will have your head if ever another device serves you as this one did.

"But prove to me that Rankin did not steal the Holy Carpet."

The darwish turned to his foaming horse, and with his poniard swiftly cut the lashing of the pack behind the cantle of the saddle. He flung the bundle at the foot of the dais, and unwound the outer covering of rags. Then he unrolled a rug somewhat over four feet wide and slightly less than ten feet long, and flung its folds upon the steps.

"Behold the Holy Carpet which Rankin did not steal!"

The Resident started as though prodded with red-hot irons.

The Sultan roared his rage.

"God, by God, by the Very God! I sent you to keep Rankin from stealing the carpet, and Allah curse your father, you stole it yourself! I sent you as a preserver of the peace, and you ride back with war at your heels! O crack-brain! Son of a camel and father of a pig!"

"*Ana dakhilak, ya sultan,*" murmured the darwish, and grinned.

Sir John was choking, but he finally managed to articulate.

"Your majesty, protection or not protection, this fellow must be surrendered to the Amir, and the carpet returned."

"Your Excellency," interposed the darwish, "I am his protected, and his captains and lords bear witness. And he will protect me to the uttermost."

Sir John knew that Ismeddin spoke the truth.

And Sir John knew that no explanations would be acceptable to his superiors. He wondered just how soon his successor would report for duty. He saw the concessions sacked and burned by horsemen from the hills.

"My good man," resumed Sir John, "I understand His Majesty's obligation to his protected. But you have served His Majesty so faithfully you simply couldn't hold out for protection at the cost of war. And your life isn't in danger. Return the accursed carpet, and go your way. I will reward you richly."

"Hear His Excellency seek favors of old Ismeddin!" mocked the darwish.

And Sir John endured his misery in silence.

"My lord," continued the darwish, "I obeyed your command concerning *Sidi* Rankin. As to the Holy Carpet, it came without reprisal in its wake.

"I warned the Amri before witnesses that I had come to steal the carpet from the shrine of Imam Ismail, Allah curse the heretic! And the Amir laughed, and invited me to spend as much of my life as I cared to devote to the enterprise. He posted a company of the guard before the shrine, with orders to shoot me down if I crossed their line with as little as my finger tip. And he swore that if I could take it, then it was mine.

"And here is the Holy Carpet. By your beard, *ya sultan*, this is the truth."

The Sultan and Sir John listened to Ismeddin's account of the taking of the carpet, and of the fighting in the hills, and of feasting of the vultures . . .

Then said Ismeddin, "Your servant offers you a throne carpet worthy of a prince. And the sight of it is like listening to exalting music."

The darwish attempted to fling the carpet across the throne from which the Sultan had risen; but the Sultan stopped him with a gesture.

"Ismeddin," he said, "that carpet is red with the blood of the Companions of the Old Tiger. In the old days when I tossed away the lives of my men, I rode leading them; but now I sit safely on my throne. So I will not sit on that blood-stained rug!"

"So be it, and the thought is worthy of you, my lord," said the darwish. Then, with a lordly gesture, "Permit me then to give it to my faithful servant with whose blood this carpet is reddest."

He beckoned to the groom.

"Take it, Saoud, and my blessing with it!"

The purple tinge left Sir John's face, and he sighed his satisfaction.

"My word, your Majesty," said Sir John as he turned from the throne to leave the audience hall, "an unusual fellow, this Ismeddin. A bit irregular, you know, this keeping the stolen carpet, but since Captain Rankin isn't involved, it will be quite satisfactory. Entirely so, your Majesty."

Then, as the Resident passed the sentries at the door of the audience hall, the Sultan said to Ismeddin, "Why did you demand protection you didn't need? And who is this groom of yours? He's so loaded with bandages I couldn't recognize him."

"I demanded protection," replied the darwish, "for the purpose of giving that ass of a Resident a few unhappy moments for making me thwart an honest looting.

"As to the groom: that is *Sidi* Rankin in one of his disguises."

And Ismeddin told the Sultan the unrelated portions of the quest of the Holy Carpet as a bandaged, sword-slashing groom with a bundle on his shoulder led a foaming horse toward the excavations not far from the city wall.

22
The Seed from the Sepulchre
Clark Ashton Smith
(1933)

This fun little weird menace story from one of the *Weird Tales* trinity (the others being, of course, Howard and Lovecraft) was published in the October 1933 issue. Although the story was well received by several readers, as reported in the reader's forum "The Eyrie," Smith lost out on the favorite story status to some guy named Robert E. Howard, whose "The Pool of the Black One" appeared in the same issue. Howard himself, however, liked the story, for as he wrote Smith in a letter, "I enjoyed your story in October *Weird Tales*, as always."

"Yes, I found the place," said Falmer. "It's a queer sort of place, pretty much as the legends describe it." He spat quickly into the fire, as if the act of speech had been physically distasteful to him, and, half averting his face from the scrutiny of Thone, stared with morose and somber eyes into the jungle-matted Venezuelan darkness.

Thone, still weak and dizzy from the fever that had incapacitated him for continuing their journey to its end, was curiously puzzled. Falmer, he thought, had under-gone an inexplicable change during the three days of his absence: a change that was too elusive in some of its phases to be fully defined or delimited.

Other phases, however, were all too obvious. Falmer, even during extreme hardship or illness, had heretofore been unquenchably loquacious and cheerful. Now he seemed sullen, uncommunicative, as if preoccupied with far-off things of disagreeable import. His bluff face had grown hollow—even pointed—and his eyes had narrowed to secretive slits. Thone was troubled by these changes, though he tried to dismiss his impressions as mere distempered fancies due to the influence of the ebbing fever.

"But can't you tell me what the place was like?" he persisted.

"There isn't much to tell," said Falmer, in a queer grumbling tone. "Just a few crumbling walls and falling pillars."

"But didn't you find the burial-pit of the Indian legend, where the gold was supposed to be?"

"I found it . . . but there was no treasure." Falmer's voice had taken on a forbidding surliness; and Thone decided to refrain from further questioning.

"I guess," he commented lightly, "that we had better stick to orchid hunting. Treasure trove doesn't seem to be in our line. By the way, did you see any unusual flowers or plants during the trip?"

"Hell, no," Falmer snapped. His face had gone suddenly ashen in the firelight, and his eyes had assumed a set glare that might have meant either fear or anger. "Shut up, can't you? I don't want to talk. I've had a headache all day—some damned Venezuelan fever coming on, I suppose. We'd better head for the Orinoco tomorrow. I've had all I want of this trip."

James Falmer and Roderick Thone, professional orchid hunters, with two Indian guides, had been following an obscure tributary of the upper Orinoco. The country was rich in rare flowers; and, beyond its floral wealth, they had been drawn by vague but persistent rumors among the local tribes concerning the existence of a ruined city somewhere on this tributary; a city that contained a burial pit in which vast treasures of gold, silver, and jewels had been interred together with the dead of some nameless people. The two men had thought it worthwhile to investigate these rumors. Thone had fallen sick while they were still a full day's journey from the site of the ruins, and Falmer had gone on in a canoe with one of the Indians, leaving the other to attend to Thone. He had returned at nightfall of the third day following his departure.

Thone decided after a while, as he lay staring at his companion, that the latter's taciturnity and moroseness were perhaps due to disappointment over his failure to find the treasure. It must have been that, together with some tropical infection working in the man's blood. However, he admitted doubtfully to himself, it was not like Falmer to be disappointed or downcast under such circumstances.

Falmer did not speak again, but sat glaring before him as if he saw something invisible to others beyond the labyrinth of fire-touched boughs and lianas in which the whispering, stealthy darkness crouched. Somehow, there was a shadowy fear in his aspect. Thone continued to watch him, and saw that the Indians, impassive and cryptic, were also watching him, as if with some obscure expectancy. The riddle was too much for Thone, and he gave it up after a while, lapsing into restless, fever-turbulent slumber from which he awakened at intervals, to see the set face of Falmer, dimmer and more distorted each time with the slowly dying fire and the invading shadows.

Thone felt stronger in the morning: his brain was clear, his pulse tranquil once more; and he saw with mounting concern the indisposition of Falmer, who seemed to rouse and exert himself with great difficulty, speaking hardly a word and moving with singular stiffness and sluggishness. He appeared to have forgotten his announced project of returning toward the Orinoco, and Thone took entire charge of the preparations for departure. His companion's condition puzzled him more and more: apparently there was no fever and the symptoms were wholly ambiguous. However, on general principles, he administered a stiff dose of quinine to Falmer before they started.

The paling saffron of sultry dawn sifted upon them through the jungle tops as they loaded their belongings into the dugouts and pushed off down the slow current. Thone sat near the bow of one of the boats, with Falmer in the rear, and a large bundle of orchid roots and part of their equipment filling the middle. The two Indians occupied the other boat, together with the rest of the supplies.

It was a monotonous journey. The river wound like a sluggish olive snake between dark, interminable walls of forest, from which the goblin faces of orchids leered. There were no sounds other than the splash of paddles, the furious chattering of monkeys, and petulant cries of fiery-colored birds. The sun rose above the jungle and poured down a tide of torrid brilliance.

Thone rowed steadily looking back over his shoulder at times to address Falmer with some casual remark or friendly question. The latter, with dazed eyes and features queerly pale and pinched in the sunlight, sat dully erect and made no effort to use his paddle. He offered no reply to the queries of Thone, but shook his head at intervals, with a sort of shuddering motion that was plainly involuntary. After a while he began to moan thickly, as if in pain or delirium.

They went on in this manner for hours. The heat grew more oppressive between' the stifling walls of jungle. Thone became aware of a shriller cadence in the moans of his companion. Looking back, he saw that Falmer had removed his sun-helmet, seemingly oblivious of the murderous heat, and was clawing at the crown of his head with frantic fingers. Convulsions shook his entire body, and the dugout began to rock dangerously as he tossed to and fro in a paroxysm of manifest agony. His voice mounted to a high unhuman shrieking.

Thone made a quick decision. There was a break in the lining palisade of somber forest, and he headed the boat for shore immediately. The Indians followed, whispering between themselves and eyeing the sick man with glances of apprehensive awe and terror that puzzled Thone tremendously. He felt that there was some devilish mystery about the whole affair; and he could not imagine what was wrong with Falmer. All the known manifestations of malignant tropical diseases rose before him like a rout of hideous fantasms; but, among them, he could not recognize the thing that had assailed his companion.

Having gotten Falmer ashore on a semicircle of liana-latticed beach without the aid of the guides, who seemed unwilling to approach the sick man, Thone administered a heavy hypodermic injection of morphine from his medicine-chest. This appeared to ease Falmer's suffering, and the convulsions ceased. Thone, taking advantage of their remission, proceeded to examine the crown of Falmer's head.

He was startled to find amid the thick disheveled hair, a hard and pointed lump which resembled the tip of a beginning horn, rising under the still unbroken skin. As if endowed with erectile and resistless life, it seemed to grow beneath his fingers.

At the same time, abruptly and mysteriously, Falmer opened his eyes and appeared to regain full consciousness. For a few minutes he was more his normal self than at any time since his return from the ruins. He began to talk, as if anxious to relieve his mind of some oppressing burden. His voice was peculiarly thick and toneless, but Thone was able to follow his mutterings and piece them together.

"The pit! The pit!" said Falmer—"the infernal thing that was in the pit, in the deep sepulcher! . . . I wouldn't go back there for the treasure of a dozen El Dorados . . . I didn't tell you much about those ruins, Thone. Somehow it was hard—impossibly hard—to talk . . .

"I guess the Indian knew there was something wrong with the ruins. He led me to the place . . . but he wouldn't tell me anything about it; and he waited by the riverside while I searched for the treasure.

"Great gray walls there were, older than the jungle—old as death and time. They must have been quarried and reared by people from some lost planet. They loomed and leaned at mad, unnatural angles, threatening to crush the trees about them.

And there were columns, too: thick, swollen columns of unholy form, whose abominable carvings the jungle had not wholly screened from view.

"There was no trouble finding that accursed burial-pit. The pavement above had broken through quite recently, I think. A big tree had pried with its boa-like roots between the flagstones that were buried beneath centuries of mold. One of the flags had been tilted back on the pavement, and another had fallen through into the pit. There was a large hole, whose bottom I could see dimly in the forest-strangled light. Something glimmered palely at the bottom; but I could not be sure what it was.

"I had taken along a coil of rope, as you remember. I tied one end of it to a main root of the tree, dropped the other through the opening, and went down like a monkey. When I got to the bottom I could see little at first in the gloom, except the whitish glimmering all around me, at my feet. Something that was unspeakably brittle and friable crunched beneath me when I began to move. I turned on my flashlight, and saw that the place was fairly littered with bones. Human skeletons lay tumbled everywhere. They must have been very old, for they broke into powder at a touch.

"It was the burial-chamber of the legend. Looking about with a flashlight, I found the steps that led to the blocked-up entrance. But if any treasure had been buried with the bodies, it must have been removed long ago. I groped around amid the bones and dust, feeling pretty much like a ghoul, but couldn't find anything of value, not even a bracelet or a finger-ring on any of the skeletons.

"It wasn't until I thought of climbing out that I noticed the real horror. In one of the corners—the corner nearest to the opening in the roof—I looked up and saw it in the webby shadows. Ten feet above my head it hung, and I had almost touched it, unknowingly, when I descended the rope.

"It looked like a sort of white lattice-work at first. Then I saw that the lattice was partly formed of human bones—a complete skeleton, very tall and stalwart, like that of a warrior. A pale withered thing grew out of the skull, like a set of fantastic antlers ending in myriads of long and stringy tendrils that had spread upward till they reached the roof. They must have lifted the skeleton, or body, along with them as they climbed.

"I examined the thing with my flashlight. It must have been a plant of some sort, and apparently it had started to grow in the cranium. Some of the branches had issued from the cloven crown, others through the eye-holes, the mouth, and the nose-hole, to flare upward. And the roots of the blasphemous thing had gone downward, trellising themselves on every bone. The very toes and fingers were ringed with them, and they drooped in writhing coils. Worst of all, the ones that had issued from the toe-ends *were rooted in a second skull*, which dangled just below, with fragments of the broken-off root system. There was a litter of fallen bones on the floor in the corner . . .

"The sight made me feel a little weak, somehow, and more than a little nauseated—that abhorrent, inexplicable mingling of the human and the plant. I started to climb the rope, in a feverish hurry to get out, but the thing fascinated me in its abominable fashion, and I couldn't help pausing to study it a little more when I had climbed half-way. I leaned toward it too far, I guess, and the rope began to sway, bringing my face lightly against the leprous, antler-shaped boughs above the skull.

"Something broke—possibly a sort of pod on one of the branches. I found my head enveloped in a cloud of pearl-grey powder, very light, fine, and scentless. The stuff settled on my hair, it got into my nose and eyes, nearly choking and blinding me. I shook it off as well as I could. Then I climbed on and pulled myself through the opening . . ."

As if the effort of coherent narration had been too heavy a strain, Falmer lapsed into disconnected mumblings. The mysterious malady, whatever it was, returned upon him, and his delirious ramblings were mixed with groans of torture. But at moments he regained a flash of coherence.

"My head! my head!" he muttered. "There must be something in my brain, something that grows and spreads; I tell you, I can feel it there. I haven't felt right at any time since I left the burial pit. . . . My mind has been queer ever since . . . It must have been the spores of the ancient devil-plant . . . The spores have taken root . . . the thing is splitting my skull, going down into my brain—a plant that springs out of a human cranium, as if from a flower pot!"

The dreadful convulsions began once more, and Falmer writhed uncontrollably in his companion's arms, shrieking with agony. Thone, sick at heart and shocked by his sufferings, abandoned all effort to restrain him and took up the hypodermic. With much difficulty, he managed to inject a triple dose, and Falmer grew quiet by degrees, and lay with open glassy eyes, breathing stertorously. Thone, for the first time, perceived an odd protrusion of his eyeballs, which seemed about to start from their sockets, making it impossible for the lids to close, and lending the drawn features an expression of mad horror. It was as if something were pushing Falmer's eyes from his head.

Thone, trembling with sudden weakness and terror, felt that he was involved in some unnatural web of nightmare. He could not, dared not, believe the story Falmer had told him, and its implications. Assuring himself that his companion had imagined it all, had been ill throughout with the incubation of some strange fever, he stooped over and found that the horn-shaped lump on Falmer's head had now broken through the skin.

With a sense of unreality, he stared at the object that his prying fingers had revealed amid the matted hair. It was unmistakably a plant-bud of some sort, with involuted folds of pale green and bloody pink that seemed about to expand. The thing issued from above the central suture of the skull.

A nausea swept upon Thone, and he recoiled from the lolling head and its baleful outgrowth, averting his gaze. His fever was returning, there was a woeful debility in all his limbs, and he heard the muttering voice of delirium through the quinine-induced ringing in his ears. His eyes blurred with a deathly and miasmal mist.

He fought to subdue his illness and impotence. He must not give way to it wholly; he must go on with Falmer and the Indians and reach the nearest trading-station, many days away on the Orinoco, where Falmer could receive aid.

As if through sheer volition, his eyes cleared, and he felt a resurgence of strength. He looked around for the guides, and saw, with a start of uncomprehending surprise, that they had vanished. Peering further, he observed that one of the boats— the dugout used by the Indian—had also disappeared. It was plain that he and Falmer had been deserted. Perhaps the Indians had known what was wrong with the sick man, and had been afraid. At any rate, they were gone, and they had taken much of the camp equipment and most of the provisions with them.

Thone turned once more to the supine body of Falmer, conquering his repugnance with effort. Resolutely he drew out his clasp-knife and, stooping over the stricken man, he excised the protruding bud, cutting as close to the scalp as he could with safety. The thing was unnaturally tough and rubbery; it exuded a thin, sanious fluid; and he shuddered when he saw its internal structure, full of nerve-like filaments, with a core that suggested cartilage. He flung it aside, quickly, on, the river sand. Then, lifting Falmer in his arms, he lurched and staggered towards the remaining boat. He fell more than once, and lay half swooning across the inert body. Alternately carrying and dragging his burden, he reached the boat at last. With the remnant of his failing strength, he contrived to prop Falmer in the stern against the pile of equipment.

His fever was mounting apace. After much delay, with tedious, half-delirious exertions, he pushed off from the shore and got the boat into midstream. He paddled with nerveless strokes, till the fever mastered him wholly and the oar slipped from oblivious fingers . . .

He awoke in the yellow glare of dawn, with his brain and his senses comparatively clear. His illness had left a great languor, but his first thought was of Falmer. He twisted about, nearly falling overboard in his debility, and sat facing his companion.

Falmer still reclined, half sitting, half lying, against the pile of blankets and other impedimenta. His knees were drawn up, his hands clasping them as if in tetanic rigor. His features had grown as stark and ghastly as those of a dead man, and his whole aspect was one of mortal rigidity. It was this, however, that caused Thone to gasp with unbelieving horror.

During the interim of Thone's delirium and his lapse into slumber, the monstrous plant-bud, merely stimulated, it would seem, by the act of excision, had grown again with preternatural rapidity, from Falmer's head. A loathsome pale-green stem was mounting thickly, and had started to branch like antlers after attaining a height of six or seven inches.

More dreadful than this, if possible, similar growths had issued from the eyes, and their stems, climbing vertically across the forehead, had entirely displaced the eyeballs. Already they were branching like the thing from the crown. The antlers were all tipped with pale vermilion. They appeared to quiver with repulsive animations, nodding rhythmically in the warm, windless air . . . From the mouth another stem protruded, curling upward like a long and whitish tongue. It had not yet begun to bifurcate.

Thone closed his eyes to shut away the shocking vision. Behind his lids, in a yellow dazzle of light, he still saw the cadaverous features, the climbing stems that quivered against the dawn like ghastly hydras of tomb-etiolated green. They seemed to be waving toward him, growing and lengthening as they waved. He opened his eyes again, and fancied, with a start of new terror, that the antlers were actually taller than they had been a few moments previous.

After that, he sat watching them in a sort of baleful hypnosis. The illusion of the plant's visible growth, and freer movement—if it were illusion—increased upon him. Falmer, however, did not stir, and his parchment face appeared to shrivel and fall in, as if the roots of the growth were draining his blood, were devouring his very flesh in their insatiable and ghoulish hunger.

Thone wrenched his eyes away and stared at the river shore. The stream had widened and the current had grown more sluggish. He sought to recognize their location, looking vainly for some familiar landmark in the monotonous dull-green cliffs of jungle that lined the margin. He felt hopelessly lost and alienated. He seemed to be drifting on an unknown tide of madness and nightmare, accompanied by something more frightful than corruption itself.

His mind began to wander with an odd inconsequence, coming back always, in a sort of closed circle, to the thing that was devouring Falmer. With a flash of scientific curiosity, he found himself wondering to what genus it belonged. It was neither fungus nor pitcher-plant, nor anything that he had ever encountered or heard of in his explorations. It must have come, as Falmer had suggested, from an alien world: it was nothing that the earth could conceivably have nourished

He felt, with a comforting assurance, that Falmer was dead. That at least, was a mercy. But, even as he shaped the thought, he heard a low, guttural moaning, and, peering at Falmer in a horrible startlement, saw that his limbs and body were twitching slightly. The twitching increased, and took on a rhythmic regularity, though at no time did it resemble the agonized and violent convulsions of the previous day. It was plainly automatic, like a sort of galvanism; and Thone saw that it was timed with the languorous and loathsome swaying of the plant. The effect on the watcher was insidiously mesmeric and somnolent; and once he caught himself beating the detestable rhythm with his foot.

    He tried to pull himself together, groping desperately for something to which his sanity could cling. Ineluctably, his illness returned: fever, nausea, and revulsion worse than the loathliness of death. But, before he yielded to it utterly, he drew his loaded revolver from the holster and fired six times into Falmer's quivering body. He knew that he had not missed, but, after the final bullet, Falmer still moaned and twitched in unison with the evil swaying of the plant, and Thone, sliding into delirium, heard still the ceaseless, automatic moaning.

There was no time in the world of seething unreality and shoreless oblivion through which he drifted. When he came to himself again, he could not know if hours or weeks had elapsed. But he knew at once that the boat was no longer moving; and lifting himself dizzily, he saw that it had floated into shallow water and mud and was nosing the beach of a tiny, jungle-tufted isle in mid-river. The putrid odor of slime was about him like a stagnant pool; and he heard a strident humming of insects.

    It was either late morning or early afternoon, for the sun was high in the still heavens. Lianas were drooping above him from the island trees like uncoiled serpents, and epiphytic orchids, marked with ophidian mottlings, leaned toward him grotesquely from lowering boughs. Immense butterflies went past on sumptuously spotted wings.

    He sat up, feeling very giddy and lightheaded, and faced again the horror that accompanied him. The thing had grown incredibly: the three-antlered stems, mounting above Falmer's head, had become gigantic and had put out masses of ropy feelers that tossed uneasily in the air, as if searching for support—or new provender. In the topmost antlers, a prodigious blossom had opened—a sort of fleshy disk, broad as a man's face and white as leprosy.

Falmer's features had shrunken till the outlines of every bone were visible as if beneath tightened paper. He was a mere death's-head in a mask of human skin; and beneath his clothing, the body was little more than a skeleton. He was quite still now, except for the communicated quivering of the stems. The atrocious plant had sucked-him dry, had eaten his vitals and his flesh.

Thone wanted to hurl himself forward in a mad impulse to grapple with the growth. But a strange paralysis held him back. The plant was like a living and sentient thing—a thing that watched him, that dominated him with its unclean but superior will. And the huge blossom, as he stared, took on the dim, unnatural semblance of a face. It was somehow like the face of Falmer, but the lineaments were twisted all awry, and were mingled with those of something wholly devilish and nonhuman. Thone could not move—he could not take his eyes from the blasphemous abnormality.

By some miracle, his fever had left him; and it did not return. Instead, there came an eternity of frozen fright and madness, in which he sat facing the mesmeric plant. It towered before him from the dry, dead shell that had been Falmer, its swollen, glutted stems and branches swaying gently, its huge flower leering perpetually upon him with its impious travesty of a human face. He thought that he heard a low, singing sound, ineffably sweet, demonically sweet, but whether it emanated from the plant or was a mere hallucination of his overwrought senses, he could not know.

The sluggish hours went by, and a gruelling sun poured down its beams like molten lead from some titanic vessel of torture. His head swam with weakness and the fetor-laden heat, but he could not relax the rigor of his posture. There was no change in the nodding monstrosity, which seemed to have attained its full growth above the head of its victim. But after a long interim Thone's eyes were drawn to the shrunken hands of Falmer, which still clasped the drawn-up knees in a spasmodic clutch. Through the ends of the fingers, tiny white rootlets had broken and were writhing slowly in the air—groping, it seemed, for a new source of nourishment. Then from the neck and chin, other tips were breaking, and over the whole body the clothing stirred in a curious manner, as if with the crawling and lifting of hidden lizards.

At the same time the singing grew louder, sweeter, more imperious, and the swaying of the great plant assumed an indescribably seductive tempo. It was like the allurement of voluptuous sirens, the deadly languor of dancing cobras. Thone felt an irresistible compulsion: a summons was being laid upon him, and his drugged mind and body must obey it. The very fingers of Falmer, twisting viperishly, seemed beckoning to him. Suddenly he was on his hands and knees in the bottom of the boat.

Inch by inch, with terror and fascination contending in his brain, he crept forward, dragging himself over the disregarded bundle of orchid-plants—inch by inch, foot by foot, till his head was against the withered hands of Falmer, from which hung and floated the questing roots.

Some cataleptic spell had made him helpless. He felt the rootlets as they moved like delving fingers through his hair and over his face and neck, and started to strike in with agonizing, needle-sharp tips. He could not stir, he could not even close his lids. In a frozen stare, he saw the gold and carmine flash of a hovering butterfly as the roots began to pierce his pupils.

Deeper and deeper went the greedy roots, while new filaments grew out to enmesh him like a witch's net . . . For a while, it seemed that the dead and the living writhed together in leashed convulsions . . . At last Thone hung supine amid the lethal, ever-growing web. Bloated and colossal, the plant lived on; and in its upper branches, through the still, stifling afternoon, a second flower began to unfold.

Robert E. Howard's

23
The Festival
H.P. Lovecraft
(1933)

H.P. Lovecraft originally published this short story in the January 1925 issue of *Weird Tales* magazine. Reprinted in the October 1933 issue, it was that issue in which, it appears, Robert E. Howard first read "The Festival." In a letter to Lovecraft that September, Howard wrote, "I like your 'Festival' reprint in the current *Weird Tales*. Indeed, I believe I like it as well as anything I ever read of yours. It will quite overshadow my Conan yarn." Howard's "The Pool of the Black One," was the Conan yarn to which he referred.

"*Efficiunt Daemones, ut quae non sunt, sic tamen quasi sint, conspicienda hominibus exhibeant.*"
("Devils so work that men perceive things which do not exist as if they were real.")
—Lactantius.

I was far from home, and the spell of the eastern sea was upon me. In the twilight I heard it pounding on the rocks, and I knew it lay just over the hill where the twisting willows writhed against the clearing sky and the first stars of evening. And because my fathers had called me to the old town beyond, I pushed on through the shallow, new-fallen snow along the road that soared lonely up to where Aldebaran twinkled among the trees; on toward the very ancient town I had never seen but often dreamed of.

It was the Yuletide, which men call Christmas though they know in their hearts it is older than Bethlehem and Babylon, older than Memphis and mankind. It was the Yuletide, and I had come at last to the ancient sea town where my people had dwelt and kept festival in the elder time when festival was forbidden; where also they had commanded their sons to keep festival once every century, that the memory of primal secrets might not be forgotten. Mine were an old people, and were old even when this land was settled three hundred years before. And they were strange, because they had come as dark furtive folk from opiate southern gardens of orchids, and spoken another tongue before they learnt the tongue of the blue-eyed fishers. And now they were scattered, and shared only the rituals of mysteries that none living could understand. I was the only one who came back that night to the old fishing town as legend bade, for only the poor and the lonely remember.

Then beyond the hill's crest I saw Kingsport outspread frostily in the gloaming; snowy Kingsport with its ancient vanes and steeples, ridgepoles and chimney-pots, wharves and small bridges, willow-trees and graveyards; endless labyrinths of steep, narrow, crooked streets, and dizzy church-crowned central peak that time durst not touch; ceaseless mazes of colonial houses piled and scattered at all angles and levels like a child's disordered blocks; antiquity hovering on grey wings over winter-whitened gables and gambrel roofs; fanlights and small-paned windows one by one gleaming out in the cold dusk to join Orion and the archaic stars. And against the rotting wharves the sea pounded; the secretive, immemorial sea out of which the people had come in the elder time.

Beside the road at its crest a still higher summit rose, bleak and wind-swept, and I saw that it was a burying-ground where black gravestones stuck ghoulishly through the snow like the decayed fingernails of a gigantic corpse. The printless road was very lonely, and sometimes I thought I heard a distant horrible creaking as of a gibbet in the wind. They had hanged four kinsmen of mine for witchcraft in 1692, but I did not know just where.

As the road wound down the seaward slope I listened for the merry sounds of a village at evening, but did not hear them. Then I thought of the season, and felt that these old Puritan folk might well have Christmas customs strange to me, and full of silent hearthside prayer. So after that I did not listen for merriment or look for wayfarers, but kept on down past the hushed lighted farmhouses and shadowy stone walls to where the signs of ancient shops and seataverns creaked in the salt breeze, and the grotesque knockers of pillared doorways glistened along deserted, unpaved lanes in the light of little, curtained windows.

I had seen maps of the town, and knew where to find the home of my people. It was told that I should be known and welcomed, for village legend lives long; so I hastened through Back Street to Circle Court, and across the fresh snow on the one full flagstone pavement in the town, to where Green Lane leads off behind the Market house. The old maps still held good, and I had no trouble; though at Arkham they must have lied when they said the trolleys ran to this place, since I saw not a wire overhead. Snow would have hid the rails in any case. I was glad I had chosen to walk, for the white village had seemed very beautiful from the hill; and now I was eager to knock at the door of my people, the seventh house on the left in Green Lane, with an ancient peaked roof and jutting second story, all built before 1650.

There were lights inside the house when I came upon it, and I saw from the diamond window-panes that it must have been kept very close to its antique state. The upper part overhung the narrow grass-grown street and nearly met the overhanging part of the house opposite, so that I was almost in a tunnel, with the low stone doorstep wholly free from snow. There was no sidewalk, but many houses had high doors reached by double flights of steps with iron railings. It was an odd scene, and because I was strange to New England I had never known its like before. Though it pleased me, I would have relished it better if there had been footprints in the snow, and people in the streets, and a few windows without drawn curtains.

When I sounded the archaic iron knocker I was half afraid. Some fear had been gathering in me, perhaps because of the strangeness of my heritage, and the bleakness of the evening, and the queerness of the silence in that aged town of curious customs. And when my knock was answered I was fully afraid, because I had not heard any footsteps before the door creaked open. But I was not afraid long, for the gowned, slippered old man in the doorway had a bland face that reassured me; and though he made signs that he was dumb, he wrote a quaint and ancient welcome with the stylus and wax tablet he carried.

He beckoned me into a low, candle-lit room with massive exposed rafters and dark, stiff, sparse furniture of the seventeenth century. The past was vivid there, for not an attribute was missing. There was a cavernous fireplace and a spinning-wheel at which a bent old woman in loose wrapper and deep poke-bonnet sat back toward me, silently spinning despite the festive season. An indefinite dampness seemed upon the place, and I marvelled that no fire should be blazing. The high-backed settle faced the row of curtained windows at the left, and seemed to be occupied, though I was not sure. I did not like everything about what I saw, and felt again the fear I had had. This fear grew stronger from what had before lessened it, for the more I looked at the old man's bland face the more its very blandness terrified me. The eyes never moved, and the skin was too like wax. Finally I was sure it was not a face at all, but a fiendishly cunning mask. But the flabby hands, curiously gloved, wrote genially on the tablet and told me I must wait a while before I could be led to the place of festival.

Pointing to a chair, table, and pile of books, the old man now left the room; and when I sat down to read I saw that the books were hoary and mouldy, and that they included old

Morryster's wild *Marvells of Science*, the terrible *Saducismus Triumphatus* of Joseph Glanvil, published in 1681, the shocking *Dæmonolatreia* of Remigius, printed in 1595 at Lyons, and worst of all, the unmentionable *Necronomicon* of the mad Arab Abdul Alhazred, in Olaus Wormius' forbidden Latin translation; a book which I had never seen, but of which I had heard monstrous things whispered. No one spoke to me, but I could hear the creaking of signs in the wind outside, and the whir of the wheel as the bonneted old woman continued her silent spinning, spinning.

I thought the room and the books and the people very morbid and disquieting, but because an old tradition of my fathers had summoned me to strange feastings, I resolved to expect queer things. So I tried to read, and soon became tremblingly absorbed by something I found in that accursed *Necronomicon*; a thought and a legend too hideous for sanity or consciousness. But I disliked it when I fancied I heard the closing of one of the windows that the settle faced, as if it had been stealthily opened. It had seemed to follow a whirring that was not of the old woman's spinning-wheel. This was not much, though, for the old woman was spinning very hard, and the aged clock had been striking. After that I lost the feeling that there were persons on the settle, and was reading intently and shudderingly when the old man came back booted and dressed in a loose antique costume, and sat down on that very bench, so that I could not see him. It was certainly nervous waiting, and the blasphemous book in my hands made it doubly so. When eleven struck, however, the old man stood up, glided to a massive carved chest in a corner, and got two hooded cloaks; one of which he donned, and the other of which he draped round the old woman, who was ceasing her monotonous spinning. Then they both started for the outer door; the woman lamely creeping, and the old man, after picking up the very book I had been reading, beckoning me as he drew his hood over that unmoving face or mask.

We went out into the moonless and tortuous network of that incredibly ancient town; went out as the lights in the curtained windows disappeared one by one, and the Dog Star leered at the throng of cowled, cloaked figures that poured silently from every doorway and formed monstrous processions up this street and that, past the creaking signs and antediluvian gables, the thatched roofs and diamond-paned windows; threading precipitous lanes where decaying houses overlapped and crumbled together, gliding across open courts and churchyards where the bobbing lanthorns made eldritch drunken constellations.

Amid these hushed throngs I followed my voiceless guides; jostled by elbows that seemed preternaturally soft, and pressed by chests and stomachs that seemed abnormally pulpy; but seeing never a face and hearing never a word. Up, up, up the eery columns slithered, and I saw that all the travellers were converging as they flowed near a sort of focus of crazy alleys at the top of a high hill in the centre of the town, where perched a great white church. I had seen it from the road's crest when I looked at Kingsport in the new dusk, and it had made me shiver because Aldebaran had seemed to balance itself a moment on the ghostly spire.

There was an open space around the church; partly a churchyard with spectral shafts, and partly a half-paved square swept nearly bare of snow by the wind, and lined with unwholesomely archaic houses having peaked roofs and overhanging gables. Death-fires danced over the tombs, revealing gruesome vistas, though queerly failing to cast any shadows. Past the churchyard, where there were no houses, I could see over the hill's summit and watch the glimmer of stars on the harbour, though the town was invisible in the dark. Only once in a while a lanthorn bobbed horribly through serpentine alleys on its way to overtake the throng that was now slipping speechlessly into the church.

I waited till the crowd had oozed into the black doorway, and till all the stragglers had followed. The old man was pulling at my sleeve, but I was determined to be the last. Then I finally went, the sinister man and the old spinning woman before me. Crossing the threshold into that swarming temple of unknown darkness, I turned once to look at the outside world as the churchyard phosphorescence cast a sickly glow on the hill-top pavement. And as I did so I shuddered. For though the wind had not left much snow, a few patches did remain on the path near the door; and in that fleeting backward look it seemed to my troubled eyes that they bore no mark of passing feet, not even mine.

The church was scarce lighted by all the lanthorns that had entered it, for most of the throng had already vanished. They had streamed up the aisle between the high white pews to the trap-door of the vaults which yawned loathsomely open just before the pulpit, and were now squirming noiselessly in. I followed dumbly down the footworn steps and into the dank, suffocating crypt. The tail of that sinuous line of night-marchers seemed very horrible, and as I saw them wriggling into a venerable tomb they seemed more horrible still. Then I noticed that the tomb's floor had an aperture down which the throng was sliding, and in a moment we were all descending an ominous staircase of rough-hewn stone; a narrow spiral staircase damp and peculiarly odorous, that wound endlessly down into the bowels of the hill past monotonous walls of dripping stone blocks and crumbling mortar. It was a silent, shocking descent, and I observed after a horrible interval that the walls and steps were changing in nature, as if chiselled out of the solid rock. What mainly troubled me was that the myriad footfalls made no sound and set up no echoes.

After more eons of descent I saw some side passages or burrows leading from unknown recesses of blackness to this shaft of nighted mystery. Soon they became excessively numerous, like impious catacombs of nameless menace; and their pungent odor of decay grew quite unbearable. I knew we must have passed down through the mountain and beneath the earth of Kingsport itself, and I shivered that a town should be so aged and maggoty with subterraneous evil.

Then I saw the lurid shimmering of pale light, and heard the insidious lapping of sunless waters. Again I shivered, for I did not like the things that the night had brought, and wished bitterly that no forefather had summoned me to this primal rite. As the steps and the passage grew broader, I heard another sound, the thin, whining mockery of a feeble flute; and suddenly there spread out before me the boundless vista of an inner world—a vast fungous shore litten by a belching column of sick greenish flame and washed by a wide oily river that flowed from abysses frightful and unsuspected to join the blackest gulfs of immemorial ocean.

Fainting and gasping, I looked at that unhallowed Erebus of titan toadstools, leprous fire, and slimy water, and saw the cloaked throngs forming a semicircle around the blazing pillar. It was the Yule-rite, older than man and fated to survive him; the primal rite of the solstice and of spring's promise beyond the snows; the rite of fire and evergreen, light and music. And in the Stygian grotto I saw them do the rite, and adore the sick pillar of flame, and throw into the water handfuls gouged out of the viscous vegetation which glittered green in the chlorotic glare. I saw this, and I saw something amorphously squatted far away from the light, piping noisomely on a flute; and as the thing piped I thought I heard noxious muffled flutterings in the foetid darkness where I could not see. But what frightened me most was that flaming column; spouting volcanically from depths profound and inconceivable, casting no shadows as healthy flame should, and coating the nitrous stone above with a nasty, venomous verdigris. For in all that seething combustion no warmth lay, but only the clamminess of death and corruption.

The man who had brought me now squirmed to a point directly beside the hideous flame, and made stiff ceremonial motions to the semicircle he faced. At certain stages of the ritual they did grovelling obeisance, especially when he held above his head that abhorrent *Necronomicon* he had taken with him; and I shared all the obeisances because I had been summoned to this festival by the writings of my forefathers. Then the old man made a signal to the half-seen flute-player in the darkness, which player thereupon changed its feeble drone to a scarce louder drone in another key; precipitating as it did so a horror unthinkable and unexpected. At this horror I sank nearly to the lichened earth, transfixed with a dread not of this nor any world, but only of the mad spaces between the stars.

Out of the unimaginable blackness beyond the gangrenous glare of that cold flame, out of the Tartarean leagues through which that oily river rolled uncanny, unheard, and unsuspected, there flopped rhythmically a horde of tame, trained, hybrid winged things that no sound eye could ever wholly grasp, or sound brain ever wholly remember. They were not altogether crows, nor moles, nor buzzards, nor ants, nor vampire bats, nor decomposed human beings; but something I cannot and must not recall. They flopped limply along, half with their webbed feet and half with their membraneous wings; and as they reached the throng of celebrants the cowled figures seized and mounted them, and rode off one by one along the reaches of that unlighted river, into pits and galleries of panic where poison springs feed frightful and undiscoverable cataracts.

The old spinning woman had gone with the throng, and the old man remained only because I had refused when he motioned me to seize an animal and ride like the rest. I saw when I staggered to my feet that the amorphous flute-player had rolled out of sight, but that two of the beasts were patiently standing by. As I hung back, the old man produced his stylus and tablet and wrote that he was the true deputy of my fathers who had founded the Yule worship in this ancient place; that it had been decreed I should come back, and that the most secret mysteries were yet to be performed. He wrote this in a very ancient hand, and when I still hesitated he pulled from his loose robe a seal ring and a watch, both with my family arms, to prove that he was what he said. But it was a hideous proof, because I knew from old papers that that watch had been buried with my great-great-great-great-grandfather in 1698.

Presently the old man drew back his hood and pointed to the family resemblance in his face, but I only shuddered, because I was sure that the face was merely a devilish waxen mask. The flopping animals were now scratching restlessly at the lichens, and I saw that the old man was nearly as restless himself. When one of the things began to waddle and edge away, he turned quickly to stop it; so that the suddenness of his motion dislodged the waxen mask from what should have been his head. And then, because that nightmare's position barred me from the stone staircase down which we had come, I flung myself into the oily underground river that bubbled somewhere to the caves of the sea; flung myself into that putrescent juice of earth's inner horrors before the madness of my screams could bring down upon me all the charnel legions these pest-gulfs might conceal.

At the hospital they told me I had been found half frozen in Kingsport Harbour at dawn, clinging to the drifting spar that accident sent to save me. They told me I had taken the wrong fork of the hill road the night before, and fallen over the cliffs at Orange Point—a thing they deduced from prints found in the snow. There was nothing I could say, because everything was wrong. Everything was wrong, with the broad window shewing a sea of roofs in which only about one in five was ancient, and the sound of trolleys and motors in the streets below. They insisted that this was Kingsport, and I could not deny it.

When I went delirious at hearing that the hospital stood near the old churchyard on Central Hill, they sent me to St. Mary's Hospital in Arkham, where I could have better care. I liked it there, for the doctors were broad-minded, and even lent me their influence in obtaining the carefully sheltered copy of Alhazred's objectionable *Necronomicon* from the library of Miskatonic University. They said something about a "psychosis", and agreed I had better get any harassing obsessions off my mind.

So I read again that hideous chapter, and shuddered doubly because it was indeed not new to me. I had seen it before, let footprints tell what they might; and where it was I had seen it were best forgotten. There was no one—in waking hours—who could remind me of it; but my dreams are filled with terror, because of phrases I dare not quote. I dare quote only one paragraph, put into such English as I can make from the awkward Low Latin.

"The nethermost caverns," wrote the mad Arab, "are not for the fathoming of eyes that see; for their marvels are strange and terrific. Cursed the ground where dead thoughts live new and oddly bodied, and evil the mind that is held by no head. Wisely did Ibn Schacabac say, that happy is the tomb where no wizard hath lain, and happy the town at night whose wizards are all ashes. For it is of old rumour that the soul of the devil-bought hastes not from his charnel clay, but fats and instructs *the very worm that gnaws*; till out of corruption horrid life springs, and the dull scavengers of earth wax crafty to vex it and swell monstrous to plague it. Great holes secretly are digged where earth's pores ought to suffice, and things have learnt to walk that ought to crawl."

Robert E. Howard's

24
Revenant
Clark Ashton Smith
(1934)

In July 1933, Howard wrote to Clark Ashton Smith who had apparently sent him a personalized and signed copy of this poem. Howard stated, "First let me thank you very much indeed for the magnificent poem 'Revenant' which is as splendid as anything of its kind that I ever read, and which I have placed among my most treasured possessions. It is indeed an honor to receive an addressed and signed copy of such a poem." The poem then appeared in the *Fantasy Fan* magazine in their March 1934 issue. Howard took the time to praise Smith in a letter to the magazine in May 1934. "Smith's poem in the March issue was splendid, as always. By all means, publish as many of his poems as possible."

I am the spectre who returns
Unto some desolate world in min borne afar
On the black flowing of Lethean skies:
Ever I search, in cryptic galleries,
The void sarcophagi, the broken urns
Of many a vanished avatar;
Or haunt the gloom of crumbling pylons vast
In temples that enshrine the shadowy past.
Viewless, impalpable, and fleet,
I roam stupendous avenues, and greet
Familiar sphinxes carved from everlasting stone,
Or the fair, brittle gods of long ago,
Decayed and fallen low.
And there I mark the tail clepsammiae
That time has overthrown,
And empty clepsydrae,

And dials drowned in umbrage never-lifting;
And there, on rusty parapegms,
I read the ephemerides
Of antique stars and eider planets drifting
Oblivionward in night;
And there, with purples of the tomb bedlight
And crowned with funereal gems,
I bold awhile the throne
Whereon mine immemorial selves have sate,
Canopied by the triple-tinted glory
Of the three suns forever paled and flown.

I am the spectre who returns
And dwells content with his forlorn estate
In mansions lost and hoary
Where no lamp burns;
Who trysts within the sepulchre,
And finds the ancient shadows lovelier
Than gardens all emblazed with sevenfold noon,
Or topaz-builded towers
That throng below some iris-pouring moon.
Exiled and homeless in the younger stars,
Henceforth I shah inhabit that grey clime
Whose days belong to primal calendars;
Nor would I come again
Back to the garish terrene hours:
For I am free of vaults unfathomable
And treasures lost from time:
With bat and vampire there
I fit through sombre skies immeasurable
Or fly adown the unending subterranes;
Mummied and ceremented,
I sit in councils of the kingly dead,
And oftentimes for vestiture I wear
The granite of great idols looming darkly

In atlantean fanes;
Or closely now and starkly
I ding as dings the attenuating air
About the ruins bare.

Robert E. Howard's

25
The Dweller
William Lumley
(1934)

William Lumley was a latecomer to the Lovecraft circle. Described by Lovecraft as "old" and a cat lover who lived in Buffalo, New York, around the time this poem was written, not much else is known about him. Lumley is only known to have authored two poems and the short story, "The Diary of Alonzo Typer," all of which were edited and revised by Lovecraft. This poem saw publication in the February 1934 issue of *Fantasy Fan*, and Howard commented in the May issue, "I would like to see more by Lumley, and it would be a fine thing if you could get some of Lovecraft's poetry."

Dread and potent broods a Dweller
   In an evil twilight space,
Formless as a daemon's shadow,
   Void of members and of face.

Heeding not the shaped or human,
   Past the reach of time or law—
Never may our minds conceive It
   Save as clouds of fright and awe.

When It crawls malignly on us,
   Lethal mists of leaden grey,
Rising vaguely in the distance,
   Veil its hideous bulk away.

And Its mutterings of horror,
    Foul with lore of charnel ground,
Lose themselves in troubled thunders
    That from far horizons sound.

26
Through the Gates of the Silver Key
H. P. Lovecraft & E. Hoffmann Price
(1934)

Co-written between October 1932 and April 1933, "Through the Gates of the Silver Key" is a sequel to Lovecraft's short story "Silver Key," which was published in the January 1929 issue of *Weird Tales* magazine. "Through the Gates," which focuses on Lovecraft's character Randolph Carter, appeared in the July 1934 issue of *Weird Tales.* The story came from E. Hoffmann Price's love of the first yarn which he described as "one of my favorite HPL stories" and, after "telling him of the pleasure I had in rereading it, I suggested a sequel to account for Randolph Carter's doings after his disappearrance." Lovecraft reluctantly agreed, and Price fired off a 6,000 word draft to Lovecraft, who then rewrote it creating a 14,000 word version. As Price later estimated, Lovecraft had left "fewer than fifty of my original words." After reading the story, Howard wrote to Lovecraft saying, "I hardly know how to express my admiration for the splendid work you and Mr. Price have accomplished. I was most intrigued by the personalities of 'Etienne de Marigny' and 'Ward Phillips'! And hope these fine characters will be used again." "My sensations while reading this story are rather difficult to describe," Howard continued. "The effect of reality was remarkable. Some of the speculations were over my head, at the first reading—not from any lack of clarity, but simply because of their cosmic depth. The Dhole-haunted planet of Yaddith conjures up tantalizing vistas of surmise, and I hope you will use it in future stories. I hope, too, that you'll decide to get poor Randolph Carter out of his frightful predicament."

Robert E. Howard's

Chapter 1

In a vast room hung with strangely figured arras and carpeted with Boukhara rugs of impressive age and workmanship four men were sitting around a document-strown table. From the far corners, where odd tripods of wrought-iron were now and then replenished by an incredibly aged negro in somber livery, came the hypnotic fumes of olibanum; while in a deep niche on one side there ticked a curious coffin-shaped clock whose dial bore baffling hieroglyphs and whose four hands did not move in consonance with any time system known on this planet. It was a singular and disturbing room, but well fitted to the business now at hand. For here, in the New Orleans home of this continent's greatest mystic, mathematician, and orientalist, there was being settled at last the estate of a scarcely less great mystic, scholar, author, and dreamer who had vanished from the face of the earth four years before.

Randolph Carter, who had all his life sought to escape from the tedium and limitations of waking reality in the beckoning vistas of dreams and fabled avenues of other dimensions, disappeared from the sight of man on the seventh of October, 1928, at the age of fifty-four. His career had been a strange and lonely one, and there were those who inferred from his curious novels many episodes more bizarre than any in his recorded history. His association with Harley Warren, the South Carolina mystic whose studies in the primal Naacal language of the Himalayan priests had led to such outrageous conclusions, had been close. Indeed, it was he who—one mist-mad, terrible night in an ancient graveyard—had seen Warren descend into a dank and nitrous vault, never to emerge. Carter lived in Boston, but it was from the wild, haunted hills behind hoary and witch-accursed Arkham that all his forbears had come. And it was amid those ancient, cryptically brooding hills that he had ultimately vanished.

His old servant Parks—who died early in 1930—had spoken of the strangely aromatic and hideously carven box he had found in the attic, and of the undecipherable parchments and queerly figured silver key which that box had contained; matters of which Carter had also written to others. Carter, he said, had told him that this key had come down from his ancestors, and that it would help him to unlock the gate to his lost boyhood, and to strange dimensions and fantastic realms which he had hitherto visited only in vague, brief, and elusive dreams. Then one day Carter took the box and its contents and rode away in his car, never to return.

Later on, people found the car at the side of an old, grass-grown road in the hills behind crumbling Arkham—the hills where Carter's forbears had once dwelt, and where the ruined cellar of the great Carter homestead still gaped to the sky. It was in a grove of tall elms near by that another of the Carters had mysteriously vanished in 1781, and not far away was the half-rotted cottage where Goody Fowler, the witch, had brewed her ominous potions still earlier. The region had been settled in 1692 by fugitives from the witchcraft trials in Salem, and even now it bore a name for vaguely ominous things scarcely to be envisaged. Edmund Carter had fled from the shadow of Gallows Hill just in time, and the tales of his sorceries were many. Now, it seemed, his lone descendant had gone somewhere to join him!

In the car they found the hideously carved box of fragrant wood, and the parchment which no man could read. The silver key was gone—presumably with Carter. Further than that there was no certain clue. Detectives from Boston said that the fallen timbers of the old Carter place seemed oddly disturbed, and somebody found a handkerchief on the rock-ridged, sinisterly wooded slope behind the ruins near the dreaded cave called the Snake Den.

It was then that the country legends about the Snake Den gained a new vitality. Farmers whispered of the blasphemous uses to which old Edmund Carter the wizard had put that horrible grotto, and added later tales about the fondness which

Randolph Carter himself had had for it when a boy. In Carter's boyhood the venerable gambrel-roofed homestead was still standing and tenanted by his great-uncle Christopher. He had visited there often, and had talked singularly about the Snake-Den. People remembered what he had said about a deep fissure and an unknown inner cave beyond, and speculated on the change he had shewn after spending one whole memorable day in the cavern when he was nine. That was in October, too—and ever after that he had seemed to have an uncanny knack at prophesying future events.

It had rained late in the night that Carter vanished, and no one was quite able to trace his footprints from the car. Inside the Snake Den all was amorphous liquid mud owing to copious seepage. Only the ignorant rustics whispered about the prints they thought they spied where the great elms overhang the road, and on the sinister hillside near the Snake Den, where the handkerchief was found. Who could pay attention to whispers that spoke of stubby little tracks like those which Randolph Carter's square-toed boots made when he was a small boy? It was as crazy a notion as that other whisper—that the tracks of old Benijah Corey's peculiar heel-less boots had met the stubby little tracks in the road. Old Benijah had been the Carters' hired man when Randolph was young—but he had died thirty years ago.

It must have been these whispers—plus Carter's own statement to Parks and others that the queerly arabesqued silver key would help him unlock the gate of his lost boyhood—which caused a number of mystical students to declare that the missing man had actually doubled back on the trail of time and returned through forty-five years to that other October day in 1883 when he had stayed in the Snake Den as a small boy. When he came out that night, they argued, he had somehow made the whole trip to 1928 and back; for did he not thereafter know of things which were to happen later? And yet he had never spoken of anything to happen after 1928.

One student—an elderly eccentric of Providence, Rhode Island, who had enjoyed a long and close correspondence with Carter—had a still more elaborate theory, and believed that Carter had not only returned to boyhood, but achieved a further liberation, roving at will through the prismatic vistas of boyhood dream. After a strange vision this man published a tale of Carter's vanishing, in which he hinted that the lost one now reigned as king on the opal throne of Ilek-Vad, that fabulous town of turrets atop the hollow cliffs of glass overlooking the twilight sea wherein the bearded and finny Gnorri build their singular labyrinths.

It was this old man, Ward Phillips, who pleaded most loudly against the apportionment of Carter's estate to his heirs—all distant cousins—on the ground that he was still alive in another time-dimension and might well return some day. Against him was arrayed the legal talent of one of the cousins, Ernest K. Aspinwall of Chicago, a man ten years Carter's senior, but keen as a youth in forensic battles. For four years the contest had raged, but now the time for apportionment had come, and this vast, strange room in New Orleans was to be the scene of the arrangements.

It was the home of Carter's literary and financial executor—the distinguished Creole student of mysteries and Eastern antiquities, Etienne-Laurent de Marigny. Carter had met de Marigny during the war, when they both served in the French Foreign Legion, and had at once cleaved to him because of their similar tastes and outlook. When, on a memorable joint furlough, the learned young Creole had taken the wistful Boston dreamer to Bayonne, in the south of France, and had shown him certain terrible secrets in the nighted and immemorial crypts that burrow beneath that brooding, eon-weighted city, the friendship was forever sealed. Carter's will had named de Marigny as executor, and now that vivid scholar was reluctantly presiding over the settlement of the estate. It was sad work for him, for like the old Rhode-Islander he did not believe that Carter was dead. But what weight have the dreams of mystics against the harsh wisdom of the world?

Around the table in that strange room in the old French quarter sat the men who claimed an interest in the proceedings. There had been the usual legal advertisements of the conference in papers wherever Carter heirs were thought to live, yet only four now sat listening to the abnormal ticking of that coffin-shaped clock which told no earthly time, and to the bubbling of the courtyard fountain beyond half-curtained, fanlighted windows. As the hours wore on the faces of the four were half-shrouded in the curling fumes from the tripods, which, piled recklessly with fuel, seemed to need less and less attention from the silently gliding and increasingly nervous old negro.

There was Etienne de Marigny himself—slim, dark, handsome, mustached, and still young. Aspinwall, representing the heirs, was white-haired, apoplectic-faced, side-whiskered, and portly. Phillips, the Providence mystic, was lean, grey, long-nosed, clean-shaven, and stoop-shouldered. The fourth man was non-committal in age—lean, and with a dark, bearded, singularly immobile face of very regular contour, bound with the turban of a high-caste Brahmin and having night-black, burning, almost irisless eyes which seemed to gaze out from a vast distance behind the features. He had announced himself as the Swami Chandraputra, an adept from Benares with important information to give; and both de Marigny and Phillips—who had corresponded with him—had been quick to recognize the genuineness of his mystical pretensions. His speech had an oddly forced, hollow, metallic quality, as if the use of English taxed his vocal apparatus; yet his language was as easy, correct, and idiomatic as any native Anglo-Saxon's. In general attire he was the normal European civilian, but his loose clothes sat peculiarly badly on him, while his bushy black beard, Eastern turban, and large white mittens gave him an air of exotic eccentricity.

De Marigny, fingering the parchment found in Carter's car, was speaking.

"No, I have not been able to make anything of the parchment. Mr. Phillips, here, also gives it up. Colonel Churchward declares it is not Naacal, and it looks nothing at all like the hieroglyphs on that Easter Island wooden club. The carvings on that box, though, do strongly suggest Easter Island images. The nearest thing I can recall to these parchment characters—notice how all the letters seem to hang down from horizontal word-bars—is the writing in a book poor Harley Warren once had. It came from India while Carter and I were visiting him in 1919, and he never would tell us anything about it. Said it would be better if we didn't know, and hinted that it might have come originally from some place other than the earth. He took it with him in December when he went down into the vault in that old graveyard—but neither he nor the book ever came to the surface again. Some time ago I sent our friend here—the Swami Chandraputra—a memory-sketch of some of those letters, and also a photostatic copy of the Carter parchment. He believes he may be able to shed light on them after certain references and consultations.

"But the key—Carter sent me a photograph of that. Its curious arabesques were not letters, but seem to have belonged to the same culture-tradition as the hieroglyphs on the parchment. Carter always spoke of being on the point of solving the mystery, though he never gave details. Once he grew almost poetic about the whole business. That antique silver key, he said, would unlock the successive doors that bar our free march down the mighty corridors of space and time to the very Border which no man has crossed since Shaddad with his terrific genius built and concealed in the sands of Arabia Petraea the prodigious domes and uncounted minarets of thousand-pillared Irem. Half-starved dervishes—wrote Carter—and thirst-crazed nomads have returned to tell of that monumental portal, and of the Hand that is sculptured above the keystone of the arch, but no man has passed and returned to say that his footprints on the garnet-strown sands within bear witness to his visit. The key, he surmised, was that for which the cyclopean sculptured Hand vainly grasps.

"Why Carter didn't take the parchment as well as the key, we cannot say. Perhaps he forgot it—or perhaps he forbore to take it through recollection of one who had taken a book of like characters into a vault and never returned. Or perhaps it was really immaterial to what he wished to do."

As de Marigny paused, old Mr. Phillips spoke in a harsh, shrill voice.

"We can know of Randolph Carter's wandering only what we dream. I have been to many strange places in dreams, and have heard many strange and significant things in Ulthar, beyond the river Skai. It does not appear that the parchment was needed, for certainly Carter reentered the world of his boyhood dreams, and is now a king in Ilek-Vad."

Mr. Aspinwall grew doubly apoplectic-looking as he sputtered: "Can't somebody shut that old fool up? We've had enough of these moonings. The problem is to divide the property, and it's about time we got to it."

For the first time Swami Chandraputra spoke in his queerly alien voice.

"Gentlemen, there is more to this matter than you think. Mr. Aspinwall does not do well to laugh at the evidence of dreams. Mr. Phillips has taken an incomplete view—perhaps because he has not dreamed enough. I, myself, have done much dreaming. We in India have always done that, just as all the Carters seem to have done it. You, Mr. Aspinwall, as a maternal cousin, are naturally not a Carter. My own dreams, and certain other sources of information, have told me a great deal which you still find obscure. For example, Randolph Carter forgot that parchment which he couldn't then decipher—yet it would have been well for him had he remembered to take it. You see, I have really learned pretty much what happened to Carter after he left his car with the silver key at sunset on that seventh of October, four years ago."

Aspinwall audibly sneered, but the others sat up with heightened interest. The smoke from the tripods increased, and the crazy ticking of that coffin-shaped clock seemed to fall into bizarre patterns like the dots and dashes of some alien and insoluble telegraph message from outer space. The Hindoo leaned back, half closed his eyes, and continued in that oddly laboured yet idiomatic voice, while before his audience there began to float a picture of what had happened to Randolph Carter.

Chapter 2

The hills behind Arkham are full of a strange magic—something, perhaps, which the old wizard Edmund Carter called down from the stars and up from the crypts of nether earth when he fled there from Salem in 1692. As soon as Randolph Carter was back among them he knew that he was close to one of the gates which a few audacious, abhorred, and alien-souled men have blasted through titan walls betwixt the world and the outside absolute. Here, he felt, and on this day of the year, he could carry out with success the message he had deciphered months before from the arabesques of that tarnished and incredibly ancient silver key. He knew now how it must be rotated, how it must be held up to the setting sun, and what syllables of ceremony must be intoned into the void at the ninth and last turning. In a spot as close to a dark polarity and induced gate as this, it could not fail in its primary function. Certainly, he would rest that night in the lost boyhood for which he had never ceased to mourn.

He got out of the car with the key in his pocket, walking uphill deeper and deeper into the shadowy core of that brooding, haunted countryside of winding road, vine-grown stone wall, black woodland, gnarled, neglected orchard, gaping-windowed, deserted farmhouse, and nameless ruin. At the sunset hour, when the distant spires of Kingsport gleamed in the ruddy blaze, he took out the key and made the needed turnings and intonations. Only later did he realize how soon the ritual had taken effect.

Then in the deepening twilight he had heard a voice out of the past. Old Benijah Corey, his great-uncle's hired man. Had not old Benijah been dead for thirty years? Thirty years before *when*? What was time? Where had he been? Why was it strange that Benijah should be calling him on this seventh of October, 1883? Was he not out later than Aunt Martha had told him to stay? What was this key in his blouse pocket, where his little telescope—given him by his father on his ninth birthday two months before—ought to be? Had he found it in the attic at home? Would it unlock the mystic pylon which his sharp eye had traced amidst the jagged rocks at the back of that inner cave behind the Snake Den on the hill? That was the place they always coupled with old Edmund Carter the wizard. People wouldn't go there, and nobody but him had ever noticed or squirmed through the root-choked fissure to that great black inner chamber with the pylon. Whose hands had carved that hint of a pylon out of the living rock? Old Wizard Edmund's—or *others* that he had conjured up and commanded?

That evening little Randolph ate supper with Uncle Chris and Aunt Martha in the old gambrel-roofed farmhouse.

Next morning he was up early, and out through the twisted-boughed apple orchard to the upper timber-lot where the mouth of the Snake Den lurked black and forbidding amongst grotesque, over-nourished oaks. A nameless expectancy was upon him, and he did not even notice the loss of his handkerchief as he fumbled in his blouse pocket to see if the queer silver key was safe. He crawled through the dark orifice with tense, adventurous assurance, lighting his way with matches taken from the sitting-room. In another moment he had wriggled through the root-choked fissure at the farther end, and was in the vast, unknown inner grotto whose ultimate rock wall seemed half like a monstrous and consciously shapen pylon. Before that dank, dripping wall he stood silent and awestruck, lighting one match after another as he gazed. Was that stony bulge above the keystone of the imagined arch really a gigantic sculptured hand? Then he drew forth the silver key, and made motions and intonations whose source he could only dimly remember. Was anything forgotten? He knew only that he wished to cross the barrier to the untrammelled land of his dreams and the gulfs where all dimensions dissolve in the absolute.

Chapter 3

What happened then is scarcely to be described in words. It is full of those paradoxes, contradictions, and anomalies which have no place in waking life, but which fill our more fantastic dreams, and are taken as matters of course till we return to our narrow, rigid, objective world of limited causation and tri-dimensional logic. As the Hindoo continued his tale, he had difficulty in avoiding what seemed—even more than the notion of a man transferred through the years to boyhood—an air of trivial, puerile extravagance. Mr. Aspinwall, in disgust, gave an apoplectic snort and virtually stopped listening.

For the rite of the silver key, as practiced by Randolph Carter in that black, haunted cave within a cave, did not prove unavailing. From the first gesture and syllable an aura of strange, awesome mutation was apparent—a sense of incalculable disturbance and confusion in time and space, yet one which held no hint of what we recognize as motion and duration. Imperceptibly, such things as age and location ceased to have any significance whatever. The day before, Randolph Carter had miraculously leaped a gulf of years. Now there was no distinction between boy and man. There was only the entity

Randolph Carter, with a certain store of images which had lost all connection with terrestrial scenes and circumstances of acquisition. A moment before, there had been an inner cave with vague suggestions of a monstrous arch and gigantic sculptured hand on the farther wall. Now there was neither cave nor absence of cave; neither wall nor absence of wall. There was only a flux of impressions not so much visual as cerebral, amidst which the entity that was Randolph Carter experienced perceptions or registrations of all that his mind revolved on, yet without any clear consciousness of the way in which he received them.

By the time the rite was over Carter knew that he was in no region whose place could be told by earth's geographers, and in no age whose date history could fix. For the nature of what was happening was not wholly unfamiliar to him. There were hints of it in the cryptical Pnakotic fragments, and a whole chapter in the forbidden *Necronomicon* of the mad Arab, Abdul Alhazred, had taken on significance when he had deciphered the designs graven on the silver key. A gate had been unlocked—not indeed the Ultimate Gate, but one leading from earth and time to that extension of earth which is outside time, and from which in turn the Ultimate Gate leads fearsomely and perilously to the Last Void which is outside all earths, all universes, and all matter.

There would be a Guide—and a very terrible one; a Guide who had been an entity of earth millions of years before, when man was undreamed of, and when forgotten shapes moved on a steaming planet building strange cities among whose last, crumbling ruins the earliest mammals were to play. Carter remembered what the monstrous *Necronomicon* had vaguely and disconcertingly adumbrated concerning that Guide.

"And while there are those," the mad Arab had written, *"who have dared to seek glimpses beyond the Veil, and to accept HIM as guide, they would have been more prudent had they avoided commerce with HIM; for it is written in the* Book

of Thoth *how terrific is the price of a single glimpse. Nor may those who pass ever return, for in the Vastnesses transcending our world are Shapes of darkness that seize and bind. The Affair that shambleth about in the night, the Evil that defieth the Elder Sign, the Herd that stand watch at the secret portal each tomb is known to have, and that thrive on that which groweth out of the tenants within—all these Blacknesses are lesser than HE WHO guardeth the Gateway: HE WHO will guide the rash one beyond all the worlds into the Abyss of unnamable Devourers. For HE is 'UMR AT-TAWIL, the Most Ancient One, which the scribe rendereth as THE PROLONGED OF LIFE."*

Memory and imagination shaped dim half-pictures with uncertain outlines amidst the seething chaos, but Carter knew that they were of memory and imagination only. Yet he felt that it was not chance which built these things in his consciousness, but rather some vast reality, ineffable and undimensioned, which surrounded him and strove to translate itself into the only symbols he was capable of grasping. For no mind of earth may grasp the extensions of shape which interweave in the oblique gulfs outside time and the dimensions we know.

There floated before Carter a cloudy pageantry of shapes and scenes which he somehow linked with earth's primal, aeon-forgotten past. Monstrous living things moved deliberately through vistas of fantastic handiwork that no sane dream ever held, and landscapes bore incredible vegetation and cliffs and mountains and masonry of no human pattern. There were cities under the sea, and denizens thereof; and towers in great deserts where globes and cylinders and nameless winged entities shot off into space or hurtled down out of space. All this Carter grasped, though the images bore no fixed relation to one another or to him. He himself had no stable form or position, but only such shifting hints of form and position as his whirling fancy supplied.

He had wished to find the enchanted regions of his boyhood dreams, where galleys sail up the river Oukranos past the gilded spires of Thran, and elephant caravans tramp through perfumed jungles in Kled, beyond forgotten palaces with veined ivory columns that sleep lovely and unbroken under the moon. Now, intoxicated with wider visions, he scarcely knew what he sought. Thoughts of infinite and blasphemous daring rose in his mind, and he knew he would face the dreaded Guide without fear, asking monstrous and terrible things of him.

All at once the pageant of impressions seemed to achieve a vague kind of stabilization. There were great masses of towering stone, carven into alien and incomprehensible designs and disposed according to the laws of some unknown, inverse geometry. Light filtered down from a sky of no assignable color in baffling, contradictory directions, and played almost sentiently over what seemed to be a curved line of gigantic hieroglyphed pedestals more hexagonal than otherwise and surmounted by cloaked, ill-defined shapes.

There was another shape, too, which occupied no pedestal, but which seemed to glide or float over the cloudy, floor-like lower level. It was not exactly permanent in outline, but held transient suggestions of something remotely preceding or paralleling the human form, though half as large again as an ordinary man. It seemed to be heavily cloaked, like the Shapes on the pedestals, with some neutral-colored fabric; and Carter could not detect any eye-holes through which it might gaze. Probably it did not need to gaze, for it seemed to belong to an order of being far outside the merely physical in organization and faculties.

A moment later Carter knew that this was so, for the Shape had spoken to his mind without sound or language. And though the name it uttered was a dreaded and terrible one, Randolph Carter did not flinch in fear. Instead, he spoke back, equally without sound or language, and made those obeisances which the hideous *Necronomicon* had taught him to make. For this Shape was nothing less than that which all the world has feared since Lomar rose out of the sea and the Winged Ones came to earth to teach the Elder Lore to man. It was indeed the frightful Guide and Guardian of the Gate—'UMR AT-TAWIL, the ancient one, which the scribe rendereth the PROLONGED OF LIFE.

The Guide knew, as he knew all things, of Carter's quest and coming, and that this seeker of dreams and secrets stood before him unafraid. There was no horror or malignity in what he radiated, and Carter wondered for a moment whether the mad Arab's terrific blasphemous hints, and extracts from the Book of Thoth, might not have come from envy and a baffled wish to do what was now about to be done. Or perhaps the Guide reserved his horror and malignity for those who feared. As the radiations continued, Carter mentally interpreted them in the form of words.

"I am indeed that Most Ancient One," said the Guide, "of whom you know. We have awaited you—the Ancient Ones and I. You are welcome, even though long delayed. You have the Key, and have unlocked the First Gate. Now the Ultimate Gate is ready for your trial. If you fear, you need not advance. You may still go back unharmed the way you came. But if you choose to advance—"

The pause was ominous, but the radiations continued to be friendly. Carter hesitated not a moment, for a burning curiosity drove him on.

"I will advance," he radiated back, "and I accept you as my Guide."

At this reply the Guide seemed to make a sign by certain motions of his robe which may or may not have involved the lifting of an arm or some homologous member. A second sign followed, and from his well-learnt lore Carter knew that he was at last very close to the Ultimate Gate. The light now changed to another inexplicable color, and the Shapes on the quasi-hexagonal pedestals became more clearly defined. As they sat more erect, their outlines became more like those of men, though Carter knew that they could not be men. Upon their cloaked heads there now seemed to rest tall, uncertainly colored mitres, strangely suggestive of those on certain nameless figures chiseled by a forgotten sculptor along the living cliffs of a high, forbidden mountain in Tartary; while grasped in certain folds of their swathings were long scepters whose carven heads bodied forth a grotesque and archaic mystery.

Carter guessed what they were, whence they came, and Whom they served; and guessed, too, the price of their service. But he was still content, for at one mighty venture he was to learn all. Damnation, he reflected, is but a word bandied about by those whose blindness leads them to condemn all who can see, even with a single eye. He wondered at the vast conceit of those who had babbled of the *malignant* Ancient Ones, as if They could pause from their everlasting dreams to wreak a wrath upon mankind. As well, he thought, might a mammoth pause to visit frantic vengeance on an angleworm. Now the whole assemblage on the vaguely hexagonal pillars was greeting him with a gesture of those oddly carven scepters, and radiating a message which he understood:

"We salute you, Most Ancient One, and you, Randolph Carter, whose daring has made you one of us."

Carter saw now that one of the pedestals was vacant, and a gesture of the Most Ancient One told him it was reserved for him. He saw also another pedestal, taller than the rest, and at the center of the oddly curved line—neither semicircle nor ellipse, parabola nor hyperbola—which they formed. This, he guessed, was the Guide's own throne. Moving and rising in a manner hardly definable, Carter took his seat; and as he did so he saw that the Guide had likewise seated himself.

Gradually and mistily it became apparent that the Most Ancient One was holding something—some object clutched in the outflung folds of his robe as if for the sight, or what answered for sight, of the cloaked Companions. It was a large sphere or apparent sphere of some obscurely iridescent metal, and as the Guide put it forward a low, pervasive half-impression of *sound* began to rise and fall in intervals which seemed to be rhythmic even though they followed no rhythm of earth. There was a suggestion of chanting—or what human imagination might interpret as chanting. Presently the quasi-sphere began to grow luminous, and as it gleamed up into a cold, pulsating light of unassignable colour Carter saw that its flickerings conformed to the alien rhythm of the chant. Then all the mitered, scepter-bearing Shapes on the pedestals commenced a slight, curious swaying in the same inexplicable rhythm, while nimbuses of unclassifiable light—resembling that of the quasi-sphere—played round their shrouded heads.

The Hindoo paused in his tale and looked curiously at the tall, coffin-shaped clock with the four hands and hieroglyphed dial, whose crazy ticking followed no known rhythm of earth.

"You, Mr. de Marigny," he suddenly said to his learned host, "do not need to be told the particular alien rhythm to which those cowled Shapes on the hexagonal pillars chanted and nodded. You are the only one else—in America—who has had a taste of the Outer Extension. That clock—I suppose it was sent you by the Yogi poor Harley Warren used to talk about—the seer who said that he alone of living men had been to Yian-Ho, the hidden legacy of sinister, aeon-old Leng, and had borne certain things away from that dreadful and forbidden city. I wonder how many of its subtler properties you know? If my dreams and readings be correct, it was made by those who knew much of the First Gateway. But let me go on with my tale."

At last, continued the Swami, the swaying and the suggestion of chanting ceased, the lambent nimbuses around the now drooping and motionless heads faded away, while the cloaked Shapes slumped curiously on their pedestals. The quasi-sphere, however, continued to pulsate with inexplicable light. Carter felt that the Ancient Ones were sleeping as they had been when he first saw them, and he wondered out of what cosmic dreams his coming had wakened them. Slowly there filtered into his mind the truth that this strange chanting ritual had been one of instruction, and that the Companions had been chanted by the Most Ancient One into a new and peculiar kind of sleep, in order that their dreams might open the Ultimate Gate to which the silver key was a passport. He knew that in the profundity of this deep sleep they were contemplating unplumbed vastnesses of utter and absolute outsideness with which the earth had nothing to do, and that they were to accomplish that which his presence had demanded.

The Guide did not share this sleep, but seemed still to be giving instructions in some subtle, soundless way. Evidently he was implanting images of those things which he wished the Companions to dream; and Carter knew that as each of the Ancient Ones pictured the prescribed thought, there would be born the nucleus of a manifestation visible to his own earthly eyes. When the dreams of all the Shapes had achieved a oneness, that manifestation would occur, and everything he required be materialized, through concentration. He had seen such things on earth—in India, where the combined, projected will of a circle of adepts can make a thought take tangible substance, and in hoary Atlaanât, of which few men dare speak.

Just what the Ultimate Gate was, and how it was to be passed, Carter could not be certain; but a feeling of tense expectancy surged over him. He was conscious of having a kind of body, and of holding the fateful Silver Key in his hand. The masses of towering stone opposite him seemed to possess the evenness of a wall, toward the center of which his eyes were irresistibly drawn. And then suddenly he felt the mental currents of the Most Ancient One cease to flow forth.

For the first time Carter realized how terrific utter silence, mental and physical, may be. The earlier moments had never failed to contain some perceptible rhythm, if only the faint, cryptical pulse of the earth's dimensional extension, but now the hush of the abyss seemed to fall upon everything. Despite his intimations of body, he had no audible breath; and the glow of 'Umr at-Tawil's quasi-sphere had grown petrifiedly fixed and unpulsating. A potent nimbus, brighter than those which had played round the heads of the Shapes, blazed frozenly over the shrouded skull of the terrible Guide.

A dizziness assailed Carter, and his sense of lost orientation waxed a thousandfold. The strange lights seemed to hold the quality of the most impenetrable blacknesses heaped upon blacknesses, while about the Ancient Ones, so close on their pseudo-hexagonal thrones, there hovered an air of the most stupefying remoteness. Then he felt himself wafted into immeasurable depths, with waves of perfumed warmth lapping against his face. It was as if he floated in a torrid, rose-tinctured sea; a sea of drugged wine whose waves broke foaming against shores of brazen fire. A great fear clutched him as he half saw that vast expanse of surging sea lapping against its far-off coast. But the moment of silence was broken—the surgings were speaking to him in a language that was not of physical sound or articulate words.

"The man of Truth is beyond good and evil," intoned a voice that was not a voice. *"The Man of Truth has ridden to All-Is-One. The Man of Truth has learnt that Illusion is the One Reality, and that Substance is the Great Impostor."*

And now, in that rise of masonry to which his eyes had been so irresistibly drawn, there appeared the outline of a titanic arch not unlike that which he thought he had glimpsed so long ago in that cave within a cave, on the far, unreal surface of the three-dimensioned earth. He realised that he had been using the silver key—moving it in accord with an unlearnt and instinctive ritual closely akin to that which had opened the Inner Gate. That rose-drunken sea which lapped his cheeks was, he realised, no more or less than the adamantine mass of the solid wall yielding before his spell, and the vortex of thought with which the Ancient Ones had aided his spell. Still guided by instinct and blind determination, he floated forward—and through the Ultimate Gate.

Chapter 4

Randolph Carter's advance through that cyclopean bulk of abnormal masonry was like a dizzy precipitation through the measureless gulfs between the stars. From a great distance he felt triumphant, god-like surges of deadly sweetness, and after that the rustling of great wings, and impressions of sound like the chirpings and murmurings of objects unknown on earth or in the solar system. Glancing backward, he saw not one gate alone, but a multiplicity of gates, at some of which clamored Forms he strove not to remember.

And then, suddenly, he felt a greater terror than that which any of the Forms could give—a terror from which he could not flee because it was connected with himself. Even the First Gateway had taken something of stability from him, leaving him uncertain about his bodily form and about his relationship to the mistily defined objects around him, but it had not disturbed his sense of unity. He had still been Randolph Carter, a fixed point in the dimensional seething. Now, beyond the Ultimate Gateway, he realized in a moment of consuming fright that he was not one person, but many persons.

He was in many places at the same time. On Earth, on October 7, 1883, a little boy named Randolph Carter was leaving the Snake Den in the hushed evening light and running down the rocky slope and through the twisted-boughed orchard toward his Uncle Christopher's house in the hills beyond Arkham; yet at that same moment, which was also somehow in the earthly year of 1928, a vague shadow not less

Randolph Carter was sitting on a pedestal among the Ancient Ones in Earth's transdimensional extension. Here, too, was a third Randolph Carter in the unknown and formless cosmic abyss beyond the Ultimate Gate. And elsewhere, in a chaos of scenes whose infinite multiplicity and monstrous diversity brought him close to the brink of madness, were a limitless confusion of beings which he knew were as much himself as the local manifestation now beyond the Ultimate Gate.

There were Carters in settings belonging to every known and suspected age of Earth's history, and to remoter ages of earthly entity transcending knowledge, suspicion, and credibility; Carters of forms both human and non-human, vertebrate and invertebrate, conscious and mindless, animal and vegetable. And more, there were Carters having nothing in common with earthly life, but moving outrageously amidst backgrounds of other planets and systems and galaxies and cosmic continua; spores of eternal life drifting from world to world, universe to universe, yet all equally himself. Some of the glimpses recalled dreams—both faint and vivid, single and persistent—which he had had through the long years since he first began to dream, and a few possessed a haunting, fascinating, and almost horrible familiarity which no earthly logic could explain.

Faced with this realization, Randolph Carter reeled in the clutch of supreme horror—horror such as had not been hinted even at the climax of that hideous night when two had ventured into an ancient and abhorred necropolis under a waning moon and only one had emerged. No death, no doom, no anguish can arouse the surpassing despair which flows from a loss of *identity*. Merging with nothingness is peaceful oblivion; but to be aware of existence and yet to know that one is no longer a definite being distinguished from other beings—that one no longer has a *self*—that is the nameless summit of agony and dread.

He knew that there had been a Randolph Carter of Boston, yet could not be sure whether he—the fragment or facet of an earthly entity beyond the Ultimate Gate—had been that one or some other. His *self* had been annihilated; and yet he—if indeed there could, in view of that utter nullity of individual existence, be such a thing as *he*—was equally aware of being in some inconceivable way a legion of selves. It was as though his body had been suddenly transformed into one of those many-limbed and many-headed effigies sculptured in Indian temples, and he contemplated the aggregation in a bewildered attempt to discern which was the original and which the additions—if indeed (supremely monstrous thought!) there *were* any original as distinguished from other embodiments.

Then, in the midst of these devastating reflections, Carter's beyond-the-gate fragment was hurled from what had seemed the nadir of horror to black, clutching pits of a horror still more profound. This time it was largely external—a force or personality which at once confronted and surrounded and pervaded him, and which in addition to its local presence, seemed also to be a part of himself, and likewise to be co-existent with all time and coterminous with all space. There was no visual image, yet the sense of entity and the awful concept of combined localism, identity, and infinity lent a paralyzing terror beyond anything which any Carter-fragment had hitherto deemed capable of existing.

In the face of that awful wonder, the quasi-Carter forgot the horror of destroyed individuality. It was an All-in-One and One-in-All of limitless being and self—not merely a thing of one Space-Time continuum, but allied to the ultimate animating essence of existence's whole unbounded sweep—the last, utter sweep which has no confines and which outreaches fancy and mathematics alike. It was perhaps that which certain secret cults of earth have whispered of as *Yog-Sothoth*, and which has been a deity under other names; that which the crustaceans of Yuggoth worship as the Beyond-One, and which the vaporous brains of the spiral nebulae know by an untranslatable Sign—yet in a flash the Carter-facet realized how slight and fractional all these conceptions are.

And now the Being was addressing the Carter-facet in prodigious waves that smote and burned and thundered—a concentration of energy that blasted its recipient with well-nigh unendurable violence, and that followed, with certain definite variations, the singular unearthly rhythm which had marked the chanting and swaying of the Ancient Ones, and the flickering of the monstrous lights, in that baffling region beyond the First Gate. It was as though suns and worlds and universes had converged upon one point whose very position in space they had conspired to annihilate with an impact of resistless fury. But amidst the greater terror one lesser terror was diminished; for the searing waves appeared somehow to isolate the Beyond-the-Gate Carter from his infinity of duplicates—to restore, as it were, a certain amount of the illusion of identity. After a time the hearer began to translate the waves into speech-forms known to him, and his sense of horror and oppression waned. Fright became pure awe, and what had seemed blasphemously abnormal seemed now only ineffably majestic.

"Randolph Carter," it seemed to say, "my manifestations on your planet's extension, the Ancient Ones, have sent you as one who would lately have returned to small lands of dream which he had lost, yet who with greater freedom has risen to greater and nobler desires and curiosities. You wished to sail up golden Oukranos, to search out forgotten ivory cities in orchid-heavy Kled, and to reign on the opal throne of Ilek-Vad, whose fabulous towers and numberless domes rise mighty toward a single red star in a firmament alien to your earth and to all matter. Now, with the passing of two Gates, you wish loftier things. You would not flee like a child from a scene disliked to a dream beloved, but would plunge like a man into that last and inmost of secrets which lies behind all scenes and dreams.

"What you wish, I have found good; and I am ready to grant that which I have granted eleven times only to beings of your planet—five times only to those you call men, or those resembling them. I am ready to shew you the Ultimate Mystery, to look on which is to blast a feeble spirit. Yet before you gaze full at that last and first of secrets you may still wield a free choice, and return if you will through the two Gates with the Veil still unrent before your eyes."

Chapter 5

A sudden shutting-off of the waves left Carter in a chilling and awesome silence full of the spirit of desolation. On every hand pressed the illimitable vastness of the void, yet the seeker knew that the Being was still there. After a moment he thought of words whose mental substance he flung into the abyss: "I accept. I will not retreat."

The waves surged forth again, and Carter knew that the Being had heard. And now there poured from that limitless Mind a flood of knowledge and explanation which opened new vistas to the seeker, and prepared him for such a grasp of the cosmos as he had never hoped to possess. He was told how childish and limited is the notion of a tri-dimensional world, and what an infinity of directions there are besides the known directions of up-down, forward-backward, right-left. He was shewn the smallness and tinsel emptiness of the little gods of earth, with their petty, human interests and connections— their hatreds, rages, loves, and vanities; their craving for praise and sacrifice, and their demands for faith contrary to reason and nature.

While most of the impressions translated themselves to Carter as words, there were others to which other senses gave interpretation. Perhaps with eyes and perhaps with imagination he perceived that he was in a region of dimensions beyond those conceivable to the eye and brain of man. He saw now, in the brooding shadows of that which had been first a vortex of power and then an illimitable void, a sweep of creation that dizzied his senses. From some inconceivable vantage-point he looked upon prodigious forms whose multiple extensions transcended any conception of being, size, and boundaries which his mind had hitherto been able to hold, despite a lifetime of cryptical study. He began to understand dimly why there could exist at the same time the little boy Randolph Carter in the Arkham farmhouse in 1883, the misty form on the vaguely hexagonal pillar beyond the First Gate, the fragment now facing the Presence in the limitless abyss, and all the other Carters his fancy or perception envisaged.

Then the waves increased in strength, and sought to improve his understanding, reconciling him to the multiform entity of which his present fragment was an infinitesimal part. They told him that every figure of space is but the result of the intersection by a plane of some corresponding figure of one more dimension—as a square is cut from a cube or a circle from a sphere. The cube and sphere, of three dimensions, are thus cut from corresponding forms of four dimensions that men know only through guesses and dreams; and these in turn are cut from forms of five dimensions, and so on up to the dizzy and reachless heights of archetypal infinity. The world of men and of the gods of men is merely an infinitesimal phase of an infinitesimal thing—the three-dimensional phase of that small wholeness reached by the First Gate, where 'Umr at-Tawil dictates dreams to the Ancient Ones. Though men hail it as reality and brand thoughts of its many-dimensioned original as unreality, it is in truth the very opposite. That which we call substance and reality is shadow and illusion, and that which we call shadow and illusion is substance and reality.

Time, the waves went on, is motionless, and without beginning or end. That it has motion, and is the cause of change, is an illusion. Indeed, it is itself really an illusion, for except to the narrow sight of beings in limited dimensions there are no such things as past, present, and future. Men think of time only because of what they call change, yet that too is illusion. All that was, and is, and is to be, exists simultaneously.

These revelations came with a god-like solemnity which left Carter unable to doubt. Even though they lay almost beyond his comprehension, he felt that they must be true in the light of that final cosmic reality which belies all local perspectives and narrow partial views; and he was familiar enough with profound speculations to be free from the bondage of local and partial conceptions. Had his whole quest not been based upon a faith in the unreality of the local and partial?

After an impressive pause the waves continued, saying that what the denizens of few-dimensioned zones call change is merely a function of their consciousness, which views the external world from various cosmic angles. As the Shapes produced by the cutting of a cone seem to vary with the angles of cutting—being circle, ellipse, parabola, or hyperbola according to that angle, yet without any change in the cone itself—so do the local aspects of an unchanged and endless reality seem to change with the cosmic angle of regarding. To this variety of angles of consciousness the feeble beings of the inner worlds are slaves, since with rare exceptions they cannot learn to control them. Only a few students of forbidden things have gained inklings of this control, and have thereby conquered time and change. But the entities outside the Gates command all angles, and view the myriad parts of the cosmos in terms of fragmentary, change-involving perspective, or of the changeless totality beyond perspective, in accordance with their will.

As the waves paused again, Carter began to comprehend, vaguely and terrifiedly, the ultimate background of that riddle of lost individuality which had at first so horrified him. His intuition pieced together the fragments of revelation, and brought him closer and closer to a grasp of the secret. He understood that much of the frightful revelation would have come upon him—splitting up his ego amongst myriads of earthly counterparts—inside the First Gate, had not the magic of 'Umr at-Tawil kept it from him in order that he might use the Silver Key with precision for the Ultimate Gate's opening. Anxious for clearer knowledge, he sent out waves of thought, asking more of the exact relationship between his various facets—the fragment now beyond the Ultimate Gate, the fragment still on the quasi-hexagonal pedestal beyond the First Gate, the boy of 1883, the man of 1928, the various ancestral beings who had formed his heritage and the bulwark of his ego, and the nameless denizens of the other aeons and other worlds which that first hideous flash of ultimate perception had identified with him. Slowly the waves of the Being surged out in reply, trying to make plain what was almost beyond the reach of an earthly mind.

All descended lines of beings of the finite dimensions, continued the waves, and all stages of growth in each one of these beings, are merely manifestations of one archetypal and eternal being in the space outside dimensions. Each local being—son, father, grandfather, and so on—and each stage of individual being—infant, child, boy, young man, old man—is merely one of the infinite phases of that same archetypal and eternal being, caused by a variation in the angle of the consciousness-plane which cuts it. Randolph Carter at all ages; Randolph Carter and all his ancestors both human and pre-human, terrestrial and pre-terrestrial; all these were only phases of one ultimate, eternal "Carter" outside space and time—phantom projections differentiated only by the angle at which the plane of consciousness happened to cut the eternal archetype in each case.

A slight change of angle could turn the student of today into the child of yesterday; could turn Randolph Carter into that wizard Edmund Carter who fled from Salem to the hills behind Arkham in 1692, or that Pickman Carter who in the year 2169 would use strange means in repelling the Mongol hordes from Australia; could turn a human Carter into one of those earlier entities which had dwelt in primal Hyperborea and worshipped black, plastic Tsathoggua after flying down from Kythamil, the double planet that once revolved around Arcturus; could turn a terrestrial Carter to a remotely ancestral and doubtfully shaped dweller on Kythamil itself, or a still remoter creature of trans-galactic Stronti, or a four-dimensional gaseous consciousness in an older space-time continuum, or a vegetable brain of the future on a dark radioactive comet of inconceivable orbit—and so on, in the endless cosmic circle.

The archetypes, throbbed the waves, are the people of the ultimate abyss—formless, ineffable, and guessed at only by rare dreamers on the low-dimensioned worlds. Chief among such was this informing Being itself . . . *which indeed was Carter's own archetype.* The glutless zeal of Carter and all his forbears for forbidden cosmic secrets was a natural result of derivation from the Supreme Archetype. On every world all great wizards, all great thinkers, all great artists, are facets of It.

Almost stunned with awe, and with a kind of terrifying delight, Randolph Carter's consciousness did homage to that transcendent Entity from which it was derived. As the waves paused again he pondered in the mighty silence, thinking of strange tributes, stranger questions, and still stranger requests. Curious concepts flowed conflictingly through a brain dazed with unaccustomed vistas and unforeseen disclosures. It occurred to him that, if those disclosures were literally true, he might bodily visit all those infinitely distant ages and parts of the universe which he had hitherto known only in dreams, could he but command the magic to change the angle of his consciousness-plane. And did not the silver key supply that magic? Had it not first changed him from a man in 1928 to a boy in 1883, and then to something quite outside time? Oddly, despite his present apparent absence of body, he knew that the Key was still with him.

While the silence still lasted, Randolph Carter radiated forth the thoughts and questions which assailed him. He knew that in this ultimate abyss he was equidistant from every facet of his archetype—human or non-human, earthly or extra-earthly, galactic or trans-galactic; and his curiosity regarding the other phases of his being—especially those phases which were farthest from an earthly 1928 in time and space, or which had most persistently haunted his dreams throughout life—was at fever heat. He felt that his archetypal Entity could at will send him bodily to any of these phases of bygone and distant life by changing his consciousness-plane, and despite the marvels he had undergone he burned for the further marvel of walking in the flesh through those grotesque and incredible scenes which visions of the night had fragmentarily brought him.

Without definite intention he was asking the Presence for access to a dim, fantastic world whose five multicolored suns, alien constellations, dizzy black crags, clawed, tapir-snouted denizens, bizarre metal towers, unexplained tunnels, and cryptical floating cylinders had intruded again and again upon his slumbers. That world, he felt vaguely, was in all the conceivable cosmos the one most freely in touch with others; and he longed to explore the vistas whose beginnings he had glimpsed, and to embark through space to those still remoter worlds with which the clawed, snouted denizens trafficked. There was no time for fear. As at all crises of his strange life, sheer cosmic curiosity triumphed over everything else.

When the waves resumed their awesome pulsing Carter knew that his terrible request was granted. The Being was telling him of the nighted gulfs through which he would have to pass, of the unknown quintuple star in an unsuspected galaxy around which the alien world revolved, and of the burrowing inner horrors against which the clawed, snouted race of that world perpetually fought. It told him, too, of how the angle of his personal consciousness-plane, and the angle of his consciousness-plane regarding the space-time elements of the sought-for world, would have to be tilted simultaneously in order to restore to that world the Carter-facet which had dwelt there.

The Presence warned him to be sure of his symbols if he wished ever to return from the remote and alien world he had chosen, and he radiated back an impatient affirmation; confident that the silver key, which he felt was with him and which he knew had tilted both world and personal planes in throwing him back to 1883, contained those symbols which were meant. And now the Being, grasping his impatience, signified Its readiness to accomplish the monstrous precipitation. The waves abruptly ceased, and there supervened a momentary stillness tense with nameless and dreadful expectancy.

Then, without warning, came a whirring and drumming that swelled to a terrific thundering. Once again Carter felt himself the focal point of an intense concentration of energy which smote and hammered and seared unbearably in the now-familiar alien rhythm of outer space, and which he could not classify as either the blasting heat of a blazing star or the all-petrifying cold of the ultimate abyss. Bands and rays of color utterly foreign to any spectrum of our universe played and wove and interlaced before him, and he was conscious of a frightful velocity of motion. He caught one fleeting glimpse of a figure sitting *alone* upon a cloudy throne more hexagonal than otherwise....

Chapter 6

As the Hindoo paused in his story he saw that de Marigny and Phillips were watching him absorbedly. Aspinwall pretended to ignore the narrative, and kept his eyes ostentatiously on the papers before him. The alien-rhythmed ticking of the coffin-shaped clock took on a new and portentous meaning, while the fumes from the choked, neglected tripods wove themselves into fantastic and inexplicable shapes, and formed disturbing combinations with the grotesque figures of the draught-swayed tapestries. The old negro who had tended them was gone—perhaps some growing tension had frightened him out of the house. An almost apologetic hesitancy hampered the speaker as he resumed in his oddly labored yet idiomatic voice.

"You have found these things of the abyss hard to believe," he said, "but you will find the tangible and material things ahead still harder. That is the way of our minds. Marvels are doubly incredible when brought into three dimensions from the vague regions of possible dream. I shall not try to tell you much—that would be another and very different story. I will tell only what you absolutely have to know."

Carter, after that final vortex of alien and polychromatic rhythm, had found himself in what for a moment he thought was his old insistent dream. He was, as many a night before, walking amidst throngs of clawed, snouted beings through the streets of a labyrinth of inexplicably fashioned metal under a blaze of diverse solar color; and as he looked down he saw that his body was like those of the others—rugose, partly squamous, and curiously articulated in a fashion mainly insect-like yet not without a caricaturish resemblance to the human outline. The silver key was still in his grasp—though held by a noxious-looking claw.

In another moment the dream-sense vanished, and he felt rather as one just awaked from a dream. The ultimate abyss—the Being—an entity of absurd, outlandish race called Randolph Carter on a world of the future not yet born—some of these things were parts of the persistent, recurrent dreams of the wizard Zkauba on the planet Yaddith. They were too persistent—they interfered with his duties in weaving spells to keep the frightful dholes in their burrows, and became mixed up with his recollections of the myriad real worlds he had visited in his light-beam envelope. And now they had become quasi-real as never before. This heavy, material silver key in his right upper claw, exact image of one he had dreamt about, meant no good. He must rest and reflect, and consult the Tablets of Nhing for advice on what to do. Climbing a metal wall in a lane off the main concourse, he entered his apartment and approached the rack of tablets.

Seven day-fractions later Zkauba squatted on his prism in awe and half-despair, for the truth had opened up a new and conflicting set of memories. Nevermore could he know the peace of being one entity. For all time and space he was two: Zkauba the Wizard of Yaddith, disgusted with the thought of the repellent earth-mammal Carter that he was to be and had been, and Randolph Carter, of Boston on the earth, shivering with fright at the clawed, snouted thing which he had once been, and had become again.

The time-units spent on Yaddith, croaked the Swami— whose labored voice was beginning to shew signs of fatigue— made a tale in themselves which could not be related in brief compass. There were trips to Shonhi and Mthura and Kath, and other worlds in the twenty-eight galaxies accessible to the light-beam envelopes of the creatures of Yaddith, and trips back and forth through aeons of time with the aid of the Silver Key and various other symbols known to Yaddith's wizards. There were hideous struggles with the bleached, viscous Dholes in the primal tunnels that honeycombed the planet. There were awed sessions in libraries amongst the massed lore of ten thousand worlds living and dead. There were tense conferences with other minds of Yaddith, including that of the Arch-Ancient Buo. Zkauba told no one of what had befallen his personality, but when the Randolph Carter facet was uppermost he would study furiously every possible means of returning to the earth and to human form, and would desperately practice human speech with the buzzing, alien throat-organs so ill adapted to it.

The Carter-facet had soon learned with horror that the Silver Key was unable to effect his return to human form. It was, as he deduced too late from things he remembered, things he dreamed, and things he inferred from the lore of Yaddith, a product of Hyperborea on Earth; with power over the personal consciousness-angles of human beings alone. It could, however, change the planetary angle and send the user at will through time in an unchanged body. There had been an added spell which gave it limitless powers it otherwise lacked; but this, too, was a human discovery—peculiar to a spatially unreachable region, and not to be duplicated by the wizards of Yaddith. It had been written on the undecipherable parchment in the hideously carven box with the silver key, and Carter bitterly lamented that he had left it behind. The now inaccessible Being of the abyss had warned him to be sure of his symbols, and had doubtless thought he lacked nothing.

As time wore on he strove harder and harder to utilise the monstrous lore of Yaddith in finding a way back to the abyss and the omnipotent Entity. With his new knowledge he could have done much toward reading the cryptic parchment; but that power, under present conditions, was merely ironic. There were times, however, when the Zkauba-facet was uppermost, and when he strove to erase the conflicting Carter-memories which troubled him.

Thus long spaces of time wore on—ages longer than the brain of man could grasp, since the beings of Yaddith die only after prolonged cycles. After many hundred revolutions the Carter-facet seemed to gain on the Zkauba-facet, and would spend vast periods calculating the distance of Yaddith in space and time from the human earth that was to be. The figures were staggering—eons of light-years beyond counting—but the immemorial lore of Yaddith fitted Carter to grasp such things. He cultivated the power of dreaming himself momentarily earthward, and learned many things about our planet that he had never known before. But he could not dream the needed formula on the missing parchment.

Then at last he conceived a wild plan of escape from Yaddith—which began when he found a drug that would keep his Zkauba-facet always dormant, yet without dissolution of the knowledge and memories of Zkauba. He thought that his calculations would let him perform a voyage with a light-wave envelope such as no being of Yaddith had ever performed—a *bodily* voyage through nameless aeons and across incredible galactic reaches to the solar system and the earth itself. Once on Earth, though in the body of a clawed, snouted thing, he might be able somehow to find—and finish deciphering—the strangely hieroglyphed parchment he had left in the car at Arkham; and with its aid—and the key's—resume his normal terrestrial semblance.

He was not blind to the perils of the attempt. He knew that when he had brought the planet-angle to the right aeon (a thing impossible to do while hurtling through space), Yaddith would be a dead world dominated by triumphant Dholes, and that his escape in the light-wave envelope would be a matter of grave doubt. Likewise was he aware of how he must achieve suspended animation, in the manner of an adept, to endure the aeon-long flight through fathomless abysses. He knew, too, that—assuming his voyage succeeded—he must immunize himself to the bacterial and other earthly conditions hostile to a body from Yaddith. Furthermore, he must provide a way of feigning human shape on earth until he might recover and decipher the parchment and resume that shape in truth. Otherwise he would probably be discovered and destroyed by the people in horror as a thing that should not be. And there must be some gold—luckily obtainable on Yaddith—to tide him over that period of quest.

Slowly Carter's plans went forward. He provided a light-wave envelope of abnormal toughness, able to stand both the prodigious time-transition and the unexampled flight through space. He tested all his calculations, and sent forth his earthward dreams again and again, bringing them as close as possible to 1928. He practiced suspended animation with marvelous success. He discovered just the bacterial agent he needed, and worked out the varying gravity-stress to which he must become used. He artfully fashioned a waxen mask and loose costume enabling him to pass among men as a human being of a sort, and devised a doubly potent spell with which to hold back the Dholes at the moment of his starting from the black, dead Yaddith of the inconceivable future. He took care, too, to assemble a large supply of the drugs—unobtainable on earth—which would keep his Zkauba-facet in abeyance till he might shed the Yaddith body, nor did he neglect a small store of gold for earthly use.

The starting-day was a time of doubt and apprehension. Carter climbed up to his envelope-platform, on the pretext of sailing for the triple star Nython, and crawled into the sheath of shining metal. He had just room to perform the ritual of the Silver Key, and as he did so he slowly started the levitation of his envelope. There was an appalling seething and darkening of the day, and a hideous racking of pain. The cosmos seemed to reel irresponsibly, and the other constellations danced in a black sky.

All at once Carter felt a new equilibrium. The cold of interstellar gulfs gnawed at the outside of his envelope, and he could see that he floated free in space—the metal building from which he had started having decayed ages before. Below him the ground was festering with gigantic Dholes; and even as he looked, one reared up several hundred feet and levelled a bleached, viscous end at him. But his spells were effective, and in another moment he was falling away from Yaddith unharmed.

Chapter 7

In that bizarre room in New Orleans, from which the old black servant had instinctively fled, the odd voice of Swami Chandraputra grew hoarser still.

"Gentlemen," he continued, "I will not ask you to believe these things until I have shewn you special proof. Accept it, then, as a myth, when I tell you of *the thousands of light-years—thousands of years of time, and uncounted billions of miles* that Randolph Carter hurtled through space as a nameless, alien entity in a thin envelope of electron-activated metal. He timed his period of suspended animation with utmost care, planning to have it end only a few years before the time of landing on the Earth in or near 1928.

"He will never forget that awakening. Remember, gentlemen, that before that aeon-long sleep *he had lived consciously for thousands of terrestrial years amidst the alien and horrible wonders of Yaddith.* There was a hideous gnawing of cold, a cessation of menacing dreams, and a glance through the eye-plates of the envelope. Stars, clusters, nebulae, on every hand—*and at last their outlines bore some kinship to the constellations of earth that he knew.*

"Some day his descent into the solar system may be told. He saw Kynarth and Yuggoth on the rim, passed close to Neptune and glimpsed the hellish white fungi that spot it, learned an untellable secret from the close-glimpsed mists of Jupiter and saw the horror on one of the satellites, and gazed at the Cyclopean ruins that sprawl over Mars' ruddy disc. When the earth drew near he saw it as a thin crescent which swelled alarmingly in size. He slackened speed, though his sensations of homecoming made him wish to lose not a moment. I will not try to tell you of those sensations as I learned them from Carter.

"Well, toward the last Carter hovered about in the earth's upper air waiting till daylight came over the western hemisphere. He wanted to land where he had left—near the

Snake Den in the hills behind Arkham. If any of you have been away from home long—and I know one of you has—I leave it to you how the sight of New England's rolling hills and great elms and gnarled orchards and ancient stone walls must have affected him.

"He came down at dawn in the lower meadow of the old Carter place, and was thankful for the silence and solitude. It was autumn, as when he had left, and the smell of the hills was balm to his soul. He managed to drag the metal envelope up the slope of the timber-lot into the Snake Den, though it would not go through the weed-choked fissure to the inner cave. It was there also that he covered his alien body with the human clothing and waxen mask which would be necessary. He kept the envelope here for over a year, till certain circumstances made a new hiding-place necessary.

"He walked to Arkham—incidentally practicing the management of his body in human posture and against terrestrial gravity—and got his gold changed to money at a bank. He also made some inquiries—posing as a foreigner ignorant of much English—and found that the year was 1930, only two years after the goal he had aimed at.

"Of course, his position was horrible. Unable to assert his identity, forced to live on guard every moment, with certain difficulties regarding food, and with a need to conserve the alien drug which kept his Zkauba-facet dormant, he felt that he must act as quickly as possible. Going to Boston and taking a room in the decaying West End, where he could live cheaply and inconspicuously, he at once established inquiries concerning Randolph Carter's estate and effects. It was then that he learned how anxious Mr. Aspinwall, here, was to have the estate divided, and how valiantly Mr. de Marigny and Mr. Phillips strove to keep it intact."

The Hindoo bowed, though no expression crossed his dark, tranquil, and thickly bearded face.

"Indirectly," he continued, "Carter secured a good copy of the missing parchment and began work on its deciphering. I am glad to say that I was able to help in all this—for he appealed to me quite early, and through me came in touch with other mystics throughout the world. I went to live with him in Boston—a wretched place in Chambers St. As for the parchment—I am pleased to help Mr. de Marigny in his perplexity. To him let me say that the language of those hieroglyphics is not Naacal but R'lyehian, which was brought to earth by the spawn of Cthulhu countless cycles ago. It is, of course, a translation—there was an Hyperborean original millions of years earlier in the primal tongue of Tsath-yo.

"There was more to decipher than Carter had looked for, but at no time did he give up hope. Early this year he made great strides through a book he imported from Nepal, and there is no question but that he will win before long. Unfortunately, however, one handicap has developed—the exhaustion of the alien drug which keeps the Zkauba-facet dormant. This is not, however, as great a calamity as was feared. Carter's personality is gaining in the body, and when Zkauba comes uppermost—for shorter and shorter periods, and now only when evoked by some unusual excitement—he is generally too dazed to undo any of Carter's work. He cannot find the metal envelope that would take him back to Yaddith, for although he almost did, once, Carter hid it anew at a time when the Zkauba-facet was wholly latent. All the harm he has done is to frighten a few people and create certain nightmare rumors among the Poles and Lithuanians of Boston's West End. So far, he has never injured the careful disguise prepared by the Carter-facet, though he sometimes throws it off so that parts have to be replaced. I have seen what lies beneath—and it is not good to see.

"A month ago Carter saw the advertisement of this meeting, and knew that he must act quickly to save his estate.

He could not wait to decipher the parchment and resume his human form. Consequently he deputed me to act for him.

"Gentlemen, I say to you that Randolph Carter is not dead; that he is temporarily in an anomalous condition, but that within two or three months at the outside he will be able to appear in proper form and demand the custody of his estate. I am prepared to offer proof if necessary. Therefore I beg that you adjourn this meeting for an indefinite period."

Chapter 8

De Marigny and Phillips stared at the Hindoo as if hypnotized, while Aspinwall emitted a series of snorts and bellows. The old attorney's disgust had by now surged into open rage, and he pounded the table with an apoplectically veined fist. When he spoke, it was in a kind of bark.

"How long is this foolery to be borne? I've listened an hour to this madman—this faker—and now he has the damned effrontery to say that Randolph Carter is alive—to ask us to postpone the settlement for no good reason! Why don't you throw the scoundrel out, de Marigny? Do you mean to make us all the butts of a charlatan or idiot?"

De Marigny quietly raised his hands and spoke softly.

"Let us think slowly and clearly. This has been a very singular tale, and there are things in it which I, as a mystic not altogether ignorant, recognize as far from impossible. Furthermore—since 1930 I have received letters from the Swami which tally with his account."

As he paused, old Mr. Phillips ventured a word.

"Swami Chandraputra spoke of proofs. I, too, recognize much that is significant in this story, and I have myself had many oddly corroborative letters from the Swami during the last two years; but some of these statements are very extreme. Is there not something tangible which can be shewn?"

At last the impassive-faced Swami replied, slowly and hoarsely, and drawing an object from the pocket of his loose coat as he spoke.

"While none of you here has ever seen the silver key itself, Messrs. de Marigny and Phillips have seen photographs of it. *Does this look familiar to you?*"

He fumblingly laid on the table, with his large, white-mittened hand, a heavy key of tarnished silver—nearly five inches long, of unknown and utterly exotic workmanship, and covered from end to end with hieroglyphs of the most bizarre description. De Marigny and Phillips gasped.

"That's it!" cried de Marigny. "The camera doesn't lie. I couldn't be mistaken!"

But Aspinwall had already launched a reply.

"Fools! What does it prove? If that's really the key that belonged to my cousin, it's up to this foreigner—this damned nigger—to explain how he got it! Randolph Carter vanished with the key four years ago. How do we know he wasn't robbed and murdered? He was half-crazy himself, and in touch with still crazier people.

"Look here, you nigger—where did you get that key? Did you kill Randolph Carter?"

The Swami's features, abnormally placid, did not change; but the remote, irisless black eyes behind them blazed dangerously. He spoke with great difficulty.

"Please control yourself, Mr. Aspinwall. There is another form of proof that I *could* give, but its effect upon everybody would not be pleasant. Let us be reasonable. Here are some papers obviously written since 1930, and in the unmistakable style of Randolph Carter."

He clumsily drew a long envelope from inside his loose coat and handed it to the sputtering attorney as de Marigny and Phillips watched with chaotic thoughts and a dawning feeling of supernal wonder.

"Of course the handwriting is almost illegible—but remember that Randolph Carter now has no hands well adapted to forming human script."

Aspinwall looked through the papers hurriedly, and was visibly perplexed, but he did not change his demeanor. The room was tense with excitement and nameless dread, and the alien rhythm of the coffin-shaped clock had an utterly diabolic sound to de Marigny and Phillips—though the lawyer seemed affected not at all.

Aspinwall spoke again. "These look like clever forgeries. If they aren't, they may mean that Randolph Carter has been brought under the control of people with no good purpose. There's only one thing to do—have this faker arrested. De Marigny, will you telephone for the police?"

"Let us wait," answered their host. "I do not think this case calls for the police. I have a certain idea. Mr. Aspinwall, this gentleman is a mystic of real attainments. He says he is in the confidence of Randolph Carter. Will it satisfy you if he can answer certain questions which could be answered only by one in such confidence? I know Carter, and can ask such questions. Let me get a book which I think will make a good test."

He turned toward the door to the library, Phillips dazedly following in a kind of automatic way. Aspinwall remained where he was, studying closely the Hindoo who confronted him with abnormally impassive face. Suddenly, as Chandraputra clumsily restored the Silver Key to his pocket, the lawyer emitted a guttural shout which stopped de Marigny and Phillips in their tracks.

"Hey, by Heaven, I've got it! This rascal is in disguise. I don't believe he's an East Indian at all. That face—it isn't a face, but a *mask!* I guess his story put that into my head, but it's true. It never moves, and that turban and beard hide the edges. This fellow's a common crook! He isn't even a foreigner—I've been watching his language. He's a Yankee of some sort. And look at those mittens—he knows his finger-prints could be spotted. Damn you, I'll pull that thing off—"

"Stop!" The hoarse, oddly alien voice of the Swami held a tone beyond all mere earthly fright. "I told you there was *another form of proof which I could give if necessary*, and I warned you not to provoke me to it. This red-faced old meddler is right—I'm not really an East Indian. *This face is a mask, and what it covers is not human.* You others have guessed—I felt that minutes ago. It wouldn't be pleasant if I took that mask off—let it alone, Ernest. I may as well tell you that *I am Randolph Carter*."

No one moved. Aspinwall snorted and made vague motions. De Marigny and Phillips, across the room, watched the workings of his red face and studied the back of the turbaned figure that confronted him. The clock's abnormal ticking was hideous, and the tripod fumes and swaying arras danced a dance of death. The half-choking lawyer broke the silence.

"No you don't, you crook—you can't scare me! You've reasons of your own for not wanting that mask off. Maybe we'd know who you are. Off with it—"

As he reached forward, the Swami seized his hand with one of his own clumsily mittened members, evoking a curious cry of mixed pain and surprise. De Marigny started toward the two, but paused confused as the pseudo-Hindoo's shout of protest changed to a wholly inexplicable rattling and buzzing sound. Aspinwall's red face was furious, and with his free hand he made another lunge at his opponent's bushy beard. This time he succeeded in getting a hold, and at his frantic tug the whole waxen visage came loose from the turban and clung to the lawyer's apoplectic fist.

As it did so, Aspinwall uttered a frightful gurgling cry, and Phillips and de Marigny saw his face convulsed with a wilder, deeper, and more hideous epilepsy of stark panic than ever they had seen on human countenance before. The pseudo-

Swami had meanwhile released his other hand and was standing as if dazed, making buzzing noises of a most abnormal quality. Then the turbaned figure slumped oddly into a posture scarcely human, and began a curious, fascinated sort of shuffle toward the coffin-shaped clock that ticked out its cosmic and abnormal rhythm. His now uncovered face was turned away, and de Marigny and Phillips could not see what the lawyer's act had disclosed. Then their attention was turned to Aspinwall, who was sinking ponderously to the floor. The spell was broken—but when they reached the old man he was dead.

Turning quickly to the shuffling Swami's receding back, de Marigny saw one of the great white mittens drop listlessly off a dangling arm. The fumes of the olibanum were thick, and all that could be glimpsed of the revealed hand was something long and black. Before the Creole could reach the retreating figure, old Mr. Phillips laid a restraining hand on his shoulder.

"Don't!" he whispered. "We don't know what we're up against—that other facet, you know—Zkauba, the wizard of Yaddith...."

The turbaned figure had now reached the abnormal clock, and the watchers saw through the dense fumes a blurred black claw fumbling with the tall, hieroglyphed door. The fumbling made a queer clicking sound. Then the figure entered the coffin-shaped case and pulled the door shut after it.

De Marigny could no longer be restrained, but when he reached and opened the clock it was empty. The abnormal ticking went on, beating out the dark cosmic rhythm which underlies all mystical gate-openings. On the floor the great white mitten, and the dead man with a bearded mask clutched in his hand, had nothing further to reveal.

* * * * *

A year has passed, and nothing has been heard of Randolph Carter. His estate is still unsettled. The Boston address from which one "Swami Chandraputra" sent inquiries to various mystics in 1930–31–32 was indeed tenanted by a strange Hindoo, but he left shortly before the date of the New Orleans conference and has never been seen since. He was said to be dark, expressionless, and bearded, and his landlord thinks the swarthy mask—which was duly exhibited—looks very much like him. He was never, however, suspected of any connection with the nightmare apparitions whispered of by local Slavs. The hills behind Arkham were searched for the "metal envelope", but nothing of the sort was ever found. However, a clerk in Arkham's First National Bank does recall a queer turbaned man who cashed an odd bit of gold bullion in October, 1930.

De Marigny and Phillips scarcely know what to make of the business. After all, what was proved? There was a story. There was a key which might have been forged from one of the pictures Carter had freely distributed in 1928. There were papers—all indecisive. There was a masked stranger, but who now living saw behind the mask? Amidst the strain and the olibanum fumes that act of vanishing in the clock might easily have been a dual hallucination. Hindoos know much of hypnotism. Reason proclaims the "Swami" a criminal with designs on Randolph Carter's estate. But the autopsy said that Aspinwall had died of shock. Was it rage *alone* which caused it? And some things in that story . . .

In a vast room hung with strangely figured arras and filled with olibanum fumes, Etienne-Laurent de Marigny often sits listening with vague sensations to the abnormal rhythm of that hieroglyphed, coffin-shaped clock.

27
Out of the Eons
Hazel Heald (& H. P. Lovecraft)
(1935)

The short story "Out of the Eons," first published in the April 1935 issue of *Weird Tales* magazine, is attributed to Hazel Heald. Little is known about Heald, only that H.P. Lovecraft so heavily edited the handful of stories she is said to have authored that many consider Lovecraft to have been the real author of the stories. Heald, who lived in Somerville, Massachusetts, only published four other Lovecraftian stories before disappearing from the scene. Howard evidently recognized Lovecraft's hand in the writing because he wrote Lovecraft in May of 1935, saying, "I enjoyed very much the story 'Out of the Eons'. It might as well have carried your name beneath the title, for it was yours, all the way through." In a follow-up letter to Lovecraft in July of that year, Howard again praised the story, writing, "Yes, I found 'Out of the Eons' fascinating and tantalizing—tantalizing because it roused my always voracious appetite for more of your stories. I felt greatly complimented that Von Juntz's hellish book should play such a prominent part in it." The book to which Howard referred was his own addition to the Cthulhu Mythos collection of forbidden books, the *Black Book* or *Nameless Cults*, which soon became *Unaussprechlichen Kulten,* later used by Lovecraft in his own Mythos stories, include the yarn reprinted here.

(*Mss. found among the effects of the late Richard H. Johnson, Ph.D., curator of the Cabot Museum of Archaeology, Boston, Mass.*)

It is not likely that any one in Boston—or any alert reader elsewhere—will ever forget the strange affair of the Cabot Museum. The newspaper publicity given to that hellish mummy, the antique and terrible rumors vaguely linked with it, the morbid wave of interest and cult activities during 1932, and the frightful fate of the two intruders on December first of that year, all combined to form one of those classic mysteries which go down for generations as folklore and become the nuclei of whole cycles of horrific speculation.

Every one seems to realize, too, that something very vital and unutterably hideous was suppressed in the public accounts of the culminant horrors. Those first disquieting hints as to the *condition* of one of the two bodies were dismissed and ignored too abruptly—nor were the singular *modifications* in the mummy given the following-up which their news value would normally prompt. It also struck people as queer that the mummy was never restored to its case. In these days of expert taxidermy the excuse that its disintegrating condition made exhibition impracticable seemed a peculiarly lame one.

As curator of the museum I am in a position to reveal all the suppressed facts, but this I shall not do during my lifetime. There are things about the world and universe which it is better for the majority not to know, and I have not departed from the opinion in which all of us—museum staff, physicians, reporters, and police—concurred at the period of the horror itself. At the same time it seems proper that a matter of such overwhelming scientific and historic importance should not remain wholly unrecorded—hence this account which I have prepared for the benefit of serious students. I shall place it among various papers to be examined after my death, leaving its fate to the discretion of my executors. Certain threats and unusual events during the past weeks have led me to believe that my life—as well as that of other museum officials—is in some peril through the enmity of several widespread secret cults of Asiatics, Polynesians, and heterogeneous mystical devotees; hence it is possible that the work of the executors may not be long postponed. [Executor's note: Dr. Johnson died suddenly and rather mysteriously of heart failure on April 22, 1933. Wentworth Moore, taxidermist of the museum, disappeared around the middle of the preceding month. On February 18 of the same year Dr. William Minot, who superintended a dissection connected with the case, was stabbed in the back, dying the following day.]

The real beginning of the horror, I suppose, was in 1879—long before my term as curator—when the museum acquired that ghastly, inexplicable mummy from the Orient Shipping Company. Its very discovery was monstrous and menacing, for it came from a crypt of unknown origin and fabulous antiquity on a bit of land suddenly upheaved from the Pacific's floor.

On May 11, 1878, Captain Charles Weatherbee of the freighter *Eridanus*, bound from Wellington, New Zealand, to Valparaiso, Chile, had sighted a new island unmarked on any chart and evidently of volcanic origin. It projected quite boldly out of the sea in the form of a truncated cone. A landing-party under Captain Weatherbee noted evidences of long submersion on the rugged slopes which they climbed, while at the summit there were signs of recent destruction, as by an earthquake. Among the scattered rubble were massive stones of manifestly artificial shaping, and a little examination disclosed the presence of some of that prehistoric cyclopean masonry found on certain Pacific islands and forming a perpetual archaeological puzzle.

Finally the sailors entered a massive stone crypt—judged to have been part of a much larger edifice, and to have originally lain far underground—in one corner of which the frightful mummy crouched. After a short period of virtual panic, caused partly by certain carvings on the walls, the men were induced to move the mummy to the ship, though it was only with fear and loathing that they touched it. Close to the body, as if once thrust into its clothes, was a cylinder of an unknown metal containing a roll of thin, bluish-white membrane of equally unknown nature, inscribed with peculiar characters in a greyish, indeterminable pigment. In the center of the vast stone floor was a suggestion of a trap-door, but the party lacked apparatus sufficiently powerful to move it.

The Cabot Museum, then newly established, saw the meagre reports of the discovery and at once took steps to acquire the mummy and the cylinder. Curator Pickman made a personal trip to Valparaiso and outfitted a schooner to search for the crypt where the thing had been found, though meeting with failure in this matter. At the recorded position of the island nothing but the sea's unbroken expanse could be discerned, and the seekers realized that the same seismic forces which had suddenly thrust the island up had carried it down again to the watery darkness where it had brooded for untold eons. The secret of that immovable trap-door would never be solved.

The mummy and the cylinder, however, remained—and the former was placed on exhibition early in November, 1879, in the museum's hall of mummies.

The Cabot Museum of Archaeology, which specializes in such remnants of ancient and unknown civilizations as do not fall within the domain of art, is a small and scarcely famous institution, though one of high standing in scientific circles. It stands in the heart of Boston's exclusive Beacon Hill district—in Mt. Vernon Street, near Joy—housed in a former private mansion with an added wing in the rear, and was a source of pride to its austere neighbors until the recent terrible events brought it an undesirable notoriety.

The hall of mummies on the western side of the original mansion (which was designed by Bulfinch and erected in 1819), on the second floor, is justly esteemed by historians and anthropologists as harboring the greatest collection of its kind in America. Here may be found typical examples of Egyptian embalming from the earliest Sakkarah specimens to the last

Coptic attempts of the eighth century; mummies of other cultures, including the prehistoric Indian specimens recently found in the Aleutian Islands; agonized Pompeian figures molded in plaster from tragic hollows in the ruin-choking ashes; naturally mummified bodies from mines and other excavations in all parts of the earth—some surprised by their terrible entombment in the grotesque postures caused by their last, tearing death-throes—everything, in short, which any collection of the sort could well be expected to contain. In 1879, of course, it was much less ample than it is now; yet even then it was remarkable. But that shocking thing from the primal cyclopean crypt on an ephemeral sea-spawned island was always its chief attraction and most impenetrable mystery.

The mummy was that of a medium-sized man of unknown race, and was cast in a peculiar crouching posture. The face, half shielded by claw-like hands, had its under jaw thrust far forward, while the shriveled features bore an expression of fright so hideous that few spectators could view them unmoved. The eyes were closed, with lids clamped down tightly over eyeballs apparently bulging and prominent. Bits of hair and beard remained, and the color of the whole was a sort of dull neutral grey. In texture the thing was half leathery and half stony, forming an insoluble enigma to those experts who sought to ascertain how it was embalmed. In places bits of its substance were eaten away by time and decay. Rags of some peculiar fabric, with suggestions of unknown designs, still clung to the object.

Just what made it so infinitely horrible and repulsive one could hardly say. For one thing, there was a subtle, indefinable sense of limitless antiquity and utter alienage which affected one like a view from the brink of a monstrous abyss of unplumbed blackness—but mostly it was the expression of crazed fear on the puckered, prognathous, half-shielded face. Such a symbol of infinite, inhuman, cosmic fright could not help communicating the emotion to the beholder amidst a disquieting cloud of mystery and vain conjecture.

Among the discriminating few who frequented the Cabot Museum this relic of an elder, forgotten world soon acquired an unholy fame, though the institution's seclusion and quiet policy prevented it from becoming a popular sensation of the "Cardiff Giant" sort. In the last century the art of vulgar ballyhoo had not invaded the field of scholarship to the extent it has now succeeded in doing. Naturally, savants of various kinds tried their best to classify the frightful object, though always without success. Theories of a bygone Pacific civilization, of which the Easter Island images and the megalithic masonry of Ponape and Nan-Matal are conceivable vestiges, were freely circulated among students, and learned journals carried varied and often conflicting speculations on a possible former continent whose peaks survive as the myriad islands of Melanesia and Polynesia. The diversity in dates assigned to the hypothetical vanished culture—or continent—was at once bewildering and amusing; yet some surprisingly relevant allusions were found in certain myths of Tahiti and other islands.

Meanwhile the strange cylinder and its baffling scroll of unknown hieroglyphs, carefully preserved in the museum library, received their due share of attention. No question could exist as to their association with the mummy; hence all realized that in the unravelling of their mystery the mystery of the shriveled horror would in all probability be unraveled as well. The cylinder, about four inches long by seven-eighths of an inch in diameter, was of a queerly iridescent metal utterly defying chemical analysis and seemingly impervious to all reagents. It was tightly fitted with a cap of the same substance, and bore engraved figurings of an evidently decorative and possibly symbolic nature—conventional designs which seemed to follow a peculiarly alien, paradoxical, and doubtfully describable system of geometry.

Not less mysterious was the scroll it contained—a neat roll of some thin, bluish-white, unanalyzable membrane, coiled round a slim rod of metal like that of the cylinder, and unwinding to a length of some two feet. The large, bold hieroglyphs, extending in a narrow line down the center of the scroll and penned or painted with a grey pigment defying analysis, resembled nothing known to linguists and paleographers, and could not be deciphered despite the transmission of photographic copies to every living expert in the given field.

It is true that a few scholars, unusually versed in the literature of occultism and magic, found vague resemblances between some of the hieroglyphs and certain primal symbols described or cited in two or three very ancient, obscure, and esoteric texts such as the *Book of Eibon*, reputed to descend from forgotten Hyperborea; the Pnakotic fragments, alleged to be pre-human; and the monstrous and forbidden *Necronomicon* of the mad Arab Abdul Alhazred. None of these resemblances, however, was beyond dispute; and because of the prevailing low estimation of occult studies, no effort was made to circulate copies of the hieroglyphs among mystical specialists. Had such circulation occurred at this early date, the later history of the case might have been very different; indeed, a glance at the hieroglyphs by any reader of von Junzt's horrible *Nameless Cults* would have established a linkage of unmistakable significance. At this period, however, the readers of that monstrous blasphemy were exceedingly few; copies having been incredibly scarce in the interval between the suppression of the original Düsseldorf edition (1839) and of the Bridewell translation (1845) and the publication of the expurgated reprint by the Golden Goblin Press in 1909. Practically speaking, no occultist or student of the primal past's esoteric lore had his attention called to the strange scroll until the recent outburst of sensational journalism which precipitated the horrible climax.

2

Thus matters glided along for a half-century following the installation of the frightful mummy at the museum. The gruesome object had a local celebrity among cultivated Bostonians, but no more than that; while the very existence of the cylinder and scroll—after a decade of futile research—was virtually forgotten. So quiet and conservative was the Cabot Museum that no reporter or feature writer ever thought of invading its uneventful precincts for rabble-tickling material.

The invasion of ballyhoo commenced in the spring of 1931, when a purchase of somewhat spectacular nature—that of the strange objects and inexplicably preserved bodies found in crypts beneath the almost vanished and evilly famous ruins of Château Faussesflammes, in Averoigne, France—brought the museum prominently into the news columns. True to its "hustling" policy, the *Boston Pillar* sent a Sunday feature writer to cover the incident and pad it with an exaggerated general account of the institution itself; and this young man—Stuart Reynolds by name—hit upon the nameless mummy as a potential sensation far surpassing the recent acquisitions nominally forming his chief assignment. A smattering of theosophical lore, and a fondness for the speculations of such writers as Colonel Churchward and Lewis Spence concerning lost continents and primal forgotten civilizations, made Reynolds especially alert toward any eonian relic like the unknown mummy.

At the museum the reporter made himself a nuisance through constant and not always intelligent questionings and endless demands for the movement of encased objects to permit photographs from unusual angles. In the basement library room he pored endlessly over the strange metal cylinder and its membranous scroll, photographing them from every angle and securing pictures of every bit of the weird hieroglyphed text. He likewise asked to see all books with any bearing whatever on the subject of primal cultures and sunken continents—sitting for three hours taking notes, and leaving only in order to hasten to Cambridge for a sight (if permission were granted) of the abhorred and forbidden *Necronomicon* at the Widener Library.

On April fifth the article appeared in the Sunday *Pillar*, smothered in photographs of mummy, cylinder, and hieroglyphed scroll, and couched in the peculiarly simpering, infantile style which the *Pillar* affects for the benefit of its vast and mentally immature clientele. Full of inaccuracies, exaggerations, and sensationalism, it was precisely the sort of thing to stir the brainless and fickle interest of the herd—and as a result the once quiet museum began to be swarmed with chattering and vacuously staring throngs such as its stately corridors had never known before.

There were scholarly and intelligent visitors, too, despite the puerility of the article—the pictures had spoken for themselves—and many persons of mature attainments sometimes see the *Pillar* by accident. I recall one very strange character who appeared during November—a dark, turbaned, and bushily bearded man with a labored, unnatural voice, curiously expressionless face, clumsy hands covered with absurd white mittens, who gave a squalid West End address and called himself "Swami Chandraputra." This fellow was unbelievably erudite in occult lore and seemed profoundly and solemnly moved by the resemblance of the hieroglyphs on the scroll to certain signs and symbols of a forgotten elder world about which he professed vast intuitive knowledge.

By June, the fame of the mummy and scroll had leaked far beyond Boston, and the museum had inquiries and requests for photographs from occultists and students of arcana all over the world. This was not altogether pleasing to our staff, since we are a scientific institution without sympathy for fantastic dreamers; yet we answered all questions with civility. One result of these catechisms was a highly learned article in *The Occult Review* by the famous New Orleans mystic Etienne-Laurent de

Marigny, in which was asserted the complete identity of some of the odd geometrical designs on the iridescent cylinder, and of several of the hieroglyphs on the membranous scroll, with certain ideographs of horrible significance (transcribed from primal monoliths or from the secret rituals of hidden bands of esoteric students and devotees) reproduced in the hellish and suppressed *Black Book* or *Nameless Cults* of von Junzt.

De Marigny recalled the frightful death of von Junzt in 1840, a year after the publication of his terrible volume at Düsseldorf, and commented on his blood-curdling and partly suspected sources of information. Above all, he emphasized the enormous relevance of the tales with which von Junzt linked most of the monstrous ideographs he had reproduced. That these tales, in which a cylinder and scroll were expressly mentioned, held a remarkable suggestion of relationship to the things at the museum, no one could deny; yet they were of such breath-taking extravagance—involving such unbelievable sweeps of time and such fantastic anomalies of a forgotten elder world—that one could much more easily admire than believe them.

Admire them the public certainly did, for copying in the press was universal. Illustrated articles sprang up everywhere, telling or purporting to tell the legends in the *Black Book*, expatiating on the horror of the mummy, comparing the cylinder's designs and the scroll's hieroglyphs with the figures reproduced by von Junzt, and indulging in the wildest, most sensational, and most irrational theories and speculations. Attendance at the museum was trebled, and the widespread nature of the interest was attested by the plethora of mail on the subject—most of it inane and superfluous—received at the museum. Apparently the mummy and its origin formed—for imaginative people—a close rival to the depression as chief topic of 1931 and 1932. For my own part, the principal effect of the furor was to make me read von Junzt's monstrous volume in the Golden Goblin edition—a perusal which left me dizzy and nauseated, yet thankful that I had not seen the utter infamy of the unexpurgated text.

3

The archaic whispers reflected in the *Black Book*, and linked with designs and symbols so closely akin to what the mysterious scroll and cylinder bore, were indeed of a character to hold one spellbound and not a little awestruck. Leaping an incredible gulf of time—behind all the civilizations, races, and lands we know—they clustered round a vanished nation and a vanished continent of the misty, fabulous dawn-years . . . that to which legend has given the name of Mu, and which old tablets in the primal Naacal tongue speak of as flourishing 200,000 years ago, when Europe harbored only hybrid entities, and lost Hyperborea knew the nameless worship of black amorphous Tsathoggua.

There was mention of a kingdom or province called K'naa in a very ancient land where the first human people had found monstrous ruins left by those who had dwelt there before— vague waves of unknown entities which had filtered down from the stars and lived out their eons on a forgotten, nascent world. K'naa was a sacred place, since from its midst the bleak basalt cliffs of Mount Yaddith-Gho soared starkly into the sky, topped by a gigantic fortress of Cyclopean stone, infinitely older than mankind and built by the alien spawn of the dark planet Yuggoth, which had colonized the earth before the birth of terrestrial life.

The spawn of Yuggoth had perished eons before, but had left behind them one monstrous and terrible living thing which could never die—their hellish god or patron daemon Ghatanothoa, which lowered and brooded eternally though unseen in the crypts beneath that fortress on Yaddith-Gho. No human creature had ever climbed Yaddith-Gho or seen that blasphemous fortress except as a distant and geometrically abnormal outline against the sky; yet most agreed that

Ghatanothoa was still there, wallowing and burrowing in unsuspected abysses beneath the megalithic walls. There were always those who believed that sacrifices must be made to Ghatanothoa, lest it crawl out of its hidden abysses and waddle horribly through the world of men as it had once waddled through the primal world of the Yuggoth-spawn.

People said that if no victims were offered, Ghatanothoa would ooze up to the light of day and lumber down the basalt cliffs of Yaddith-Gho bringing doom to all it might encounter. For no living thing could behold Ghatanothoa, or even a perfect graven image of Ghatanothoa, however small, without suffering a change more horrible than death itself. Sight of the god, or its image, as all the legends of the Yuggoth-spawn agreed, meant paralysis and petrifaction of a singularly shocking sort, in which the victim was turned to stone and leather on the outside, while the brain within remained perpetually alive—horribly fixed and prisoned through the ages, and maddeningly conscious of the passage of interminable epochs of helpless inaction till chance and time might complete the decay of the petrified shell and leave it exposed to die. Most brains, of course, would go mad long before this aeon-deferred release could arrive. No human eyes, it was said, had ever glimpsed Ghatanothoa, though the danger was as great now as it had been for the Yuggoth-spawn.

And so there was a cult in K'naa which worshipped Ghatanothoa and each year sacrificed to it twelve young warriors and twelve young maidens. These victims were offered up on flaming altars in the marble temple near the mountain's base, for none dared climb Yaddith-Gho's basalt cliffs or draw near to the Cyclopean pre-human stronghold on its crest. Vast was the power of the priests of Ghatanothoa, since upon them alone depended the preservation of K'naa and of all the land of Mu from the petrifying emergence of Ghatanothoa out of its unknown burrows.

There were in the land an hundred priests of the Dark God, under Imash-Mo the High-Priest, who walked before King Thabon at the Nath-feast, and stood proudly whilst the King knelt at the Dhoric shrine. Each priest had a marble house, a chest of gold, two hundred slaves, and an hundred concubines, besides immunity from civil law and the power of life and death over all in K'naa save the priests of the King. Yet in spite of these defenders there was ever a fear in the land lest Ghatanothoa slither up from the depths and lurch viciously down the mountain to bring horror and petrification to mankind. In the latter years the priests forbade men even to guess or imagine what its frightful aspect might be.

It was in the Year of the Red Moon (estimated as B. C. 173,148 by von Junzt) that a human being first dared to breathe defiance against Ghatanothoa and its nameless menace. This bold heretic was T'yog, High-Priest of Shub-Niggurath and guardian of the copper temple of the Goat with a Thousand Young. T'yog had thought long on the powers of the various gods, and had had strange dreams and revelations touching the life of this and earlier worlds. In the end he felt sure that the gods friendly to man could be arrayed against the hostile gods, and believed that Shub-Niggurath, Nug, and Yeb, as well as Yig the Serpent-god, were ready to take sides with man against the tyranny and presumption of Ghatanothoa.

Inspired by the Mother Goddess, T'yog wrote down a strange formula in the hieratic Naacal of his order, which he believed would keep the possessor immune from the Dark God's petrifying power. With this protection, he reflected, it might be possible for a bold man to climb the dreaded basalt cliffs and—first of all human beings—enter the Cyclopean fortress beneath which Ghatanothoa reputedly brooded. Face to face with the god, and with the power of Shub-Niggurath and her sons on his side, T'yog believed that he might be able to bring it to terms and at last deliver mankind from its brooding menace. With humanity freed through his efforts, there would be no limits to the honors he might claim. All the honors of the priests of Ghatanothoa would perforce be transferred to him; and even kingship or godhood might conceivably be within his reach.

So T'yog wrote his protective formula on a scroll of *pthagon* membrane (according to von Junzt, the inner skin of the extinct yakith-lizard) and enclosed it in a carven cylinder of *lagh* metal—the metal brought by the Elder Ones from Yuggoth, and found in no mine of earth. This charm, carried in his robe, would make him proof against the menace of Ghatanothoa—it would even restore the Dark God's petrified victims if that monstrous entity should ever emerge and begin its devastations. Thus he proposed to go up the shunned and man-untrodden mountain, invade the alien-angled citadel of Cyclopean stone, and confront the shocking devil-entity in its lair. Of what would follow, he could not even guess; but the hope of being mankind's savior lent strength to his will.

He had, however, reckoned without the jealousy and self-interest of Ghatanothoa's pampered priests. No sooner did they hear of his plan than—fearful for their prestige and privilege in case the Daemon-God should be dethroned—they set up a frantic clamor against the so-called sacrilege, crying that no man might prevail against Ghatanothoa, and that any effort to seek it out would merely provoke it to a hellish onslaught against mankind which no spell or priestcraft could hope to avert. With those cries they hoped to turn the public mind against T'yog; yet such was the people's yearning for freedom from Ghatanothoa, and such their confidence in the skill and zeal of T'yog, that all the protestations came to naught. Even the King, usually a puppet of the priests, refused to forbid T'yog's daring pilgrimage.

It was then that the priests of Ghatanothoa did by stealth what they could not do openly. One night Imash-Mo, the High-Priest, stole to T'yog in his temple chamber and took from his sleeping form the metal cylinder; silently drawing out the potent scroll and putting in its place another scroll of great similitude, yet varied enough to have no power against any god or daemon. When the cylinder was slipped back into the sleeper's cloak Imash-Mo was content, for he knew T'yog was little likely to study that cylinder's contents again. Thinking himself protected by the true scroll, the heretic would march up the forbidden mountain and into the Evil Presence—and Ghatanothoa, unchecked by any magic, would take care of the rest.

It would no longer be needful for Ghatanothoa's priests to preach against the defiance. Let T'yog go his way and meet his doom. And secretly, the priests would always cherish the stolen scroll—the true and potent charm—handing it down from one High-Priest to another for use in any dim future when it might be needful to contravene the Devil-God's will. So the rest of the night Imash-Mo slept in great peace, with the true scroll in a new cylinder fashioned for its harborage.

It was dawn on the Day of the Sky-Flames (nomenclature undefined by von Junzt) that T'yog, amidst the prayers and chanting of the people and with King Thabon's blessing on his head, started up the dreaded mountain with a staff of tlath-wood in his right hand. Within his robe was the cylinder holding what he thought to be the true charm—for he had indeed failed to find out the imposture. Nor did he see any irony in the prayers which Imash-Mo and the other priests of Ghatanothoa intoned for his safety and success.

All that morning the people stood and watched as T'yog's dwindling form struggled up the shunned basalt slope hitherto alien to men's footsteps, and many stayed watching long after he had vanished where a perilous ledge led round to the mountain's hidden side. That night a few sensitive dreamers thought they heard a faint tremor convulsing the hated peak; though most ridiculed them for the statement. Next day vast crowds watched the mountain and prayed, and wondered how soon T'yog would return. And so the next day, and the next. For weeks they hoped and waited, and then they wept. Nor did anyone ever see T'yog, who would have saved mankind from fears, again.

Thereafter men shuddered at T'yog's presumption, and tried not to think of the punishment his impiety had met. And the priests of Ghatanothoa smiled to those who might resent the god's will or challenge its right to the sacrifices. In later years the ruse of Imash-Mo became known to the people; yet the knowledge availed not to change the general feeling that Ghatanothoa were better left alone. None ever dared to defy it again. And so the ages rolled on, and King succeeded King, and High-Priest succeeded High-Priest, and nations rose and decayed, and lands rose above the sea and returned into the sea. And with many millennia decay fell upon K'naa—till at last on a hideous day of storm and thunder, terrific rumbling, and mountain-high waves, all the land of Mu sank into the sea forever.

Yet down the later eons thin streams of ancient secrets trickled. In distant lands there met together grey-faced fugitives who had survived the sea-fiend's rage, and strange skies drank the smoke of altars reared to vanished gods and daemons. Though none knew to what bottomless deep the sacred peak and Cyclopean fortress of dreaded Ghatanothoa had sunk, there were still those who mumbled its name and offered to it nameless sacrifices lest it bubble up through leagues of ocean and shamble among men spreading horror and petrifaction.

Around the scattered priests grew the rudiments of a dark and secret cult—secret because the people of the new lands had other gods and devils, and thought only evil of elder and alien ones—and within that cult many hideous things were done, and many strange objects cherished. It was whispered that a certain line of elusive priests still harbored the true charm against Ghatanothoa which Imash-Mo stole from the sleeping T'yog; though none remained who could read or understand the cryptic syllables, or who could even guess in what part of the world the lost K'naa, the dreaded peak of Yaddith-Gho, and the titan fortress of the Devil-God had lain.

Though it flourished chiefly in those Pacific regions around which Mu itself had once stretched, there were rumors of the hidden and detested cult of Ghatanothoa in ill-fated Atlantis, and on the abhorred plateau of Leng. Von Junzt implied its presence in the fabled subterrene kingdom of K'n-yan, and gave clear evidence that it had penetrated Egypt, Chaldaea, Persia, China, the forgotten Semite empires of Africa, and Mexico and Peru in the New World. That it had a strong connection with the witchcraft movement in Europe, against which the bulls of popes were vainly directed, he more than strongly hinted. The West, however, was never favorable to its growth; and public indignation—aroused by glimpses of hideous rites and nameless sacrifices—wholly stamped out many of its branches. In the end it became a hunted, doubly furtive underground affair—yet never could its nucleus be quite exterminated. It always survived somehow, chiefly in the Far East and on the Pacific Islands, where its teachings became merged into the esoteric lore of the Polynesian *Areoi*.

Von Junzt gave subtle and disquieting hints of actual contact with the cult; so that as I read I shuddered at what was rumored about his death. He spoke of the growth of certain ideas regarding the appearance of the Devil-God—a creature which no human being (unless it were the too-daring T'yog, who had never returned) had ever seen—and contrasted this habit of speculation with the taboo prevailing in ancient Mu against any attempt to imagine what the horror looked like. There was a peculiar fearfulness about the devotees' awed and fascinated whispers on this subject—whispers heavy with morbid curiosity concerning the precise nature of what T'yog might have confronted in that frightful pre-human edifice on the dreaded and now-sunken mountains before the end (if it was an end) finally came—and I felt oddly disturbed by the German scholar's oblique and insidious references to this topic.

Scarcely less disturbing were von Junzt's conjectures on the whereabouts of the stolen scroll of cantrips against Ghatanothoa, and on the ultimate uses to which this scroll might be put. Despite all my assurance that the whole matter was purely mythical, I could not help shivering at the notion of a latter-day emergence of the monstrous god, and at the picture of an humanity turned suddenly to a race of abnormal statues, each encasing a living brain doomed to inert and helpless consciousness for untold eons of futurity. The old Düsseldorf savant had a poisonous way of suggesting more than he stated, and I could understand why his damnable book was suppressed in so many countries as blasphemous, dangerous, and unclean.

I writhed with repulsion, yet the thing exerted an unholy fascination; and I could not lay it down till I had finished it. The alleged reproductions of designs and ideographs from Mu were marvelously and startlingly like the markings on the strange cylinder and the characters on the scroll, and the whole account teemed with details having vague, irritating suggestions of resemblance to things connected with the hideous mummy. The cylinder and scroll—the Pacific setting—the persistent notion of old Capt. Weatherbee that the Cyclopean crypt where the mummy was found had once lain under a vast building . . . somehow I was vaguely glad that the volcanic island had sunk before that massive suggestion of a trap-door could be opened.

4

What I read in the *Black Book* formed a fiendishly apt preparation for the news items and closer events which began to force themselves upon me in the spring of 1932. I can scarcely recall just when the increasingly frequent reports of police action against the odd and fantastical religious cults in the

Orient and elsewhere commenced to impress me; but by May or June I realized that there was, all over the world, a surprising and unwonted burst of activity on the part of bizarre, furtive, and esoteric mystical organizations ordinarily quiescent and seldom heard from.

It is not likely that I would have connected these reports with either the hints of von Junzt or the popular furor over the mummy and cylinder in the museum, but for certain significant syllables and persistent resemblances—sensationally dwelt upon by the press—in the rites and speeches of the various secret celebrants brought to public attention. As it was, I could not help remarking with disquiet the frequent recurrence of a name—in various corrupt forms—which seemed to constitute a focal point of all the cult worship, and which was obviously regarded with a singular mixture of reverence and terror. Some of the forms quoted were G'tanta, Tanotah, Than-Tha, Gatan, and Ktan-Tah—and it did not require the suggestions of my now numerous occultist correspondents to make me see in these variants a hideous and suggestive kinship to the monstrous name rendered by von Junzt as Ghatanothoa.

There were other disquieting features, too. Again and again the reports cited vague, awestruck references to a "true scroll"—something on which tremendous consequences seemed to hinge, and which was mentioned as being in the custody of a certain "Nagob", whoever and whatever he might be. Likewise, there was an insistent repetition of a name which sounded like Tog, Tiok, Yog, Zob, or Yob, and which my more and more excited consciousness involuntarily linked with the name of the hapless heretic T'yog as given in the *Black Book*. This name was usually uttered in connection with such cryptical phrases as "It is none other than he," "He had looked upon its face," "He knows all, though he can neither see nor feel," "He has brought the memory down through the eons," "The true scroll will release him," "Nagob has the true scroll," "He can tell where to find it."

Something very queer was undoubtedly in the air, and I did not wonder when my occultist correspondents, as well as the sensational Sunday papers, began to connect the new abnormal stirrings with the legends of Mu on the one hand, and with the frightful mummy's recent exploitation on the other hand. The widespread articles in the first wave of press publicity, with their insistent linkage of the mummy, cylinder, and scroll with the tale in the *Black Book*, and their crazily fantastic speculations about the whole matter, might very well have roused the latent fanaticism in hundreds of those furtive groups of exotic devotees with which our complex world abounds. Nor did the papers cease adding fuel to the flames—for the stories on the cult-stirrings were even wilder than the earlier series of yarns.

As the summer drew on, attendants noticed a curious new element among the throngs of visitors which—after a lull following the first burst of publicity—were again drawn to the museum by the second furor. More and more frequently there were persons of strange and exotic aspect—swarthy Asiatics, long-haired nondescripts, and bearded brown men who seemed unused to European clothes—who would invariably inquire for the hall of mummies and would subsequently be found staring at the hideous Pacific specimen in a veritable ecstasy of fascination. Some quiet, sinister undercurrent in this flood of eccentric foreigners seemed to impress all the guards, and I myself was far from undisturbed. I could not help thinking of the prevailing cult-stirrings among just such exotics as these—and the connection of those stirrings with myths all too close to the frightful mummy and its cylinder scroll.

At times I was half tempted to withdraw the mummy from exhibition—especially when an attendant told me that he had several times glimpsed strangers making odd obeisances before it, and had overheard sing-song mutterings which sounded like chants or rituals addressed to it at hours when the visiting throngs were somewhat thinned. One of the guards acquired a queer nervous hallucination about the petrified horror in the lone glass case, alleging that he could see from day to day certain vague, subtle, and infinitely slight changes in the frantic flexion of the bony claws, and in the fear-crazed expression of the leathery face. He could not get rid of the loathsome idea that those horrible, bulging eyes were about to pop suddenly open.

It was early in September, when the curious crowds had lessened and the hall of mummies was sometimes vacant, that the attempt to get at the mummy by cutting the glass of its case was made. The culprit, a swarthy Polynesian, was spied in time by a guard, and was overpowered before any damage occurred. Upon investigation the fellow turned out to be an Hawaiian notorious for his activity in certain underground religious cults, and having a considerable police record in connection with abnormal and inhuman rites and sacrifices. Some of the papers found in his room were highly puzzling and disturbing, including many sheets covered with hieroglyphs closely resembling those on the scroll at the museum and in the *Black Book* of von Junzt; but regarding these things he could not be prevailed upon to speak.

Scarcely a week after this incident, another attempt to get at the mummy—this time by tampering with the lock of his case—resulted in a second arrest. The offender, a Cingalese, had as long and unsavory a record of loathsome cult activities as the Hawaiian had possessed, and displayed a kindred unwillingness to talk to the police. What made this case doubly and darkly interesting was that a guard had noticed this man several times before, and had heard him addressing to the mummy a peculiar chant containing unmistakable repetitions of the word "T'yog." As a result of this affair I doubled the guards in the hall of mummies, and ordered them never to leave the now notorious specimen out of sight, even for a moment.

As may well be imagined, the press made much of these two incidents, reviewing its talk of primal and fabulous Mu, and claiming boldly that the hideous mummy was none other than the daring heretic T'yog, petrified by something he had seen in the pre-human citadel he had invaded, and preserved intact through 175,000 years of our planet's turbulent history. That the strange devotees represented cults descended from Mu, and that they were worshipping the mummy—or perhaps even seeking to awaken it to life by spells and incantations—was emphasized and reiterated in the most sensational fashion.

Writers exploited the insistence of the old legends that the *brain* of Ghatanothoa's petrified victims remained conscious and unaffected—a point which served as a basis for the wildest and most improbable speculations. The mention of a "true scroll" also received due attention—it being the prevailing popular theory that T'yog's stolen charm against Ghatanothoa was somewhere in existence, and that cult-members were trying to bring it into contact with T'yog himself for some purpose of their own. One result of this exploitation was that a third wave of gaping visitors began flooding the museum and staring at the hellish mummy which served as a nucleus for the whole strange and disturbing affair.

It was among this wave of spectators—many of whom made repeated visits—that talk of the mummy's vaguely changing aspect first began to be widespread. I suppose—despite the disturbing notion of the nervous guard some months before—that the museum's personnel was too well used to the constant sight of odd shapes to pay close attention to details; in any case, it was the excited whispers of visitors which at length aroused the guards to the subtle mutation which was apparently in progress. Almost simultaneously the press got hold of it—with blatant results which can well be imagined.

Naturally, I gave the matter my most careful observation, and by the middle of October decided that a definite disintegration of the mummy was under way. Through some chemical or physical influence in the air, the half-stony, half-leathery fibers seemed to be gradually relaxing, causing distinct variations in the angles of the limbs and in certain details of the fear-twisted facial expression. After a half-century of perfect preservation this was a highly disconcerting development, and I had the museum's taxidermist, Dr. Moore, go carefully over the gruesome object several times. He reported a general relaxation and softening, and gave the thing two or three astringent sprayings, but did not dare to attempt anything drastic lest there be a sudden crumbling and accelerated decay.

The effect of all this upon the gaping crowds was curious. Heretofore each new sensation sprung by the press had brought fresh waves of staring and whispering visitors, but now—though the papers blathered endlessly about the mummy's changes—the public seemed to have acquired a definite sense of fear which outranked even its morbid curiosity. People seemed to feel that a sinister aura hovered over the museum, and from a high peak the attendance fell to a level distinctly below normal. This lessened attendance gave added prominence to the stream of freakish foreigners who continued to infest the place, and whose numbers seemed in no way diminished.

On November eighteenth a Peruvian of Indian blood suffered a strange hysterical or epileptic seizure in front of the mummy, afterward shrieking from his hospital cot, "It tried to open its eyes!—T'yog tried to open his eyes and stare at me!" I was by this time on the point of removing the object from exhibition, but permitted myself to be overruled at a meeting of our very conservative directors. However, I could see that the museum was beginning to acquire an unholy reputation in its austere and quiet neighborhood. After this incident I gave instructions that no one be allowed to pause before the monstrous Pacific relic for more than a few minutes at a time.

It was on November twenty-fourth, after the museum's five o'clock closing, that one of the guards noticed a minute opening of the mummy's eyes. The phenomenon was very slight—nothing but a thin crescent of cornea being visible in either eye—but it was none the less of the highest interest. Dr. Moore, having been summoned hastily, was about to study the exposed bits of eyeball with a magnifier when his handling of the mummy caused the leathery lids to fall tightly shut again. All gentle efforts to open them failed, and the taxidermist did not dare to apply drastic measures. When he notified me of all this by telephone I felt a sense of mounting dread hard to reconcile with the apparently simple event concerned. For a moment I could share the popular impression that some evil, amorphous blight from unplumbed deeps of time and space hung murkily and menacingly over the museum.

Two nights later a sullen Filipino was trying to secrete himself in the museum at closing time. Arrested and taken to the station, he refused even to give his name, and was detained as a suspicious person. Meanwhile the strict surveillance of the mummy seemed to discourage the odd hordes of foreigners from haunting it. At least, the number of exotic visitors distinctly fell off after the enforcement of the "move along" order.

It was during the early morning hours of Thursday, December first, that a terrible climax developed. At about one o'clock horrible screams of mortal fright and agony were heard issuing from the museum, and a series of frantic telephone calls from neighbors brought to the scene quickly and simultaneously a squad of police and several museum officials, including myself. Some of the policemen surrounded the building while others, with the officials, cautiously entered. In the main corridor we found the night watchman strangled to death—a bit of East Indian hemp still knotted around his neck—and realized that despite all precautions some darkly evil intruder or intruders had gained access to the place. Now, however, a tomb-like silence enfolded everything and we almost feared to advance upstairs to the fateful wing where we knew the core of the trouble must lurk. We felt a bit more steadied after flooding the building with light from the central switches in the corridor, and finally crept reluctantly up the curving staircase and through a lofty archway to the hall of mummies.

5

It is from this point onward that reports of the hideous case have been censored—for we have all agreed that no good can be accomplished by a public knowledge of those terrestrial conditions implied by the further developments. I have said that we flooded the whole building with light before our ascent. Now beneath the beams that beat down on the glistening cases and their gruesome contents, we saw outspread a mute horror whose baffling details testified to happenings utterly beyond our comprehension. There were two intruders—who we afterward agreed must have hidden in the building before closing time—but they would never be executed for the watchman's murder. They had already paid the penalty.

One was a Burmese and the other a Fiji-Islander—both known to the police for their share in frightful and repulsive cult activities. They were dead, and the more we examined them the more utterly monstrous and unnamable we felt their manner of death to be. On both faces was a more wholly frantic and inhuman look of fright than even the oldest policeman had ever seen before; yet in the state of the two bodies there were vast and significant differences.

The Burmese lay collapsed close to the nameless mummy's case, from which a square of glass had been neatly cut. In his right hand was a scroll of bluish membrane which I at once saw was covered with greyish hieroglyphs—almost a duplicate of the scroll in the strange cylinder in the library downstairs, though later study brought out subtle differences. There was no mark of violence on the body, and in view of the desperate, agonized expression on the twisted face we could only conclude that the man died of sheer fright.

It was the closely adjacent Fijian, though, that gave us the profoundest shock. One of the policemen was the first to feel of him, and the cry of fright he emitted added another shudder to that neighborhood's night of terror. We ought to have known from the lethal greyness of the once-black, fear-twisted face, and of the bony hands—one of which still clutched an electric torch—that something was hideously wrong; yet every one of us was unprepared for what that officer's hesitant touch disclosed. Even now I can think of it only with a paroxysm of dread and repulsion. To be brief—the hapless invader, who less than an hour before had been a sturdy living Melanesian bent on unknown evils, was now a rigid, ash-grey figure of stony, leathery petrification, in every respect identical with the crouching, aeon-old blasphemy in the violated glass case.

Yet that was not the worst. Crowning all other horrors, and indeed seizing our shocked attention before we turned to the bodies on the floor, was the state of the frightful mummy. No longer could its changes be called vague and subtle, for it had now made radical shifts of posture. It had sagged and slumped with a curious loss of rigidity; its bony claws had sunk until they no longer even partly covered its leathery, fear-crazed face; and—God help us!—*its hellish bulging eyes had popped wide open, and seemed to be staring directly at the two intruders who had died of fright or worse.*

That ghastly, dead-fish stare was hideously mesmerizing, and it haunted us all the time we were examining the bodies of the invaders. Its effect on our nerves was damnably queer, for we somehow felt a curious rigidity creeping over us and hampering our simplest motions—a rigidity which later vanished very oddly when we passed the hieroglyphed scroll around for inspection. Every now and then I felt my gaze drawn irresistibly toward those horrible bulging eyes in the case, and when I returned to study them after viewing the bodies I thought I detected something very singular about the glassy surface of the dark and marvelously well-preserved pupils. The more I looked, the more fascinated I became; and at last I went down to the office—despite that strange stiffness in my limbs—and brought up a strong multiple magnifying glass. With this I commenced a very close and careful survey of the fishy pupils, while the others crowded expectantly around.

I had always been rather skeptical of the theory that scenes and objects become photographed on the retina of the eye in cases of death or coma; yet no sooner did I look through the lens than I realized the presence of some sort of image other than the room's reflection in the glassy, bulging optics of this nameless spawn of the eons. Certainly, there was a dimly outlined scene on the age-old retinal surface, and I could not doubt that it formed the last thing on which those eyes had looked in life—countless millennia ago. It seemed to be steadily fading, and I fumbled with the magnifier in order to shift another lens into place. Yet it must have been accurate and clear-cut, even if infinitesimally small, when—in response to some evil spell or act connected with their visit—it had confronted those intruders who were frightened to death. With the extra lens I could make out many details formerly invisible, and the awed group around me hung on the flood of words with which I tried to tell what I saw.

For here, in the year 1932, a man in the city of Boston was looking on something which belonged to an unknown and utterly alien world—a world that vanished from existence and normal memory eons ago. There was a vast room—a chamber of cyclopean masonry—and I seemed to be viewing it from one of its corners. On the walls were carvings so hideous that even in this imperfect image their stark blasphemousness and bestiality sickened me. I could not believe that the carvers of these things were human, or that they had ever seen human beings when they shaped the frightful outlines which leered at the beholder. In the center of the chamber was a colossal trap-door of stone, pushed upward to permit the emergence of some object from below. The object should have been clearly visible—indeed, must have been when the eyes first opened before the fear-stricken intruders—though under my lenses it was merely a monstrous blur.

As it happened, I was studying the right eye only when I brought the extra magnification into play. A moment later I wished fervently that my search had ended there. As it was, however, the zeal of discovery and revelation was upon me, and I shifted my powerful lenses to the mummy's left eye in the hope of finding the image less faded on that retina. My hands, trembling with excitement and unnaturally stiff from some obscure influence, were slow in bringing the magnifier into focus, but a moment later I realized that the image was less faded than in the other eye. I saw in a morbid flash of half-distinctness the insufferable thing which was welling up through the prodigious trap-door in that cyclopean, immemorially archaic crypt of a lost world—and fell fainting with an inarticulate shriek of which I am not even ashamed.

By the time I revived there was no distinct image of anything in either eye of the monstrous mummy. Sergeant Keefe of the police looked with my glass, for I could not bring myself to face that abnormal entity again. And I thanked all the powers of the cosmos that I had not looked earlier than I did. It took all my resolution, and a great deal of solicitation, to make me relate what I had glimpsed in the hideous moment of revelation. Indeed, I could not speak till we had all adjourned to the office below, out of sight of that demoniac thing which could not be. For I had begun to harbor the most terrible and fantastic notions about the mummy and its glassy, bulging eyes—that it had a kind of hellish consciousness, seeing all that occurred before it and trying vainly to communicate some frightful message from the gulfs of time. That meant madness—but at last I thought I might be better off if I told what I had half seen.

After all, it was not a long thing to tell. Oozing and surging up out of that yawning trap-door in the cyclopean crypt I had glimpsed such an unbelievable behemothic monstrosity that I could not doubt the power of its original to kill with its mere sight. Even now I cannot begin to suggest it with any words at my command. I might call it gigantic—tentacled—proboscidian—octopus-eyed—semi-amorphous—plastic—partly squamous and partly rugose—ugh! But nothing I could say could even adumbrate the loathsome, unholy, non-human, extra-galactic horror and hatefulness and unutterable evil of that forbidden spawn of black chaos and illimitable night. As I write these words the associated mental image causes me to lean back faint and nauseated. As I told of the sight to the men around me in the office, I had to fight to preserve the consciousness I had regained.

Nor were my hearers much less moved. Not a man spoke above a whisper for a full quarter-hour, and there were awed, half-furtive references to the frightful lore in the *Black Book*, to the recent newspaper tales of cult-stirrings, and to the sinister events in the museum. Ghatanothoa . . . Even its smallest perfect image could petrify—T'yog—the false scroll—he never came back—the true scroll which could fully or partly undo the petrification—did it survive?—the hellish cults—the phrases overheard—"It is none other than he"—"He had looked upon its face"—"He knows all, though he can neither see nor feel"—"He had brought the memory down through the eons"—"The true scroll will release him"—"Nagob has the true scroll"—"He can tell where to find it." Only the healing greyness of the dawn brought us back to sanity; a sanity which made of that glimpse of mine a closed topic—something not to be explained or thought of again.

We gave out only partial reports to the press, and later on co-operated with the papers in making other suppressions. For example, when the autopsy shewed the brain and several other internal organs of the petrified Fijian to be fresh and unpetrified, though hermetically sealed by the petrification of the exterior flesh—an anomaly about which physicians are still guardedly and bewilderedly debating—we did not wish a furor to be started. We knew too well what the yellow journals, remembering what was said of the intact-brained and still-conscious state of Ghatanothoa's stony-leathery victims, would make of this detail.

As matters stood, they pointed out that the man who had held the hieroglyphed scroll—and who had evidently thrust it at the mummy through the opening in the case—was not petrified, while the man who had *not* held it was. When they demanded that we make certain experiments—applying the scroll both to the stony-leathery body of the Fijian and to the mummy itself—we indignantly refused to abet such superstitious notions. Of course, the mummy was withdrawn from public view and transferred to the museum laboratory awaiting a really scientific examination before some suitable medical authority. Remembering past events, we kept it under a strict guard; but even so, an attempt was made to enter the museum at 2:25 a.m. on December fifth. Prompt working of the burglar alarm frustrated the design, though unfortunately the criminal or criminals escaped.

That no hint of anything further ever reached the public, I am profoundly thankful. I wish devoutly that there were nothing more to tell. There will, of course, be leaks, and if anything happens to me I do not know what my executors will do with this manuscript; but at least the case will not be painfully fresh in the multitude's memory when the revelation comes. Besides, no one will believe the facts when they are finally told. That is the curious thing about the multitude. When their yellow press makes hints, they are ready to swallow anything; but when a stupendous and abnormal revelation is actually made, they laugh it aside as a lie. For the sake of general sanity it is probably better so.

I have said that a scientific examination of the frightful mummy was planned. This took place on December eighth, exactly a week after the hideous culmination of events, and was conducted by the eminent Dr. William Minot, in conjunction with Wentworth Moore, Sc.D., taxidermist of the museum. Dr. Minot had witnessed the autopsy of the oddly petrified Fijian the week before. There were also present Messrs. Lawrence Cabot and Dudley Saltonstall of the museum's trustees, Drs. Mason, Wells, and Carver of the museum staff, two representatives of the press, and myself. During the week the condition of the hideous specimen had not visibly changed, though some relaxation of its fibers caused the position of the glassy, open eyes to shift slightly from time to time. All of the staff dreaded to look at the thing—for its suggestion of quiet, conscious watching had become intolerable—and it was only with an effort that I could bring myself to attend the examination.

Doctor Minot arrived shortly after 1:00 p.m., and within a few minutes began his survey of the mummy. Considerable disintegration took place under his hands, and in view of this—and of what we told him concerning the gradual relaxation of the specimen since the first of October—he decided that a thorough dissection ought to be made before the substance was further impaired. The proper instruments being present in the laboratory equipment, he began at once; exclaiming aloud at the odd, fibrous nature of the grey, mummified substance.

But his exclamation was still louder when he made the first deep incision, for out of that cut there slowly trickled a thick crimson stream whose nature—despite the infinite ages dividing this hellish mummy's lifetime from the present—was utterly unmistakable. A few more deft strokes revealed various organs in astonishing degrees of non-petrified preservation—

all, indeed, being intact except where injuries to the petrified exterior had brought about malformation or destruction. The resemblance of this condition to that found in the fright-killed Fiji-Islander was so strong that the eminent physician gasped in bewilderment. The perfection of those ghastly bulging eyes was uncanny, and their exact state with respect to petrification was very difficult to determine.

At 3:30 p.m. the brain-case was opened—and ten minutes later our stunned group took an oath of secrecy which only such guarded documents as this manuscript will ever modify. Even the two reporters were glad to confirm the silence. *For the opening had revealed a pulsing, living brain.*

28
Dominion
Clark Ashton Smith
(1935)

This poem appeared in the June 1935 issue of *Weird Tales* Magazine. Howard had been corresponding with Clark Ashton Smith for several years and always mentioned how much he enjoyed Smith's poetry. In a July 23, 1935, letter to Smith, Howard wrote, "But I have, as always, followed your work in *Weird Tales*." He continued by providing a list of his favorites. "I very much enjoyed 'The Dark Eidolon,' 'The Last Hieroglyph,' 'The Flower Women,' and the splendid poem: 'Dominion.'" He then added an additional comment regarding the last poem, "I am not exaggerating when I say that I do not consider that I ever read a finer poem than that. I'd give my trigger-finger for the ability to make words flame and burn as you do." With a comment like that coming from Howard, this poem had to be included.

Empress of all my life, it is not known to thee
What hidden world thou holdest evermore in fee;
  What muffled levies rise, from mist and Lethe drawn,

Waging some goblin war at thy forgotten whim;
What travelers in lone Cimmeria, drear and dim,
  Follow the rumor of thy face toward the dawn.

Plain are those nearer lands whereon thou lookest forth:
Thy fields upon the south, thy cities in the north:
  But vaster is that sealed and subterraneous realm:

High towers are built for thee with hushed demonian toil
In dayless lands, and furrows drawn through a dark soil,
   And sable oceans crossed by many an unstarred helm.

Though unto thee is sent a tribute of wrought gold
By them that delve therein, never shalt thou behold
   How the ore is digged from mines too near to Erebus;

Though strange Sabean myrrh within thy censers fume,
Thou shalt not ever guess the Afrit-haunted gloom
   Whence the rich balm was won with labor perilous.

Occulted still from thee, thy power is on lost things,
On alien seraphim that seek with desperate wings,
   Flown from their dying orb, the confines of thy heaven;

Yea, still thy whisper moves, and magically stirs
To life the shapeless dust in shattered sepulchers;
   And in dark bread and wine thou art the untold leaven.

But never shalt thou dream how in some far abysm
Thy lightly spoken word has been an exorcism
   Driving foul spirits from a wanderer bewrayed;

With eyes fulfilled of noon, haply thou shalt not see
How, in a land illumed by suns of ebony,
   Beneath thy breath the fiery shadows flame and fade.

29
The Haunter of the Dark
H. P. Lovecraft
(1936)

"The Haunter of the Dark" is believed to be one of the last stories written by H.P. Lovecraft. Penned in early November of 1935, it was published in the December 1936 issue of *Weird Tales* magazine (alongside Howard's "The Fire of Asshurbanipal"). The yarn was dedicated to fellow *Weird Tales* author Robert Bloch (of "Psycho" fame years later), because he had previously authored a story titled, "The Shambler from the Stars" (*Weird Tales*, September 1935), in which the Lovecraft character dies. This is Lovecraft's response to that story. The epigraph to the yarn is the second stanza of Lovecraft's 1917 poem "Nemesis." Howard did not live long enough to see the actual yarn in print, but rather, he received a circulating copy of the manuscript, as did fellow *Weird Tales* authors E. Hoffmann Price and Duane W. Rimel. Howard, writing to Lovecraft, told him, "I received 'Haunter of the Dark' from Price and sent it on to Rimel as instructed. I consider it a splendid piece of work. As a weird story and a work of art I have no criticism to offer. I enjoyed reading it immensely and see no reason why it should not be accepted by any magazine dealing in the fantastic."

(Dedicated to Robert Bloch)
I have seen the dark universe yawning
   Where the black planets roll without aim—
Where they roll in their horror unheeded,
   Without knowledge or luster or name.
        —*Nemesis.*

Cautious investigators will hesitate to challenge the common belief that Robert Blake was killed by lightning, or by some profound nervous shock derived from an electrical discharge. It is true that the window he faced was unbroken, but Nature has shewn herself capable of many freakish performances. The expression on his face may easily have arisen from some obscure muscular source unrelated to anything he saw, while the entries in his diary are clearly the result of a fantastic imagination aroused by certain local superstitions and by certain old matters he had uncovered. As for the anomalous conditions at the deserted church on Federal Hill—the shrewd analyst is not slow in attributing them to some charlatanry, conscious or unconscious, with at least some of which Blake was secretly connected.

For after all, the victim was a writer and painter wholly devoted to the field of myth, dream, terror, and superstition, and avid in his quest for scenes and effects of a bizarre, spectral sort. His earlier stay in the city—a visit to a strange old man as deeply given to occult and forbidden lore as he—had ended amidst death and flame, and it must have been some morbid instinct which drew him back from his home in Milwaukee. He may have known of the old stories despite his statements to the contrary in the diary, and his death may have nipped in the bud some stupendous hoax destined to have a literary reflection.

Among those, however, who have examined and correlated all this evidence, there remain several who cling to less rational and commonplace theories. They are inclined to take much of Blake's diary at its face value, and point significantly to certain facts such as the undoubted genuineness of the old church record, the verified existence of the disliked and unorthodox Starry Wisdom sect prior to 1877, the recorded disappearance of an inquisitive reporter named Edwin M. Lillibridge in 1893, and—above all—the look of monstrous, transfiguring fear on the face of the young writer when he died. It was one of these believers who, moved to fanatical extremes, threw into the bay the curiously angled stone and its strangely adorned metal box found in the old church steeple—the black windowless steeple, and not the tower where Blake's diary said those things originally were. Though widely censured both officially and unofficially, this man—a reputable physician with a taste for odd folklore—averred that he had rid the earth of something too dangerous to rest upon it.

Between these two schools of opinion the reader must judge for himself. The papers have given the tangible details from a skeptical angle, leaving for others the drawing of the picture as Robert Blake saw it—or thought he saw it—or pretended to see it. Now, studying the diary closely, dispassionately, and at leisure, let us summarize the dark chain of events from the expressed point of view of their chief actor.

Young Blake returned to Providence in the winter of 1934–5, taking the upper floor of a venerable dwelling in a grassy court off College Street—on the crest of the great eastward hill near the Brown University campus and behind the marble John Hay Library. It was a cozy and fascinating place, in a little garden oasis of village-like antiquity where huge, friendly cats sunned themselves atop a convenient shed. The square Georgian house had a monitor roof, classic doorway with fan carving, small-paned windows, and all the other earmarks of early nineteenth-century workmanship. Inside were six-paneled doors, wide floor-boards, a curving colonial staircase, white Adam-period mantels, and a rear set of rooms three steps below the general level.

Blake's study, a large southwest chamber, overlooked the front garden on one side, while its west windows—before one of which he had his desk—faced off from the brow of the hill and commanded a splendid view of the lower town's outspread roofs and of the mystical sunsets that flamed behind them. On the far horizon were the open countryside's purple slopes. Against these, some two miles away, rose the spectral hump of Federal Hill, bristling with huddled roofs and steeples whose remote outlines wavered mysteriously, taking fantastic forms as the smoke of the city swirled up and enmeshed them. Blake had a curious sense that he was looking upon some unknown, ethereal world which might or might not vanish in dream if ever he tried to seek it out and enter it in person.

Having sent home for most of his books, Blake bought some antique furniture suitable to his quarters and settled down to write and paint—living alone, and attending to the simple housework himself. His studio was in a north attic room, where the panes of the monitor roof furnished admirable lighting. During that first winter he produced five of his best-known short stories—*The Burrower Beneath, The Stairs in the Crypt, Shaggai, In the Vale of Pnath,* and *The Feaster from the Stars*—and painted seven canvases; studies of nameless, unhuman monsters, and profoundly alien, non-terrestrial landscapes.

At sunset he would often sit at his desk and gaze dreamily off at the outspread west—the dark towers of Memorial Hall just below, the Georgian court-house belfry, the lofty pinnacles of the downtown section, and that shimmering, spire-crowned mound in the distance whose unknown streets and labyrinthine gables so potently provoked his fancy. From his few local acquaintances he learned that the far-off slope was a vast Italian quarter, though most of the houses were remnants of older Yankee and Irish days. Now and then he would train his field-glasses on that spectral, unreachable world beyond the curling smoke; picking out individual roofs and chimneys and steeples, and speculating upon the bizarre and curious mysteries they might house. Even with optical aid Federal Hill seemed somehow alien, half fabulous, and linked to the unreal, intangible marvels of Blake's own tales and pictures. The feeling would persist long after the hill had faded into the violet, lamp-starred twilight, and the court-house floodlights and the red Industrial Trust beacon had blazed up to make the night grotesque.

Of all the distant objects on Federal Hill, a certain huge, dark church most fascinated Blake. It stood out with especial distinctness at certain hours of the day, and at sunset the great tower and tapering steeple loomed blackly against the flaming sky. It seemed to rest on especially high ground; for the grimy facade, and the obliquely seen north side with sloping roof and the tops of great pointed windows, rose boldly above the tangle of surrounding ridgepoles and chimney-pots. Peculiarly grim and austere, it appeared to be built of stone, stained and weathered with the smoke and storms of a century and more. The style, so far as the glass could shew, was that earliest experimental form of Gothic revival which preceded the stately Upjohn period and held over some of the outlines and proportions of the Georgian age. Perhaps it was reared around 1810 or 1815.

As months passed, Blake watched the far-off, forbidding structure with an oddly mounting interest. Since the vast windows were never lighted, he knew that it must be vacant. The longer he watched, the more his imagination worked, till at length he began to fancy curious things. He believed that a vague, singular aura of desolation hovered over the place, so that even the pigeons and swallows shunned its smoky eaves. Around other towers and belfries his glass would reveal great flocks of birds, but here they never rested. At least, that is what he thought and set down in his diary. He pointed the place out to several friends, but none of them had even been on Federal Hill or possessed the faintest notion of what the church was or had been.

In the spring a deep restlessness gripped Blake. He had begun his long-planned novel—based on a supposed survival of the witch-cult in Maine—but was strangely unable to make progress with it. More and more he would sit at his westward window and gaze at the distant hill and the black, frowning steeple shunned by the birds. When the delicate leaves came out on the garden boughs the world was filled with a new beauty, but Blake's restlessness was merely increased. It was then that he first thought of crossing the city and climbing bodily up that fabulous slope into the smoke-wreathed world of dream.

Late in April, just before the aeon-shadowed Walpurgis time, Blake made his first trip into the unknown. Plodding through the endless downtown streets and the bleak, decayed squares beyond, he came finally upon the ascending avenue of century-worn steps, sagging Doric porches, and blear-paned cupolas which he felt must lead up to the long-known, unreachable world beyond the mists. There were dingy blue-and-white street signs which meant nothing to him, and presently he noted the strange, dark faces of the drifting crowds, and the foreign signs over curious shops in brown, decade-weathered buildings. Nowhere could he find any of the objects he had seen from afar; so that once more he half fancied that the Federal Hill of that distant view was a dream-world never to be trod by living human feet.

Now and then a battered church facade or crumbling spire came in sight, but never the blackened pile that he sought. When he asked a shopkeeper about a great stone church the man smiled and shook his head, though he spoke English freely. As Blake climbed higher, the region seemed stranger and stranger, with bewildering mazes of brooding brown alleys leading eternally off to the south. He crossed two or three broad avenues, and once thought he glimpsed a familiar tower. Again he asked a merchant about the massive church of stone, and this time he could have sworn that the plea of ignorance was feigned. The dark man's face had a look of fear which he tried to hide, and Blake saw him make a curious sign with his right hand.

Then suddenly a black spire stood out against the cloudy sky on his left, above the tiers of brown roofs lining the tangled southerly alleys. Blake knew at once what it was, and plunged toward it through the squalid, unpaved lanes that climbed from the avenue. Twice he lost his way, but he somehow dared not ask any of the patriarchs or housewives who sat on their doorsteps, or any of the children who shouted and played in the mud of the shadowy lanes.

At last he saw the tower plain against the southwest, and a huge stone bulk rose darkly at the end of an alley. Presently he stood in a windswept open square, quaintly cobblestoned, with a high bank wall on the farther side. This was the end of his quest; for upon the wide, iron-railed, weed-grown plateau which the wall supported—a separate, lesser world raised fully six feet above the surrounding streets—there stood a grim, titan bulk whose identity, despite Blake's new perspective, was beyond dispute.

The vacant church was in a state of great decrepitude. Some of the high stone buttresses had fallen, and several delicate finials lay half lost among the brown, neglected weeds and grasses. The sooty Gothic windows were largely unbroken, though many of the stone mullions were missing. Blake wondered how the obscurely painted panes could have survived so well, in view of the known habits of small boys the world over. The massive doors were intact and tightly closed. Around the top of the bank wall, fully enclosing the grounds, was a rusty iron fence whose gate—at the head of a flight of steps from the square—was visibly padlocked. The path from the gate to the building was completely overgrown. Desolation and decay hung like a pall above the place, and in the birdless eaves and black, ivyless walls Blake felt a touch of the dimly sinister beyond his power to define.

There were very few people in the square, but Blake saw a policeman at the northerly end and approached him with questions about the church. He was a great wholesome Irishman, and it seemed odd that he would do little more than make the sign of the cross and mutter that people never spoke of that building. When Blake pressed him he said very hurriedly that the Italian priests warned everybody against it, vowing that a monstrous evil had once dwelt there and left its mark. He himself had heard dark whispers of it from his father, who recalled certain sounds and rumors from his boyhood.

There had been a bad sect there in the ould days—an outlaw sect that called up awful things from some unknown gulf of night. It had taken a good priest to exorcise what had come, though there did be those who said that merely the light could do it. If Father O'Malley were alive there would be many the thing he could tell. But now there was nothing to do but let it alone. It hurt nobody now, and those that owned it were dead or far away. They had run away like rats after the threatening talk in '77, when people began to mind the way folks vanished now and then in the neighborhood. Some day the city would step in and take the property for lack of heirs, but little good would come of anybody's touching it. Better it be left alone for the years to topple, lest things be stirred that ought to rest forever in their black abyss.

After the policeman had gone Blake stood staring at the sullen steepled pile. It excited him to find that the structure seemed as sinister to others as to him, and he wondered what grain of truth might lie behind the old tales the bluecoat had repeated. Probably they were mere legends evoked by the evil look of the place, but even so, they were like a strange coming to life of one of his own stories.

The afternoon sun came out from behind dispersing clouds, but seemed unable to light up the stained, sooty walls of the old temple that towered on its high plateau. It was odd that the green of spring had not touched the brown, withered growths in the raised, iron-fenced yard. Blake found himself edging nearer the raised area and examining the bank wall and rusted fence for possible avenues of ingress. There was a terrible lure about the blackened fane which was not to be resisted. The fence had no opening near the steps, but around on the north side were some missing bars. He could go up the steps and walk around on the narrow coping outside the fence till he came to the gap. If the people feared the place so wildly, he would encounter no interference.

He was on the embankment and almost inside the fence before anyone noticed him. Then, looking down, he saw the few people in the square edging away and making the same sign with their right hands that the shopkeeper in the avenue had made. Several windows were slammed down, and a fat woman darted into the street and pulled some small children inside a rickety, unpainted house. The gap in the fence was very easy to pass through, and before long Blake found himself wading amidst the rotting, tangled growths of the deserted yard. Here and there the worn stump of a headstone told him that there had once been burials in this field; but that, he saw, must have been very long ago. The sheer bulk of the church was oppressive now that he was close to it, but he conquered his mood and approached to try the three great doors in the facade. All were securely locked, so he began a circuit of the Cyclopean building in quest of some minor and more penetrable opening. Even then he could not be sure that he wished to enter that haunt of desertion and shadow, yet the pull of its strangeness dragged him on automatically.

A yawning and unprotected cellar window in the rear furnished the needed aperture. Peering in, Blake saw a subterrene gulf of cobwebs and dust faintly litten by the western sun's filtered rays. Debris, old barrels, and ruined boxes and furniture of numerous sorts met his eye, though over everything lay a shroud of dust which softened all sharp outlines. The rusted remains of a hot-air furnace shewed that the building had been used and kept in shape as late as mid-Victorian times.

Acting almost without conscious initiative, Blake crawled through the window and let himself down to the dust-carpeted and debris-strewn concrete floor. The vaulted cellar was a vast one, without partitions; and in a corner far to the right, amid dense shadows, he saw a black archway evidently leading upstairs. He felt a peculiar sense of oppression at being actually within the great spectral building, but kept it in check as he cautiously scouted about—finding a still-intact barrel amid the dust, and rolling it over to the open window to provide for his exit. Then, bracing himself, he crossed the wide, cobweb-festooned space toward the arch. Half choked with the omnipresent dust, and covered with ghostly gossamer fibers, he reached and began to climb the worn stone steps which rose into the darkness. He had no light, but groped carefully with his hands. After a sharp turn he felt a closed door ahead, and a little fumbling revealed its ancient latch. It opened inward, and beyond it he saw a dimly illumined corridor lined with worm-eaten paneling.

Once on the ground floor, Blake began exploring in a rapid fashion. All the inner doors were unlocked, so that he freely passed from room to room. The colossal nave was an almost eldritch place with its drifts and mountains of dust over box pews, altar, hourglass pulpit, and sounding-board, and its titanic ropes of cobweb stretching among the pointed arches of the gallery and entwining the clustered Gothic columns. Over all this hushed desolation played a hideous leaden light as the declining afternoon sun sent its rays through the strange, half-blackened panes of the great apsidal windows.

The paintings on those windows were so obscured by soot that Blake could scarcely decipher what they had represented, but from the little he could make out he did not like them. The designs were largely conventional, and his knowledge of obscure symbolism told him much concerning some of the ancient patterns. The few saints depicted bore expressions distinctly open to criticism, while one of the windows seemed to shew merely a dark space with spirals of curious luminosity scattered about in it. Turning away from the windows, Blake noticed that the cobwebbed cross above the altar was not of the ordinary kind, but resembled the primordial ankh or crux ansata of shadowy Egypt.

In a rear vestry room beside the apse Blake found a rotting desk and ceiling-high shelves of mildewed, disintegrating books. Here for the first time he received a positive shock of objective horror, for the titles of those books told him much. They were the black, forbidden things which most sane people have never even heard of, or have heard of only in furtive, timorous whispers; the banned and dreaded repositories of equivocal secrets and immemorial formulae which have trickled down the stream of time from the days of man's youth, and the dim, fabulous days before man was. He had himself read many of them—a Latin version of the abhorred *Necronomicon,* the sinister *Liber Ivonis,* the infamous *Cultes des Goules* of Comte d'Erlette, the *Unaussprechlichen Kulten* of von Junzt, and old Ludvig Prinn's hellish *De Vermis Mysteriis.* But there were others he had known merely by reputation or not at all—the *Pnakotic Manuscripts,* the *Book of Dzyan,* and a crumbling volume in wholly unidentifiable characters yet with certain symbols and diagrams shudderingly recognizable to the occult student. Clearly, the lingering local rumors had not lied. This place had once been the seat of an evil older than mankind and wider than the known universe.

In the ruined desk was a small leather-bound record-book filled with entries in some odd cryptographic medium. The manuscript writing consisted of the common traditional symbols used today in astronomy and anciently in alchemy, astrology, and other dubious arts—the devices of the sun, moon, planets, aspects, and zodiacal signs—here massed in solid pages of text, with divisions and paragraphings suggesting that each symbol answered to some alphabetical letter.

In the hope of later solving the cryptogram, Blake bore off this volume in his coat pocket. Many of the great tomes on the shelves fascinated him unutterably, and he felt tempted to borrow them at some later time. He wondered how they could have remained undisturbed so long. Was he the first to conquer the clutching, pervasive fear which had for nearly sixty years protected this deserted place from visitors?

Having now thoroughly explored the ground floor, Blake ploughed again through the dust of the spectral nave to the front vestibule, where he had seen a door and staircase presumably leading up to the blackened tower and steeple—objects so long familiar to him at a distance. The ascent was a choking experience, for dust lay thick, while the spiders had done their worst in this constricted place. The staircase was a spiral with high, narrow wooden treads, and now and then Blake passed a clouded window looking dizzily out over the city. Though he had seen no ropes below, he expected to find a bell or peal of bells in the tower whose narrow, louver-boarded lancet windows his field-glass had studied so often. Here he was doomed to disappointment; for when he attained the top of the stairs he found the tower chamber vacant of chimes, and clearly devoted to vastly different purposes.

The room, about fifteen feet square, was faintly lighted by four lancet windows, one on each side, which were glazed within their screening of decayed louver-boards. These had been further fitted with tight, opaque screens, but the latter were now largely rotted away. In the center of the dust-laden floor rose a curiously angled stone pillar some four feet in height and two in average diameter, covered on each side with bizarre, crudely incised, and wholly unrecognizable hieroglyphs. On this pillar rested a metal box of peculiarly asymmetrical form; its hinged lid thrown back, and its interior holding what looked beneath the decade-deep dust to be an egg-shaped or irregularly spherical object some four inches through. Around the pillar in a rough circle were seven high-backed Gothic chairs still largely intact, while behind them, ranging along the dark-paneled walls, were seven colossal images of crumbling, black-painted plaster, resembling more than anything else the cryptic carven megaliths of mysterious Easter Island. In one corner of the cobwebbed chamber a ladder was built into the wall, leading up to the closed trap-door of the windowless steeple above.

As Blake grew accustomed to the feeble light he noticed odd bas-reliefs on the strange open box of yellowish metal. Approaching, he tried to clear the dust away with his hands and handkerchief, and saw that the figurings were of a monstrous and utterly alien kind; depicting entities which, though seemingly alive, resembled no known life-form ever evolved on this planet. The four-inch seeming sphere turned out to be a nearly black, red-striated polyhedron with many irregular flat surfaces; either a very remarkable crystal of some sort, or an artificial object of carved and highly polished mineral matter. It did not touch the bottom of the box, but was held suspended by means of a metal band around its center, with seven queerly designed supports extending horizontally to angles of the box's inner wall near the top. This stone, once exposed, exerted upon Blake an almost alarming fascination. He could scarcely tear his eyes from it, and as he looked at its glistening surfaces he almost fancied it was transparent, with half-formed worlds of wonder within. Into his mind floated pictures of alien orbs with great stone towers, and other orbs with titan mountains and no mark of life, and still remoter spaces where only a stirring in vague blacknesses told of the presence of consciousness and will.

When he did look away, it was to notice a somewhat singular mound of dust in the far corner near the ladder to the steeple. Just why it took his attention he could not tell, but something in its contours carried a message to his unconscious mind. Ploughing toward it, and brushing aside the hanging cobwebs as he went, he began to discern something grim about it. Hand and handkerchief soon revealed the truth, and Blake gasped with a baffling mixture of emotions. It was a human skeleton, and it must have been there for a very long time. The clothing was in shreds, but some buttons and fragments of cloth bespoke a man's grey suit. There were other bits of evidence—shoes, metal clasps, huge buttons for round cuffs, a stickpin of bygone pattern, a reporter's badge with the name of the old *Providence Telegram*, and a crumbling leather pocket-book. Blake examined the latter with care, finding within it several bills of antiquated issue, a celluloid advertising calendar for 1893, some cards with the name "Edwin M. Lillibridge," and a paper covered with penciled memoranda.

This paper held much of a puzzling nature, and Blake read it carefully at the dim westward window. Its disjointed text included such phrases as the following:

"Prof. Enoch Bowen home from Egypt May 1844—buys old Free-Will Church in July—his archaeological work & studies in occult well known."

"Dr. Drowne of 4th Baptist warns against Starry Wisdom in sermon Dec. 29, 1844."

"Congregation 97 by end of '45."

"1846—3 disappearances—first mention of Shining Trapezohedron."

"7 disappearances 1848—stories of blood sacrifice begin."

"Investigation 1853 comes to nothing—stories of sounds."

"Fr. O'Malley tells of devil-worship with box found in great Egyptian ruins—says they call up something that can't exist in light. Flees a little light, and banished by strong light. Then has to be summoned again. Probably got this from deathbed confession of Francis X. Feeney, who had joined Starry Wisdom in '49. These people say the Shining Trapezohedron shows them heaven & other worlds, & that the Haunter of the Dark tells them secrets in some way."

"Story of Orrin B. Eddy 1857. They call it up by gazing at the crystal, & have a secret language of their own."

"200 or more in cong. 1863, exclusive of men at front."

"Irish boys mob church in 1869 after Patrick Regan's disappearance."

"Veiled article in J. March 14, '72, but people don't talk about it."

"6 disappearances 1876—secret committee calls on Mayor Doyle."

"Action promised Feb. 1877—church closes in April."

"Gang—Federal Hill Boys—threaten Dr. —— and vestrymen in May."

"181 persons leave city before end of '77—mention no names."

"Ghost stories begin around 1880—try to ascertain truth of report that no human being has entered church since 1877."

"Ask Lanigan for photograph of place taken 1851." . . .

Restoring the paper to the pocketbook and placing the latter in his coat, Blake turned to look down at the skeleton in the dust. The implications of the notes were clear, and there could be no doubt but that this man had come to the deserted edifice forty-two years before in quest of a newspaper sensation which no one else had been bold enough to attempt. Perhaps no one else had known of his plan—who could tell? But he had never returned to his paper. Had some bravely suppressed fear risen to overcome him and bring on sudden heart-failure? Blake stooped over the gleaming bones and noted their peculiar state. Some of them were badly scattered, and a few seemed oddly *dissolved* at the ends. Others were strangely yellowed, with vague suggestions of charring. This charring extended to some of the fragments of clothing. The skull was in a very peculiar state—stained yellow, and with a charred aperture in the top as if some powerful acid had eaten through the solid bone. What had happened to the skeleton during its four decades of silent entombment here Blake could not imagine.

Before he realized it, he was looking at the stone again, and letting its curious influence call up a nebulous pageantry in his mind. He saw processions of robed, hooded figures whose outlines were not human, and looked on endless leagues of desert lined with carved, sky-reaching monoliths. He saw towers and walls in nighted depths under the sea, and vortices of space where wisps of black mist floated before thin shimmerings of cold purple haze. And beyond all else he glimpsed an infinite gulf of darkness, where solid and semi-solid forms were known only by their windy stirrings, and cloudy patterns of force seemed to superimpose order on chaos and hold forth a key to all the paradoxes and arcana of the worlds we know.

Then all at once the spell was broken by an access of gnawing, indeterminate panic fear. Blake choked and turned away from the stone, conscious of some formless alien presence close to him and watching him with horrible intentness. He felt entangled with something—something which was not in the stone, but which had looked through it at him—something which would ceaselessly follow him with a cognition that was not physical sight. Plainly, the place was getting on his nerves—as well it might in view of his gruesome find. The light was waning, too, and since he had no illuminant with him he knew he would have to be leaving soon.

It was then, in the gathering twilight, that he thought he saw a faint trace of luminosity in the crazily angled stone. He had tried to look away from it, but some obscure compulsion drew his eyes back. Was there a subtle phosphorescence of radio-activity about the thing? What was it that the dead man's notes had said concerning a *Shining Trapezohedron*? What, anyway, was this abandoned lair of cosmic evil? What had been done here, and what might still be lurking in the bird-shunned shadows? It seemed now as if an elusive touch of fetor had arisen somewhere close by, though its source was not apparent. Blake seized the cover of the long-open box and snapped it down. It moved easily on its alien hinges, and closed completely over the unmistakably glowing stone.

At the sharp click of that closing a soft stirring sound seemed to come from the steeple's eternal blackness overhead, beyond the trap-door. Rats, without question—the only living things to reveal their presence in this accursed pile since he had entered it. And yet that stirring in the steeple frightened him horribly, so that he plunged almost wildly down the spiral stairs, across the ghoulish nave, into the vaulted basement, out amidst the gathering dusk of the deserted square, and down through the teeming, fear-haunted alleys and avenues of Federal Hill toward the sane central streets and the home-like brick sidewalks of the college district.

During the days which followed, Blake told no one of his expedition. Instead, he read much in certain books, examined long years of newspaper files downtown, and worked feverishly at the cryptogram in that leather volume from the cobwebbed vestry room. The cipher, he soon saw, was no simple one; and after a long period of endeavor he felt sure that its language could not be English, Latin, Greek, French, Spanish, Italian, or German. Evidently he would have to draw upon the deepest wells of his strange erudition.

Every evening the old impulse to gaze westward returned, and he saw the black steeple as of yore amongst the bristling roofs of a distant and half-fabulous world. But now it held a fresh note of terror for him. He knew the heritage of evil lore it masked, and with the knowledge his vision ran riot in queer new ways. The birds of spring were returning, and as he watched their sunset flights he fancied they avoided the gaunt, lone spire as never before. When a flock of them approached it, he thought, they would wheel and scatter in panic confusion— and he could guess at the wild twitterings which failed to reach him across the intervening miles.

It was in June that Blake's diary told of his victory over the cryptogram. The text was, he found, in the dark Aklo language used by certain cults of evil antiquity, and known to him in a halting way through previous researches. The diary is strangely reticent about what Blake deciphered, but he was patently awed and disconcerted by his results. There are references to a Haunter of the Dark awaked by gazing into the Shining Trapezohedron, and insane conjectures about the black gulfs of chaos from which it was called. The being is spoken of as holding all knowledge, and demanding monstrous sacrifices. Some of Blake's entries shew fear lest the thing, which he seemed to regard as summoned, stalk abroad; though he adds that the street-lights form a bulwark which cannot be crossed.

Of the Shining Trapezohedron he speaks often, calling it a window on all time and space, and tracing its history from the days it was fashioned on dark Yuggoth, before ever the Old Ones brought it to earth. It was treasured and placed in its curious box by the crinoid things of Antarctica, salvaged from their ruins by the serpent-men of Valusia, and peered at aeons later in Lemuria by the first human beings. It crossed strange lands and stranger seas, and sank with Atlantis before a Minoan fisher meshed it in his net and sold it to swarthy merchants from nighted Khem. The Pharaoh Nephren-Ka built around it a temple with a windowless crypt, and did that which caused his name to be stricken from all monuments and records. Then it slept in the ruins of that evil fane which the priests and the new Pharaoh destroyed, till the delver's spade once more brought it forth to curse mankind.

Early in July the newspapers oddly supplement Blake's entries, though in so brief and casual a way that only the diary has called general attention to their contribution. It appears that a new fear had been growing on Federal Hill since a stranger had entered the dreaded church. The Italians whispered of unaccustomed stirrings and bumpings and scrapings in the dark windowless steeple, and called on their priests to banish an entity which haunted their dreams. Something, they said, was constantly watching at a door to see if it were dark enough to venture forth. Press items mentioned the long-standing local superstitions, but failed to shed much light on the earlier background of the horror. It was obvious that the young reporters of today are no antiquarians. In writing of these things in his diary, Blake expresses a curious kind of remorse, and talks of the duty of burying the Shining Trapezohedron and of banishing what he had evoked by letting daylight into the hideous jutting spire. At the same time, however, he displays the dangerous extent of his fascination, and admits a morbid longing—pervading even his dreams—to visit the accursed tower and gaze again into the cosmic secrets of the glowing stone.

Then something in the *Journal* on the morning of July 17 threw the diarist into a veritable fever of horror. It was only a variant of the other half-humorous items about the Federal Hill restlessness, but to Blake it was somehow very terrible indeed. In the night a thunderstorm had put the city's lighting-system out of commission for a full hour, and in that black interval the Italians had nearly gone mad with fright. Those living near the dreaded church had sworn that the thing in the steeple had taken advantage of the street-lamps' absence and gone down into the body of the church, flopping and bumping around in a viscous, altogether dreadful way. Toward the last it had bumped up to the tower, where there were sounds of the shattering of glass. It could go wherever the darkness reached, but light would always send it fleeing.

When the current blazed on again there had been a shocking commotion in the tower, for even the feeble light trickling through the grime-blackened, louver-boarded windows was too much for the thing. It had bumped and slithered up into its tenebrous steeple just in time—for a long dose of light would have sent it back into the abyss whence the crazy stranger had called it. During the dark hour praying crowds had clustered round the church in the rain with lighted candles and lamps somehow shielded with folded paper and umbrellas—a guard of light to save the city from the nightmare that stalks in darkness. Once, those nearest the church declared, the outer door had rattled hideously.

But even this was not the worst. That evening in the *Bulletin* Blake read of what the reporters had found. Aroused at last to the whimsical news value of the scare, a pair of them had defied the frantic crowds of Italians and crawled into the church through the cellar window after trying the doors in vain. They found the dust of the vestibule and of the spectral nave ploughed up in a singular way, with bits of rotted cushions and satin pew-linings scattered curiously around. There was a bad odor everywhere, and here and there were bits of yellow stain and patches of what looked like charring. Opening the door to the tower, and pausing a moment at the suspicion of a scraping sound above, they found the narrow spiral stairs wiped roughly clean.

In the tower itself a similarly half-swept condition existed. They spoke of the heptagonal stone pillar, the overturned Gothic chairs, and the bizarre plaster images; though strangely enough the metal box and the old mutilated skeleton were not mentioned. What disturbed Blake the most—except for the hints of stains and charring and bad odors—was the final detail that explained the crashing glass. Every one of the tower's lancet windows was broken, and two of them had been darkened in a crude and hurried way by the stuffing of satin pew-linings and cushion-horsehair into the spaces between the slanting exterior louver-boards. More satin fragments and bunches of horsehair lay scattered around the newly swept floor, as if someone had been interrupted in the act of restoring the tower to the absolute blackness of its tightly curtained days.

Yellowish stains and charred patches were found on the ladder to the windowless spire, but when a reporter climbed up, opened the horizontally sliding trap-door, and shot a feeble flashlight beam into the black and strangely fetid space, he saw nothing but darkness, and an heterogeneous litter of shapeless fragments near the aperture. The verdict, of course, was charlatanry. Somebody had played a joke on the superstitious hill-dwellers, or else some fanatic had striven to bolster up their fears for their own supposed good. Or perhaps some of the younger and more sophisticated dwellers had staged an elaborate hoax on the outside world. There was an amusing aftermath when the police sent an officer to verify the reports. Three men in succession found ways of evading the assignment, and the fourth went very reluctantly and returned very soon without adding to the account given by the reporters.

From this point onward Blake's diary shews a mounting tide of insidious horror and nervous apprehension. He upbraids himself for not doing something, and speculates wildly on the consequences of another electrical breakdown. It has been verified that on three occasions—during thunderstorms—he telephoned the electric light company in a frantic vein and asked that desperate precautions against a lapse of power be taken. Now and then his entries shew concern over the failure of the reporters to find the metal box and stone, and the strangely marred old skeleton, when they explored the shadowy tower room. He assumed that these things had been removed— whither, and by whom or what, he could only guess. But his worst fears concerned himself, and the kind of unholy rapport he felt to exist between his mind and that lurking horror in the distant steeple—that monstrous thing of night which his rashness had called out of the ultimate black spaces. He seemed to feel a constant tugging at his will, and callers of that period remember how he would sit abstractedly at his desk and stare out of the west window at that far-off, spire-bristling mound beyond the swirling smoke of the city. His entries dwell monotonously on certain terrible dreams, and of a strengthening of the unholy rapport in his sleep. There is mention of a night when he awaked to find himself fully dressed, outdoors, and headed automatically down College Hill toward the west.

Again and again he dwells on the fact that the thing in the steeple knows where to find him.

The week following July 30 is recalled as the time of Blake's partial breakdown. He did not dress, and ordered all his food by telephone. Visitors remarked the cords he kept near his bed, and he said that sleep-walking had forced him to bind his ankles every night with knots which would probably hold or else waken him with the labour of untying.

In his diary he told of the hideous experience which had brought the collapse. After retiring on the night of the 30th he had suddenly found himself groping about in an almost black space. All he could see were short, faint, horizontal streaks of bluish light, but he could smell an overpowering fetor and hear a curious jumble of soft, furtive sounds above him. Whenever he moved he stumbled over something, and at each noise there would come a sort of answering sound from above—a vague stirring, mixed with the cautious sliding of wood on wood.

Once his groping hands encountered a pillar of stone with a vacant top, whilst later he found himself clutching the rungs of a ladder built into the wall, and fumbling his uncertain way upward toward some region of intenser stench where a hot, searing blast beat down against him. Before his eyes a kaleidoscopic range of phantasmal images played, all of them dissolving at intervals into the picture of a vast, unplumbed abyss of night wherein whirled suns and worlds of an even profounder blackness. He thought of the ancient legends of Ultimate Chaos, at whose center sprawls the blind idiot god Azathoth, Lord of All Things, encircled by his flopping horde of mindless and amorphous dancers, and lulled by the thin monotonous piping of a demoniac flute held in nameless paws.

Then a sharp report from the outer world broke through his stupor and roused him to the unutterable horror of his position. What it was, he never knew—perhaps it was some belated peal from the fireworks heard all summer on Federal Hill as the dwellers hail their various patron saints, or the saints of their native villages in Italy. In any event he shrieked aloud, dropped frantically from the ladder, and stumbled blindly across the obstructed floor of the almost lightless chamber that encompassed him.

He knew instantly where he was, and plunged recklessly down the narrow spiral staircase, tripping and bruising himself at every turn. There was a nightmare flight through a vast cobwebbed nave whose ghostly arches reached up to realms of leering shadow, a sightless scramble through a littered basement, a climb to regions of air and street-lights outside, and a mad racing down a spectral hill of gibbering gables, across a grim, silent city of tall black towers, and up the steep eastward precipice to his own ancient door.

On regaining consciousness in the morning he found himself lying on his study floor fully dressed. Dirt and cobwebs covered him, and every inch of his body seemed sore and bruised. When he faced the mirror he saw that his hair was badly scorched, while a trace of strange, evil odour seemed to cling to his upper outer clothing. It was then that his nerves broke down. Thereafter, lounging exhaustedly about in a dressing-gown, he did little but stare from his west window, shiver at the threat of thunder, and make wild entries in his diary.

The great storm broke just before midnight on August 8th. Lightning struck repeatedly in all parts of the city, and two remarkable fireballs were reported. The rain was torrential, while a constant fusillade of thunder brought sleeplessness to thousands. Blake was utterly frantic in his fear for the lighting system, and tried to telephone the company around 1 a.m., though by that time service had been temporarily cut off in the interest of safety. He recorded everything in his diary—the large, nervous, and often undecipherable hieroglyphs telling their own story of growing frenzy and despair, and of entries scrawled blindly in the dark.

He had to keep the house dark in order to see out the window, and it appears that most of his time was spent at his desk, peering anxiously through the rain across the glistening miles of downtown roofs at the constellation of distant lights marking Federal Hill. Now and then he would fumblingly make an entry in his diary, so that detached phrases such as "The lights must not go"; "It knows where I am"; "I must destroy it"; and "It is calling to me, but perhaps it means no injury this time"; are found scattered down two of the pages.

Then the lights went out all over the city. It happened at 2:12 a.m. according to power-house records, but Blake's diary gives no indication of the time. The entry is merely, "Lights out—God help me." On Federal Hill there were watchers as anxious as he, and rain-soaked knots of men paraded the square and alleys around the evil church with umbrella-shaded candles, electric flashlights, oil lanterns, crucifixes, and obscure charms of the many sorts common to southern Italy. They blessed each flash of lightning, and made cryptical signs of fear with their right hands when a turn in the storm caused the flashes to lessen and finally to cease altogether. A rising wind blew out most of the candles, so that the scene grew threateningly dark. Someone roused Father Merluzzo of Spirito Santo Church, and he hastened to the dismal square to pronounce whatever helpful syllables he could. Of the restless and curious sounds in the blackened tower, there could be no doubt whatever.

For what happened at 2:35 we have the testimony of the priest, a young, intelligent, and well-educated person; of Patrolman William J. Monahan of the Central Station, an officer of the highest reliability who had paused at that part of his beat to inspect the crowd; and of most of the seventy-eight men who had gathered around the church's high bank wall— especially those in the square where the eastward facade was visible. Of course there was nothing which can be proved as being outside the order of Nature. The possible causes of such an event are many. No one can speak with certainty of the obscure chemical processes arising in a vast, ancient, ill-aired, and long-deserted building of heterogeneous contents. Mephitic vapors—spontaneous combustion—pressure of gases born of long decay—any one of numberless phenomena might be responsible. And then, of course, the factor of conscious charlatanry can by no means be excluded. The thing was really quite simple in itself, and covered less than three minutes of actual time. Father Merluzzo, always a precise man, looked at his watch repeatedly.

It started with a definite swelling of the dull fumbling sounds inside the black tower. There had for some time been a vague exhalation of strange, evil odours from the church, and this had now become emphatic and offensive. Then at last there was a sound of splintering wood, and a large, heavy object crashed down in the yard beneath the frowning easterly facade. The tower was invisible now that the candles would not burn, but as the object neared the ground the people knew that it was the smoke-grimed louver-boarding of that tower's east window.

Immediately afterward an utterly unbearable fetor welled forth from the unseen heights, choking and sickening the trembling watchers, and almost prostrating those in the square. At the same time the air trembled with a vibration as of flapping wings, and a sudden east-blowing wind more violent than any previous blast snatched off the hats and wrenched the dripping umbrellas of the crowd. Nothing definite could be seen in the candleless night, though some upward-looking spectators thought they glimpsed a great spreading blur of denser blackness against the inky sky—something like a formless cloud of smoke that shot with meteor-like speed toward the east.

That was all. The watchers were half numbed with fright, awe, and discomfort, and scarcely knew what to do, or whether to do anything at all. Not knowing what had happened, they did not relax their vigil; and a moment later they sent up a prayer as a sharp flash of belated lightning, followed by an earsplitting crash of sound, rent the flooded heavens. Half an hour later the rain stopped, and in fifteen minutes more the street-lights sprang on again, sending the weary, bedraggled watchers relievedly back to their homes.

The next day's papers gave these matters minor mention in connection with the general storm reports. It seems that the great lightning flash and deafening explosion which followed the Federal Hill occurrence were even more tremendous farther east, where a burst of the singular fetor was likewise noticed. The phenomenon was most marked over College Hill, where the crash awaked all the sleeping inhabitants and led to a bewildered round of speculations. Of those who were already awake only a few saw the anomalous blaze of light near the top of the hill, or noticed the inexplicable upward rush of air which almost stripped the leaves from the trees and blasted the plants in the gardens. It was agreed that the lone, sudden lightning-bolt must have struck somewhere in this neighborhood, though no trace of its striking could afterward be found. A youth in the Tau Omega fraternity house thought he saw a grotesque and hideous mass of smoke in the air just as the preliminary flash burst, but his observation has not been verified. All of the few observers, however, agree as to the violent gust from the west and the flood of intolerable stench which preceded the belated stroke; whilst evidence concerning the momentary burned odor after the stroke is equally general.

These points were discussed very carefully because of their probable connexion with the death of Robert Blake. Students in the Psi Delta house, whose upper rear windows looked into Blake's study, noticed the blurred white face at the westward window on the morning of the 9th, and wondered what was wrong with the expression. When they saw the same face in the same position that evening, they felt worried, and watched for the lights to come up in his apartment. Later they rang the bell of the darkened flat, and finally had a policeman force the door.

The rigid body sat bolt upright at the desk by the window, and when the intruders saw the glassy, bulging eyes, and the marks of stark, convulsive fright on the twisted features, they turned away in sickened dismay. Shortly afterward the coroner's physician made an examination, and despite the unbroken window reported electrical shock, or nervous tension induced by electrical discharge, as the cause of death. The hideous expression he ignored altogether, deeming it a not improbable result of the profound shock as experienced by a person of such abnormal imagination and unbalanced emotions. He deduced these latter qualities from the books, paintings, and manuscripts found in the apartment, and from the blindly scrawled entries in the diary on the desk. Blake had prolonged his frenzied jottings to the last, and the broken-pointed pencil was found clutched in his spasmodically contracted right hand.

The entries after the failure of the lights were highly disjointed, and legible only in part. From them certain investigators have drawn conclusions differing greatly from the materialistic official verdict, but such speculations have little chance for belief among the conservative. The case of these imaginative theorists has not been helped by the action of superstitious Dr. Dexter, who threw the curious box and angled stone—an object certainly self-luminous as seen in the black windowless steeple where it was found—into the deepest channel of Narragansett Bay. Excessive imagination and neurotic unbalance on Blake's part, aggravated by knowledge of the evil bygone cult whose startling traces he had uncovered, form the dominant interpretation given those final frenzied jottings. These are the entries—or all that can be made of them.

"Lights still out—must be five minutes now. Everything depends on lightning. Yaddith grant it will keep up! . . . Some influence seems beating through it. . . . Rain and thunder and wind deafen. . . . The thing is taking hold of my mind. . . .

"Trouble with memory. I see things I never knew before. Other worlds and other galaxies . . . Dark . . . The lightning seems dark and the darkness seems light. . . .

"It cannot be the real hill and church that I see in the pitch-darkness. Must be retinal impression left by flashes. Heaven grant the Italians are out with their candles if the lightning stops!

"What am I afraid of? Is it not an avatar of Nyarlathotep, who in antique and shadowy Khem even took the form of man? I remember Yuggoth, and more distant Shaggai, and the ultimate void of the black planets. . . .

"The long, winging flight through the void . . . cannot cross the universe of light . . . re-created by the thoughts caught in the Shining Trapezohedron . . . send it through the horrible abysses of radiance. . . .

"My name is Blake—Robert Harrison Blake of 620 East Knapp Street, Milwaukee, Wisconsin. . . . I am on this planet. . . .

"Azathoth have mercy!—the lightning no longer flashes—horrible—I can see everything with a monstrous sense that is not sight—light is dark and dark is light . . . those people on the hill . . . guard . . . candles and charms . . . their priests. . . .

"Sense of distance gone—far is near and near is far. No light—no glass—see that steeple—that tower—window—can hear—Roderick Usher—am mad or going mad—the thing is stirring and fumbling in the tower—I am it and it is I—I want to get out . . . must get out and unify the forces. . . . It knows where I am. . . .

"I am Robert Blake, but I see the tower in the dark. There is a monstrous odour . . . senses transfigured . . . boarding at that tower window cracking and giving way. . . . Iä . . . ngai . . . ygg. . . .

"I see it—coming here—hell-wind—titan blur—black wings—Yog-Sothoth save me—the three-lobed burning eye. . ."

Robert E. Howard's

30
Ennui
Clark Ashton Smith
(1936)

Smith was apparently fascinated with the word "ennui,"—a feeling of listlessness—for he had both a prose poem and the poem reprinted here bearing the same title. This poem was published in the May 1936 issue of *Weird Tales,* and despite all that was going on in his life at the time, Howard still found time to read the issue. In a letter to August Derleth, dated May 9, 1936, approximately one month before Howard's death, he wrote, "I enjoyed your 'Lesandro's Familiar' a lot. It was the best yarn in an issue otherwise not remarkable. I did like Smith's poem, and Kramer's." Here is Smith's poem.

Thou art immured in some sad garden sown with dust
Of fruit of Sodom that bedims the summer ground,
And burdenously bows the lilies many-crowned,
Or fills the pale and ebon mouths of sleepy lust
The poppies raise . . . And, falling there imponderously,
Dull ashes emptied from the urns of all the dead
Have stilled the fountain and have sealed the fountain-head
And pall-wise draped the pine and flowering myrtle-tree . . .

Thou art becalmed upon that slothful ancient main
Where Styx and Lethe fall; where skies of stagnant gray
With the gray stagnant waters meet and merge as one:
How tardily thy torpid heart remembers pain,
And love itself, as aureate islands far away
On seas refulgent with the incredible red sun.

Robert E. Howard's

31
Bride of Baal
Edgar Daniel Kramer
(1936)

Kramer did not start publishing his poetry in *Weird Tales* until 1935, but he made up for lost time, publishing 17 poems in just over five years. He places 6th in most poems for the unique magazine (though he is tied with four others). In the same letter to August Derleth, dated May 9, 1936, in which Howard praised Clark Ashton Smith's poem "Ennui," he also praised Kramer's poem. "I enjoyed your 'Lesandro's Familiar' a lot. It was the best yarn in an issue otherwise not remarkable. I did like Smith's poem, and Kramer's." Here is Kramer's poem.

They have left me alone in the stillness where the cold, grim shadows start,
And there is no sound in the silence save the wild, mad beat of my heart;
They have sealed up the doors of the temple and Beauty is glorified,
For here in the gloom great Baal is holding his virgin bride.

Anointed with oils and perfumes and class in the night of my hair,
I tremble here in the shadows alone with my black despair;
Cold are the arms that hold me and ever I softly weep,
For a lad in a fragrant valley and a trysting I cannot keep.

My body is whiter than snow is, and redder than blood is my mouth;
My breasts are as soft as the breezes from the lotus groves of the south;
My hands are the white rose petals that fall in the time of dew,
But hunger and thirst are my portion, and gone is the joy I knew.

The hours are all unending, as I harken each smothered howl
That lifts to me from the blackness, where the hungry lions prowl;
They have left me alone in the darkness, where the lions have been unleashed,
And I weep in the arms of Baal—in terror of God and Beast!

32
Night-Gaunts
H.P. Lovecraft
(1936)

The poem "Night-Gaunts" was first published in the spring 1936 issue of *The Phantagraph*. Originally written around 1930 as chapter "XX" of his poem cycle *Fungi From Yuggoth*, it was published independently in *The Phantagraph*, then revised again for publication in *Weird Tales* magazine (December 1939). Howard read the poem in *The Phantagraph* and in his last letter to H.P. Lovecraft dated May 13, 1936, he wrote, "And I got a big kick out of your sonnet in the current issue of the Phantagraph, which is the first copy of that publication I'd seen." Unable to secure *The Phantagraph* version, the following comes from *Weird Tales*.

Out of what crypt they crawl, I cannot tell,
But every night I see the rubbery things:
Black, horned, and slender, with membranous wings,
And tails that bear the bifid barb of hell.
They come in legions on the north wind's swell
With obscene clutch that titillates and stings,
Snatching me off on monstrous voyagings
To gray worlds hidden deep in nightmare's well.

Over the jagged peaks of Thok they sweep,
Heedless of all the cries I try to make,
And down the nether pits to that foul lake
Where the puffed shoggoths splash in doubtful sleep.
But oh! If only they would make some sound,
Or wear a face where faces should be found!

Robert E. Howard's

About the Editor

Willard M. Oliver is—in the words of Robert E. Howard—just "some line-faced scrivener." A life-long Robert E. Howard fan since discovering him in 1979, Oliver is currently a member of REHupa, has published articles on Howard for *The Dark Man: The Journal of Robert E. Howard and Pulp Studies,* and is currently working on a biography of Robert E. Howard. He lives with his family in Huntsville, Texas.

Made in the USA
Columbia, SC
27 May 2025